The Eyes of Sandala

by Cathy Benedetto

a BlackWyrm book
Louisville, Kentucky

THE EYES OF SANDALA

A BlackWyrm Book
BlackWyrm Publishing
10307 Chimney Ridge Ct, Louisville, KY 40299

Printed in the United States of America.

ISBN: 978-1-61318-115-7
LCCN: 2011910299

Cover Design by Cathy Benedetto

First edition: February 2010
Second edition: July 2011

There are always folks behind the scenes who offer encouragement and support. Without them, the entire process of writing and publishing would be difficult if not impossible. Jeff and Dave, your ideas and suggestions enriched the story; the Games Gang, being there during a challenging time made daily living easier; and, Nancy, because without you there would be no book.

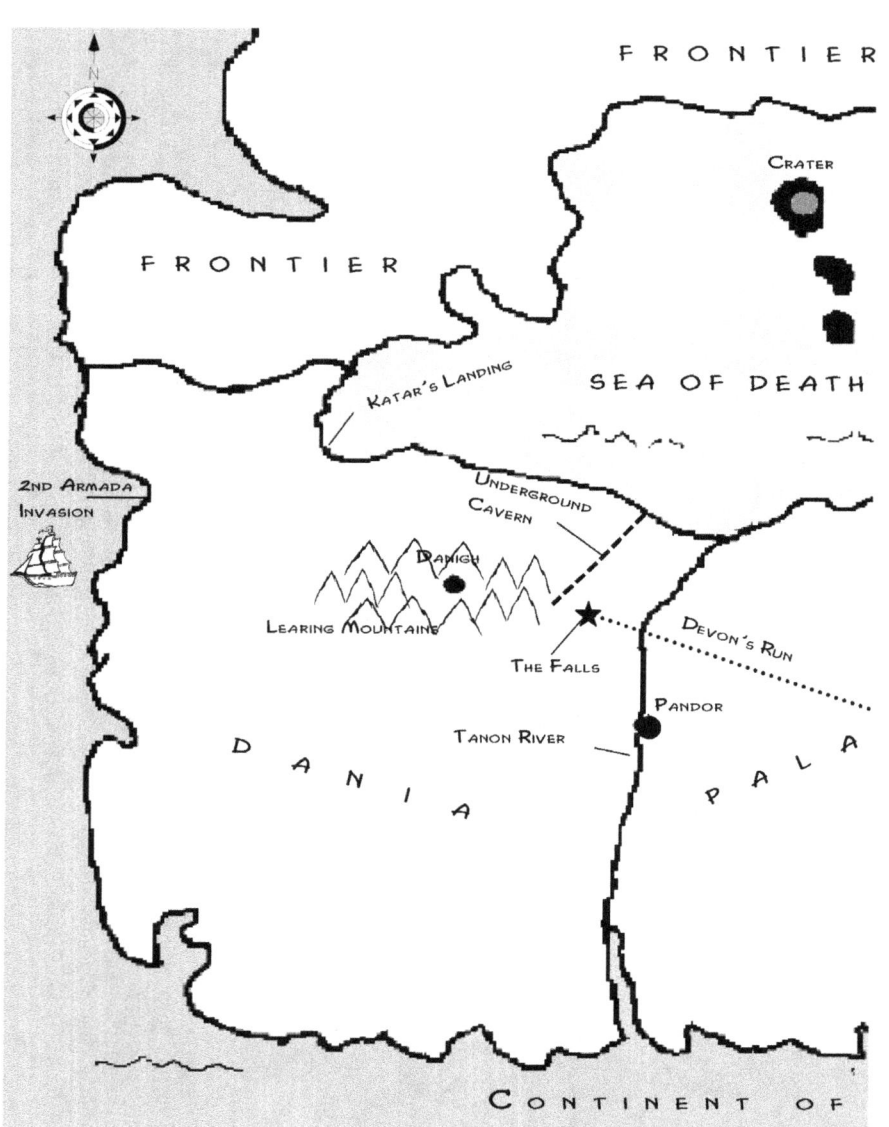

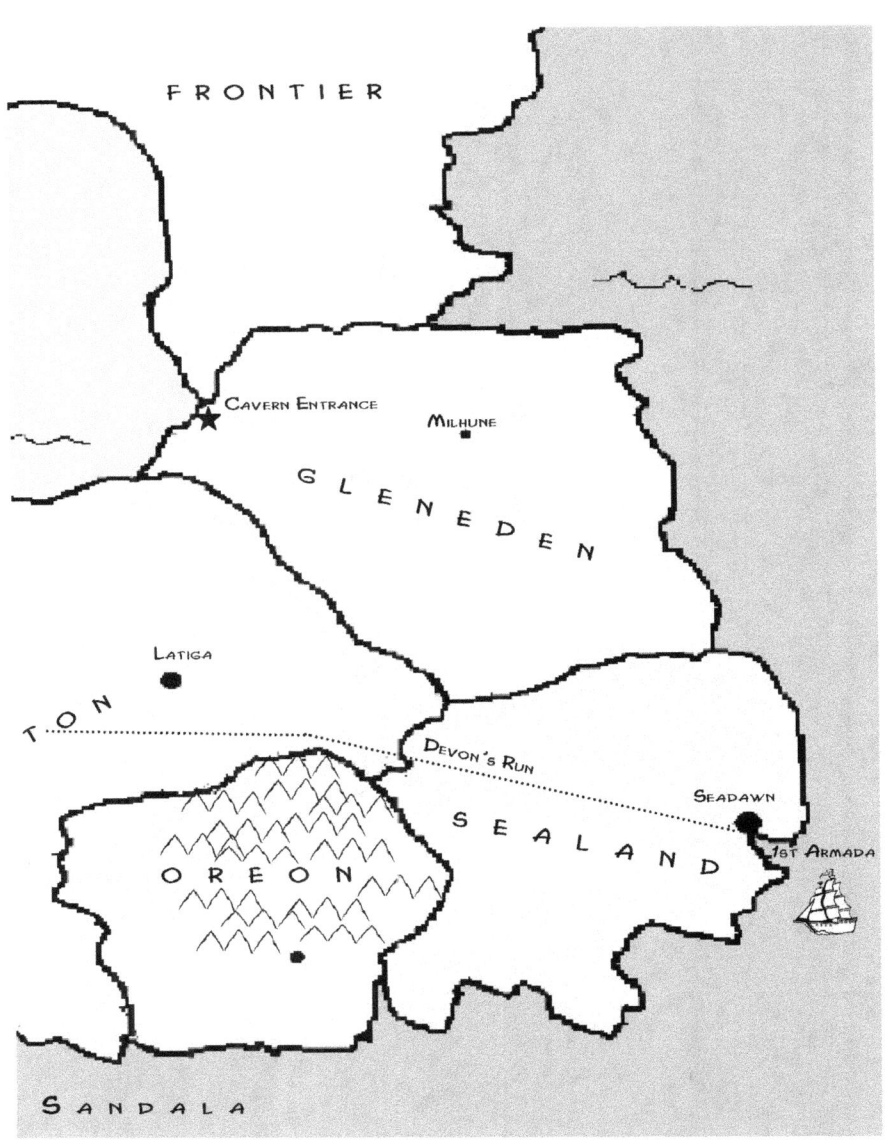

FRONTIER

CAVERN ENTRANCE ★   MILHUNE ▪

G L E N E D E N

LATIGA ●

T O N

DEVON'S RUN

SEADAWN ●

O R E O N   S E A L A N D

1ST ARMADA

●

S A N D A L A

To former students, players,
and teammates for their inspiration.

Dedication

To former students, players, and teammates for their inspiration.

Acknowledgements

There are always folks behind the scenes who offer encouragement and support. Without them, the entire process of writing and publishing would be difficult if not impossible. Jeff and Dave, your ideas and suggestions enriched the story; the Games Gang, being there during a challenging time made daily living easier; and, Nancy, without you there would be no meaning.

CHAPTER 1

SIX MONTHS EARLIER...

They came from the sea, slipping quietly into the small channel. The silver moonlight faded behind them as one by one the sleek boats disappeared under the moss laden branches of gnarled trees along the bank. Blackened faces hid the oarsmen's fair-skinned features and blunted any moonlight that seeped through the thick cypress. Inside the boats, metallic weapons laid bundled in dark cloth.

For nearly a mile, the crafts glided forward, barely disturbing the dark water. The rugged men who powered the muffled oars studied the heavy tropical foliage surrounding them. It was dark and forbidding. Who knew what lay hidden there?

An unpleasant odor of exotic flowers mixed with the stench of rotting trees assailed them. It drenched the air, making it heavy and pungent, and dropped on the boats as if trying to engulf them.

As the inlet narrowed, a figure in the lead boat stood, swaying gracefully, the craft dipping in response. He gestured to the other boats and after two more pulls, the rowers quietly shipped their oars, turning to the left with the last stroke. Each boat found purchase in the soft silt, and whispered to a halt.

The leader, Galt, a chiseled man with hard features, listened for any indication their arrival was detected, but the nightly racket of the crickets and frogs droned on. He waved them forward and the men rose quickly, stepping softly into the shallow water. Lines were formed from each craft to a small clearing several boat lengths away. Bundles were passed from one set of hands to the next until all the provisions were stacked on dry land.

Galt took pride in their precision, evidence of his role in their demanding training. He ordered them to divide the provisions and weapons while he joined the two other leaders. He kept his voice low, but there was little to say. Each knew their area of responsibility. He realized it was more an unspoken need for last minute companionship, a comfort in kind, before they went their separate ways.

High in the canopy of trees that loomed over them, an owl hooted. Galt froze everyone with a raised hand then turned his gaze upward. The rest waited, muscles bunched with tension, trying to see beyond the shadows. Finally, Galt shook his head, whispering to a man beside him."Grelag."

The man went to a nearby crate, opened a small cage and reached inside. He turned back and saw Galt point to a large tree at the edge of a clearing. Gingerly, he removed a hood from the creature he held.

The grelag was a half snake, half lizard abomination. As long as a man's forearm, its appendages ended in needle sharp claws. The venom from its bite could kill a man in less than a dozen breaths.

"Hunt," the man said to it, gesturing upward as he set it on the trunk of the tree. Quickly, it began to slither toward the top.

The men stood rooted to the ground then Galt heard a noise from above and shared a knowing look with the others. Something small hit the dirt in front of them. It was the grelag, what was left of it. The head was sliced off and blood oozed from the torn tissue around its neck. From overhead the owl hooted its mellow call once again.

Galt stared disbelieving at the dead creature. Sweat dampened his forehead. Abruptly, he pointed to two men beside him and pointed up the same tree. Sharing a fierce look, they placed knives between their teeth and began to climb. Galt judged they were halfway to the top when he heard a grunt. One of the men came crashing down, bouncing hard off several branches until he landed with a thud at the base of the tree. Galt hurried to the still form and turned him over. Eyes looked back vacantly.

Galt muttered an oath and looked back toward the tree heights, waiting. Seconds later, the second man tumbled down, landing in an awkward heap. Blood gushed from an ugly gash that ran from ear to ear.

The rest of the men began to grumble but Galt's quick, slashing hand silenced them. Their fear was betrayed by their wide, unblinking eyes. Disgusted, he spat, chancing another glance toward the forbidding treetops. What kind of creature was up there?

Finally, a man beside him broke the silence. "Do we pull back?"

"No," Galt said harshly, "but send two men back to tell the captain we have been discovered."

"But I thought..."

"Keep your wits," Galt spewed."This changes nothing."

Tight with tension, the men gathered their gear and moved out. A large group headed northeast towards lush valleys filled with abundant crops. Another angled sharply east. They would skirt the shoreline until they came to a daunting mountain range dotted with the gold and silver mining communities of Oreon. Galt led his company due west towards countryside marked by rolling hills and wealthy farmlands. For a long time, his worried gaze drifted frequently to the tree tops.

High above, orange eyes watched the two remaining men retrace their steps to the inlet before they shoved off in one of the crafts and head back out the river to the sea.

When they disappeared from view, the owl hooted once again, its cry haunting the night. A few seconds later, its call was answered, and that call re-echoed across the land.

Gradually, a thick part of the tree's main trunk changed color and the orange eyed 'owl' became identifiable as a small person. Satisfied the alarm had been raised, the 'owl' wiped blood from a knife before scurrying down the towering tree.

A lean, athletic figure, its physique showed the subtle beginnings of maturity. Clad in a leather tunic, a light spear was clutched in one hand. A jagged knife hung from one hip, and a full water skin dangled from the other. A bow and quiver filled with arrows lay strapped across its back.

Avoiding the invader's tracks, the figure started north at a steady trot, a tuft-eared lynx keeping pace nearby. The runner's eyes turned coal black as they adjusted to the darkness under the trees. The significance of the mysterious interlopers was obvious. The invasion had long been foretold. No one knew when it would begin, only that it was inevitable. So the watcher raced for home to warn of the strange men who had entered Sandala under the cloak of darkness. They were enemies, to be sure, because anyone who stole ashore in the dark of night was no friend.

The journey of several hundred miles was of no concern. The watcher could run for hours, rarely stopping for rest or water, taking nourishment on the move. Hard training underscored the importance of the task. Hundreds of watchers were posted throughout Sandala, entrusted with the safety and livelihood of thousands.

Obstacles that would trip a less-skilled individual were dodged because of a special lens that produced keen nightvision. Gradually, the darkness of the night passed into the hazy dimness of a chilly dawn. The sun would rise in another hour, and the midnight marauders would be miles away. Home called to the ten year old so she increased her pace. She remained calm, almost stoic, despite the drama of her first kill.

CHAPTER 2

TROUBLED LANDS

Devon Longstreet's blade flashed from his side, cutting the first ruffian deeply in the shoulder. As the man fell, Devon wheeled his horse about, crashing into the second mounted figure, driving him back. Before the man could respond, Devon drove his sword between the attacker's ribs. Pulling his blade free, Longstreet whirled in time to deflect a thrust at his own midsection then shoved the man away. Suddenly cautious, a fourth aggressor backed his horse off and joined the remaining attacker in circling warily, searching for an opening to launch their assault anew. The opportunity never came. In a blur of movement, Devon drew, and then cast a knife strapped at his side. As the man fell, the slim blade buried in his throat, the last foe spurred his horse in an attempt to flee.

When there's a choice, Devon reminded himself, never leave an enemy alive. In a practiced motion, he took a bow from his back, notched and then loosed an arrow. His aim was true and the last marauder tumbled from his horse.

Devon studied the carnage. One by one, they had died. Young men, foolish men, who would never again draw warmth from a friendly fire, bask in the glow of a proud father's praise, or smile at the antics of a playful child. They had mistaken him for a weary traveler, ignoring the possibility of weapons beneath a bulky blanket, blind to the exquisite bearing of his warhorse. And so in their eager rush, they paid the final price exacted of foolish men.

He wiped the blood from his sword and sighed. A ruggedly handsome man, his strong chin was hidden beneath a finely trimmed beard. His simple, peasant garb gave him a rumpled look, making him appear older than his thirty six years and cloaked his prime fighting condition. The sweat and grime accumulated while defending himself did not disguise the disgusted look that had settled on his face. Life was precious and these impulsive young men had wasted theirs. He didn't like killing or seek it out, but he was very good at it. During his decade as a sentinel followed by another ten years of service to King Sorbonne of Dania, he'd had a great deal of practice.

He dismounted, going from body to body, taking the best weapons and tossing the rest aside. Three of their mounts had scattered, but the fourth was nearby, pacing nervously. He calmed it with a whisper, and then checked for provisions. Lack of food indicated a scouting party that was dependent upon a larger force nearby. Someone would be expecting their return. Best to move on, Devon thought and whistled for his horse.

He tied the reins of the captured horse to his saddle horn before he leapt astride his big roan. He urged Shadow into a loping gallop while considering the recent events.

Nearly a month had passed since King Sorbonne had ordered him to investigate reports that wandering bands of marauders were wrecking havoc in the countryside. The king wanted to know if the attacks were limited to his kingdom or if they were plaguing the other lands as well. Scouts were dispatched to all the kingdoms and to Devon fell the task of scouting Sealand, the realm of King Dawad.

After weeks of traveling, as the eyes and ears of his worried king, Devon had learned little that was new. It was only now, deep inside Sealand territory, that things had changed. Near the border, everything had been normal. Farmers and townsmen were friendly, and often as not, he spent his nights in barns on fresh hay, after he shared a meal with the owner and his family. But as he moved further east, telling differences began to manifest.

Wary peasants resisted offering food or shelter. Villages closed up their businesses early in the day and enforced nuisance curfews in the evening. On two occasions, he had run across tracks of a band of men. The attempt to cover up their trail might have worked against less skilled eyes, but Longstreet was not an ordinary man. Cautiously, he followed the FirstGroup for several miles, witnessed their raid on a small farm and watched as they slaughtered the cattle and burned the barn.

The second time was late this afternoon. After discovering the trail of four riders, he deliberately offered himself as bait, hoping to draw them out. His strategy worked, and the soldiers, eager to fight, did not realize he was aware of their presence; that he was one of a prestigious group of men known as sentinels and well-trained in the art of war. They took his bait, interpreting his slumping posture and graying hair as the mark of an easy prey.

"Ah, Shadow," Devon spoke aloud to his four-footed companion."I've decided they're soldiers, though they dressed like ruffians. What do you think about that?"

Devon's eyes narrowed. There was too much precision behind the movement of the marauding bands. Organization meant training which usually implied military. Yet whose, he wondered? Where did they come from? What was their purpose? Sowing such unrest would only serve as an early alarm to a king as diligent as Sorbonne. If they were lead scouts for a larger military force, perhaps they were mapping the major roads and trade routes and determining the presence of any local militia. They could probe the defensive precautions of major villages and disrupt harvests with their random attacks on the farmers.

"Too much speculation, Shadow. We need real answers to relay to the King." Devon frowned. If the king didn't hear from him soon, he would be more than worried. Slowed by unusually heavy spring rains and forced to backtrack while avoiding some of the marauders, he was nearly two weeks behind schedule."C'mon, boy," he said, increasing the stallion's pace."We need to get to Seadawn."

After another hour of riding, Devon recognized the countryside outside of Claypool. It was one of Sealand's smaller villages but a welcome sight nonetheless. Wisps of smoke curled skyward and within minutes, Devon smelled the aroma of suppers cooking over welcoming fires. His stomach rumbled in anticipation. He slowed his mount to a trot and smiled at the thought of a hot bath.

As he rounded a bend in the road, he was surprised to find a wagon blocking the way. A handful of villagers brandishing pitchforks and torches stood on either side. The faces caught in the fires' reflections were not friendly.

"Whoa, Shadow," Devon said, bringing the horse to a stop a dozen feet from the nearest men. Slowly, his eyes never leaving the group before him, he dismounted.

"A strange greeting to a friendly traveler," Devon said.

A large, heavy browed man separated himself from the crowd and stepped forward."Who might you be?" he asked tersely.

For a moment, Devon looked at the scowling men. They were edgy, in a mood to fight."An emissary from King Sorbonne," he finally answered."My name's Longstreet."

"And what proof do you have of that?" the man challenged.

Devon took a few steps forward, until he came into the light cast by the torches. His eyes traveled from man to man, meeting the gaze of each in turn."My word," he said. "Which is enough." His voice was steel. The men noted his strong jaw and the scar that ran from the corner of one eye to his ear.

"In other times, maybe," the man said. The others shifted uneasily, and Devon's hand dropped slowly to his sword. There was some murmuring until another finally moved forward.

"I've heard of a sentinel named Longstreet," the man said.

Devon moved his hand away from the weapon."One and the same," he said and gave the man a curt nod.

"The inn is locked up for the night," the initial villager informed him."You'd best move on."

Devon turned to Shadow and motioned him forward. The men retreated several steps at the sight of the imposing warhorse. Devon watched them closely as he retrieved a purse from his saddle pack. He pivoted towards them, and gave it a meaningful shake.

"There's plenty in here for a room, a meal and a hot bath, and," he added gesturing behind him, "a stable for my horses. Or is Danian coin no longer accepted here?" he challenged.

"A sentinel is always welcome," the second man said at last."These are strange times. We've had some unfriendlies skulking about; smaller villages have been raided, people gone missing. That sort of thing. Just so you know we haven't forgotten our manners."

Devon nodded, grabbed Shadow's reins, and began to move through the small crowd."I understand. Four men came at me about ten miles back."

The man's eyes widened as he looked at Devon and his horse."What happened?"

Devon continued walking."It didn't go as they'd planned."

After the horses were stabled and plenty of water and hay provided, Devon was led to the inn by his one-man welcoming committee. The tall, skinny villager introduced himself."The name's Varner. I'm sorry about that back there, but we are all pretty jumpy these days. The bandits have spooked the lot of us."

"I understand," Devon offered. As they walked down the main street, he noted that no one else was outside, though it was barely dusk. All the buildings were boarded up and the only indication of life was light that escaped between narrow gaps in the wood.

When they approached the inn, Varner moved up the steps and rapped heavily on the door. In moments, a small opening was exposed as a cover slid aside and the villager identified himself. "Master Flinn, it's me, Varner. I be escorting an official emissary from King Sorbonne. His name's Longstreet and he needs a room for the night."

The opening disappeared and Devon heard the scrape of wooden bars being lifted before the inn door opened and Varner motioned him inside.

The innkeeper did not offer his hand."I'm Huart Flinn. Not much call for rooms lately so take whatever you want on the second floor."

"I'll need a bath and a meal to go along with the room," Devon informed Flinn. He held up his purse."I've the money today." The taciturn inn keeper frowned and nodded. He turned and grabbed a lantern, leading the way across the large room and up the stairs. Devon took the first room he came to and Flinn placed the lantern on a small table before he left to heat Devon's bath.

The room was good sized, though sparsely furnished, and the bed shoved up against the far wall promised an improvement over the dirt floor of a barn, no matter how much hay was tossed on it. Devon dropped his pack near the foot of the bed and sat down. Undressing slowly, he stopped to rub his tired feet and aching muscles. He was sorry that the inn was deserted. After weeks of traveling alone, he had been looking forward to the company and entertainment that a busy tavern usually offered.

A knock on the door interrupted his thoughts."Master Longstreet," the innkeeper hollered through the wood, "your bath is ready."

Moments later, after a brisk walk down the hall, Devon lowered himself into a steaming tub. The water loosened muscles stiffened by the earlier combat and the lengthy ride that had followed. He allowed himself the luxury of a good soak before he scrubbed at the dirt accumulated from nearly a week since his last bath. After he rinsed and toweled off, he dressed then made his way down the stairs to the kitchen.

He was settling himself at a large table when a woman came out with a plateful of food. She was small, with a pinched look and left quickly without meeting his eyes. Soon, Flinn returned, carrying a large mug of frothy ale which he placed in front of Devon. Devon, in turn, wasted no time and drank deeply.

"Ah," Devon said and lifted his glass in thanks.

The innkeeper waited to be sure the woman was gone before turning back to Devon."So. You're King Sorbonne's emissary?"

His mouth full of food, Devon nodded.

"Varner says you're a sentinel."

Devon wasn't sure if the innkeeper was asking or making a statement, so he said nothing.

"You have the look of one – the scarring on your hands, well-cared for weapons, a grace to your movements." Flinn studied him for several moments before he spoke again."And eyes that have stared death in the face on more than one occasion."

"A lot of men can say that," Devon rasped.

"True enough," the innkeeper replied."But most of them return home to a wife and children, and that puts some warmth in their gaze that sentinels lack."

Devon laughed."Some of us have families, loved ones. Some don't. But all of us know firsthand how cruel men can be. We've learned to not hesitate to rid the world of such men."

"And that makes you harder than most," Flinn concluded.

Devon studied the interesting man for a moment before he eventually nodded."That's true enough."

"Let me ask you," Master Flinn said leaning forward, suddenly eager."Is anything amiss in Dania? Or in Palaton?"the innkeeper asked, referring to the two kingdoms west of Sealand.

"In what respect?"

The innkeeper took a deep breath and shook his head."We haven't been getting food supplies from the local farms. Someone went to look into it, but he never returned. A shipment of dry goods from Seadawn is weeks overdue. Since you're the Danian king's emissary, I thought you might know something."

Devon saw the concern etched on the man's face and wished he could reassure him. But he could not, and there was no reason to keep him in the dark. He had as much right to know the current state of affairs as any man.

"The journey through Palaton was uneventful, but there are signs elsewhere. Gleneden's fishermen have been harassed by strange vessels; Dania is plagued by random marauders. And, your King has withdrawn his ambassador from the Gleneden court. It does not bode well."

The innkeeper rubbed his forehead with his hands then grabbed a chair and slumped into it."King Dawad isn't popular, but he's left us alone for the most part. But his greediness is legendary. He could be positioning for war against Gleneden."

Devon raised his eyebrows."Dania, Palaton and Oreon would ally with Gleneden. Surely you know that?"

"Oh, indeed," the innkeeper replied, nodding."Most Sealanders would oppose it, but an army does what it's ordered. The common people could not stop such a war."

Devon bobbed his head.

Flinn looked at Devon, as if searching for hope."You will continue on to Seadawn? What if the king refuses to see you?"

Devon looked soberly at the worried man."If that happens, the mystery won't be solved, but I'll have an answer to take to my king."

Pounding from the front of the inn interrupted them. With Devon following close behind, the host hurried over, pushed a board aside that blocked the door, gaping at the bloodied few who stood before him.

"Master Flinn, there's fighting at the edge of town," Devon's original escort gushed."We need help. Now!"

Devon raced back up the stairs to his room, grabbed his knife and sword then sprinted back to the wounded messengers.

"How many?" he asked as he brushed past them.

"A dozen, more or less," one man replied. "On foot," another offered.

"It took all three of you to come for help?" Devon challenged.

They heard the rebuke in his voice."We're not cowards."

Devon didn't bother to waste additional words. He wheeled around, a weapon in both hands and ran toward the sounds of men fighting. The three men hesitated and then ran after him.

As his small group rounded the corner, he saw one last townsman, pitchfork in hand, stabbing at several attackers. Another half dozen antagonists looked on. They turned at the sound of their approach.

Devon charged the nearest man, using his sword to knock one weapon aside and slashing that foe's throat with a backhanded slice of his knife. The three townsmen with Devon drew heart and leapt into the fray.

Others raced to join them, roused from their beds by the innkeeper. Their appearance distracted the enemy long enough for Devon to run his sword through a second attacker then throw his knife into the heart of a third.

With their advantage slipping away, the strangers drew together in a defensive circle. In moments, the townspeople had them badly outnumbered. For several tense seconds, the two sides faced each other."You've no chance," Master Flinn, the innkeeper, claimed."Drop your weapons."

Devon saw the flash of resolve on the oldest opponent's face and tightened the grip on his sword. "Watch yourselves," he told the townsmen.

Recognizing him as the deadliest foe, the man launched himself at Longstreet. The two swords rang with sound as they clashed violently as each man fought for leverage. Devon became oblivious to the struggles around him. He grunted, needing all his concentration and strength to keep the man at bay. Time stretched as each fought for an advantage. Sweat began pouring down both their faces.

Suddenly, Devon relaxed one leg. Falling backward, he used the man's momentum to flip him overhead. Before the man could regain his feet, Devon spun around then impaled him with his sword. He let go of it and grabbed the attacker by his tunic.

"Who are you?" Devon demanded, but life faded from the man's eyes. Frustrated, he threw the body aside.

Growing aware of the silence, he looked up to see the townsmen staring at him. The innkeeper's meat cleaver was dripping blood and the iron skillet in his other hand was covered with clumps of red matter. Flinn roused himself from the numbing stupor resulting from the violence."We must bury our dead," he said. His voice propelled the others into action.

"What about them?" Varner asked, pointing to the attackers.

Longstreet grunted and then spat."Start a fire and burn them." He left the men to their sober task and started to trudge back toward the inn, ignoring the frightened stares of gathering townsfolk. He heard a woman weeping behind him and knew she would not be the last to mourn the loss of a loved one on this dark night. He lumbered up the steps and shoved the inn door open, making his way across the room to the stairs. He longed for a lengthy sleep but knew he must rise early and be on the road before dawn. He needed answers for his king and they lay in Seadawn. His sentinel instinct was telling him there was no time to waste. Something big was brewing in this troubled land and he needed answers fast.

CHAPTER 3

THE SHALA RISE

Alone, at the rooftop of his world, Tahjeen Tier stroked the black panther stretched out beside him. He and his *fel* relaxed atop a stone outcropping, perched several hundred feet above the city, and gazed out at a broad expanse that stretched for miles.

The afternoon was gorgeous, pregnant with the promise of a beautiful sunset. But the moment was bittersweet. If Tahjeen's dream was a true foretelling, the Shala were not likely to enjoy many more days like this.

No, Tahjeen thought. There must to be more to life than unquestioning obedience to a centuries old prophecy. Why had the original words been written? A long time ago someone had deemed it necessary for the Shala to be chained to an eternal obligation of protecting the human population of Sandala. Who had made that decision, and more importantly, why?

One purpose, to dance with death – to fight and perhaps die, for humans. With all his heart, Tahjeen believed this was not enough. He wanted real answers, not just a rote response about duty.

He stood, his seven foot frame casting a long shadow. Normally a long, colorful robe gave him a lean appearance. But now, dressed in his fighting tunic, his arms were bared and his striking musculature showed. He stepped further out on the ledge, his white blond hair in sharp contrast to his bronzed skin. He marveled at the geography carved long ago by the eruption of the now extinct volcano. The entire Shala population lay nestled inside the expanse which measured over eight miles from rim to rim.

He studied the city below where people went about their daily routines. Around a circular dwelling, sumptuous stew was cooking in vat-sized batches while hundreds of pans filled with sweet biscuits were cooking in baking ovens as big as small homes. His keen eyesight took in the cats and kittens watching, hoping a delicious scrap would be tossed their way. The aroma drifted up to him, a reminder that dinner was in less than an hour though he was hardly hungry.

At a large cistern, people were busy folding up leather and cloth tunics, light sleepwear and soft undergarments that had been washed and set out to dry earlier that morning. Occasional laughter from the workers floated up, and Tahjeen was gratified his people could find joy in mundane tasks.

He shifted his gaze to a huge arena fenced by tall bundles of grass. Languishing on the bales were dozens of leopards, panthers, tigers and mountain lions, *fels* that belonged to the individual warriors. The felines watched as young men, women, boys and girls, trained at one of a dozen or more stations. They were learning the arts of war – wrestling, hand-to-hand combat, sword work, knife throwing, bow and arrow, and other techniques. Skilled warriors taught everything. There wasn't a person in the village unable to defend himself.

To the right sat a large stone building spanning several stories. It was the library and learning center. Inside those walls, the lore of his people was passed from one generation to the next. Courses in geography, writing, reading and mathematics were taught as well. More advanced studies and the arts had buildings of their own. Spread throughout the population center, master craftsmen and women trained all-comers regardless of age.

Tahjeens's people lived a relatively simple, harmonious life. Yet his heart ached, for his dream foretold that the serenity produced by five centuries of peace was ending. He stared hard at the scene below, wondering who would have to make the ultimate sacrifice and pay with his life in order to fulfill the prophecy's promise. Bitterness, however, was coupled with immense dignity and pride that came from being given the sacred responsibility of protecting the humans of Sandala. As the ancient lore stated and the elders taught, the Shala existed for one purpose - to keep the human beings of Sandala alive. And, until that sacrifice was called for they were to remain detached, living apart, never to meddle in the affairs of men.

Still, he was conflicted. Several years earlier when he had traveled in disguise among the humans, he had found them less worthy than the prophecy indicated. His own people were far more civilized and just. Once again, he questioned, what made humans so special that the Shala bore the burden of protecting them?

He watched the blazing marigold orb hanging low in the sky. Soon, it would dip below the western rim of the crater. He heard footsteps and his *fel* announced, *"your mother approaches."*

Tahjeen turned to face her then knelt and bowed his head."Vigilance, oh queen."

He looked up to see an affectionate smile cover her face. Her age was difficult to determine. She might be thirty, or forty, or sixty. Her long blond hair was interspersed with gray and hung in a single braid and her skin was a deep brown, smooth and unlined."I thought I might find you here." She gestured all around."It is a wonderful place to come for peace of mind."

Tahjeen stood, looking down a little at his mother, Mardra Tier, Shala Queen."Yet, I have found none this day. No answers...just more questions."

"It does not surprise me that serenity eludes you. I have spoken to our sage and he confirmed that your dream was a foretelling." He saw her eyes glisten with pride, or was it determination?

"Another watcher has returned. His report mirrors the others. That makes ten in all," she added quietly. She paused. Grave concern etched lines on her face. "The prophecy unfolds."

Watchers' reports were limited, but thanks to their diligence, they knew several things. The kingdom of Sealand had withdrawn within itself, its usual hospitality turned aside, replaced by suspicion and hostility. Throughout Sandala, raiding parties of unknown origin were creating unrest and suspicion. Add those facts to his dream of a vast armada approaching the warm waters off Seadawn's coast and it was clear war was coming to Sandala.

"As commander of our warriors, there is something you must do. Alone," the Queen added.

Tahjeen gave her a puzzled look then changed the subject to his older brother, Drayen, heir to the Shala throne."What of Drayen? Will he be returning home?" Tahjeen asked.

She shook her head."His duty lies elsewhere. He and his wife are on their way to Dania, where King Sorbonne has called a clave."

Tahjeen was surprised."A clave? That's fortunate. It is rare to call the rulers of Sandala's five kingdoms together."

His mother nodded."King Sorbonne is intuitive. He is not blind to the oddity of strange marauding bands inside his borders. Having all the rulers gathered there will save us time."

She paused, a rare look of fear passed so quickly across her face that Tahjeen was uncertain he saw it.

She took a deep breath."You must come with me now."

At the floor of the basin, she turned and entered the path leading to her home. A few moments later, they walked through the door of her private chamber. She quickened her step and Tahjeen lengthened his stride to keep pace. Once inside her quarters, she turned to him.

"You must leave your *fel* here. This is one task you must undertake alone."

He nodded then gave Paca a silent command to obey. The queen headed across the room, turning to enter an alcove. Inside, various weapons lay within easy reach. A gleaming bronze shield was the central figure on the wall. Around it, razor sharp spears pointed inwards offset by dozens of knives of different lengths. Circling them all were swords. They lay tip to end and varied in size and weight.

"You will face a series of daunting trials. There is no predicting what obstacles lay in wait or what form they might take. Select a weapon but do not encumber yourself. A small token of protection is best."

He removed a long knife from its ornamental stand and rejoined her as she hurried across the room to the far wall.

"This is a picture of my father that I drew when I was quite young," she said, pointing up at a crude sketch scrawled by a childish hand. Still, you could tell that the figure was tall and robust."Pray that his spirit accompanies you now."

For a moment Tahjeen studied his grandfather. Out of the corner of his eye, he saw his mother slip her hand behind the portrait and push against the stone it covered. There was a loud click as a latch was tripped and the wall began to rumble open. It ground its way laterally for several feet, scraping across the floor.

"Be ever vigilant, my son," she said, briefly resting her hands on his forearms. She met his eyes and he saw the colors change, reflecting fear and hope and pride. She gave him a squeeze, released him, and turned to leave.

Without looking back at his mother, Tahjeen stepped through the opening in front of him. A long stone stairway stretched below, lit by small, flickering torches every thirty feet. He wondered who lit them as he wound his way in a twisting descent. The air stayed surprisingly warm even as he sensed he was dropping hundreds of feet down into the bowels of the earth. He was even more puzzled by the secrecy behind his destination. His mother had never mentioned it to him. The steps seemed to go on forever as the stairs weaved their way along the narrow passage.

Smooth stone walls surrounded him. Surprisingly, they were not damp. There was no smell of mold or decay. Instead, the passage appeared to be used regularly, which he found curious. Drawings adorned the walls, barely illuminated by the meager light. Despite the shadows, he could tell they were colorful, almost majestic, depicting heroes of past wars going back hundreds, maybe thousands of years. Sketches showed creatures he had never seen before. They were attacking his forefathers along with other humans he did not recognize. They were a fair-skinned enemy with light hair.

He worked his way down, passing many such drawings, as time seemed to lose itself. At long last the stairs ended and he came to a huge cavern, its ceiling disappearing far above him. The torches that circled it cast eerie shadows along the walls. He shivered.

Across the cavern were three entryways. He had no idea which one to choose. With no reason for hesitation, he walked to the one on his right simply because it was closest.

He started forward into the passageway, tightening the grip on his knife. After a hundred steps another cavern opened before him. This one was smaller and very cold. His breath froze before him and his lungs ached when he inhaled.

Something shattered off to his left and he spun quickly in that direction. Glassy ice lay in a pile on the floor below an icicle that was at least ten feet in height. More ice broke behind him and again on his right as two more impressive icicles seemed to lean against the wall. Then all three began to move.

The ice in each screeched apart, separating into arms and legs. In slow, jerky steps they lurched towards him. As they drew near, the cold intensified, ice forming on the stones they touched. They circled him, forcing Tahjeen to turn constantly, and he felt certain that if one of those creatures enfolded him he would die. He readied himself and raised his knife.

Instantly one of the creatures reached out with frigid fingers. Tahjeen slashed downward, severing the limb. When its arm hit the floor it did not shatter, but melted into harmless water. He stepped away, gaining room to face the two other frozen attackers.

He charged the closest one, his knife a blur of movement, lashing through the coldness, cutting it from crotch to head then slicing off its legs. It disappeared entirely into a small pool of chalky water. But the first figure had continued moving forward and he sensed its awful nearness. Spinning left, he leapt high, his knife arching down toward the strange, pointed head. But as his knife delivered the mortal blow, the falling creature's remaining arm reached out and brushed his leg.

He screamed then watched in horror as his leg grew cold and began to freeze solid. But there was no time to waste on pain for the third icicle was nearly on top of him. Crippled, Tahjeen's movements were restricted and he was forced to toss his knife from one hand to the next, each time rendering a damaging blow until the creature was nothing more than rapidly melting shards.

Panting heavily, he leaned on his good leg. The chill in the room began to dissipate. Slowly, the feeling returned to his leg until it was as if nothing had happened.

"Games!" he cried."Why must I play such games?"

His challenge echoed off walls.

Grimly, Tahjeen moved toward the far opening and entered. There was no point wasting time contemplating what challenge lay ahead. Instead, he focused on the area immediately surrounding him.

The passageway narrowed, the walls drawing uncomfortably close. The torches began to flicker and in the gloom he felt the ceiling pressing down on him. He gagged on a breath of air that whispered past him, its sickening odor, warm and foul, trapped between the walls.

The breeze stiffened, raising the hem of his tunic as a whistling sound came from somewhere ahead. The noise swelled. It seemed to bounce along the walls and surround him. Through the stiff wind and putrid stench, he forged on until at last, he saw them.

Misty wraiths floated towards him, moving on the wind, their mouths agape and wailing. Where one touched a wall the stone begin to sizzle with bubbles and start to melt. Acid! Then they dipped and swooped and were upon him.

As they swirled around him, he slashed his knife in lightning quick motions. One of the creatures, cut in half, completely dissipated. Another floated near and he slit it once, spun and raked through another while spiraling back and slicing the head off of the first. It evaporated and was gone.

Before he could whirl back and destroy the other, its wispy tendrils laced about his arm. A scream tore from his throat and he fell back against the wall, fighting to remain conscious. Through eyes teary with excruciating pain, he watched as acid ate its way through his skin then reached the bone.

With his one remaining, arm he pushed away from the wall, forcing himself to rise and confront the final assailant. Again and again, he swung the short blade. He ducked and jumped aside as the wraith reached out, trying to envelope him. It howled, frustrated, and drew back, gathering itself for a final assault. It grew and spread, covering the ceiling and walls. His knife sparked against the stone as he whipped and cut and slashed and thrust until finally, all was quiet and he was once again alone.

Sweat rolled down his forehead. His tunic dragged at him, soaked through with perspiration. His eyes narrowed, turning from a brilliant orange into a fiery red as anger coursed through him. Now did not seem the time for such tests and trials. What purpose did it serve?

Again, as before with his icy nemesis, his injured limb restored itself, leaving no sign of injury. Magically, the dampness in his clothes evaporated. Resolute and irritated, he trudged toward the light at the end of the passageway.

He stepped out into a gigantic cavern. It was lined with hundreds of shelves filled with books. They stretched as far as he could see.

It appeared to be a library. Row upon row marched across the cavernous space, disappearing into the ceiling high above. He wound his way through them until he came to an opening in the middle. At a small table, a strange creature sat staring. Tahjeen wasn't sure what it was – a ground hog, or nutria? It was difficult to tell because most of its brown fur was covered by a striped woolen cape that was tied in the middle. A cap sat lopsided on its head.

"Oh, my!" the creature said, startled."Who are you? What do you want? What are you doing here?" It stood up on its back legs, a quill pen trembled in one of its paws.

Tahjeen was having none of the absurdity. Marching quickly across the open space, he raised his knife high."Enough!" he shouted."This ends now!" He started to bring the knife down when a voice thundered all around him.

"Hold!"

The creature before him scurried away into the night, leaving behind its silly cap. Then the wall behind the table melted away, replaced by shimmering, semi-translucent drapes. They rippled slowly as something huge moved behind them. He caught a fleeting glimpse of spots and stripes - something pacing on four legs.

He sensed *It* watching...waiting. Well, let it wait no more.

"Why the games? The challenges? What if I had failed, hadn't survived to reach the surface?" he said, his voice filled with outrage.

The curtains moved again as they creature whipped about."You are brave, but unwise," the powerful voice rumbled."Think!" *It* bellowed, the sound loud enough to hurt his ears.

Tahjeen forced himself to stand his ground."What exactly would you have me think?" he said simply.

The creature roared its impatience, the noise deafening as it echoed off the walls. He felt the sound blowing past him, trying to push him back but he stayed rooted to the floor and waited. A long brown tail, marked by a tuft of hair at its end, swished briefly outside the curtain.

"More than one entrance exists. What if someone else stumbled on to one and gained access?" *It* finally explained."There have to be tests that only you can pass."

Tahjeen chewed over the answer. It was far from satisfying.

"You are here now," the creature continued."In the defense of the humans of Sandala, I can help you in three ways. One tied to the past, one to the present and one to the future."There was a pause as if he was being given time to consider, but the words were charged with double meaning. Tahjeen's mind worked furiously. Was this still some game? Why three questions? What was he supposed to ask? What kind of creature was this?

Dampness formed on his brow as he recalled words uttered by his mother and teachers. They floated through his mind - lessons from military sages, political philosophers and endless classes on leadership. 'Know your enemy...trust sparingly...expect surprise...plan for the future'.   After long moments, he took a deep breath then slowly exhaled.

"I seek knowledge of my enemy, guidance among allies and awareness of the future," he said, fervently hoping that he had neither underplayed nor overplayed his hand, that whatever information the creature chose to share would be useful.

Suddenly, the curtains drew aside and before him stood the largest male lion he had ever seen. Its head was massive. A rich, full mane trailed down its neck, its brilliant brown hue complimented by a glorious golden coat. The paws were as big across as he was tall. The lion moved closer, the powerful shoulders rippling with muscle. The ground vibrated with each step and his golden hide reflected the stripes of tigers and the spots of leopards as he moved. He seemed to be a composite of all three, though the lion in him dominated. Tahjeen collapsed to his knees and bowed humbly, completely awed.

"Look at me," the lion commanded, "and witness the recent past."

He obeyed instantly and was lost in the depths of the cat's large eyes. They were fathomless and hypnotic. Slowly, a vision began to form. Hundreds of ships, perhaps thousands, were sailing from a harbor he did not recognize. This was the enemy's armada, he realized. It was even larger than reported, filling the seas as it moved toward the horizon. Then it parted, half entering Seadawn's great harbor while the remainder continued in a southwesterly direction. Two armadas! One in Sealand, as the watchers had reported. The other – to Dania? Was another army headed for Dania? It was the only possibility that made any sense. Then the vision was gone.

"For the present," the gigantic lion said, "know that a trusted ally will betray you."

His mind whirled. A traitor? Yes, Dawad, King of Sealand seemed to welcome the enemy to his shores. But that was too obvious and he had never been trustworthy. It must be another. There had to be another! But whom?

"Finally," the regal beast concluded, "in the future, a twin's deceit threatens your entire race."

He was deeply shocked. Twins were common among his people. Who could it be? Shala? Human? Perhaps the enemy? Oh, he wailed silently, such information was nearly useless, the possibilities endless.

"You have asked and I have answered," the King of beasts said. His voice had grown softer, almost sad. "My days as guardian and guide are almost at an end. I can serve the Shala only one more time. But you must find me in the city of *fels,* deep within the frontier."

He did not diminish in size, but for the first time Tahjeen noticed grey amidst the tawny mane and facial whiskers. He realized the claws were torn and yellow with wear. The lion's massive shoulders now sagged with a deep weariness. How old was he, Tahjeen wondered? How long had he been here for the Shala?

He sat back, no longer doubting the truth of the creature's words or even the value of his advice. It was up to him to solve the complexity. He had asked and the lion had answered.

"Thank you," Tahjeen said humbly.

The creature bowed his huge head then turned and disappeared into the shadows.

Tahjeen returned the way he came and found his mother waiting for him. He stopped, shocked."Your hair!" he said. She gave him a puzzled look."It has gone completely gray."

She pulled at her long braid, inspecting it and saw the truth of his words."I wondered," she said."You didn't seem gone that long but I felt my heart slow and its beat become erratic."

She looked up at Tahjeen and beckoned for him to sit beside her. He bowed low then stepped toward her and covered her hands with his own. They shared a long look. Finally, he spoke. He wasted little time, ignoring the challenges he had faced and instead talked only of the answer to his three questions.

"I fear my questions were weak and led to answers that are too vague to be of help."

But his mother shook her head."It would not matter. Your questions were precise and the answer to anything you might have asked would be equally complex. We have learned things of great importance. We can prepare for the second armada and I agree that it is bound for Dania." She sighed, her shoulders lowering. In resignation, he wondered?

"And for the rest, well, it is always wise counsel to never completely trust your allies and now we know for certain that one will betray you. It will not be Dawad," she continued."His betrayal is already complete."

He watched her study him for a long moment. "But I fear the hardest will involve twins. You must never allow any close to you. Choose a companion you can confide in and let him always be present when you deal with a twin."

Tahjeen nodded, his human friend, Achates, coming quickly to mind. His loyalty was unquestioned."Mother, may I ask you something?"

"Of course."

"Who was that creature?" he asked.

A wondrous smile enveloped her features."My son, you have had the great honor and privilege of meeting the King of the *Fels.*"

His mouth fell open in surprise."He advises us?" he asked deliberately.

The queen shook her head."No, Tahjeen. He commands us. And all Shala obey."

He was rocked, the rules by which he knew his world broken apart."But we are independent, self-governing. We have our own laws."

"No people are truly independent, Tahjeen. Each society may have their own customs and laws, but there are universal truths that all must obey in order to survive. The King of the *Fels* demands that those truths be followed and the Shala are the tools he uses to enforce them."

Tahjeen's eyes showed colors of outrage and denial, turning crimson then rust.

"Understand," the queen continued, "we are the only race he judges worthy and capable of such a task. It is a great honor."

"But we have lived apart, independent, self-sufficient. We rely on no one," he countered.

"You force me to repeat that no race is completely independent, Tahjeen. You *must* understand that. You *must* believe it. Life is often a struggle between those who do and those who do not. Our role is to stop the ignorant from destroying us all. I say to you again, to serve as he commands is the greatest honor there is."

He sighed but the blue of serenity colored his eyes. He was

beginning to understand.

The queen stood and he rose quickly in response."Call the council and military leaders to the legal chamber. Have food served there as well." She hesitated, momentarily paralyzed by the gravity of her next command.

"What is it?" His voice was gentle.

"The village elders must do something no living Shala has ever done," she said eventually.

Tahjeen held his breath, waiting for the words that would change their lives forever.

"Tell them to light the signal fires and raise the banner."Her cat howled as she spoke the words and matching feline calls echoed all around her.

Once Tahjeen did as she asked, the village sprang into action. Centuries of lessons drilled into generations of Shala had prepared them well. At the arena's armory, older men formed a long line and began passing along a wide array of weapons that were eventually stacked in three different piles. At the food stores hundreds of people began putting together packs of dried meat, fruits and biscuits for an army who wouldn't always have the time to stop and hunt.

All the men and women who had chosen to be warriors for their life's work, raced home to don their leather fighting tunics. They grabbed their rucksacks before heading to the arena to be outfitted with short and long knives, two swords, a bow and a quiver of arrows, one axe, a shield and spear. Once armed, they would pick up their rations and then assemble outside the village. When the meeting with the Queen was over, the military leaders would join them and relay the orders.

Everyone was busy. There was little talk, many meaningful looks and family farewells, but no time was wasted, for all knew what the fires and raised banner meant: the Shala were rising.

While the rest of the population worked feverishly to prepare, the Council and military leaders gathered in the Legal Chamber. Soup and meaty sweet biscuits were eaten quickly.

As her main ruling body, the individuals now present had been kept fully apprised of events pertinent to Shalaen life, so all were aware of the different watchers racing home with reports of invaders. They had anticipated this moment, knowing that as the reports piled up one upon the other the Queen would have to make a decision.

She studied them one by one, her eyes communicating that she fully understood what she was about to order. They also understood. They knew the prophecy as well as she.

"Ever vigilant," she said, officially opening the session. Everyone present responded in kind. Then she turned to Tahjeen, addressing him formally."Tahjeen Tier, Military Commander, please announce your intentions."

"Vigilance," he repeated, though the rest remained tense and silent. His chiseled, dark features glanced at each in turn."The situation is one of great peril and the need for action is more urgent that we thought."

The men and women at the table absorbed his words in silence."Dania appears the major target. Besides Sealand, it has the most evidence of infiltration and attacks. More importantly, we have received additional information indicating that a second armada may land there as well. Because of this, I am dividing our military."

He looked directly at a lean young man seated at the opposite end."Katar, take your *kosh* across the Sea of Death and on to the northwest coast of Dania. Prepare to defend against a sea invasion." Katar nodded quickly in response. Nothing else that passed between the two men gave any indication that they had shared a close friendship since childhood.

Tahjeen shifted his gaze to a brawny male warrior and striking, statuesque woman seated to the right."Toman, Katrine, combine your *koshes* and travel the southern caverns. Your destination is Dania's capitol. I will travel with you. We will rest tonight and leave at first light."

The two leaders shared a quick glance then bowed to Tahjeen. His final penetrating look settled on an older man to his left. A golden mountain lion sat beside him, resting his huge head on the warrior's thigh. After a moment, Tahjeen smiled."Gable, the most difficult task is yours."

Gable returned the smile. Though older than the others, he was hardly feeble. He was the Master Warrior in charge of all arena training and in prime fighting condition.

"Take your *kosh,*" Tahjeen directed, "through the eastern caverns and into Gleneden. From there, split your forces and infiltrate the three remaining kingdoms. You must gather intelligence, undermine the invaders, and provide assistance to the populace whenever possible."

He paused, emphasizing the importance of his next words."Gable, we need to know what is happening in those kingdoms. What you learn will be used to form the basis of our defense. Keep your warriors alive. Do not directly engage. Be prepared to organize a large-scale retreat."

"I understand," Gable answered. Tahjeen had selected him purposefully because of his age and experience. Younger leaders might initially be excited, even eager to go to battle. His role was just as vital, but called for restraint.

"Tahjeen," spoke a handsome woman from the left, "will any additional defensive precautions be taken?"

"Yes, Madell. Though our island kingdom is basically unknown to the outside and impenetrable, we will want to be aware of any activity. You will double the number of watchers on the island shores and dispatch a half-dozen more to each of the fore islands."

Tahjeen turned to another man and ordered him to dramatically increase the number of defenders at both cavern entrances."We must on all accounts keep the caverns safe. No one can foretell how much we'll rely on them in the coming days."

Additional questions were not asked. Certainly no one challenged Tahjeen's complete autonomy to make these decisions. He had total power of the military. But they had been involved from the start, their input and advice crucial in planning this course of action. Not one of his orders came as a surprise.

The queen stood and gestured to a man across the room. He hurried to her, bearing a box which contained a shimmering crown made of black gold. He bowed low and offered it to her.

She reached inside the box and retrieved the crown then placed it on her head. It was the first time she had worn any symbol of authority since the day of her coronation many years ago.

For a moment, she stood quietly. Even though it wasn't truly possible, she seemed to grow taller. "I, Mardra Tier, Queen of the Shala, now wear the crown of war." As one the others stood and spoke the next words in unison."The Shala rise!" The big cats in the room joined the chorus with full-throated roars.

CHAPTER 4

DUTY CALLS

Studying a tanned piece of leather, Tahjeen reviewed the plans one more time. The continent of Sandala stared back at him. He looked at the hidden basin outside of the crater, where Katar's *kosh* were busy boarding the boats anchored in the harbor. A third would go below immediately and prepare to work the oars. The rest would spread across the main deck to either rest or tend the sails. They would rotate shifts every two hours allowing them to maintain a furious pace. Tahjeen estimated they would cross the Sea of Death in less than a day, and be at Dania's western shore two days later.

He didn't envy Katar's role. If, as presumed, the enemy armada landed there, Katar's task would be daunting. According to the vision of the King of the Fels, Katar would be heavily outnumbered – perhaps as much as twenty to one. Even Shala could not repel such odds. Tahjeen stared unseeing at the map before him. His eyes turned the color of a pale moon, reflecting sorrow that he might never see his childhood friend again.

He shook his head to clear the gloom, his eyes once again the emerald green of determined focus. He moved his finger to the eastern cavern entrance where Gable's *kosh* was headed. His journey through that cavern would take two days before they would enter Gleneden and begin their complex task. But Gable was proficient and Tahjeen had little doubt that whatever he was assigned to do would be completed.

His finger moved to the southern cavern where Toman and Katrine's *koshes* were waiting for him. Like Gable's group, it would take two days to reach the entrance inside Dania. But Tahjeen wanted to get there far sooner. He intended to take a handful of warriors and scout ahead.

That won't happen if I keep staring at this map, he told himself. *Come Paca,* he mentally called his *fel. There is no more time to waste.*

It was not wasted, his *fel* responded. *You needed the time to steel yourself for what lies ahead.*

Tahjeen did not answer but started running towards the western cavern.

Toman and Katrine's *koshes*, ten thousand men, women and *fels*, lined both sides of the cavern's wide mouth. Set in the southwestern area of the crater, the early morning sun had yet to reach it. The wide entrance lay in the shadows, its mouth a gaping black hole. Tahjeen and Paca loped towards the two leaders and stopped in front of them.

"I am going on ahead with a small party to scout the area outside of the Danian entrance," Tahjeen told them."You know what to do."

Katrine nodded, pulling her plentiful blonde hair behind her head and tying by a leather string. Impressive muscles rippled across her long arms as she worked."Are you going to implore the *blurl* for aid?" she asked.

"Yes. Cantankerous or not, I doubt they will refuse. They care about Sandala as much as we do."

"Who's going with you?" Toman asked. His stoic features showed no concern at this new development.

In response, Tahjeen waved four young warriors and two additional *fels* forward.

"Achates and Morgan will help if we encounter any humans, plus they know the area well. Dutong and Langwyn will be the Shala bodyguard my mother insists upon."

"Your mother is wise, Tahjeen. You are not invulnerable," Katrine reminded him.

Tahjeen shrugged."Destiny can be delayed but in the end, it's unavoidable, regardless of bodyguards."

Toman and Katrine looked away and Tahjeen regretted his gloomy words. He stepped forward and placed his hands on their shoulders."We'll be careful. May the spirits of our ancestors watch over you both. Be vigilant. My eyes are always yours. We'll meet again soon." With that, Tahjeen and his small party turned away and raced into the entrance.

After several hours of hard running, they could hear the sound of splashing water. A few moments later, Tahjeen and his companions stopped at small waterfall deep inside the cavern. The tunnel was wider here and several pools formed along the edge. Off to one side, a worn rock ledge extended along the wall, inviting dozens to sit and languish. In a large alcove, Tahjeen saw several rafts, each large enough for him and his companions. He nodded to himself, turning and approaching the waterfall. Leaning forward, he placed his palms against the rock behind the falls. Water splashed off his tunic and ran down his forearms. He closed his eyes then began to chant, his voice low and tinged with hope.

Keeper of the sea, come to me, come to me.
Lover of this land, run to me, run to me.
A humble Shala needs your aid, be not afraid.
Keeper of the sea, come to me, come to me.

He repeated the refrain for several minutes. Then the cascading water parted, avoiding his hands as it ran down the wall, splattering onto the floor in the center of the cavern. It stopped there and began pushing upward, gurgling as it formed into a tall, liquid being not unlike the Shala in stature. Torches along the cavern walls cast the form in a yellowish hue.

Tahjeen pushed away from the falls and faced the watery form."Greetings *blurl*. You honor me by answering my call."

"Hmmph," it rumbled in a bubbly fashion."For a royal son of a Queen, you asked quite politely, though we must say that we have never regarded you as humble. How can we help you?"

Tahjeen ignored the jibe."My companions and I need to reach Dania quickly and request that you transport us on your honored waters."

The *blurl* bubbled rapidly."Shala can run fast enough without our help."

The tall form started to collapse toward the floor.

"Please wait," Tahjeen implored, throwing out a hand."Sandala is under siege. The land is being invaded. For the first time in over five hundred years, the Shala rise."

The creature reformed quickly."Why didn't you say so in the first place?"

It turned to the waterfall and in moments a roaring echoed through the cavern as the flow increased ten-fold. While his friends hurried to retrieve one of the rafts, Tahjeen watched a big wave begin to form. He thought he heard the *blurl* mutter 'wasting time' and 'inarticulate'.

Within a few minutes the wave almost reached the ceiling of the cavern. The raft was placed in front of it and at the *blurl's* urging, the small company of warriors stepped aboard. Water flooded beneath them lifting the raft. Moments later the wave pushed forward and began propelling them at lightning speed down the cavern.

Tahjeen and the rest huddled in the middle as the sides of the tunnel began racing by. The speed increased until the walls seemed to disappear altogether. Never comfortable on or in water, the three *fels* mewed their displeasure. Tahjeen and the two other Shala petted them urging calm.

After several minutes, a human near his own age with dark, curly hair that ended mid-neckline spoke up."What is it you have in mind?" Achates asked.

Tahjeen turned and faced the young man who had lived among the Shala for three years. He was married to Katrine's sister and had adopted the Shala ways."I'm not sure. I just don't like the idea of ten thousand of us bursting from the cavern without having some sense of what might be waiting for us."

Achates nodded."You think someone might actually know about us?"

"I have no idea. We'll get some horses from the corral just inside the entrance then scout the area to make sure no enemy is nearby. We need to get to Dania unimpeded."

"What of the armada landing at Seadawn?"Achates asked.

"Based on Sealand's behavior, they are already siding with the invaders if not working with them overtly. Rather than face them head on, we'll defend Dania. It's the real plum of the five kingdoms. And, as it happens, their king has called a clave so all the rulers will be there. It's an opportunity to reveal ourselves and work directly with the Sandalese."

Tahjeen saw Achates nod."Dania is wealthy, their army is formidable and King Sorbonne has a sterling reputation," Achates said.

Langwyn and Dutong, the two Shala bodyguards, had leaned closer to listen to the discussion. Both were close to Tahjeen in age, though Dutong, the larger of the two, would turn twenty in a matter of weeks. His dark auburn hair flowed halfway down his back."Will we scout in several directions?"Langwyn asked.

"We'll stay together and sweep a crescent shape about fifty miles around the cavern opening. Toman and Katrine will wait for us before they begin moving their *koshes* on to Danigh," Tahjeen answered."For now," he continued, "grab what rest you can."

Dutong and Langwyn glanced at the walls flashing band shared a doubtful look. Tahjeen smiled then leaned against Paca and closed his eyes.

After several hours, a change in the raft's speed roused Tahjeen. The raft was slowing. They drifted forward until the water subsided altogether. Most of it disappeared into the earthy floor until only the original *blurl* remained.

Tahjeen stood up and bowed to the watery, translucent creature."The Shala are grateful for your assistance."

"You should be," the *blurl* said; then it disappeared as well.

The others laughed as Tahjeen retrieved his pack from the raft.

"Achates, take the lead. If any humans await us, I don't want a Shala to be the first thing they see."

As Achates hurried on ahead Tahjeen turned to Dutong."Go just inside the entrance. Reach out with your senses. Try and detect anything unusual." Dutong nodded, and glanced quickly at his *fel*. Shawna, his lithe cheetah, raced off ahead of him.

"You're being doubly cautious," Langwyn said. A small, jagged scar that ran across his forehead, bunched as his brows furrowed in consternation.

"With ten thousand Shala lives at stake, not to mention the human population, we can't afford any mistakes," Tahjeen reminded him."Now let's fetch the horses."

CHAPTER 5

FATHER AND SONS

Sorbonne Augustus Hargreave, King of Dania, shielded his eyes from the morning sun as he stood on his balcony and looked out at the thriving city he loved. He glanced up at the heavily treed Learing Mountains which ringed Danigh and provided it with some modest safety behind the steep façade. A few of the taller peaks were capped with snow. They loomed over two narrow passes that were located to the east and west of the city. Should an attack ever occur that the mountains failed to deter, townsfolk could find safety behind the walls of his stalwart castle.

As the capital, Danigh was the hub of a bustling trade and home to the kingdom's artisans and scholars. From here the king oversaw the enterprises that made his kingdom the wealthiest in Sandala. Busy shops lined the main street that stretched for nearly a mile. Young men throughout Dania came here to become an apprentice, or begin military training. Those who had an aptitude and interest came to attend a fine school that graduated scribes for civil service, traveling teachers charged with spreading literacy throughout his realm, and the occasional author of plays that entertained the populace. Danigh was the cultural center of all Sandala.

Sorbonne's gaze drifted lower as he watched the late afternoon sun drop towards the horizon, casting long shadows across the courtyard. On the far side a group of laborers were busy constructing an outdoor stage for Roland's wedding. In a few weeks his eldest son would be married to Princess Leona Obair from Oreon, giving Sorbonne the political alliance he sought.

Almost directly below him, Roland was ending a training session with Cullen, the Master at Arms. The king watched as the young man dunked his head in a bucket of water then whipped his black hair to and fro. The pair then made their way across the yard, pausing to exchange words with the pigeon master before they continued on inside.

A blur of movement caught the king's eye. Sorbonne looked up and saw his other son racing along the parapet. A smile spread across his face. What a bundle of inquisitive energy that one was. Full of mischief, a playful rogue with an impish look – a little devil according to Cullen. He had inherited his mother's red, curly hair and good humor.

A homing pigeon caught his eye and his mood shifted. He watched, anxious, as the bird glided toward its roost in the pigeon barn. His chest swelled with hope. Pray it is news from Devon, the king mused. He has been gone far too long. He turned and hurried from his chamber.

Sorbonne watched the other males eat with gusto. The only female among them was the old serving woman who brought their dinner. It had been many hours since the noon repast, and breakfast was always spartan. The evening meal was hearty, and the only one with hot food. There was little talk while they ate, though the king barely touched his food.

Sorbonne and the others sat at a long, planked wooden table scarred from hot plates, misaimed knives and food stains, but the red oak still shined thanks to patient buffing by caring hands. Plucked from the richest forest in the kingdom, the tree had been finely crafted into the table that had been his wedding gift nearly twenty years ago. A large chandelier, hanging from along chain, was centered over the table. It held a dozen candles whose bright glow made shadows dance along the walls.

Absently, King Sorbonne scratched at his chest, his long red woolen smock irritating him as usual. He took in the empty place where his queen once sat. It was still hard for him to believe she had been gone ten years. The tall, strong woman from Sealand was more than a wife. She had also been his best friend. Though their marriage had the political purpose of binding the two kingdoms closer, within weeks the king and his young bride had found themselves deeply in love.

She had been strong, but not for child bearing. Roland's birth had been difficult, and two daughters that followed died within hours of delivery. Irene had barely recovered when she again became pregnant. The result was Aldo, who survived the terrible birth that sent his mother to the grave.

The king studied his sons, Irene's commendable legacy, Sorbonne thought, and yet there were times, though rare, when her presence would have been worth the sacrifice of youngest son.

He chastised himself. Such thoughts bred discontent and led to trouble.

"Sire?" Cullen asked, noting the king's distant look.

Sorbonne's gaze traveled to him. Three years ago he appeared bringing letters of reference from Gleneden's Queen. She recommended him as an excellent trainer of young soldiers. It wasn't long before he became Roland's personal trainer. In time he became Sorbonne's trusted advisor and friend, someone to talk with; and someone who would listen. At his insistence, Cullen took a place at the table.

Sorbonne shook his head. "Just wandering thoughts."

Cullen pushed his chair back, giving his long legs more room. His shaved head made his age difficult to determine, but there were enough gray hairs in his short-trimmed beard and deep lines in his face to suggest several decades of living. The tunic and leggings he had changed into for dinner bore the signs of heavy use as well.

The meal over, the old woman reappeared with a tray filled with steaming cups of rich, strong coffee. As she began clearing the table, Cullen spoke. "Your Majesty, Roland inquired about the scouting parties."

The king turned his attention to his oldest son. Interpreting the look as permission to speak, Roland plunged ahead.

"Yes, father. I was surprised you sent out more patrols. I'm unaware of anything that warrants that degree of response, but you are not one to act rashly."

It took some time for Sorbonne to reply.

"One envoy has yet to return," the king finally said.

"Who?" Roland asked, a curious expression on his face.

The King's face sobered. "Devon."

Roland paled. "My God," he said in a mere whisper. Everyone at the table was quiet. For Sorbonne, the idea that something might have happened to Devon Longstreet was unthinkable. He was Sorbonne's best scout – a former sentinel, elusive, brilliant, and skilled.

Roland broke the silence. "Where did you send him?"

"To Seadawn," Sorbonne answered simply.

"It is a long way and there are two mountain ranges to cross," Roland replied.

"A reasonable explanation," Sorbonne said. "But Gleneden is even further, and that scout returned ten days ago." When the latest pigeon had failed to bring a message from Longstreet, the king's anxiety had deepened.

Sorbonne looked around the table, his gaze stopping at his younger son. What he had to say wasn't for a child's ears. "Cullen, Roland, join me in my library."

"Father," Aldo said abruptly, "I found something today."

"Not now, Aldo," he said, waving his hand. "You can show me later." He saw desperation flash across his youngest son's face, and realized that the lad knew he was being deliberately excluded.

"But it is important!" Aldo complained loudly. "Here, look!" he said, retrieving a book from inside his shirt and tossing it on the table in front of his father.

Sorbonne took one look at the tattered log and sank back in his chair. He stared at it in silence." Where did you find this?" he finally asked.

"It was in the old dungeon buried under some rubble. It's important, isn't it? And look at this drawing, father," he said, grabbing the book back, "let me show you." He leafed through some moldy pages until he found the sketch of a tall, well-muscled, athletic looking individual, who appeared to be male except he lacked the sexual organs that would define him so. Aldo handed the dusty manuscript back to the king. "What kind of man is that?"

Before the king could answer, the sound of breaking dishes startled them. Behind Sorbonne, the old serving woman had dropped the tray filled with their dirty plates. Her eyes were wide and her fear palpable.

King Sorbonne rose at once and went to her. "What is it, Mathilda?" he asked, searching her terror stricken face.

For a moment, he thought she wouldn't answer, but then with a trembling finger she pointed toward the picture. "Shala," she said then turned and fled.

The king paled. He looked at Aldo then Roland, trying to make up his mind. The lad was still too young. "Aldo," Sorbonne ordered. "Go to your room and remain there. Roland, Cullen, come with me."

"Why do you always send me away?" Aldo blurted. "Just because Roland's the oldest.. "

"That's enough!" the king interrupted. "Go to your room at once!"

Surprisingly, Aldo did not look cowed. When Aldo's gaze switched to Roland, Sorbonne saw an ugly sneer of resentment flash across his face. "Now, Aldo," he said gently. "I will come and talk with you about this later."

The three men were in Sorbonne's private library. They sat in large wooden padded chairs that encircled a big square table. Roland and Cullen waited, silent and patient, while the King thumbed through the book. At long last, he closed it and set it down in front of them.

"I saw this book once before," the king finally said, "When I was Aldo's age. My grandfather was king then. He called my father into a private meeting," he said, looking around him, "in this very room." He paused as poignant memories surfaced.

"I was father's only son and from the age of eight he kept me at his side constantly, teaching me how to be king."

Cullen sat quietly, little expression on his face. "What is the book about, Father?" Roland asked. Sorbonne saw curiosity play with his son's face.

The king took a deep breath then began to relate what his grandfather had told him – about an ancient, mystical warrior race called Shala. "There is a prophecy," the King said, "which says that in time of great peril, when the five lands are seriously threatened, the Shala will rise and come to Sandala's defense."

Sorbonne rose and went to the fire. Leaning against the huge mantel, he went on. "Grandfather never saw a Shala...had never known anyone who had. The same was true for my father and is for me as well. Whether or not they actually exist, I do not know." He gestured to the old volume on the table,"That book describes them in detail and contains the prophecy I spoke of earlier."

Sorbonne began describing the warrior race who shared some human traits but not others. "According to legend, Shala are worth ten men in battle, strong enough to lift a horse and they move like lightning. They are masters in hand-to-hand combat and supposedly have been blessed with mystical powers and enhanced senses. They can even talk with one another without words and with no regard for distance. But strangest of all are their eyes - they change color."

Roland and Cullen remained silent, perhaps in disbelief, Sorbonne mused. "Each warrior also has a unique relationship with a huge cat that fights at their side in battle. The pair is inseparable, bonded for life, and communicates in some fashion."

Roland finally found his voice. "Do you believe the book is factual, Father?"

"A few months ago I would have said no," the King answered,"but its rediscovery at this point seems more than coincidence. Initially, that is why I wanted to talk with you then Aldo discovers this." Sorbonne waved some unspoken thought away. "But I am confusing the issue." He paused and moved closer to Roland and Cullen.

"Two months ago Queen Endoreen sent word that some of her fishermen had disappeared, in calm seas no less. Then a ship with foreign sails pursued another one of her boats until they escaped into a fog bank. She felt the incidents merited investigation. I had the bird master send a pigeon, informing her that we had reports of bands of men sneaking outside some of our towns, and that I had dispatched my best scouts to all the corners of the land."

"Last month," Sorbonne went on, "one of our birds returned from Gleneden carrying a message that King Dawad had not attended their yearly trade conference. And soon after, his ambassador packed up and left."

"Sire," Roland asked, "do you think that Sealand is planning an attack?"

"I have no idea, but it bothers me greatly that Devon was sent there and has not returned," Sorbonne said.

Cullen offered two plausible explanations. "Either Devon has discovered something of significance in Seadawn and is staying longer to investigate, or something far worse has happened to him."

"I agree," the King said, nodding. "And because of that I have called a Clave. Queen Endoreen and her husband are on their way and should be arriving tomorrow. King Baldor and Dawad have also been informed, and of course King Darvus is already in route because of the wedding."

Roland brows rose in surprise but Cullen's face remained unreadable. Sorbonne knew that calling for a Clave was a serious step, but the monarchs of Sandala needed to meet and decide on a course of action.

"Father, I am surprised you invited Dawad. Even if he does not come, you have made him aware of your suspicions."

"I want him aware, Roland. If he is up to something or plotting with a foreign power, I want him very aware that the rest of us will not be caught by surprise."

Cullen spoke again. "So this is why you find the book about the Shala more credible." It was a statement, not a question.

The King nodded. "Some believe it to be rubbish, the imagination of some ancient storyteller, entertaining his relatives as they hunkered down around a fire. But the words of the prophecy are haunting. They are clearly a warning."

"What does the prophecy say, Father?" Roland asked.

"I want you to read it for yourself," the King said, pointing to the book once again. "Read it tonight then keep it hidden so it will not disappear again."

Sorbonne then assigned additional tasks. "Roland, arrange accommodations for all the visitors, and organize a banquet befitting people of their stature." He watched his oldest son nod then turned his attention to Cullen.

"Intensify the army's training, get some more recruits from the outlying farms and talk to the blacksmith about increasing our supply of weapons. Roland," he said, turning back to the dark-haired prince, "I want you at Cullen's side whenever possible. You need command experience, a role you may soon have to undertake.

When he finished, the king's mood was dark. "I pray with everything I hold dear that it will never happen, but I have no intention of being unprepared."

Both men bowed to the King then Roland bent down and picked up the dusty book.

Eavesdropping, Aldo barely had time to retreat and disappear into a storage closet. He wanted that book back! It was his; he had found it. He could hear the two men pass by on the way to their private chambers. Somehow, he would find a way to get the book away from his brother.

Once inside his room, Roland sat down on his bed. He dreaded opening the old manuscript, yet his curiosity was piqued. He turned several tattered pages, yellow with age, until he came to the picture Aldo had been so excited about. This Shala, he thought, was an imposing figure. His skin was uncharacteristically dark, but perhaps the book had faded with time. But his hair was so blond it was almost white. The eyes, though, struck him the most. They were solid black. Most strange.

He turned another page, and there was the Prophecy:

Vigilant guardians of all the lands,
Remain a myth until the time,
Foreign soldiers come,
Bringing death.
Live, learn, love and toil;
Generations pass unto the soil.
Train for the time when invaders come
So you can dance with death.
Live apart from humankind;
But learn their heart and mind.
Raise your children until it's time
To dance with death.
We have one purpose and it is clear
With foreign soldiers spreading fear,
When humans weep and war is near,
The Shala rise...
To dance with death.

He read through it twice then closed the book. The words disturbed him. They offered the promise to appear when foreigners invade, but the words were vague, and difficult to interpret. He would read more, but not now, not after that sobering lament. He wondered if they put it to song, or chanted it to the rhythmic beat of drums. He tried to imagine a people, another race, whose main purpose in life was to protect him and others like him.

He undressed, washed himself, and climbed into bed. Sleep was a long time coming.

CHAPTER 6

SEADAWN

The sentinel slogged his way through garbage encrusted alleys, surprised they weren't also littered with beggars and drunks. Devon was working his way to Falcon's Inn, his favorite tavern in Seadawn. He emerged into a street bustling with wagons hauling wares for the market, sharing the crowded space with noisy hawkers, and shoppers, shouting back and forth as they argued quality and price. Soldiers appeared every fifty feet or so, their eyes busy scanning the crowd. The presence of the guards bothered him, it was unusual. So he drifted towards the shoppers and immersed himself among them.

Soon Falcon's Inn loomed before him, its two stories casting a shadow that stretched past the middle of the street. Devon pushed through the tavern's doors and was buffeted by the raucous sounds of drinking men. He spotted a table in a dim corner and headed for it, casually observing the clientele. They were mostly locals, another oddity since the Falcon usually drew in traders and younger lords from border kingdoms. Though a few were well dressed, the rest appeared to be local street fare from Seadawn. Bawdy laughter erupted followed by curses then more laughter. Devon sensed eyes watching him as he made his way across the room.

Once he settled, it was the owner, an old friend, who arrived to serve him. "Good evening, sir. What may I bring you?" Devon lowered his hood and noted the alarm that passed across the man's ruddy face.

"Sit, Talgar," Devon invited, "and tell me if the world's been kind to you."

Talgar glanced around nervously then sat down. His face was haggard and strained. Talgar's red hair was cut short and flecked with far more gray than Devon remembered. Even his burly physique seemed reduced. Devon wondered if the man was ill.

"Devon, how in Sandala...how did you get into the city?" Talgar spoke quietly. "How did you get past the guards?"

Devon studied the man, granting him a brief smile, as he searched his face for the meaning behind the questions. Finally he spoke. "Not the hospitality I'd hoped for." His face was grim. "Talgar, what is going on?"

Worry blanketed his friend's ruddy face. "The city's closed, locked up tighter than a maiden's pleasure chamber. It's been that way for weeks." He paused, gathering his thoughts. "I must be brief. This place is not safe for you. All foreigners are being turned back at the gates, some even arrested and tossed in the brink." Talgar shifted in his chair. "So how did you avoid the guards?"

Devon smiled. "Remember the old, unused storm sewer?"

"Ah. Well, all the same," Talgar went on, "you are bound to be recognized and turned in. You are too well known. It's likely that someone has already reported your presence. You must leave. Now!"

But Devon refused. "Not until I get some answers!" he barked.

"All right, but keep your voice down." Talgar's eyes flicked around the room again. "But not here. Meet me in the usual place later tonight."

Talgar stood up and forced the veins in his face to pulse. "Get out! I don't serve your kind! Not the front entrance. Go outback into the alley where your mother birthed you!"

Following the lead Talgar's insult dictated, Devon rose swiftly, knocking his chair aside then scrambled toward the rear door. He seemed to diminish in size as he slinked away, hoping his demeanor would convince watchful eyes that he was a pitiful peasant who had overstepped his station.

Talgar went back behind the bar. Near the front, a man nodded to his companions then stood and left.

Behind the tavern, Devon hurried to a drainpipe. He began pulling himself up, hand over hand, praying the pipe's cleats would hold. After twenty feet he heard a noise from below and froze. He looked down and saw a big tomcat pawing through garbage. Relieved, Devon let his breath out and renewed climbing. After a few more feet he reached the top of the roof, found purchase then hauled himself up.

He crept toward the peak. Near the middle there was a raised shingle. He pried it aside then used his fingers to reach under the tar paper and push a small lever. A trap door opened and he lowered himself inside.

"Where is he?" King Dawad demanded. Though stooped shouldered and slightly built, his icy eyes radiated power and a growing fury.

Before him, the magistrate, a little man with ferret-like eyes, was sweating nervously. "Your majesty," he blurted,"he was at the Falcon, but he left. We are not certain where he is. I have alerted guards and they are combing the city for him."

The King nodded, slightly mollified. He waved his hand in dismissal and the magistrate scurried away, wanting to be out of the castle and Dawad's sight as fast as possible. The king waited until the door closed, before he stood and pulled aside the curtain near the far wall. There, hidden in the alcove, sat two men. Both were militaristic in bearing and dress, fair-skinned and severe looking. Neither seemed pleased.

"This is a problem?" Taro, the elder by two decades, asked. His deep purple uniform was neatly trimmed with gold braid. Numerous ribbons and star-shaped gold pins would have seemed gaudy had they not been subdued by the man's harsh features and ice blue eyes.

The King nodded deferentially. "Yes, General. Devon Longstreet is a former Sentinel. He is close to Dania's ruler and no doubt here to spy on us. As you have mentioned many times, the element of surprise is essential. It is why we have locked the city down. If Longstreet were somehow able to get word to his king, it could prove disastrous. We must find him!"

King Dawad was hardly subtle in his hostility toward Dania. He held King Sorbonne responsible for the death of his beloved sister Irene, and Taro knew he was not one to forgive. It was yet another trait that made him pliable to Taro's demands.

Taro stared back at the ruler, masking his distaste for the man's incessant whining. He hid it because Dawad, Sealand's king, was essential to the success of the invasion. With the greedy king as a willing partner, Seadawn was the launching area for the empire's massive invasion of Sandala's east coast. He looked forward to the day when he could end it. "Explain 'Sentinel,'" he finally said.

King Dawad began to pace as his fretting continued. "During

the inland wars, there was a band of thirty, special men, great trackers and assassins. They were chosen because they were the best, regardless of kingdom. They operated independently and were critical in turning the tide of the insurrection. There are only a half dozen or so left," Dawad concluded, "and Longstreet is one of them."

"Then he must be stopped!" Taro explained, realizing the danger. If Longstreet were able to warn the Danian king, they would have weeks to prepare a defense. He glanced quickly at his comrade behind the curtain who in turn looked to the King.

"Have you an artist who can sketch his countenance?" the younger man named Raston asked. He was handsome and blond, but ruthlessness marred his good looks.

King Dawad nodded. "Then call for him at once. Have the sketch in my hands within the hour." The King, contradicting his regal title, sped from the chamber.

Taro, scars from battle etched across his face and hands, got up and walked to the balcony window. He studied the harbor below him. After several moments, he turned back to his companion.

"We must be very careful, Raston. Our fleet arrives tomorrow and if this sentinel was to see it and report...." He let his words trail off, the implications clear.

Raston rose quickly. "I understand."

Taro nodded. "You had better. Dania is the most powerful of the five kingdoms. Surprise is crucial. We will sweep through Palaton and Gleneden in mere days, leaving Dania without allies."

"What of Oreon, sir?" Raston asked of the mountainous kingdom.

"Pah," Taro uttered with disgust. "They are simple mountain people. Dania is the threat. A few days warning is one thing, but if they have time to fully arm and move in mass to their borders, it could become a costly war."

"And we would win!"

"Of course, but that is not the point." Taro fought irritation while he eyed Raston. "I suppose now is a good time to tell you."

He could see that Raston was puzzled, thinking that war is war, limited by a young man's simplistic vision of the world. Taro waved for him to sit then walked over and joined him.

"The Emperor wants a second capital," he said. "Expansion

requires another center of government to supervise the people and the wealth in this region of the empire. It will be an elaborate venture requiring an entirely new infrastructure. Dania is the perfect site. So, we do not want a long, destructive war with them. We want their resources intact."

Taro studied the confident young man. "This man cannot be allowed to take word to his ruler."

Taro stood and walked once again to the window. With his back to Raston he ordered, "Find this Sentinel. Find him and kill him!"

Raston jumped to his feet and saluted. "Yes, Commander General!"

Devon propped open the access to let in fresh air, pulling some biscuits, cheese and water from his rucksack. He ate then settled back against some dusty crates and closed his eyes and recalled his cautious approach to Seadawn.

Hidden a safe distance away, he had used his spyglass to watch as travelers neared the main gate. He had been surprised – not just to find the gates closed and heavily guarded, but also because every wagonload and person was searched before they gained entrance. More alarming was that after a half-day of observation, he had not seen one person leave. For this reason, he had hidden his war horse outside the city walls, tethering him loosely in a dense copse of trees then entering through the forgotten storm sewer.

Knowing Talgar wouldn't show until after dark, he willed himself to relax, taking rest while he could. Who knew what revelations tomorrow might bring?

"It was nearly two moons ago," Talgar said over a mug of his finest ale. He had arrived moments before, bringing food, refreshments, and a tall candle with him.

"An unknown ship entered the harbor. After it anchored out in the bay, two men rowed ashore. They were soldiers, carried themselves like commanders. Once in the military you do not forget the look."

"I was curious so I followed them," Talgar went on. "They went straight to the palace. I returned to the inn, and more or less forgot about it. But several days later there were dozens of foreign soldiers prowling the streets, looking stern and taking the measure of any man who met their gaze. It was very unsettling."

Devon interrupted him with a question. "Are they still here?"

Talgar nodded. "That ship left a few days later, but another one arrived in its place. I don't think anyone was supposed to see that, but I was out on the roof daubing fresh tar on a leak. It slid into port with muffled oars, as quiet as you please. Over the next hour hundreds of armed soldiers came ashore."

Talgar paused, stroking his beard, a puzzled look on his face. "The devil of it is I've seen no sign of them since".

"It would appear that the King has made a pact with some foreign power," Devon said.

Talgar nodded. "That would be my guess. The question is, what kind of deal?"

Devon leaned back, tossing down the last of his draft. King Dawad's hostility toward Dania was hardly subtle. He was consumed with envy which can lead to greed, which often leads to far worse.

Devon ended his sober thoughts. "If he has, I doubt it's an economic one."

"By the gods, he would be crazy to enter into a military alliance. The four other kingdoms would stand against him!" Talgar proclaimed.

Devon leaned forward. "Describe these foreigners."

Talgar shrugged. "Fair haired, light skinned. That's the best I could tell under the moonlight."

Devon sat back, pondering Talgar's answer. Then with a sense of urgency he asked, "Did you know that many of the towns are under curfew, shutting down business early and not welcoming travelers?"

Alarmed, Talgar sat up. "No. All I know is that few travelers get into the city and no one, I mean no one, gets out."

The two men exchanged looks. Taken singly, none of the evidence was damning, but to war veterans capable of grasping a bigger picture, they both knew the implication was sinister. King Dawad was only a step away from martial law. Ina kingdom used to benevolent rule, he was looking more like a dictator every day.

A chill moved down Devon's spine. "I think he has a major ally to back him in a war, and knowing that an attack on any of the lands will constitute an attack on all, the ally is powerful."

"Surely not the Surmese? He couldn't be that daft!"

"You'd best hope not. They do not back anyone in a war for long before they turn and eat their allies. But, it fits...your description, the clandestine arrival and Dawad's short-sightedness."

"Then we are doomed. Their war machine is massive. I never dreamed the Surmese would range this far," Talgar said despondently.

"I need more information before I return to Dania," Devon said. "All we have now is speculation. "You are taking a terrible risk," Talgar warned. "Every hour you spend here increases the chance of capture. I was right, you know. Someone turned you in. They are looking for you everywhere."

Devon nodded, appreciative of the warning. "I won't stay long, my friend. Watch your own back as well."

They stood as one, clasping forearms before Talgar left.

Just before dawn Devon moved to the roof, laying low as he used his glass to scan the harbor. In the distance, emerging from the fog's tendrils, an armada crept into view. He counted ships until the sheer number made it pointless. There were hundreds. Once the fog lifted, sails filled the water as far as he could see.

For the better part of the morning he watched the ships come in. Most anchored some distance offshore. They were packed with men, and within minutes longboats were lowered, and headed towards shore. Once on solid ground, most of the men formed ranks and marched into the city's interior, but some trotted to the harbor where other ships had docked.

Those vessels were laden with provisions. The soldiers unloaded them so other ships could have their turn at disengorging supplies. While the men worked, wagons began appearing. Once loaded, Surmese soldiers climbed aboard and guided the oxen that pulled the carts away from the wharf.

Strangest of all were vessels whose main decks had roofs over them. When they came near enough to see, Devon realized the ships carried large cages filled with the oddest creatures he had ever seen. They were huge, the size of a small cottage, with horns protruding from the middle of their face and sides. He watched as a half dozen men strapped a heavy leather harness and seat over one of the creatures. One of the soldiers grabbed the horns and hoisted himself up on the beast's back. Devon's stomach roiled at the thought of those beasts knocking down walls and trampling innocent civilians.

From the bowels of the hold more cages appeared filled with hounds that made Devon's skin crawl. They looked like the Hell hounds that wandered throughout Sandala's frontier slavering poison from fangs that could rip a man apart. They could run forever and once they had the scent, they never gave up the chase until their prey, or they, were dead.

Then hundreds of smaller crates were brought ashore. Given the distance, it was difficult to see what they held. It looked somewhat like lizards though their elongated torsos were more like a snake. What in Sandala's name are those for? Devon wondered. It was time to leave. Devon hoped he had not waited too long.

He descended from the roof carefully, not wanting to dislodge any shingles and draw attention from below. The information he had was too important for him to risk capture. He must get word back to Dania and King Sorbonne.

Shouting from the street level led him to peer cautiously over the side. A group of soldiers had Talgar trussed up between them, but the big innkeeper still struggled. It was clear Talgar had fallen under suspicion. He fought the urge to leap to his friend's aid, watching helplessly as he was dragged away. Things would not go easy for him and both anger and sadness rolled through Devon's heart. Once Talgar disappeared from sight, he dropped over the side and into the alley.

Traveling through the back streets, he avoided detection from prying eyes. In a careful half-hour, he reached the storm sewer he had traveled through less than two days ago. Carefully stepping over muddy debris deposited from recent rainstorms, he entered the drain pipe.

He trudged through as quickly as he could and in a few minutes reached the outer entrance. It was as he had left it, covered with overgrown ivy and weeds. He pushed the greenery aside. Peering through, he cursed under his breath.

The foreigners had taken additional precautions. The guard around the perimeter had been doubled and more soldiers were lolling about in the distance. It was at least fifty yards to the grove of trees that hid his horse. He said a quick prayer that it was still there. Any attempt at escape would futile if they had already discovered his stallion.

He figured the trees could be reached in less than ten seconds. None of the off duty soldiers were near enough to intercept him, but the guards on patrol were another matter. He watched, counting the seconds it took them to make their silent rounds. He waited several minutes, wanting to be sure of their routine before he burst from his hiding place.

He covered half the distance before soldiers began shouting as they raised the alarm. Under his racing feet, he could hear the crunch of breaking twigs and from the corner of his vision he saw other movement. No doubt the sentries had raced back to investigate. Then, he was through the bushes and into the trees.

"Steady, Shadow," he said, calming his horse that had started at the sound of his crashing through the underbrush. He untied the reins then leapt into the saddle. Drawing his sword he urged his horse forward.

"Throw him in the dungeon!" Taro ordered. "He will die before he tells us anything." He watched several guards drag the beaten man away. He had seen his kind before, and knew that no kind of torture would get the inn keeper to talk. He turned and glared at Raston.

The younger man was quick to respond. "General, we are searching house to house, room to room, and outside the gates. The perimeter guard has been tripled. He will not escape," Raston assured him.

Taro grumbled. "If he is as tough as that tavern owner, he will get outside the walls. You have the copies of Longstreet's likeness?"

"Yes, sir. It is in the hands of all the captains. My own horse is ready if a chase proves necessary." He was about to say something more when the door to Taro's chamber burst open.

Despite the evening's chill, the soldier was sweating and breathing hard. He waited for permission to speak and began as soon as Taro gave the signal.

"Commander General, Tallic's patrol nearly caught him but he made it to a thicket west of town. He had a war-horse hidden there, and before they could stop him he burst out and rode right through them. Three men are dead and several more wounded. Tallic's in pursuit."

Raston bolted for the door. "Take the hounds with you, "Taro called after him. "I don't care if they tear him to pieces. I don't need him alive. I need him dead!" Taro was furious. The man had no doubt observed the armada's arrival. Who knew how much he'd seen, but he would certainly put whatever information he had gleaned to good use. Taro's success relied heavily on subterfuge. The more the enemy knew, the greater the potential for prolonging the war and complicating his mission. As his anger intensified, Taro vowed that someone would pay for allowing Devon Longstreet to escape.

CHAPTER 7

THE WEDDING PARTY

Settled comfortably on a small bed inside the wagon, Ariann Obair looked up from her reading when her older sister sighed. Princess Leona Obair, heir to the throne of Oreon, did not bother to hide her irritation. Her dark brown hair, hanging down well past her shoulders, was unkempt, the unfortunate result of weeks of traveling.

"Do not look at me like that," Leona said. "I'm tired from being on the road and getting tossed about in the back of this wagon. I am sore all over; every set of clothes I brought is soiled; and I haven't eaten properly in weeks. I hope Roland is worth it."

Ariann laughed. The attractive traveling dress Leona wore looked relatively fresh, all things considered. Ariann's own thick mane of shoulder-length blond hair still glistened, thanks to her daily ritual of three hundred strokes with her hairbrush. Her own garment, a rumpled blue taffeta, still managed to be attractive.

"What, pray tell, is so amusing?"

"You," Ariann replied. "We are riding in a luxurious wagon, sleeping on fine linens, with a pleasant cover to shade us from the heat, and you can only complain. I find that ironic and amusing."

"Well, I don't see how."

Ariann stared at her sister, amazed by her negative take on life and her air of expectation. Pampered was an apt description, Ariann mused. The rest of their party slept on unpadded wooden boards, or outside exposed to nature's elements. Soldiers hunted for them and servants did all the cooking. The two sisters had only to sit back and be waited on.

"If you would poke your head outside once in a while, or ride up front with the driver," at the last statement Leona's eyebrows lifted in alarm, "or ride up front with the driver," Ariann repeated, trying to override Leona's distaste, "you would see some beautiful country, maybe even learn a thing or two about our people."

"I think you forget that we are rulers, not part of the common populace," Leona interrupted and Ariann detected the irritation in her voice. "We are royalty, and our position merits the treatment you seem to disdain."

"It is not disdain, and I do think members of the ruling class are entitled to certain amenities. However, I also believe we have a responsibility to not presume too much. As father often says, we serve at the whim of the people."

"Oh, please! We intrude very little on the lives of our subjects, and we make their lives..." She was stopped mid-sentence by another mind-jarring jolt from the wagon.

"Driver!" Leona raised her voice. "Do you think it possible to avoid some of the larger holes, or are you intent on rolling over every one?"

"I am without pity," Ariann said. Leona answered by turning away and closing her eyes.

Ariann meant what she said. She was having a wonderful time and her sister was making a mistake walling herself off from the world. She thought about the beauty of the land and the refreshing bath the clear stream had made possible the previous day.

Six months earlier their father, King Darvus III of Oreon, had called them to his library. When they had entered the room he could hardly contain himself, elation oozing from every pore like water from a drenched sponge. Beaming with pride, he announced that he and King Sorbonne of Dania had agreed in principle on the marriage of Sorbonne's son and heir, Prince Roland, to Princess Leona. It was not lost on either princess that the marriage was an excellent move for their father, in effect making him the chief ally of the largest and most prosperous kingdom in Sandala. That his daughter would one day be Queen of both realms was no doubt thrilling for him to contemplate.

In due time, Leona informed her that she had exchanged letters with Prince Roland with positive results. Plans for a spring wedding followed. Once the heavy rains of winter subsided, announcing the onset of spring, King Darvus gathered her and Leona along with many of the royal servants, and setout on the cross-country journey to Dania. Escorting the royal

entourage were forty members of the King's Guard - fierce soldiers, the finest in all Oreon.

For the past several weeks, the Royal party had been inching
their way towards Dania. It took nearly a week to journey
through the Splay horn Mountains that ran throughout their
realm. Entering into the neighboring kingdom of Palaton,
Ariann took in the stark contrast between the mountainous
domain she called home, and the lush valleys and lowlands of
King Baldor's. She noted the difference in fashion between her
mountain folk and the Palatonian citizens. Lighter garments
were the norm in the warmer climate the people of the lower
altitudes enjoyed.

Five days later, they came to the sprawling river city of
Pandor. King Darvus decided they could all do with some rest,
some meals and hot baths. They took rooms at the finest inn
overlooking the broad, smooth flowing Tanon River. For the next
two days, Ariann toured the city with her father and sister. She
was impressed by its wealth and the care with which it had been
laid out. Streets were clean of the debris that littered larger
centers of population, and the central market boasted fruits and
vegetables that were fresh and tasty. Only the pier down at the
docks seemed like any other – foul smelling and noisy as hundreds of birds hovered and dove, seeking an easy meal.

On the third day, King Darvus hired a large boat to take
them across the Tanon. There they disembarked, stepping onto
the soil of Dania. Now, two days later, Ariann enjoyed their
westward trek across the rolling hills of southeastern Dania. In
another week or so, they would come to the Learing Mountains
that ringed Dania's capital city, Danigh.

While Leona feigned sleep, Ariann considered her own
future. She would miss Leona. They had spent sixteen years
together. Her father might focus more on Ariann's situation.
Marriage to a prince from another kingdom was a possibility,
but as far as she knew, Queen Endoreen of Gleneden was too
young to have any sons old enough, and King Dawad of Sealand
had no sons. That left only Palaton. King Baldor did have
eligible offspring, but he was also an arch rival, and astern,
rather unpleasant man. Her father might not arrange a
marriage under those circumstances.

That left a life of public service. That appealed to her and
there were causes that she could support. Education topped her

list. She believed with all her heart that every man, woman and child in the kingdom, regardless of class, should be able to read and write. Knowledge was the key to so many other issues. An educated person was more likely to understand the importance of hygiene, the need for safer waste disposal, even the logic of women owning their own property or business.

Like Leona minutes before, she sighed. Who was she fooling? Her father would never consider her as a public emissary. He was a good-hearted man but unappreciative of her intellect. He was impressed with her healing skills, but had no idea she had advanced her abilities far beyond her sister's by devoting a significant portion of her time to reading every text she could find.

No, her father doted on Leona. It had been that way for as long as she could remember. A nanny had once confided that Ariann reminded him too much of her mother who had died a dozen years ago. To avoid the pain of remembrance, he avoided her. So Leona was his favorite and that was that.

The dour thoughts darkened her mood and her mind wandered into the throes of self-pity.

Shouting and the harsh clangs of clashing metal roused her. Ariann poked her head outside the wagon's cover to see dozens of men launching themselves at the royal party's escorts. The attack from three sides was so sudden that several of the King's guard fell before they'd drawn their swords.

Terrified, the driver whipped the horses, responding to the Guard Master's call to form a circle. She heard Leona cry out as she bounced around behind her.

"Form a defense around the wagons. Pull in smartly now!" Ariann saw the Guard Master, sword held high, galloping about and forcing his men to regain order. Quickly, they folded into a tight circle around the wagons that carried the King and his daughters. For a time, their proficiency kept the marauders at bay.

Then a second force of attackers appeared in tight formation aimed directly at the King's wagon. They hacked through the first line of defenders, and were slowed only by the appearance of the King himself and three of his royal bodyguards. Ariann could hear her father grunting with effort. The King was not a young man, but what he'd lost in age he replaced with ferocity. His first blow severed a man's arm, but another marauder quickly replaced him. The fighting continued, fierce and deadly, interrupted sporadically by the horrific screams of wounded and dying men.

The guardsmen were out-numbered and the attackers very skilled. Though roughly dressed, they moved with a precision typical of professional soldiers. Being on horseback was the only advantage the King's men had, but the enemy realized that and turned their attention to the steeds. Two marauders on the left combined an attack on the nearest horse. Blows crashed against its forelegs. The stallion dodged one but a second sliced through and the horse screamed as it lurched forward, tossing its rider to the ground. A marauder's sword ran the guardsman through while another's blow brought the animal to the ground. Dust and blood filled the air as swords clanged together and horses reared about, pounding the ground with their hooves, frantically trying to avoid the enemies' swords. Slowly but steadily the advantage held by the royal soldiers began to slip away.

Another dozen ruffians appeared on a hill off to the right, and Ariann's despair deepened. Her father's men would fight until they won or all died but she feared the latter was far more likely. Grimly, she watched as the Guard Master spurred his horse toward the latest attackers, but before he covered much ground, three riders came over the far side of the hill and raced towards the enemy.

She was amazed when they unleashed arrows while still at full gallop. Three marauders fell before two of the horsemen veered off and headed for the royal wagons. The final rider continued towards the group of enemy who remained.

Ariann didn't see what happened next, as she wheeled about and saw two additional mysterious riders attacking the main force of the bandits from the rear. Whoever these new arrivals were, they knew how to fight and were on their side. That was all that mattered.

On horseback, the Guard Master charged back into the melee. Blood and bodies flew about. As he fought for his life and the life of his King, Ariann could have sworn that among the shrieks of the injured men there was a bone-chilling roar of a lion.

She looked back to the hillside where the marauders had turned toward the lone rider's horse pounding towards them. One man shouted at two others who then turned to face the stranger. The rider, with brilliant white blond hair flying out from beneath his helmet, leapt off his horse and flung his traveling cloak aside. Striding forward, he reached inside his tunic with both hands and in a blur of motion let fly with knives. Each found its target, so he unsheathed his sword and walked on. His first knife was buried in the nearer man's chest and he toppled where he stood. The second struck the neck of the other. Ariann was stunned when the tall man beheaded him with a backhanded slash of his sword as he walked past. He disappeared from view behind a thicket of trees. She stared after him, horrified.

Then Leona's hands grabbed her around the waist and pulled her back inside the wagon. "Are you trying to get yourself killed?" Leona chastised.

Ariann landed roughly on the wooden floorboards. "Of course not, but judging by the number of attackers, we should prepare to defend ourselves."

A look of horror settled on Leona's features.

Beyond Ariann's view, Tahjeen reached over his shoulder and pulled out a second sword that had been strapped along his spine. In a movement too fast to defend, he disarmed one man then ripped him open from belly to chin while he parried with another before thrusting home a killing blow. Ahead of him a man went down when Tahjeen's huge panther appeared, tearing his throat out as he raced past. Then a second man screamed as Paca took him down.

A fifth died at the end of Tahjeen's lightning swords, while the panther's sharp fangs sank into the shoulder of a new victim. The big cat shook him until he hung as limp as a pile of wet laundry.

Tahjeen faced the last man. He looked for a sign of surrender, expecting the man to toss his weapon aside. But the eyes that looked back at him were cold. For seconds they circled each other and then the attacker leapt forward and engaged. Tahjeen's white hair whipped about as he blocked the bandit's move, spinning around to plunge his sword deep into his opponent's side. Surprise registered on the man's face.

Surely now he would surrender, Tahjeen thought and removed his helmet. When the bandit saw the fiery red that filled his eyes, recognition and fear flooded his features. Rather than concede, he launched a furious assault, but Tahjeen deflected each blow, studying the man as he fought, trying to find a way to keep him alive. But a freshly exposed tree root tripped him and took the decision away. As he fell, the enemy lunged and before Tahjeen could parry, Paca ended the engagement with a vicious swipe of his claws.

He flung the corpse aside and stood up. He sighed, frustrated. He had hoped to question this man. He wanted answers. As the dust began to settle, the silence around him was filled by the smell of death. He clogged his senses and clouded his thoughts. Finally, he knew the fighting was over. Tahjeen turned and reached out to the large black beast. As the animal rubbed against him, he moved his hands over his svelte form looking for any wounds.

You were perfect, Paca. Thank you. He felt the animal's pleasure at the words of appreciation then motioned his *fel* away. The big cat moved off and disappeared into the nearby woods.

Tahjeen surveyed the carnage. His eyes turned mossy green as unfamiliar feelings coursed through him. It was the first time he had killed a man - a first for all of them. Sadness gripped him. Throughout adolescence he had trained relentlessly, but always against hay bales or with blunted weapons. His skill had never been used to drain a man of his life's blood. The moment was sobering. It disturbed him even more that he had fought automatically, oblivious of the damage he was inflicting.

He walked back to two of the dead and retrieved his knives. Two of his companions trotted up on their horses. "Did any of the living see you?" Tahjeen asked.

"Only from a distance; when it was over we sent our *fels* away."

Tahjeen nodded then studied his Shala companions. He wondered if they felt as he did. "You are uninjured?" he asked, and each nodded. "You did well. Replace your helmets then keep your distance and patrol the perimeter."

As they departed, he turned at the sound of someone else approaching. He saw the stricken look on the face of the only human he called friend. "What's wrong, Achates?" he asked.

"Morgan," Achates said. "He was fighting near one of the wagons when I saw him go down."

Grimly, Tahjeen gripped his friend's shoulder. "I'm sorry," he said, his eyes teal blue with empathy. "The travelers' fate?" he asked gently.

"I'm sure there are casualties. I'll go to them next." He paused, bothered by something. "What puzzles you?"

"Those bandits seemed unusually adept," Achates answered.

Tahjeen nodded back. He thought so too and the refusal to surrender was unusual. "One saw my eyes and responded as if he knew I was Shala." Being recognized made him uneasy. Scouting ahead of the main *koshes* had uncovered interesting information. If the marauders were an advance party for the invaders then the enemy already knew of the Shala's existence. He wondered how that might alter things.

"I have always wondered what it would feel like to kill another man," Achates said. He looked at the blood and bodies; his face was not so youthful anymore.

CHAPTER 8

AN OLD MAN

Ariann surveyed the wreckage. She felt tears forming and forced herself to be calm. Her skills would be of no use if she couldn't control her emotions. She breathed deeply before she looked at one of their overturned wagons, its contents strewn about the landscape. Another's driver's seat was drenched in blood. She winced at the thought of the desperate man fighting in defense of his cargo. The rest of the wagons, drawn in a haphazard circle, appeared undamaged.

She watched as several unharmed soldiers moved the wounded to the wagon next to hers, before she glanced at others who were digging a pit near a pile of bodies. She knew it would have been much larger had the strangers not intervened. Determined, she hurried to the injured men and moments later Leona was by her side.

"What do you want me to do?" Leona asked, deferring to her younger sister's healing skill. She appeared frantic and lost, wheeling about as she talked.

Ariann reached out, taking her hands. "First, calm yourself. Then, go among the wounded and determine who is bleeding the most, in the most pain, or unconscious. I will do the same but we must be quick."

Leona, eyes wide, nodded and headed for the rear of the wagon where she started to examine the men there. Ariann hurried to the men slumped against the front. In seconds she realized that only one of the injured looked near death, but the rest had some nasty sword slashes that were bleeding profusely. It saddened her to see such carnage. Why did men do this to each other?

Moments later Leona returned to her side. "I think one man has already died and another near death, but the rest incurred deep cuts," Leona said, pushing her disheveled hair back from her forehead.

"Tend to these men," Ariann directed. "Wash your hands then tear some strips of cloth, as clean as you can find. Tie them off above the wounds. It will slow the loss of blood." Leona nodded and raced away.

Ariann ran to the back of the wagon, oblivious to her own image, unaware of the blood spatters that were turning her blue dress into a red nightmare. Seeing the look on the faces of the uninjured soldiers, she steeled herself for the worst. Two of their comrades lay dead and another was unconscious. A quick examination revealed an ugly lump on the side of his head but no visible bleeding.

"Make him comfortable," Ariann instructed. "For this type of injury there is nothing we can do but let him rest." She saw another soldier fixing a tourniquet of sorts on a terrible leg wound. She could tell it wasn't the first time he had done so.

"Have you washed your hands?" she asked. He shook his head.

"Please do so now then repeat your efforts on the others who have severe bleeding from their limbs." The man hesitated then stood up. She moved closer to him.

"You must loosen the tourniquets every two hundred breaths. Retighten them after sixty breaths." The decisiveness in her tone ended his uncertainty.

Ariann turned to some soldiers nearby. "Move the men into this wagon and," she glanced around and pointed, saying, "and that one over there." They bent to their task as she returned to Leona. She relayed the same information regarding the tourniquets then placed heavy pads of clean cloth over several other wounds. As she worked, her own dress became heavily spotted with blood. When she finished, she turned to three of her father's royal guard.

"Hold each bandage tightly. The pressure will staunch the bleeding. Stay with them until it stops. If a bandage soaks through, come and find me," Ariann said. She turned at the sound of a horse approaching. She watched a dark-haired young man dismount in front of her father. She was close enough to hear their conversation. Her father spoke first.

"Sir, I am Darvus III, King of Oreon. Thank the gods for your timely arrival. We owe you our lives."

The younger man bowed. "I am Achates Dron, Your

Highness, from Danigh. It is fortunate we happened upon your party." Ariann watched him look towards the lifeless bodies. "I am only sorry that we did not appear sooner."

The King's gaze shifted from Achates to the dead and wounded soldiers. Bleakness flicked across his face. "Nevertheless, I would like to personally thank each man. Once we finish burying our dead and treating the wounded, would the rest of your party join us for dinner so we can thank you properly?"

"I am sorry, your Majesty. We must forego dinner. My companions have already set up a perimeter in case there are other bandits in the vicinity. They will trade watch throughout the night."

"Then you must at least let us care for your injured," the King replied.

"That is greatly appreciated. It appears that Morgan," Achates said as he pointed to his fallen companion who lay propped up against the closest wagon, "took a bad one."

"And the other wounded?" the king inquired.

"There are no others," Achates answered.

Ariann was incredulous. The fighting had been vicious. She watched Achates start towards his friend then moved to join him.

"How do you fare?" Ariann heard Achates ask his young friend. He smiled despite his pain. Blood loss had turned his face ashen. "A bit more prickly than training sessions."

Achates didn't laugh. Morgan's tunic was drenched in blood.

Ariann interrupted his examination. "We will take good care of him, Commander. We have some skills in healing."

Achates turned towards her soft, melodic voice.

"First, we must stop his bleeding. The only wagon as yet unfilled with wounded is my own. Would you be so kind as to put him there?" He seemed momentarily mesmerized. "Sir?" she said again.

Achates nodded then helped Morgan to his feet before he scooped him up. "Over there," Ariann said, pointing to the next wagon over.

After he had settled Morgan inside, Ariann joined him. She pulled aside Morgan's ruined tunic, exposing a deep gash that was pulsing a stream of blood. She handed Achates a bundle of cloth and told him to press firmly against the wound. "I will be right back," she assured him.

She reappeared in moments, still wiping her hands on some white linen. She pushed him aside and removed the cloth press. She'd seen a few hunters lose blood like this, and none had survived. Ariann reached inside the wound, probing with her fingers. In a moment, she nodded to herself and the flow of blood slowed.

"My name is Ariann," she said, wiping the blood from her hand on a clean cloth. Her fingernails were still caked with red. "I am the king's younger daughter."

"My lady," Achates responded and she saw a hopeful look settle on his face.

Tahjeen was setting up camp when Achates trotted up. His horse was tethered nearby while he hauled stones to form a circle for the fire. He had already hung his pack from some tall branches and brought his mount some water. He watched Achates dismount then asked him to describe his recent sojourn to the royal's camp.

"It is Darvus, King of Oreon," Achates began.

"The King of Oreon!" Tahjeen exclaimed. "Praise Sandala he wasn't harmed."

"I know," Achates replied. "But he is adamant that he meet us and express his thanks. He believes we saved his life. His death would have left no male heirs to his throne and tumbled his kingdom into chaos."

Tahjeen nodded then beckoned Achates to continue.

"I told him we would come this evening," Achates continued. "Morgan cannot be moved as yet. If we wait until darkness falls and you are disguised, well..." He let his voice trail off. He knew his friend wasn't pleased, but outright refusal would be unusual and raise suspicion.

Tahjeen sighed. "We will make it work, for Morgan's sake. Lanta would never forgive us if we didn't bring him home alive." He paused momentarily then asked, "How is Morgan?"

"She is amazing," Achates marveled. "She has the healing hands and a gentle way. Her voice is mesmerizing."

Tahjeen smiled sardonically. "I was asking about Morgan."

"I know," Achates said. "It's just...there is just..." At the look on the other man's face, Achates shifted his train of thought and answered. "He's lost a great deal of blood. She has stopped it for now and given him a potion of some sort. He's resting, but very pale."

Tahjeen saw sadness take hold of Achates' face. "I doubt he'll survive the night, regardless of her care."

"Then I need to see him now, Achates. Alone. You must escort me there and prevent any interference."

"Wearing a mesh-draped helmet might draw questions."

"Shield me the best you can."

Achates nodded, eager to go for Morgan's sake. Quickly, the two young men in their bloody leather tunics walked across the several hundred feet that separated their parties. It was risky for Tahjeen to expose himself this way but Morgan's life might hang in the balance.

They approached the other party and King Darvus started forward to greet them. Tahjeen heard Achates take a deep breath, "Your Majesty," Achates said, bowing low, "Please forgive us but we need to see Morgan immediately. Proper introductions must wait." And with that declaration, he hustled Tahjeen past the surprised king to the wagon where Morgan lay.

Before he climbed in, Tahjeen saw a young woman hurrying over.

"She is the healer," Achates whispered.

"Don't let her intercede. Forestall her with apologies, but do not let her pass." Tahjeen could see that she was taken aback as she stood open mouthed and uncertain, but he was firm in his resolve to forestall any interruption. He turned and stepped inside the wagon.

Tahjeen knelt beside his stricken companion. He pricked his own finger and squeezed a drop of blood on Morgan's lips then placed one hand over the injured man's heart and the other on the bandage covering his wound. Tahjeen closed his eyes and began to breathe deeply.

Reaching inside himself, into the part of his mind where images were formed, he envisioned a pathway growing and stretching until it reached down into the earth. He drew upon the healing power buried within nature's heart. Through his mind he called for chemicals to rise to the surface to fight infection. He beckoned moisture from the soil to replenish the lost blood. He willed the cool dampness from the far depths to lower Morgan's fever.

Perspiring heavily, Tahjeen's concentration rendered him immune to the voices arguing outside the wagon.

Finally, Morgan's shallow breathing grew steadier. Less pain was reflected in his features. Beneath the bandages, his wound started to heal. Slowly, he opened his eyes.

Tahjeen smiled. He let the warmth from his hands dissipate. "You'll be all right now. Try to sleep."

Tahjeen opened the flap then jumped down in front of an angry king.

"Your Majesty, My Lady, I apologize. But once Achates explained the severity of Morgan's wound, it was imperative that I see him immediately. My healing power is an ancient, secret thing that must not be observed, or interfered with."

He spoke the last sentence while looking meaningfully at Ariann. He towered over her but she did not appear the least bit cowed.

"I must return to camp and rest." He reached out and put an arm around Achates' shoulders. *Come, Paca,* Tahjeen called silently.

"I assure you, we'll return later in the evening," Achates said.

As his friend helped him to their own campsite, Tahjeen heard a panther cough somewhere in the nearby trees. The *fel* knew he was needed.

When they entered their camp, Tahjeen lay down next to the circle of rocks. In moments, the big cat came bounding in.

Tahjeen glanced back toward the royal's camp. He wondered what they thought about his strange visit. There will be many questions to answer later this evening, he mused. Close by, he heard Achates tossing wood inside the circle and his eyes closed in anticipation of the warmth that was soon to come.

Paca stretched his full length alongside him. A great paw draped across his chest and he mewed softly. Tahjeen put an arm around him then rested his head against the panther's chest. In seconds, he was asleep.

Shortly after sunset, Tahjeen awoke. While he slept, Paca served as a conduit to the healing powers deep within the earth. Tahjeen woke famished, but fully restored. He stroked Paca lovingly as Achates served him some roasted meat from the fire. He ate quickly then stood up and began donning the disguise of an old man.

Achates watched as Tahjeen affixed a gray wig and beard. "Why can't we tell them who we are and what has brought us here?"

Tahjeen's thoughts flashed back to his mother's words. Though it was logical to assume that the attack on the Oreon King's party placed him squarely on their side, he could still not afford to trust him. Tahjeen shook his head. "We know that a close ally will betray us so we have to be cautious. Things may appear to be something they're not."

"When the morning comes," Achates asked, "will we go back to the cavern and wait the *koshes*?"

"No. King Darvus may well be loyal to Sandala, so we need to escort them safely to Danigh. Tonight, I will *lais* with my cousin Katrine. When she and Toman reach the entrance in two days, they need to go on without us. We can't risk delays. We have no real idea when the armada will arrive at Dania's western coast. Those *koshes* need to get to Danigh first"

Achates grabbed a cane and handed it to Tahjeen who then put on a cloak with a heavy hood that cast a deep shadow over his face, and more importantly, his eyes. His disguise was complete. King Darvus was expecting them. He motioned to Achates and together, the two walked towards the fire flickering in the distance.

As they neared the other camp, Tahjeen had Achates hail the guard so as not to cause alarm. Two of their own companions were on guard as well, so they were confident that they were safe for the night. They walked toward the inner circle of wagons where the royal party sat at a table close to the fire. At their approach, the King rose.

"Ah, Commander, at last I get to formally thank my benefactor. Sir," he said to the bent, older man, "it is with heart-felt thanks that I greet you. I fear that had you and your men not arrived when you did, we would not be here now, to make your acquaintance and to express our gratitude. I am King Darvus III. These are my daughters, the Princess Leona, and my youngest, Ariann." The young women bowed along with the King. They were all attired in clean clothes, the bloody signs of the earlier fighting no longer in evidence.

Tahjeen, the old man, bowed in return before Achates spoke. "Your majesty, may I present our grandfather, Janus Dron."

Stooped, Tahjeen limped forward, leaning on his cane. He bowed again, acknowledging the King. "My Lord, I am grateful we arrived in time."

"I was expecting the rest of your men as well," the king said as he looked around.

"I felt it best, sire," the old man explained, "that they scout the surrounding territory. Better a live, empty stomach in the morning than a full, dead one."

The King blinked, startled by the old man's terseness. "Ah, I understand. Good thinking." Darvus recovered and smiled broadly. "Please, Sir Dron, come and sit with us." He beckoned to the table, and a padded chair that was waiting for the grandfather. After the men were seated the young women joined them.

Once everyone was comfortable, the old man spoke. "I am not royalty, Your Highness. 'Sir' is an honorific I do not deserve. I am simply 'old Dron'."

The King roared his amusement. "Nonsense. In my presence, you will always be 'Sir Dron'. Thanks to the efforts of your grandsons, you have earned it."

"They train hard, Your Highness." Tahjeen commented then added, "Please excuse my hood, but my eyes are weak and light causes me pain." He spoke in a raspy voice, his shoulders stooped, his stature diminished.

King Darvus waved away the statement. "Sir Dron, what is your destination?"

"Danigh, Your Majesty," the old man answered.

"Splendid!" The King enthused as he clapped his hands together. "We are in route there as well. Perhaps we could travel together? It would seem wise to do so in case there are other bandits about."

"I agree, Sire." Tahjeen replied. "May I ask the purpose of your visit to the capital?"

The King smiled and glanced at his oldest daughter. "Princess Leona is to be married to Dania's Prince Roland. Our two kingdoms will enjoy mutually prosperous trade, and form a military alliance." His smile broadened. "Hopefully, we will soon have a male heir to my throne."

Princess Leona appeared politely indifferent and Tahjeen inferred that it was a political marriage in which she had little say. She was pretty, but he found himself drawn more to the younger daughter. Though she knew her place and retreated within herself in her sister's presence, Tahjeen sensed an aura radiating from her that projected intelligence, wit, and, surprisingly, some unknown power. Nevertheless, he forced himself to focus on the King. "Your Highness, how does Morgan fair?"

"His condition has improved since your healer visited. "Darvus turned to his younger daughter. "Ariann has some healing skill and her ministering can work small miracles. When I first saw the young man's injury, I must confess that I feared the worst."

The direction of the King's comments gave Tahjeen the opening he sought. "My Lady, thank you for helping my grandson." He found he liked looking at her, and had to remind himself to slouch and disguise his voice.

A stunning smile transformed her face into something less than beautiful but definitely interesting. "You are quite welcome, Sir," she replied. "But I suspect that my skills worked less a miracle than your healer's." She was watching him closely, as if trying to see behind the shadows that hid much of his face.

Achates is right, Tahjeen thought. Her voice is magical. Like a magnet it draws me towards her.

"Your Highness," Achates interjected, breaking the trance and shaking Tahjeen free of his enchantment, "We should get an early start, so we must take our leave. With your permission?"

"Of course," the King replied. "We will be ready shortly after sunrise."

Achates nodded, walking over to help his 'grandfather' up. They bid the ladies goodnight as they slowly trekked back to their own camp. Tahjeen was sure he felt the eyes of Ariann on his back every step of the way.

The next day was uneventful. Since Morgan was much improved, the Lady Ariann agreed he could travel. As they decamped, Achates met with the King's men, volunteering his brothers to scout ahead and guard the perimeters. If there were another attack, the King and his party would be forewarned. After he finished talking with the guards, Ariann watched him return to his grandfather where they conversed out of hearing range.

Riding alongside her older sister, Ariann watched them from a distance. "Achates is interesting," Leona said.

Ariann wondered what Leona was up to now. "He seems like a nice man," she offered.

"Handsome, too," Leona said.

"After a fashion," Ariann replied.

Her sister laughed. "And strong and literate for one of lesser rank. I think he'd like to get to know you better. Who knows, with Father so beholding, you might find a husband on this trip too." Her eyes were dancing.

Ariann shook her head, amused by her sister's teasing but refusing further comment. She had been watching, though and what she saw puzzled her. Supposedly Achates was in charge but he was receiving subtle signals from his grandfather.

It was a contradiction that aroused her curiosity. Why not be direct? Why the subterfuge?

The healer also raised her suspicions. She knew she was a talented healer, but she had never seen a wound heal as quickly, nor a patient regain strength so fast. None of it was her doing. It happened immediately after the healer came to see him. And, where had he disappeared to? She hadn't seen him since.

Ariann was bright and, being younger, enjoyed more freedom than Leona. If she poured hours of her young life into learning, no one cared. That learning revealed a love for science and the eventual development of her medicinal skills. She had other strengths but most of all, she loved studying people. She discovered she could learn a great deal by staying quiet, watching and listening. She had a knack for hearing what was not being said, for people saying one thing when meaning something else.

That was what was bothering her now. There was something queer about Achates and his grandfather. She wasn't alarmed. She sensed no reason to be afraid. They had been quick to come to their defense and had come close to paying a very dear price. Yet, there was something. She just couldn't put her finger on it.

She kept all this to herself. Her father would not be interested in her observations. What she thought was unimportant. She was merely a pawn to be played in political games. She was not resentful, merely resigned to the fact that she had no choice.

They stopped to rest and have lunch. While the horses were being tethered, a snake spooked them. Before an alert guard killed the snake, several horses broke free. Ariann watched with growing concern. The marauders had already cost them several horses. If they lost any more, their journey would be severely hampered. But she was surprised when one of the stallions abruptly stopped. It neighed, pawed the ground, and tossed its head about. Then the powerful horse began to walk towards Achates' grandfather.

The two other horses had stopped as well, as if Sir Dron was calling them. Yet, she heard no sound save their nickering. In time, all three surrounded him. He reached out slowly and one by one, took their reigns. He handed them to Achates who was mounted on his own horse close by.

As Achates trotted them back towards her party, she gathered her skirts to avoid the dampness of the morning dew, and walked over to him. His warm smile greeted her. He climbed down off his horse and bowed. "Good day, My Lady."

"A pleasant day to you, commander. Please thank your grandfather for collecting our horses."

"Oh, well, he does have a way with animals."

Ariann thought he looked uncomfortable. She decided to be direct and see where it led. "Is he a priest or magician of some sort?"

Achates' eyebrows lifted in surprise. "Er, no. He is just..."

"An old man," she finished for him, "who seems to have a way with many things," she added.

Achates remounted quickly, raising his hand in a respectful salute. "My Lady, have a good day," he said and rode quickly away.

"You certainly scared him off," her sister called from their wagon. She yawned rather unladylike then got down. "What in Sandala did you say to him?"

"I was trying to glean information about his grandfather," Ariann replied.

"Ah, yes – your inquisitive nature at work once again. I take it he had little to say?" her sister asked.

Ariann looked at her sister, wishing they were closer and enjoyed a relationship where confidences were shared. But Leona was not like that. She was entirely the Princess, and one day she would be Queen. The gulf between them was wide, separated by political importance and the power that came with ruling a realm.

"I was probably being too nosy," Ariann said simply, recognizing that Leona's interest in the grandfather was not mutual. But her own curiosity surrounding Sir Dron only deepened.

CHAPTER 9

DESTINY

For Ariann, the afternoon dragged by as the parties inched their way towards Danigh. The gentle terrain made traveling easy. Even so, with a half dozen wagons creaking along, their advance was slow. She saw Achates check in with the King, and ride with him for awhile. But the grandfather kept his distance. Her father had offered him a more comfortable ride in one of the wagons, but he had politely declined. It made it difficult for Ariann to study him, though she occasionally saw him looking away as she turned in his direction, as if he had been watching her. Achates remained aloof as well, leaving her to conclude that he did not like a woman who spoke her mind.

Late in the afternoon, the countryside began to change. The hills loomed larger and the number of trees multiplied into a forest. The road before them became challenging as the elevation increased, slowing their progress. Game was plentiful, however, and that evening Achates' brothers delivered fresh meat for them to cook. It was a welcome change from dried meat and hard biscuits, and the King's guardsmen appreciated a break from hunting.

The next day the road burst out among the trees into an open expanse of high desert. As they passed a stream, Achates advised they stop and refill their water barrels. Fresh water might prove scarce over the next few days.

Once they began to move again, the low cloud cover lifted and a brilliant sun bore down. Before long they were layered in road dust. The heat intensified, forcing Ariann and Leona to retreat inside their wagon, hoping the cover's shade would provide relief.

They traveled thus, crossing the dusty plain, coming ever closer to the towering mountains that encircled the capital city. By mid-afternoon Ariann was dozing inside her wagon when she was jostled awake by a sudden increase in speed. She heard several of the men shouting, so she looked out the flap to see what the fuss was.

A beautiful lake sprawled before her, with the jagged Learing Mountains providing a stunning backdrop. The horses and oxen were eager to drink, explaining the sudden hurry. The lake was crystalline; the snow-capped peaks were a mirror reflection that rippled as a soft breeze whispered across the water.

She saw Achates ride up to them and call to her father. "Your Highness, grandfather suggests we stop early and camp here for the night. We could all use a bath. Would that be all right?"

"Of course," her father answered. "The pass ahead is difficult and the animals could use a rest before we push on." Achates nodded. "I'll inform my grandfather." Ariann looked at the clear water and smiled. A bath would feel wonderful indeed.

Paca, Tahjeen said, mentally calling out to his *fel.* The big leopard appeared several yards ahead, padding out of some brush overhanging the water's edge. He took note of his dripping black fur.

"So you have already been in the water," he said aloud since no one else was around. He was over a mile from the main camp, seeking privacy to bathe.

Together, he and the cat rounded a bend in the shoreline where several boulders hid them from view. He began to undress, removing the dusty cloak and tossing it aside. Boots came next then pants and undergarments, and finally the wig and grimy beard whose itchiness was proving unpleasant.

Naked, his oak colored skin was in stark contrast to his unkempt blond locks which had become thick with dirt and he was eager to wash it.

Tahjeen strode into the cold water, his tall form rippling with muscle. His abdomen tapered into lean hips, but his genitalia was hidden, tucked under a solid plate of hinged bone that was further covered by smooth, dark skin.

Stretching forward, he sliced into the water. After several powerful strokes he paused, treading water. He thought about the legends that claimed a Shala warrior had 'the strength of ten men' and smiled. Tahjeen knew it was untrue – the more likely number was two, perhaps three.

It was true, however, that he could run faster than any man and hurl a spear over twice as far. A human could not draw the bow he trained with, and the arrows it launched flew faster than the human eye could follow. Achates complained that when he trained with him, Tahjeen's movements seemed a blur.

He waded deeper and prepared to submerge. He pushed his thoughts aside then turned back to his big cat. *Guard, Paca,* he commanded. Knowing he was safer with Paca than with any man, save a fellow tribesman, he inhaled deeply then plunged into the depths.

Tahjeen took advantage of a warrior's ability to hold his breath for ten minutes or more. He gave no thought that while submerged, his heightened senses were blocked. He could not detect a scent, nor see or hear anyone approaching.

Ariann saw a small cove that promised privacy. She told the soldier guarding her to take her horse and retreat a comfortable distance. She proceeded on, eager to languish in the cleansing waters. As she rounded the corner of an outcropping, she was surprised to see a pile of clothing strewn atop one of the boulders. She was more than surprised when she stepped around the rock and nearly stumbled onto a huge black panther. Ariann froze in place, but the animal merely looked, studying her.

She had read of animals attacking when you tried to run, so she began to inch backwards. The cat did nothing. Growing braver, Ariann started to turn around, but a patch of gray near the pile of clothes caught her eye. It was the grandfather's beard! She gasped. The animal forgotten for the moment, she went to the clothes for a closer look. Yes, they definitely belonged to the old man.

What in the world, she thought looking again at the beautiful animal resting casually nearby. Was this his pet? At that precise moment, Tahjeen surfaced.

He stood up, the water barely reaching his waist. He started to shake the water out of his hair when his senses alerted him to her presence. He spun around quickly, his colorful eyes settling on Ariann's startled face.

Both momentarily speechless, she found her voice first. "Hello, grandfather," she said with no small bit of irony. "Now it all makes sense - an old man with a young man's hands; avoiding us in the daylight; the numerous conferences with Achates. You are their leader, are you not?" Her voice had remained quiet, but the challenge was unmistakable.

"You are observant," he said, then started wading towards her.

"No! Stop," she said, not wanting his maleness exposed, but upon seeing nothing her mouth fell open in disbelief. She looked up into his eyes and grew mesmerized by the multitude of vibrant colors.

A myriad of thoughts bombarded her, but she could only ask, "What are you?"

He looked back thoughtfully. Finally, he answered. "My name is Tahjeen," he said simply.

"That isn't what I asked," she said pointedly. She stood her ground, calm and unafraid, waiting.

He took longer to reply this time, perhaps studying her. "You have an inner strength," he finally said, "and deserve a truthful answer. "I am," he said standing tall and proud,"Shala."

Her eyes widened. Shala...Shala! Her mind reeled. She had read about such beings in the library archives. But until this moment, she had never known if they were real. Fascinated, she surveyed him from head to foot.

He was tall, very tall. Length added grace to his muscular arms. His face was chiseled into rugged plains, his lips full and nose well formed. Recalling some of what she'd read, she ventured a question. "The Prophecy indicates that only in times of great threat to Sandala would you appear. Is that why you're here? Are we in such peril?"

He nodded.

"And the two who ride with you that we never see? Are they also Shala?"

Tahjeen nodded again.

She looked at the panther. "Does he belong to you?" Ariann asked.

"In a manner of speaking," Tahjeen replied, glancing at his *fel*. "He was supposed to be guarding me. He picked an odd time to relax his vigilance. His name is Paca. He is my *fel*."

In response to the criticism, the panther yawned. *There was no danger,* the animal explained.

Intrigued, Ariann looked at the beautiful creature. "What does *fel* mean?"

"We are bonded, in a way that is difficult to explain. It is part of a ritual search that all warriors undertake. On the search, we..." he paused, seeking the proper words. "We find one another, and from that time forward, we can communicate mind to mind."

The big cat rose, shook the dust off and then padded over to Ariann. He walked around her, sniffing, almost stalking, a low rumble building in his throat. Momentarily unnerved, Ariann stepped away, but the cat followed and began to rub against her.

Once again at ease, the woman laughed, failing to notice the startled look on Tahjeen's face. He began to wade towards her once again. She turned at the sound of his approach, and noticed the intensity of his gaze. "What?" she asked, unsettled by his demeanor.

"Paca says you are the one," Tahjeen said as his breath grew ragged.

"Explain that to me," she said suddenly alarmed.

Tahjeen looked at her closely, searching her eyes, her face. He noted every mark that made her unique – the tiny freckles that crossed her nose; the small yellow speck near the iris that disrupted the perfection of her blue eyes; the lift of her eyebrows.

Tahjeen's skin kindled with warmth, his back arching like a courting bird. In precise, measured steps, he moved around her. He leaned close to take in her scent then paused when his face drew so near hers that he could breathe her breath. Suddenly, he backed away.

As he looked back at her, she saw the colors in his eyes began to whirl. They were flashing green, white, red, blue, yellow, until they settled into a rich, fluorescent pink. Finally, his voice raw, he answered her.

"It means that we are destined to be together, as lovers and mates."

Ariann's eyes widened in shock. His impertinence angered her and helped her find her voice. "I will be no one's lover unless I choose to be." She backed away. "And, I do not!"

She spun around, her face flushed with anger, and left him standing alone as she disappeared behind the rocks. He turned and looked at his *fel*, who came to him and licked his fingers. *She is the one,* the cat said with firm conviction.

"I believe you, Paca," Tahjeen reassured him. "You have knowledge I cannot begin to fathom."

Tahjeen looked back to where the young woman had disappeared and shook his head. *But did it have to be one so full of fire*? A smile tugged at the corner of his mouth. The big animal purred with pleasure as Tahjeen's fingers stroked his ebony fur.

The challenge will be good for you.

Tahjeen stared at his companion, wondering when the animal had developed a sense of humor. Then he walked to his clothes, frowning in mild disgust as he began to put on his stained and dusty pants.

Suddenly Paca turned in the direction of Ariann's departure and growled. His shoulder muscles bunched as he crouched in preparation for a charge. *She is in peril!* The unmistakable sound of Ariann's scream bolted both the Shala and his cat into action. Tahjeen reached for his weapons.

CHAPTER 10

PERIL

Rather than follow her exact path, Tahjeen jumped twelve feet straight up the bank then raced the last thirty feet to the crest of the hill. When he reached the top, what he saw in the ravine below chilled him.

Her guard lay crumpled, presumably dead. Ariann was cornered against a large rock. Several armed men were taunting her, laughing, as they prodded her with long spears. Like the previous raiders, they were a raggedy looking band. They wore earth-colored garments that were dirty and torn. But the clever disguise did not fool Tahjeen. The attackers were agile, skilled and disciplined - all indicators of military training. Even in the face of such a threat, Tahjeen noted her defiance and was pleased. She would fight, not faint.

"Stop!" he bellowed from high above them, his voice echoing off the rock walls.

The men turned as one to locate the source of interference. They spied him on the crest of the hill, his silhouette dark, framed from behind by the setting sun. For long moments, no one said anything. Time seemed to slow as they took stock of the situation. The armed men were glancing about, trying to locate any others who might be with the stranger. Finally, the apparent leader spoke.

"And who are you to order us?" he challenged.

Tahjeen appeared to move down the slope in slow-motion, his features and stature hidden by the darkening shadows. He stopped just short of the waning sun's light.

"Someone who can kill you where you stand," he answered, his voice low and menacing. "Put your weapons down. Now!"

At the leader's signal, the two other men began a flanking movement. Tahjeen stepped quickly into the light. "Stop," he said.

They saw him and froze. Gripped by uncertainty, they looked back to their leader, but he, too, had grown wary.

With lightning speed, Tahjeen took advantage of their indecision and charged the nearest man. He threw him down and disarmed him before the others could react. The remaining two retreated quickly to gain distance from the strange warrior and the leader lifted an odd-looking horn to his lips and blew. In another flash of movement Tahjeen knocked the horn aside with one hand and put a sword to the man's throat with his other.

"Whom were you calling?" he demanded.

The man smiled. "Death."

Tahjeen roughly shoved the leader aside. *Paca?* He called silently then stood still, concentrating.

Many come!

Tahjeen heard the urgency in the panther's words and wheeled about, throwing a nasty looking knife that killed another armed man. The leader started to lift his sword but Tahjeen disemboweled him in one efficient motion. He ignored the disarmed warrior watching all this happen.

Tahjeen turned to Ariann. "Get the horses! Paca says that many are headed this way. I cannot fight them all."

He began to run, broken tree limbs cracking as he brushed them aside. He was pleased that she did not question his choice of direction. As they passed the spot where he had been bathing, he grabbed the rest of his clothes. A few steps more and he retrieved his traveling pack that had been shoved behind a rock.

"Paca!" he called out, and tossed the pack towards the large animal. Paca put it in his jaws, turning and bounding on ahead, rocks and dust flying under his padded feet. Ariann rounded the corner astride one of the horses while gripping the reins of the other. Tahjeen raced toward her.

"Stay out of the water and keep to the rocks. It will make our trail harder to follow." He tied his clothes in a bundle around his waist, grabbed his weapons then leapt onto the second horse.

They raced along the lake's shoreline until Tahjeen heard the babbling of a small stream. When they reached it, he didn't hesitate, but took them into it, heading uphill into the trees. The noise from the water muffled the clopping of the horses' hooves and helped cover the splashing caused by their anxious movement.

They rode for several minutes but the hillside grew steeper

and the rocks in the water were slippery, slowing their progress. At a sharp turn, broken branches forged a dam against some boulders. With no easy way around, Tahjeen backtracked until the horses were able to scale the bank. Then they continued on.

The trees grew dense, providing more cover but slowing their pace. He glanced back dismayed at the trail they were leaving, but knew they had little choice. He was unfamiliar with the area, but knew that sooner or later the trees would thin out and they would be more exposed.

When he judged that they had covered over a mile, he called to his *fel* and retrieved his pack. *Paca, find out where they are.* The brush separated and rustled as the cat turned and loped down the hill.

"Rest your horse while you can," Tahjeen told Ariann.

"I assume we headed this way because the marauders were between us and the rest of our party," she stated rather than asked. "What do we do if they come after us?"

"Paca will tell us how many, and if I fight or continue running," Tahjeen answered.

"And if they are not chasing us?" she asked.

"Then I hide you while Paca and I return to help the others."

His words filled Ariann with new apprehension. Everyone had been travel weary, looking forward to rest. They would be relaxed, unprepared.

As if reading her thoughts, Tahjeen spoke. "Achates will have posted guards around the camp. They won't be taken by surprise. The other *fels* will sense intruders."

His words eased her mind. She nodded, grateful for his reassurance. It gave her time to study him, and recall how ruthlessly he had killed her tormentors, yet was surprised to discover she was no longer afraid of him.

He caught her looking at him, and raised his head in question. "Thank you for coming to my aid," she said. He bowed slightly but said nothing.

She watched him for a time, recalling his declaration that one day they would be lovers and mates. The memory rekindled her irritation and before she could stop herself, words meant to hurt spewed forth. "Are you always so efficient a killer?"

His eyes spun hues of gold, orange and yellow, until they lost all color and turned transparent. The lack of definition unsettled her. His posture tensed and his words came quietly, like the light breath of a soft breeze.

"Before it was necessary to rescue you, none of us had ever killed a man."

She was shocked and her face reddened. She felt ashamed. "I...I am sorry I said that."

He did not reply.

She wanted to say more, but before she could find the words, he glanced downhill. "Paca's coming," he said. "Now we'll learn if I must kill for you again."

CHAPTER 11

THE CHASE

Paca returned from his reconnaissance, reporting that eight warriors trailed them on horseback. Tahjeen's predicament irritated him. He wanted Ariann back with her people quickly so he could help the others make it safely to Danigh. Though his four companions would do everything in their power to protect the travelers, his presence would improve the odds greatly.

You must protect her. I know that. Paca's reminder increased Tahjeen's frustration. *You must trust.*

Tahjeen glared at the panther. Paca grunted, turned his back and walked over to Ariann, sitting down and grooming himself. Tahjeen picked up random thoughts from the cat –*impatient* and *unappreciative* were among them. The animal's sense of outrage helped alter his mood. He chuckled.

Thank you, Paca, for putting me in my place.

The *fel* looked at him and started purring.

"What did he see?" Ariann asked.

"Enough to make avoidance the wiser course." He did not add that if not for her presence he would go after the pursuers. "We must head northeast and gradually circle back around."

He saw her nod as she tucked an errant strand of hair under her head cover. His head tipped to one side as he studied her.

"What?"

For a moment, he said nothing. Finally he stood and walked over to her. "What are you wearing under your dress?"

"I beg your pardon?"

"A dress hampers you in such terrain. Are there pantaloons underneath?"

She nodded. "I am not taking off my dress."

"You don't have to." He pulled her to her feet, took his knife and before she could object, slit the dress down the front, from the waist to its bottom hem.

Ariann flinched, her face radiating outrage."What do you think you are doing?" she yelled, her voice pitched high with tension.

"Making some breeches," he replied without concern. Then ordered, twirling his finger, "Now turn around."

Tahjeen made an identical cut down the back then stepped back and looked at the once attractive outfit. A moment later he made two more cuts, one down each side.

"Weave these around your legs," he said, indicating the four strips. "They'll give you additional protection."

When Ariann bent to do so, he reached for her scarf. "Stop!" she wailed.

Surprised by her reaction, he shook his head. "Ariann," he said quietly. "Are you trying to help them find us?"

Flustered, she glanced at the forest surrounding them. "No, of course not. I just don't like to be treated roughly." Tahjeen saw tears forming in her lovely eyes.

He reached out and gently took her hands. "Let me braid your hair. It will be easier to manage, less apt to tangle." He waited, silently seeking permission.

He watched as she warred with her feelings, her unease struggling against reason. Finally, she relented. "All right."

"Sit here." Tahjeen pointed to a rock in front of him. Once Ariann did as he asked, Tahjeen took her long, honey colored hair in his strong hands.

He removed her scarf then started to weave her hair into a long braid, finding the feel of her silky tresses unnerving and intimate. He was firm, yet careful. When he finished, he told her to wait and went to his pack. Moments later, he returned with a leather tunic. It was large, one of his. She watched as he cut it, making it smaller. He helped her stand, slipping the modified garment over her head and settling it on to her shoulders.

It hung well below her knees. He cut two hand widths from the bottom then sliced a long, narrow strip from it. Next, Tahjeen made two holes in front of the tunic about waist high, and two similar ones in the back. He fed one of the strips through all four holes, cinching it up to make a knot.

"You will need better shoes." His voice was gentle.

She no longer argued, but sat down and removed the lightweight pair she wore. They were already torn and barely recognizable.

Slashing the remaining piece of leather in two, he made twelve holes down each side. Needing more material, he cut an arrow strip from the bottom of his own tunic. In a few minutes, she had shoes tied to her foot by the lace that wove back and forth through the holes he had made.

She stood and inspected her new outfit. "It's crude," Tahjeen said, "but it will keep you warm and better protected from branches and thorns."

"My father and sister would be appalled if they saw me." She smiled.

"We need to move on," Tahjeen said. She looked at him shyly, her gaze furtive. He could think of nothing to say so he retrieved the horses and helped her mount.

They continued northeasterly in a steady trot but the slope steepened. Though still in the foothills of the Learing Mountains, the incline would soon become too difficult to continue riding. Until the ground leveled, they would have to travel on foot.

A half day later, the moon high in the night sky, Tahjeen stopped, tying the horses to a low slung branch under a giant ponderosa pine. Ariann was near exhaustion and could only watch from the rough ground where she had lowered herself. She lacked the energy to resist when he pulled her back to her feet.

"There's a ledge a short ways back where we'll rest for the night. I'll take you there now then go find something for us to eat." Tahjeen guided her a hundred paces back the way they had come and helped her down the side of the mountain to a ledge thirty feet below.

"We'll be safe here, out of sight from above. Rest," he commanded then scrambled back to the top.

Horrified, Ariann watched as he bit into something raw. She had no idea what it was and didn't want to know. Tahjeen offered her a piece but she shook her head. "Take it," Tahjeen said. "You need nourishment and we cannot risk a fire. It's safe." He held bloody flesh out to her once again.

"I don't think I can."

"Think of something else while you chew."

Reluctantly, Ariann took it. The first bite roused nausea and her stomach roiled. But she was determined to show him she could master herself, so she chewed, and chewed... and chewed.

She followed his advice and tried to take her mind off the raw, bloody meal. They had been on the go for the entire day and well into the night and she was bone tired.

When they had reached the higher altitude, the footing became too precarious as their climb grew steeper. They had gotten off the exhausted horses and begun walking. Tahjeen took both of the horses' reins, leading them carefully over the loose shale and treacherous terrain. The rocky, arid ground was a mixture of hardy mountain pine and juniper scrub. Some of the evergreens seemed to emerge out of solid rock, as their roots clung to the smallest piece of earth. For a few hours she kept up a good pace then despite her protests, he dropped the reins and picked her up and carried her. Paca trailed behind the horses, forcing them to follow. For an hour or more, Tahjeen ran with her in his arms. Then he would put her down, give her some water and let her rest. But it soon, after he would pick her up and start out again.

Toward the top of the mountain, the trees thinned out, frequently forcing them into the open. Tahjeen hurried them from cover to cover, keeping their exposure to a minimum. Once they had paused to see if their chasers could be detected, but Tahjeen saw nothing. Paca went down to find out how far back the enemy was and returned within the hour to report that they were several miles behind and had stopped for the night.

Still, Tahjeen forged on, widening their lead, seeking away to lose them altogether. Laboring on, across chilly mountain streams and steep hillsides of loose shale, Ariann nearly fell twice. If not for Tahjeen's quick reactions and strength, she would have perished on the rugged slopes.

When she misstepped, he did not berate her but grew more careful and stayed close by. She felt his protectiveness and chided herself for being so difficult earlier on. Clearly, he was determined to get her safely back to civilization even at the risk of his own life.

"Are you finished?" His comments brought her musings to an end.

She looked at her hand and was surprised to find the bloody meat gone. "Yes."

"Try to sleep. I will keep watch for a time then Paca will guard while I rest."

She pushed herself closer to the side of the mountain. Her

legs nearly reached the end of the small ledge. She had no intention of falling off during the night. She wrapped her arms around herself, trying to ward off the cold then Paca jumped onto the ledge and came to her. He lay down beside her as if he knew his warmth was needed."Oh, Paca, thank you," she whispered, gratefully stroking his silky head, and fell asleep in seconds.

She woke to find strong arms wrapped around her. She tensed, forgetting where she was or who she was with. "It's all right," Tahjeen said sleepily."You were cold, as am I."

She didn't answer but gradually relaxed. His body was warm. She listened and heard his breathing slow as he drifted off to sleep. Later, he shifted position, moving one leg so it covered hers. She tried to relax but his innocent embrace was arousing sensations she had not dealt with before. He felt so good…no, stop, she told herself and took a deep, calming breath, willing her mind to think of other things.

She stared out at a perfect, star-lit night. The sky was bright and here, near the mountain peak, she felt she could reach out and touch the thousands of sparkling orbs. It was like being on the top of the world.

Where were her people tonight? Were they still alive? Who was this strange being who held her so intimately? What was happening to Sandala?

There were no answers for the questions that railed at her consciousness, only a sense of melancholy that nothing would ever be the same. She had read too much history, studied too many archives to believe that events happened randomly. There was always a cause or hidden factors that propelled events in a certain direction. Cause and effect, action and reaction – everything was linked. And what role am I to play in aloof this, she wondered?

CHAPTER 12

COMMANDER GENERAL TARO

In front of his huge command tent, on a grassy plain ten miles outside of Seadawn, Commander General Taro Schull stood rock still, watching. Dust stirred all around him as beasts lumbered forward, spurred by their trainer's lashes, shaking the ground where he stood. Men's shouts echoed across the horizon, directing hundreds of wagons loaded with weapons and supplies. Units of soldiers jogged in different directions as the various divisions began to assemble. The thick air was drenched by the odorous sweat of thousands of laboring men.

Taro's insides churned like the contents of a witches' caldron. The mobilization was taking too long as far as he was concerned. In truth, the highly disciplined, elite army was working with great efficiency and at breakneck speed. But it did not matter. They would never move fast enough to please the commander of the Surmese forces.

There was justification for his impatience. The Emperor, High Lord Klaron, fifth descendant of the Kauble line, the dynasty's founder, tolerated neither sloppiness nor failure. In large part the success of the Sandala invasion depended on the speed with which the first four kingdoms could be overrun thereby insuring Dania's isolation. Speed and precision were not just goals, they were necessities.

Still, no one watching would assume General Taro was anything other than calm. The scowl on his face never changed; his own pace never varied. He moved with a brisk, determined stride regardless of the situation. These attributes, combined with his military acuity and leadership, was why the Emperor had chosen him to lead the invasion. It was a great honor, filled with reward and rife with peril. He could return home to a hero's welcome, soon to be rich beyond his wildest dreams, or he would die on Sandalese soil. It was victory or death, and better to die in

a foreign land than face the humiliation of a public execution if
he should fail.

"Captain!" Taro shouted to an officer supervising the
placement of armaments for the different divisions.

The man hurried over and saluted smartly."Sir?"

"How much longer before the rest of the beasts arrive?"

"A few hundred breaths at most, sir. There was a slight delay
because one of the hounds had gone foul. Fortunately, we were
able to put it down before it did any damage."

A raised eyebrow was the only visible reaction from the
Commander General.

"When they arrive, Captain, divide the hounds among the
divisions, but keep all the klaghorns together. They will be held
in reserve for Dania."

"As you wish, Commander General. I will inform the
handlers." The officer saluted then headed off toward a cluster of
men.

Taro wheeled about and beckoned to a man who was
standing a dozen paces away. His personal assistant stepped
forward smartly. "Gather the division leaders and have them
come to my tent at once."

As his aide raced off, Taro took a last glance around the huge
assembly of men, weapons and supplies then turned and headed
to his command tent.

Taro paced while the last General settled himself. The man
was not late. It was just that Taro liked to start early. On top of
that, he was eager to launch the campaign that would lead to his
ultimate glory – a prized seat at the Emperor's side. To be a part
of that inner circle, to wield the power that came with it, to enjoy
the riches that would flow his way because of it, and above all,
the glory and respect that would finally be his...

Taro ended his grandiose musings. He inspected the three
men who sat before him.

General Whitehock came from a family of privilege. Despite
that, the brash, cocky, elitist was a seasoned veteran, and he
could lead. His only drawback was that Taro didn't like him but
in war, that hardly mattered. His handsome face was unmarred
by battle, adding another rung on Taro's ladder of dislike, his
own features scarred numerous times. Mentally dismissing him,
he let his gaze slide to the next man.

General Starcher had worked his way up through the ranks

despite his common background. His parents had been marginally successful grocers, but as the younger of two sons, he would inherit nothing. Rather than live off the whim of his older brother, Starcher threw himself into the army with vigor. He made a name for himself in the Island Wars and promotion followed. His victory against daunting odds in the Olandus Mountain campaign caught the eye of the Emperor, and lo, another General was born. His heavy, blunt features were far from flattering and his thick lips and turned-up nose gave rise to a nickname he so detested that he would kill the man who muttered it, the Pig.

Taro didn't mind. The man was gifted even if he suffered heavy casualties on the battlefield. Men were supposed to die in war. It was victory that counted most.

The final man, General Blugar, came from a traditional military family and knew exactly what was expected of him and of Taro as well. His uniform was stiff and his bearing as rigid as Taro's. His fair-skinned features, creased by age and years of responsibility, were sharp. A no-nonsense, disciplined leader, he was reliable, if unimaginative. Still, Taro valued reliability over imagination in this campaign, for everything was straightforward and the objectives simple - conquer Sandala, first by manipulating the petty Sealand ruler then by overrunning the three other kingdoms leaving Dania, the true prize of the continent, completely isolated.

Taro finally nodded a greeting then opened a large map of Sandala and began laying out his strategy.

"General Whitehock, you will take two divisions into Oreon. The pass here," he said as he pointed it out on the map, "is not heavily fortified. You will take it then flood into the lowlands. Concentrate on the larger centers of populations. Stay out of the mountains. It will only slow you down and the population there is insignificant. I expect you to capture the capital within the week."

Taro looked at the brash leader. "Do you have any questions?"

Whitehock shook his head. "Not at this time," he said as a smile began to play at the corners of his mouth. Taro glared at him until all semblance of amusement disappeared.

"General Blugar," Taro said, his gaze traveling to the Pig. "You will take two divisions into Gleneden. Expect modest resistance, but they will be severely outnumbered. Also in your favor is the land's geography. There are many farms and low, rolling hills. You will find plenty to eat along the way to the capital." Taro unloosed a menacing smile daring Blugar to respond, and was not surprised when he didn't.

"Milhune is on the far border, here," Taro pointed again, "but as I indicated, you will cover the terrain with ease. There are no passes to fight through, only a capital to overrun. I expect completion in five days, yes?"

"Of course." Taro contained his irritation when Blugar's face betrayed nothing.

Taro turned to General Starcher. "Palaton is your objective, general." Taro's rugged fist settled on the map where Palaton was sketched."Their ruler is a militarist so he may be the one surprise we face. But I am confident you will find a way. Am I correct?"

Taro was fully aware that Starcher was the only one who did not fear him. He was the Emperor's favorite as well and felt a degree of security. Taro dealt with him by giving him the most difficult assignment. That's how Taro always played potential rivals.

"Correct, Commander. And how many divisions will I command?"

Taro nodded, appearing pleased, though inwardly he noted Starcher's lack of intimidation which did not please him at all."Two divisions, general, just like the others. Is that not enough?" Taro chided.

"It will be more than sufficient, Commander. Thank you. Do I have a timetable as well?"

Taro's eyes narrowed, though he successfully kept the smile on his face."A full week, general. The same as General Whitehock."

Starcher nodded then turned his gaze to the map.

"Commander General," Whitehock said, "what of the other four divisions and the beasts?"

Taro glared, unappreciative of the interruption, though he had to credit Whitehock. The man did not wither under his stare.

He turned away and pointed to Sealand. "Two divisions will remain here, ensuring our continued control of the kingdom. Since Dawad's unfortunate and ill-timed assassination," he paused, smiling, and all three men joined him with quiet laughter. "We need to be sure there is no insurrection. There will be some public outcry which might lead to minor disturbances, but the presence of twenty thousand soldiers will keep them in their place."

Nods followed all around the table.

"The last two divisions as well as the beasts will travel with me. We will be a moving command center as we march toward Dania. Once you have accomplished your objectives, you will leave half a division in place and bring the rest to join me here." His index finger landed sharply on the foothills leading to the eastern pass of the Learing Mountains.

"Together, sixty thousand strong, we will unleash the beasts and attack Dania from the east while the ten divisions that land on her far coast will surprise them from the west."

Taro was pleased. He could see by their expressions that he had them, that they were anticipating a glorious victory. Dania might have its capital surrounded by mountains, but no army in the history of the Empire could hope to forestall one hundred and sixty thousand well trained soldiers.

CHAPTER 13

THE CLAVE

There was a knock on the door and Roland entered his chambers. Sorbonne was expecting him."Is everything ready?"he asked. He was seated behind a massive oak table, maps and papers strewn across it.

"Yes, Father, everyone is here except, as you feared, the Sealand King. We've received no word from him."

Sorbonne digested the last piece of information. His features tightened. So that's how it is, he thought. Dawad has turned his back on the rest of Sandala. The King sighed then glanced at his son.

The past several days had been busy ones for Dania's heir. As requested, he had rooms prepared for the travelers, and welcomed each group in a manner befitting their rank. The rulers from Palaton and Gleneden arrived the same day, so there was a joint feast for both parties. Then King Darvus of Oreon appeared two days later and received a separate welcoming dinner. Roland had seen to it that all the royals were entertained, and encouraged to enjoy the bountiful gardens of the palace and King Sorbonne's elaborate library.

At Sorbonne's request, the other monarchs agreed to wait three additional days for King Dawad. During that time, he told Roland to invite Queen Endoreen to a private dinner with him. Sorbonne told her of Devon's absence and she brought him up to date on Gleneden's situation. King Sorbonne considered Endoreen his strongest ally and he appreciated her candor and allegiance. But one could only feast so long and the other rulers began to complain as their impatience increased. The three-day deadline was over.

"They are waiting for you in the Great Room," Roland said, "Is there anything else, Father?"

Sorbonne read the concern etched across his son's face.

Roland was trained for war but wasn't eager to embrace such action. He had no idea how much Sorbonne respected him for his reticence.

"Yes. I want you with me," the King replied."You can observe and absorb."

"The opening session may be difficult," Sorbonne continued. We will all be testing the waters and determining where we stand with one another. I don't know where their loyalty lies, or if there is a traitor among them so I must proceed with care.

He looked at his son with a gaze as intense as a fire at the height of its blaze."Watch them closely. Afterwards, once they return to their rooms, we'll talk."

Sorbonne turned away."Leave me now. I'll be along in a moment. Be ready to announce me."

Roland bowed and then turned to leave the chamber. The king crossed to the balcony and took in the majestic view. The last remnant of fog was lifting from the land as the midmorning sun delivered its warmth. He looked out at the fields ripe with a full harvest, and at a populace that seemed happy and relatively carefree. He took a deep breath then slowly exhaled, hoping that the life they had come to expect, that had been blessed with so much, would continue. Then worry creased his brow. He questioned that if the situation became dire, would Roland be up to the task? "By all the gods, Devon Longstreet, be alive and well and on your way home."

The massive redwood table, carved from one of the giants found in the western mountains of Dania, seated at least twenty. It was centered in The Great Room. With the size of each kingdom's entourage, they would need all the space the table provided. Still it was dwarfed by the thirty foot ceiling. The huge fireplace in the back was laboring to provide sufficient heat for the monstrous room, and a dozen heavy, colorful draperies blocked the chill from the smooth, stone walls, while giving life to the austere setting.

After being announced, King Sorbonne entered, nodding graciously at his guests. "Your majesties, I thank you for your expeditious journeys in coming to this clave."

He glanced around the room, individually acknowledging every ruler. Queen Endoreen, standing near the roaring fire, radiated charisma. A woman of peace, wisdom, and beauty, she was quite amazing for one so young. A gorgeous, flowing, red velvet gown accented her red-blond hair. Sorbonne greeted her husband and advisor, Drayen, and the third attendee of her party, an administrator and liaison.

Then his gaze shifted to the King of Oreon. "Ah, King Darvus, I hope your journey was not too tiresome. I see that your lovely daughter is here by your side."

King Darvus, dressed in a long, royal blue gown, and his dark beard neatly trimmed, nodded back."Our journey was plagued by misfortune which I will soon relate. I'm very eager to hear what you have to tell us."

Sorbonne bowed, moving to the final member on the far side of the table, King Baldor, welcoming him as warmly as he had the others.

"Let us hope the trip is worth it," Baldor answered curtly. His sharp, dark features were almost handsome in a ruthless sort of way. His deep purple robe and finely groomed goatee added to his regal bearing."I am anxious to hear the news and your interpretations." His reply bordered on rudeness but it also cleared the way for King Sorbonne to go directly to the point.

"I hope that my reason for calling you here does not come to pass." He gestured expansively."Please, please. Seat yourselves. I am gratified that you'll also be able to attend the royal wedding, but that is not why you were asked here."

Chairs scraped against the stone floor as everyone shuffled to their seats. Sorbonne waited until everyone was comfortable before he sat down. He beckoned to nearby servants who then moved forward and presented the various monarchs with a warm beverage. Finally, he folded his hands in front of his and began.

"For the past six months, well-armed marauders have been attacking farms and villages. They removed their injured, or, if their wounds were too severe, they killed them where they lay." He reached for a steaming mug, using its heat to warm his hands.

"That gave me pause," he continued. "Could this be happening in other kingdoms? I sent my sentinels out to find the answer. They have all come back, save one. The envoy from Sealand has not returned."

The others were silent, their eyes riveted on Sorbonne. He had their complete attention. Even Baldor looked alarmed as he put his mug down and stared at Dania's king. What was happening in Sealand was a mystery deepened by their ruler's absence from this meeting."King Dawad's lack of response deeply concerns me and the scouts tell me there is no such evidence of strangers within your borders."

"Surely you are not accusing us of anything?" King Baldor shot back as his posture grew rigid.

"Certainly not," King Sorbonne assured him."But I have been well taught by my father to honor the ancient scrolls, and prophetic signs are appearing."

"Ha!" Baldor spat out, waving his hand."Your father was too superstitious. I think," he went on, sarcasm dripping from his words, "that you have some disgruntled men in the ranks of your army. Perhaps they have not been sufficiently compensated and feel justified seizing some wealth for themselves."

Sorbonne regarded him carefully. Only the tightening of age lines around his eyes indicated that he was working hard to control his anger. There was no love lost between the two men. Sorbonne knew Baldor was powerful, had a well-trained army, and was an effective ruler who was respected, if not loved, by his people. He was important to the future of Sandala.

Using measured words, King Sorbonne answered."Each kingdom has a copy of the ancient scrolls. Each ruler is free to place faith in them as he sees fit."

His gaze traveled around the room, pausing long enough for the eyes of each ruler met his in return."I have chosen to give great credence to them."

"I know that centuries have passed since the last attack on Sandala. People have grown lax as well as forgetful. Perhaps it is complacency or refusal to believe in the scrolls because memories are buried far in the past. But the men who wreck havoc in my kingdom are not my soldiers," King Sorbonne said, his tone lowering ominously at the end.

"My commanders know one another," he continued, "and each in turn knows their men. No one recognized any of the men they fought." Sorbonne let the statement hang, though he was sure Baldor had not missed the point.

"The assaults appear to be probes," Sorbonne continued, "tests to discover the soft underbelly of Dania. I think you would agree that the conquest of this kingdom would place a great hardship on the rest."

The rulers digested King Sorbonne's words, and eventually

each nodded in agreement. Queen Endoreen looked particularly thoughtful.

"King Sorbonne," she said, speaking in a melodious voice that affected them all as much as her beauty, "what you are suggesting is very serious. We have had difficulties in our trade with Sealand. A rift has come between us, and several of our ships have failed to return from major trading voyages. Adding those facts to your own, coupled with the failure of Devon to return..."

King Baldor sat up straight and interrupted her."Devon? Is Devon Longstreet the sentinel who hasn't returned?"

Sorbonne nodded solemnly.

"Why didn't say so in the first place?" Sorbonne was aware that Baldor knew of Devon and respected his abilities.

King Darvus cleared his throat, gaining everyone's attention. They all turned their eyes towards him."During our journey here we were attacked on two different occasions. We suffered heavy losses and might not be here today if it had not been for the intervention of some young men from Dania. They came to our aid in the midst of the first attack, and forestalled a second onslaught while we raced to safety at your garrison stationed at the base of Mount Loor."

He paused, as worry played across his face. "While under attack, my younger daughter and one of your soldiers were separated from us. Their fate is uncertain."

"I have firsthand knowledge," King Darvus continued, "of the marauders, bandits... whatever they are. And I assure you King Baldor, I have not seen the likes of them before. They are not to be taken lightly."

Sorbonne rose quickly."I will have Cullen send a rescue party after her immediately." He turned and signaled to his son who was seated by the near wall. Roland departed swiftly.

A din came to the room as a flurry of questions ensued as the members of the courts began to discuss what all this might mean. King Sorbonne reached inside his tunic and retrieved the book Aldo had found in the dungeon. He raised it in his hands then dropped it in the middle of the table.

The sound of it hitting the wood startled everyone and caused all eyes to turn towards the book. Queen Endoreen was first to pick it up."By the gods," she exclaimed, her face registering surprise."It is one of the ancient scrolls." She began to turn the pages until she came to the same picture that had startled and amazed Roland's brother. She studied the tall, exquisite warrior."Why, it is a Shala warrior."

King Baldor growled his displeasure as he angrily shoved himself away from the table and stood up."This is ridiculous. There may be something amiss. I do not doubt your word, Sorbonne. But Shala? We have never seen a Shala! No one alive has seen a Shala. They are pure myth. They do not exist!"

Endoreen regarded him curiously."How can you be certain?" she asked.

"I ask you to consider," Baldor replied."They appear out of nowhere then disappear never to be seen again. Their emergence, presence, and disappearance cannot be explained."

"Centuries ago," Baldor continued as he began to prowl around the table, "to preserve their independence, the five kingdoms of Sandala fought together against an invader. Many lives were lost. Cities fell and innocent people died. But it ended in victory. In time, aged warriors began to recall events, small skirmishes turned into major engagements, and the destruction of a village became the leveling of a city. Failed and exaggerated recollections turned into legends." Baldor paused and came to a stop. When he spoke again, a more sarcastic tone emerged.

"Some miracle warrior appears to save us. How preposterous does that sound? The Shala do not exist. You have no proof that they do. Have you ever seen one?"

Darvus turned away, not wanting to confront Baldor. The man was disagreeable, close-minded, and a fierce adversary. It would be to no avail."I only know for certain," Darvus said, "that we were attacked twice as we traveled."

"But you do not know who attacked you." Baldor declared.

Sorbonne threw up a hand, regaining order. "All right! We do agree there is a problem. At the very least, we must determine who they are and where they come from. Does anyone have a suggestion as to how we might do that?"

Queen Endoreen proposed that they find out what was happening in Sealand and the rest agreed. Since the sentinel Devon had not returned, they feared the worst. The lack of King Dawad's presence increased their anxiety.

"It is quite likely," Baldor concluded, reseating himself, "that Sealand's leadership has changed allegiance or been compromised altogether. Dawad is either behind the attacks, has knowledge of them, or has himself, been deposed."

"We need to send a well-armed military expedition to his borders and we need to do it now," Sorbonne concluded.

"It should be a combined expedition," King Baldor said."Not just your men."

"I never meant to imply otherwise," Sorbonne answered."Other suggestions?"

"We should all use our pigeons to contact our military leaders and strategic outposts," Queen Endoreen said. "We need confirmation and information quickly." There were nods around the table.

King Sorbonne was gratified as the monarchs began to work collectively. It showed in the way their shoulders leaned forward and bodies turned to him as their unofficial leader. Assistants began wording messages for the birds to fly to various destinations. If the answers that followed did not contain pre-ordained code words, a lack of authenticity would be substantiated. Everyone became fully engaged in the task at hand.

Queen Endoreen's husband, Drayen, had been quiet, listening to the others as they debated, but Sorbonne saw him stand and signal for attention.

"Your majesties, there is one thing we have not considered." His deep voice resonated. Sorbonne found him physically impressive, tall and broad. Though he was robed in such away that his girth was hard to determine, he gave the impression that there wasn't an ounce of fat on him. Yet, none at the table feared the man, for he was blind.

Since his marriage to Endoreen two years ago, they had seen him at the festive occasions held yearly by one of the five kingdoms. Drayen did not speak often, saving his comments for his wife, the Queen. He did not share the crown nor was he regarded as a regent. But everyone knew he was her chief advisor and confidant. Now, the fact that he spoke at all gave Sorbonne pause. Drayen had his full attention.

"If Dania were to be invaded and compromised, and their harvests confiscated, we would all suffer for it."

"With all due respect, Drayen," the King Darvus spoke up, "we have our own harvests and enough food for our people."

Drayen turned in King Darvus' general direction, dark leather patches covering his sightless eyes."For people, yes, but would you have enough to feed an army?"

That stopped them. What he said rang true. If an army could not be fed, it was ripe for defeat. The abundant crops raised in Dania and shipped every year to each outlying kingdom, were vital.

Discussions renewed over this latest concern. New tasks were assigned and a strategy debated over how to capture one of the marauders alive. The talking went on for several hours. Refreshments were brought as servants came and went until the late evening then they retired to their own chambers. Another meeting was set for the next morning.

Back in their private room, Drayen sat down while Endoreen moved about the chamber looking for any sign of disturbance."It's safe," she told her husband. He removed the patches then rubbed his eyes gingerly.

"Do you think it is possible?" she asked.

He looked up at her."The Prophecy?"

She nodded.

Drayen sighed."Devon's absence bothers me. Perhaps marauders can be explained, but his disappearance and the Sealand inconsistencies cannot." He paused, glancing around the room.

"What is it?"

Drayen shook his head."I thought I felt another presence, but it has gone."

Endoreen studied their belongings once again. The short length of hair she had placed inside a traveling bag was still in place. She looked back at her husband.

"Has your mother communicated with you?" Endoreen asked.

"Not recently," he said, shaking his head.

A frown creased the Queen's forehead."Even though I am a devout believer in the Ancient Scrolls, I still find it difficult to believe this could be happening."

"Believe it," Drayen said softly. "We may be in the gravest of danger if we ignore the signs or are slow to pursue answers." He sat down in a large chair next to her and began to massage her shoulders. He could see her gratitude when she looked back at him.

"You had to cover your eyes for longer than usual today," she said. "Are they bothering you?"

He shook his head, his eyes flashing a rich pink of affection.

Soundlessly, a man retreated down the hidden passageway

behind the rooms Endoreen and Drayen shared. The hole in the picture on the far wall of their bedroom wall was small, but it was enough. He smiled. The emperor would be pleased. Very pleased.

The candle he carried lit the way back to the entrance located inside a large linen closet. As he stepped back inside, the young boy waiting there helped him put back the bedding that hid the secret door.

"Thank you, Aldo," the man said, smiling at the beaming child."We'll keep this our little secret, all right?"

The boy nodded, pleased that this important man had befriended him instead of Roland.

CHAPTER 14

PIGEONS

The old pigeon master paused to catch his breath. He leaned against a half empty water barrel, letting his aging heart slow. His wrinkled face dripped with sweat from preparing dozens of pigeons for early morning release. Crates had to be moved, watering completed, feed disbursed, and message cylinders laid out at the ready. Norris didn't know what was going on at the monarchs' meeting inside the castle, but it had unleashed a whirlwind of activity.

He drank a few delicious moments of respite then straightened and trudged across to a crate from Oreon. "Yes, my sweet thing," he said aloud to the last pigeon as he returned it to its cage, plump and happy, "looks like you will have a ways to fly tomorrow."

He hesitated, sensing an unusual stillness. The birds had grown quiet and watchful. Norris's wary, pale blue eyes looked around the shed, but saw nothing out of sorts and resumed his work. He tossed several empty grain sacks into an open bin and was bent over a cage from Gleneden, when a blow from behind crushed the back of his skull.

The old man's body crashed into the cage, knocking it to the floor. Startled pigeons began flapping their wings in dismay. The assailant reached out and caught the old man then lowered him gently to the ground. He picked up the bloody pot he had used as the weapon and tossed it clanging into the far corner. He paused, a look of regret passing over his face then he withdrew a small flask from the inside of his tunic. He went from crate to crate, putting a few drops from the small container into the pigeons' water. With dozens of cages, he was forced to work quickly.

Anxious, wary of discovery, and fearful that the poison might not work fast enough, he tossed the flask aside and opened the next cage. He reached inside, grabbed the closest bird and gave its neck a savage twist. He snatched the next pigeon and repeated his actions, but the birds were growing alarmed by the disturbance and the startled cries of the pigeons he clutched. He began to panic as the racket crescendoed, afraid the cacophony would garner the attention of the palace guards.

In his hurry, he didn't see a water pail. His foot caught and he stumbled. He reached out to regain balance but the crate he latched on to gave way under his weight and crashed to the ground. Pigeon feathers flew about and several of the terrified creatures shrieked in protest.

Outside the barn, a soldier stopped in mid-stride. He heard the ruckus inside the building he now skirted."Norris?"he called out to the old keeper."Is that you?" He waited for an answer instead, heard something falling.

"Traxton!" the guard yelled to a second man nearby."Get over here! Something's going on in the pigeon shed." Amid-size, swarthy man rushed up and together, spears in hand, they hurried to investigate.

As they came through the front entrance, someone rushed out a side door."After him!" the first man ordered, pointing, and Traxton bolted after the fleeing figure. The remaining soldier looked around the shed's dim interior. He saw a crate lying on its side next to an upturned table. Approaching the cages his heart began to pound at the sight of birds slumped over, their necks at an impossible angle. Turning back to the front to sound the alarm, the crumpled figure of Norris caught his eye. He rushed to the old man's side but one look at the pool of blood and the sightless gaze of the pigeon keeper told him that he was far too late. He rose quickly and raced outside. Within moments, his shouts brought a half a dozen guards to his side. Five were ordered to start an immediate ground search while the final man was sent to fetch the King.

Gently, King Sorbonne closed the dead keeper's eyes. He stood up, surveying the destruction around him. Anger swelled inside him. His features tightened and his ears burned with the heat of rage. He was very fond of old Norris. The pigeon keeper had been a decent, kind soul. He kept a good home for the birds that provided Sandala with their only means for quick, long distance communication. He did not deserve to die like this.

"How many birds are left?" King Sorbonne asked the nearest soldier.

"At least half, Sire. The bugger, ah, beg your pardon, wasn't able to complete his grisly task."

"Send a man to fetch Norris's son. He can determine the extent of the damage and discover if anything else is amiss," the King ordered.

He walked over to the side door where the villain had made his escape. Staring into the night, a new worry began to grow inside his gut. How could someone gain access to the palace grounds? Under the existing conditions the outside gates were locked down early and extra guards were on patrol. It was highly doubtful that anyone could manage to break in.

He saw Queen Endoreen, King Baldor and King Darvus come into the barn. Endoreen's face slowly drained of color, while Darvus stumbled in apparent shock. Baldor's face suffused with red. He was the first to find his voice.

"How could this happen? How many birds were harmed? Are any alive?" Do you have any idea who did this?" Baldor raged.

King Sorbonne shook his head."It appears someone snuck in, murdered the pigeon master then started killing the birds. About half are dead. Fortunately, the intruder was interrupted before he could do any further damage."

Queen Endoreen moved forward."Are there any clues as to the assailant's identity?" Sorbonne felt her steady voice fill the air with calm.

He shook his head. Inhaling deeply, he held his breath for a moment before he exhaled in a burst."I can only speculate," he said in a bitter tone, "that there is a spy or traitor among us. It is inconceivable that anyone broke into the castle ground. They had to already be inside."

All the monarchs were stunned. They glanced at one another, mouths agape, looks of confusion and accusation flowing across their faces. The poison of suspicion choked the air.

Roland entered, pushing his way through the extra guards and monarchs. As he neared his father, he began to speak then saw the crumpled body of Norris lying on the ground. Crying out in anguish, he rushed to the old man's side. He started to reach out to the bloody corpse then slumped back.

Sorbonne moved to his side and laid a comforting hand on his son's shoulder. "I need to speak with you." Roland looked up at him, nodded and slowly stood. The two walked some distance away from the others in the barn.

Sorbonne's eyes were filled with a mixture of anger and sadness. "There is a real possibility that a traitor is among us. I fear this attack came from someone already inside the castle — perhaps a member of someone's entourage." Roland quickly glanced in their direction then looked back at his father and nodded.

"I want you to watch them closely but discreetly. Don't arouse suspicion. Should they discover such surveillance, it could be disastrous. It could even be construed as an act of war," the King cautioned.

"It will be my pleasure, Father, and I will be discreet. Norris was a good keeper and a decent fellow." Roland's features were grim, his eyes fierce.

As Sorbonne walked back to the other rulers, Drayen arrived with an escort and joined him. The two began to talk quietly. Across from them, King Baldor was speaking to Darvus. A few moments later, the Palatonian king left.

King Darvus appeared surprised, but was forced to move aside as Roland hurried after Baldor. Then Cullen entered and Darvus joined the arm's master as he walked over to King Sorbonne. He watched them approaching and spoke directly to Cullen.

"This is a sad night. I fear there is evil about." The warrior nodded back, grim-faced

"How can I be of service, your majesty?" Cullen asked.

"The attacker is likely someone inside the castle grounds," Sorbonne answered."I want you to personally check all the guards for authenticity. Interview every last man. Find out if any of them have seen someone they don't recognize. Ask them...forgive me, Cullen." The King shook his head as if to clear his thoughts then met Cullen's gaze."I know you do not need to be told what to do."

Cullen bowed, gripped the King's forearm to offer reassurance then hurried away. Sorbonne turned to King Darvus.

"Sir, I have sent for the pigeon keeper's son. He can help us determine how many pigeons have been destroyed. Would you ask the others to help with the inventory? We need to know who can still send messages home tomorrow morning."

"Of course," Darvus nodded."I'll tell the others to fetch their bird handlers, but there is something else you should know. Baldor's pigeons are not here. He kept them with his soldiers, separated from the rest."

Sorbonne was rocked by the news. Queen Endoreen and Drayen had joined them and heard Darvus' pronouncement as well.

"That is an interesting development," Drayen commented."Has anyone checked to see if any of his pigeons were killed?"

King Sorbonne shook his head."Not as yet, but believe me, it will be done. And soon." His voice was bleak. He paused a moment to consider this last bit of information. If Baldor was responsible, he would hardly call attention to himself. More than likely he was being cautious. He was known for his suspicious nature and had never found others easy to trust.

"This is a nasty business," King Sorbonne finally said."King Baldor is not a stupid man. It is as if someone wants to throw suspicion his way. And here we stand, hip deep in mistrust. If an enemy wanted to divide us, he can sleep well tonight for the first wedge has been firmly driven in."

Sorbonne looked around the barn one last time then left. Endoreen watched him go then turned to King Darvus. "What can we do to help?"

"Please send for your bird handlers," Darvus said. "We need to find out how many pigeons each of us has left. Hopefully, we'll still be able to send out our messages in the morning."

He was interrupted by Drayen. "What is this?" the blind man asked, bending over and feeling the ground before him then locating an object he had just kicked. He held it up to the others.

Queen Endoreen took it from his outstretched hand."It is a flask of some kind." She raised it to her nose and sniffed. She pulled her head back quickly. "Drayen, smell this."

She placed it back in his hand and he did as she asked. "Poison!" he said, frowning. "You must remove the pigeons' food and water quickly! They could all be tainted."

King Darvus and Queen Endoreen rushed to the cages. Drayen called for a guard and asked him to go to the castle and fetch the bird keepers from Oreon and Gleneden. He heard the man leave and another enter."Who are you?" Drayen asked, looking in the newcomer's general direction.

A young man of modest height and simple attire looked back at him. "I am Jonathan, son of Norris. Where is my father?

CHAPTER 15

BLURLS

"How soon will we rendezvous with the others?" Ariann asked.

Tahjeen, in the midst of ducking under a low branch, paused. He turned to face her.

"We're not going to be able to. Our pursuers forced us too far out of our way. Instead, we're going to meet with a large band of Shala warriors. They're waiting about a half a day from here."

Ariann sighed. She had awakened determined to be positive, willing herself to believe her family was safe, and that Tahjeen would get her back to them. Younger daughter or not, her father would worry and she wanted to put his mind at ease.

She also yearned for the comfort of the wagon. Nights in the open had definite drawbacks, as the welts dotting her face from mosquito bites proved. She had appreciated Tahjeen's use of some medicinal plant to ease her discomfort. Though Ariann felt safe with him, sleeping under the stars and being tracked by marauders took away her peace of mind.

The positive side, however, was that Tahjeen was open to her questions. She had learned a great deal in their brief time together. She was amazed that Shala women were regarded as peers and treated as intellectual equals. What an interesting thought.

Because of that revelation, pulling her own weight became a focus for her. She took her turn at standing guard and tended her horse. She did not want Tahjeen to think she was helpless or too prim to get her hands soiled.

She was far less pleased, however, when he told her that Shalaen youth began their military training at the age of four. What an utterly ridiculous thing to do!

Ariann was amazed that the only punishment for crime among the Shala was banishment. Where did they go? She had asked, and was stunned to find that exile meant living among humans.

In contrast, she found delight at all the colorful shades his eyes could project, and occasionally tried prodding a reaction from him that might produce a new one. As to her initial outrage at being told they would eventually marry, she remained indignant and refused any conversation that veered in that direction.

That didn't prevent him from telling her about the beautiful miracle that took place when a Shala and human joined –the mixing of the chemicals that resulted in profound changes in each individual's unique personality and physical makeup. It was as if a seed were planted within each that caused them to change into something striking and charismatic, somehow blending the best in both. Afterwards the couple seemed larger than before, a result of the new energy radiating from them. Ariann felt herself redden as she recalled the description. That he would even speak of such things was unheard of!

Her thoughts halted when she saw some fresh water. She hadn't realized her degree of thirst, and dismounted."Take care where you step," Tahjeen cautioned as he took a hold of her horse's reins.

Ariann stopped, puzzled by his warning, seeing only a small, clear pool directly in front of her. Bending forward, she cupped her hand and started to dip it into the water.

"Good luck with that," Tahjeen said laughing. Irritated, Ariann hesitated. He hadn't said why. She reached out but the water divided and moved several inches away. Startled, she scrambled backward. What in the world? Tentatively, curiosity overriding trepidation, she stretched her fingers and gasped when once again, the liquid retreated. Tahjeen jumped down from his horse and walked up beside her. Amusement tweaked the corners of his lips. "I, I don't understand?" she said. Her curiosity was piqued. "What is causing that?" Tahjeen edged closer to the water. "Reveal yourself. We intend no harm."

In answer, the water pooled together several feet in front of Ariann. Gradually, it rose, forming a liquid figure about two feet high. It looked like a wet, translucent child.

"Well, I dare say that drinking me would do a great deal of harm – to both of us." It stared indignantly back at them. Ariann smiled, captivated."What is it?" she asked Tahjeen. "I am standing right in front of you," the watery figure said. "You don't have to be rude. I can speak for myself!""Pardon me," Ariann said, trying to hide her amusement."There is no need to laugh at my expense," it huffed, "unless of course, you find humor in your own ignorance."

She couldn't help herself and giggled. The creature started to dissolve once again, but Tahjeen intervened."Stop, blurl. She's a stranger to this land and means no insult." The blurl reformed itself into the little person she saw before.

"Someone should teach her proper etiquette," the blurl snipped.

Tahjeen shook his head, crossed to Ariann, and helped her to her feet."I can smell water nearby. You can quench your thirst there."

As they walked away, Tahjeen pulling the horses behind him, Ariann quizzed him about the blurl. "What a strange creature. Is it actually made of water? Was it a male or female?"

"It's not water. It was correct when it said that drinking it would harm you both. It's poisonous to anyone or anything who tries to drink it." He took several steps before he continued. He lifted his head, sniffing the air then altered his course slightly.

"It is neither male nor female, but a small part of a very, very large entity. It takes any form it chooses, though it's always liquid and somewhat transparent." He stepped across a hollow log, reaching back to help her over it.

"They could be useful," Ariann said."Is it possible to befriend them? Make them allies?"

Tahjeen smiled."In a formal way, I doubt it. If you sneeze they run away, and getting one to hold a sensible conversation is, well, difficult. But they can be appealed to for limited help."

"How were you able to identify it?" she asked.

"It may look like water, but it doesn't have the same qualities. You can't see your reflection, for one thing. If you stare into it, you'll simply see what is on the other side."

She thought about that and realized there was a great deal she did not know about the land in which she lived. She hated that kind of ignorance. There was no excuse for it! A person had an obligation to learn, to become knowledgeable.

Her thoughts turned back to the blurl. If she could befriend one, get to know it and establish a relationship – well, the possibilities were endless. She decided to share her sentiments with Tahjeen.

Tahjeen listened to her politely and when she finished, he offered his own opinion."I've never seen it happen, though it's possible no one has really tried. The blurl is part of the land and therefore has a stake in the future of Sandala. Your idea has merit."

They reached a narrow stream where Tahjeen stopped to let the horses drink. The water was clear, rippling over small stones. More importantly to Ariann, it didn't divide itself and pull away. She looked to see if her reflection was visible and found that it was, indeed, water. After they slaked their thirst, Tahjeen turned to her.

"If time allows in the future, we'll try what you suggest."

Ariann was very pleased that he had taken the time to weigh the value of her idea. She wasn't used to anyone taking her seriously. She studied him, standing near the stream. She wondered if all Shala were like him – deadly, yet interesting. There was a wild quality about him that promised danger - a feral look that came and went.

His eyes lost focus as he froze. She recognized the look and knew he was communicating with his *fel*, Paca. There were many questions she meant to ask about that relationship. Perhaps now would be a good time. She waited until his eyes regained focus before she spcke.

"Is everything all right?" After he nodded in the affirmative, she decided to push for more.

"How long have you and Paca been, um, friends?"

Tahjeen tied both horses' reins to a tree limb then sat down on a moss-covered stump. He gestured for her to sit as well before he answered."I was older than most, almost nine. I wanted to go on my search sooner, but waited out of respect for my older brother. When he finally told me he wasn't going after one, I left the next morning. That was over ten years ago."

So, that meant, Ariann realized, that Tahjeen is nineteen or twenty. She was surprised having thought him to be older. "A search." Her interest deepened. "Where do you go?"

"North of our crater," he replied. "There's a high desert some distance from our home. It's a beautiful, rugged land but difficult for people to survive in. Animals are its only inhabitants. We call it the frontier."

She raised one eyebrow, captivated anew by the latest

revelation. Maybe someday she could explore this frontier. She shook her head and reminded herself to stay on topic."Do all Shala have *fels*?" she asked.

"Only those who try and are fortunate enough to be chosen."

Now that was interesting."Who chooses? Your ruler?"

She could tell he was surprised by her question."No. We are all free to go on a search." He stood up slowly and stretched.

Now she was confused."But you said the only Shala who have *fels* were chosen?"

"The *fel* does the choosing, Ariann. We can only hope and search for one who'll accept us." He moved towards the horses and untied their reins.

"Oh," she said, realization dawning. She leaned forward, wrapping her arms around her knees, trying to imagine a nine year old wandering through a rugged land alone. How in the world did a wild animal decide who was worthy? How did a child find his way there and back? Did some children die during their search for a *fel*?

"If someone isn't chosen, what happens?" she asked, finally standing.

He studied her for a time before he handed her the reins."A great majority are chosen. All warriors have one."

Ariann realized that he hadn't answered her question. Was there something he was hiding or was some Shala history forbidden to outsiders?

"You avoided my question," she said at last, without reprimand.

He nodded then began adjusting his horse's stirrups. She waited patiently, suddenly certain that he was going to answer her and that the answer was important.

"Few are rejected," he said as he retightened the cinch. "Those who are, have a kind of emptiness inside of them. In some way, they are lacking."

"Lacking...in what way?" She was fascinated, pleased that he was opening up the Shala world to her.

His brows furrowed."There were twin boys once - one weak, the other strong. The weaker one was quick-witted, playful and likeable. The other was hot-tempered. He was also self-centered and sometimes cruel. When the day came for their search, they went together." He reached across taking her hand, offering to help her mount before he continued. Once she was settled on top of her horse, he went on.

"As always, we waited. Searches can last a week, perhaps as long as two. But after three weeks we were very worried. A youth can be killed on the search. It's rare but it happens. The land is rugged and tests a child's ability to survive. Some feared the stronger one had done something to the weaker one, though no one said so out loud." He mounted, and paused to study the trees around them.

"After a month had passed," he continued, "their mother went into mourning. Then a few days later both of them returned. The weaker one, vibrant with new-found confidence, had a beautiful young *fel* by his side. But the older boy bore some nasty claw marks, and his bitterness and anger were plainly visible. Clearly, the *fel* had rejected him."

Ariann was totally immersed in the story and waited for him to tell more. After several moments passed and she realized he wasn't going to continue, she prodded."What happened?"

He seemed bothered, sad, and his face showed it. In quiet tones he went on with his story."His bitterness was twisted into acts of violence. He hurt several children, finally breaking a younger lad's arm. The Queen and the elders had no choice. He was exiled."

Ariann was stunned."How old was he?" she asked.

"Ten," he replied.

"Ten!" she exclaimed. She whipped her head around, her long, blond braid following along and now flowing down her chest. She glared at him. She grabbed her braid, twisting it with her hands. "Surely he deserved another chance!"

"Ariann, some souls are born damaged and cannot be altered." He urged his forward and it started off at a slow pace.

"I don't believe that." She gave her own mount a kick and started off after him. She didn't like talking to his back. "People can change." She caught herself working the braid and flung it around her to her back.

"Change is difficult," Tahjeen said, glancing back at her, "even for the best of us, even if we want to change. The rest need to be protected from predators who would victimize them."

"And so you foist him off on humans? Do you not care what he might do to us?" Her voice was tinged with anger, her eyes flashing daggers.

"It may appear that way, but in truth, the few who are exiled live apart from you, not among you. Have you ever seen one?" he asked then answered it himself."No. They live in unpopulated areas where humans seldom travel. They are no threat to you. And we keep track of them to make sure that never happens."

Despite the logic of his explanation, she was still outraged. This was a situation ripe for exploitation, yet she wasn't sure how or by whom. The belief that some people were incapable of change also troubled her. She did not accept that. It was too fatalistic and final, too lacking in hope.

"*Fels* are a wonderful gift, Ariann," Tahjeen said, interrupting her thoughts."Everyone has the opportunity to acquire one, but not all are worthy. It is that simple," he said.

She stared back at him, distressed. She shook her head."Nothing is ever that simple."

CHAPTER 16

MOTHER AND SONS

The Shala Queen entered her sleeping quarters and saw the elixir waiting for her on the bedside stand. The drink would close off the conscious world and take her mind to a higher plane where she could *lais*, or communicate with anyone with whom she shared a direct blood relationship. She could dream-speak to her own parents, siblings, and children.

Tonight, she would contact Drayen. By now all the rulers should have arrived in Danigh. She would tell him of the second armada and of Tahjeen's war plans. He could not answer but that wouldn't matter. He knew what to do. He was Shala.

For now, she had to wait until she was sure he would be asleep. Needing rest herself for the arduous days ahead, she asked her assistant to rouse her a few hours before dawn.

Mardra washed herself quickly then banked the coals that chased the evening chill from her room. It was still early, but once in bed she fell quickly asleep, relaxing herself with deep breathing and an ever narrowing focus to block the day's disturbing events.

A few hours before dawn, Artur wakened her. He pointed to a plain, golden goblet sitting on a table several feet away. She rose and walked several steps to retrieve it before she crossed the room and seated herself on the floor in front of a small fire. Mardra folded her legs beneath her, letting her free hand rest on her thigh. She lifted the goblet to her lips and swallowed.

The elixir tasted bitter, but not completely unpleasant, and it took effect rapidly. She closed her eyes and formed an image of Drayen, her oldest son and heir. In her mind she called his name repeatedly until his face grew clear.

"Vigilance, my son," she greeted."Enemies have invaded Sealand and are on the march. A second armada approaches the western shore and Katar sails to defend the Dania's coastline.

Katrine, Toman and Tahjeen travel the southern cavern then proceed to Danigh. Gable will infiltrate the other kingdoms. Inform Sorbonne and the Clave. Keep me informed. Be well, Drayen. The Shala rise."

Nearly three hundred miles away, Drayen Tier jerked awake. Beside him, Endoreen stirred."What is it?" she asked her husband.

He rose and started dressing."Mother just spoke to me. We must wake King Sorbonne immediately." He looked at his wife, his colorful eyes flashing red and black, reflecting alarm and danger.

"It is time to reveal myself to him, Endoreen. He believes the legends and knows the prophecy, but it will be easier for him to sway the others if he sees living proof."

Despite her first-hand knowledge of the Shala, gained through marriage to Drayen and a visit to his homeland; despite her complete and utter acceptance of the prophecy; despite her years of training to one day rule Gleneden, Endoreen swallowed in fear. Knowing what was and what might be did not mean she expected it to happen in her lifetime. She was prepared, yet unready. She was made of steel, yet afraid. She was intelligent and capable, but she felt at sea.

He saw these emotions play across her face and went to her. "My lovely wife, my Queen," he said as his gaze took in her red-golden hair, expressive eyes, and fair skin."Don't doubt yourself. With my strength and your wisdom and the Shala, we will prevail."

She felt her confidence returning, and her calm restored. She reached out and touched her husband's cheek."Give me a moment to dress then we will go to King Sorbonne."

The night servant was resistant to rousing the King, but Endoreen used every ounce of her regal bearing and power of voice to demand it. The imposing figure of the large blind man beside her helped to persuade him. The servant went inside the king's private chambers.

Within a minute Sorbonne himself bid them enter. He was sleep-tousled but fully clothed. Recognizing their presence as an emergency, he wasted no time. "What has happened?"

Queen Endoreen took a deep breath, choosing her words carefully. "My Lord, do you truly believe in the prophecy?" She searched his face while he looked back at her, his brows furrowing.

Finally, he nodded."Yes, I do. That was the main reason I called the Clave."

"Then I would like to introduce Drayen as not only my husband," she nodded to him and he removed his eye patches. "but as Shala, and the oldest son of their Queen."

CHAPTER 17

THE REVEALING

"Why is it necessary to drag us from our beds before the sun is up?" Baldor demanded. He was seated at the meeting table in the Great Hall, along with the other Clave members. Still dressed for bed, sleeping robes hastily thrown on, all appeared disheveled. None were pleased to have their sleep disrupted. Servants scurried around them, trying to rekindle the fire and ward off the night's chill.

"I assure you," King Sorbonne said, "there is ample reason." He looked at the monarchs and their staff as they settled in. Other servants entered, bringing coffee along with bread and cheese. He waited until everyone had food and drink in hand before he began.

"Just minutes ago we received word that an invasion began several days ago. Armies are on the march toward your kingdoms. You have decisions to make and new messages to send. As to one of the decisions, well, even if you left now, by the time you arrived at your capital it might already be under foreign rule or completely surrounded. You could be captured, or worse. You are welcome to remain here for however long that proves necessary or advisable."

Baldor scrambled to his feet, shoving his chair backward, startling everyone. Someone coughed, trying to clear his throat. "Wait just a moment. How was this discovered? Did Devon Longstreet finally return? What exactly did he say? We have the right to know!"

King Sorbonne looked back at the Palatonian ruler. He was not surprised that Baldor would leap to that conclusion. Darvus probably had as well.

"It was not Longstreet," Sorbonne said."In a manner of speaking, it was the Prophecy coming to fruition."

"Blast your Prophecy!" Baldor yelled, his face mottling with anger. "It proves nothing. Is that what you are basing this on?" Baldor roared. He stood, his body rigid, his fists clenched at his side.

"No, my Lord." Drayen said, standing. No matter what rank or lineage he held, when Queen Endoreen's husband stretched to his full height he was intimidating. That fact was not lost on any one in the room.

"I received word earlier this morning," he said, removing his patches slowly. Everyone at the table tensed."From the Shala Queen." With the last words his colorful eyes looked across at each ruler.

Darvus bolted to his feet and jumped back."By the gods!" he sputtered.

Baldor paled, and backed away from the table. His mouth fell open while his eyes blinked rapidly. He glanced from Endoreen to Drayen then stumbled against his chair and fell into it. He was breathing heavily.

"I, I don't understand." Darvus finally said, still stunned.

Finally, Queen Endoreen stood. She asked everyone else to sit down, and in a few moments, they complied.

"Several years ago when Drayen and I first met, he revealed what he was. After we married, we traveled to his homeland – to the home of the Shala." All eyes were on her, everyone so silent you could hear air move.

"So I can offer my own testimony that the Shala civilization exists, that it is not a myth," she said, looking at Baldor, "for I have been there."

A brief silence was ended by questions bombarding her from all sides, but Sorbonne interrupted."We must stay on point. We are being invaded. Details about the Shala can come later." Everyone quieted, so Endoreen continued.

"Early this morning the Queen of the Shala contacted Drayen. An ancient potion, an elixir, allows a Shala to walk in the dream world and talk with a blood relative. She told us that a foreign power is invading Sandala, and that a second invasion at Dania's west coast, is also likely."

She sat down and Sorbonne glared at all of them. "Does anyone still have doubts?" he asked. For once, no one uttered a word.

Baldor finally regained his composure and found his voice. "My pigeons should return by noon tomorrow. Then I will have a better idea of how things fare at home. I suggest we adjourn until then. It will give us time to digest this... this," he looked at Drayen, still feeling the effects of the startling revelation. "The recent events," Baldor concluded.

"Not all of us had an abundance of pigeons to send," King Darvus said meaningfully.

Baldor's neck began to suffuse with red."What do you mean by that?" he demanded.

But King Sorbonne interrupted."Please, bickering is not helpful. We must remember that the enemy is on the march. Time is precious." He looked at Baldor. "Digest things quickly."

As the attendees returned to their room, one man paused at his door, waiting until the last person had entered his quarters. He absolutely did not want to be interrupted. Taking care that no one was watching, he slipped into his room.

Once inside, he went to the small enclosure that served as his closet and pulled a curtain aside. A crate of pigeons was hidden behind it. He sat down and pulled a piece of leather and a writing implement from a pocket of his cloak. When he finished writing, he placed the message inside a small container then opened the crate and carefully withdrew one of the birds. After he attached the capsule, he went to his window and opened the wooden shutters. He leaned over the railing and looked at the courtyard. Good, no one was there. He released the bird and watched it gain altitude as it headed off to the east.

In Sorbonne's library, Cullen and Roland joined the King while servants stirred the fire and brought refreshments. King Sorbonne ordered more since others would be joining them. The servants bowed and hurried from the room. A few minutes later, Queen Endoreen and Drayen came in. They forced themselves to eat though the dire news had dampened everyone's appetite.

"Thank you for coming," Sorbonne finally said. "I thought we might talk more about the situation, even if it is premature. Hopefully, in another day when the pigeons arrive we will know more ...if they arrive," he added soberly.

"The enemy could shoot them down," Roland said.

"Yes, that's a possibility. However, some are coming from outposts where no enemy should be. Yet."

Sorbonne looked at Drayen. "My Lord, how many warriors will your mother send?"

"All we have, Your Majesty," Drayen said matter-of-factly.

"It's a fighting force of four *koshes* of five thousand each."

Irritated by the foreign sounding word, Sorbonne demanded, "What are *koshes?*"

"A *kosh*," Drayen explained, "is the Shalaen word for team. They have lived together since the age of ten. The teams are selected to insure harmony and a balance of the unique skills some Shala have."

"Indeed," Sorbonne said, regarding the concept. "How far will they have to travel to get here?" King Sorbonne asked.

"Several hundred miles, Sire."

"Then they might not arrive in time," the King lamented, his face crestfallen. He stroked his chin, a lifelong gesture of worry.

"They will be here within three days. The teams can run for hours and cover over a hundred miles a day."

"But, that is impossible!" Roland exclaimed, wide eyed and defiant.

Drayen turned toward him and stared back. He gave his shoulders a slight shrug."Not for a Shala."

The two *koshes* led by Katrine and Toman were already halfway through the cavern. The huge passage wound its way beneath the body of water the humans called the Sea of Death, so named because its acidic waters burned human skin and ate away the wood of any boat that had not been specially coated.

In another day the cavern would slope upward and eventually open in Dania. From there, they were less than a half day away from the capital.

Gable's *kosh* faced a trickier situation. It would not be easy to hide five thousand warriors in plain sight. He considered that dilemma as they traveled the eastern underground passage.

Within thirty-six hours most of the pigeons had returned. Despite the shortage of birds due to the attacker's brutality at the barn, everyone had been able to send word to the necessary locations. The return messages cast a dark cloud over those gathered in the Great Hall. It was worse than they had imagined possible.

King Sorbonne formally opened the session."My Lords and Lady, I suggest we go around the table and hear from everyone in turn. Please share whatever you can." He turned to the Gleneden monarch and motioned to her with his hand."Queen Endoreen, if you please."

Without any preliminaries, she began. "Approximately

twenty thousand of the enemy attacked our southern border. The garrison stationed there was quickly overrun, but not before they were able to get a message off to the capital." Her eyes were steady and her words frank as she calmly revealed the situation in Gleneden.

"We have a standing army of about four thousand, and my generals have issued a call to arms for every able bodied man. My second in command believes we can organize a strong defense of the capital, and citizens in the countryside, along with several other garrisons, have managed to slow the offensive." She stared at them all, grave concern plain for them to see. "He wants to know when I will return, and promises daily correspondence."

No one made any comment. Twenty thousand against four said enough. Sooner or later, the capital city of Milhune would fall, unless there was some divine intervention. Baldor looked away and shook his head.

Sorbonne turned to Darvus, noted that age had somehow taken hold of him, shrinking his frame."King Darvus?" Sorbonne asked with raised eyebrows.

Darvus looked up. Bleakness captured every inch of his face. When he spoke, even his voice was frail."They are rolling across Oreon's countryside unchecked. They ignored the mountain population centers – there are not many people there and the terrain is difficult." His voice trailed off as his shoulders slumped in defeat.

"Three pigeons returned carrying the same message. The capital will fall within the day." Endoreen looked at him with sympathy.

Though he had finished speaking, King Sorbonne wanted more information. "Your Highness, what was the size of the army reported?" he asked Darvus quietly.

Darvus stared blankly across the room. "They were guessing, but it sounded similar to the one in Gleneden."

"Thank you, sir." Sorbonne shifted his gaze to Baldor whose eyes were crackling with fire. Still, deeper lines were etched across his brow and his complexion was paler than yesterday. "King Baldor?" Sorbonne asked.

Baldor voice crackled with intensity."The same size of force also attacked us. It is likely they were all launched at the same time. However, my army was undergoing its yearly training games and, luckily, was more prepared than Gleneden or Oreon. Though the invaders were barely slowed by the mountain pass defenses, they were stalled before they got much further." He took a deep breath, and as the air inflated his lungs his determination grew in turn.

"My generals will put eight thousand men in the field and leave another four thousand to guard the capital. They are not the best odds, but by the gods we will fight! They will not have an easy time of it in Palaton."

The fury behind his words rallied them. Darvus sat up straighter then ventured to ask how the rest could help. Sorbonne looked from leader to leader, inviting someone to jumping.

It was Drayen who spoke up."My Lords, we must ask ourselves a difficult question. With Sealand already in the enemy camp, and if Oreon has fallen and Gleneden will within the week, can Dania afford to help Palaton?" He stared hard at King Darvus and Endoreen then looked directly at Baldor.

"Forgive me, King Baldor. There is nothing I would like more than to assist you," Drayen concluded.

"There is nothing to forgive, sir." Baldor said quietly, his gaze strong and steady. He was a realist."Too many soldiers would die trying to reach our borders. It makes no sense logistically. I will return home immediately because there is still a chance. But the future of Sandala," he paused, "rests in Dania."

With those words, Baldor's stature rose. Though he could be a difficult man, with that one statement any lingering doubts about his loyalty was eradicated.

Drayen looked at Baldor, appreciating his military mind and his determination then turned to the rest."There is good news, my Lords," he said. "For the first time in five hundred years, the Shala Queen has lit the bonfires and raised the banner. It means, as the Prophecy foretold, that the Shala rise to defend the people of the Sandala."

The mumbling began as monarchs and their aides began reacting to this latest revelation. Baldor looked back at him, both startled and interested. "What does that really mean?" he asked.

Drayen, standing tall and proud, answered. "Twenty thousand Shala warriors will arrive in two days. The majority have been sent here to secure this capital and to hold off a second invasion that's projected. But there will be warriors going into every kingdom."

Surprised, Baldor chewed over the reply before he finally turned to Queen Endoreen. "My Lady, it would seem logical that the largest force would be sent to Gleneden since that is where you live."

"The Shala Queen believes that Dania's survival is critical," she answered."It would be very difficult for the rest of us to survive if Dania fell." She raised her index finger."It must be our primary focus."

"My Lords, Dania is the easiest to defend," Drayen interjected as he walked over to the large map of Sandala.

"Since the capital is surrounded by mountains," he said, as his large hand rested on the capital city, "any enemy would suffer heavy losses trying to cross those passes."

But King Darvus raised a concern they all shared."But, sir, can your twenty thousand make enough difference?"

Drayen offered a grim smile as he returned to the big table. "We have a saying. Four to one is a Shala victory. Anything less is an unfair fight."

Noting the puzzled looks on many faces, Queen Endoreen spoke up. "Shala are not like us," she explained."They are stronger physically and have heightened senses that make it possible for them to hear or smell you from some distance. They are very dangerous enemies."

"But can they still die, my Lady?" Baldor asked, though his skeptical eyes bore in on her Shalaen husband.

Drayen nodded soberly."Make no mistake about that, Your Highness."

More servants entered, bringing additional food and drink. When the meeting broke off into smaller groups, Drayen made an effort to convince Baldor to remain in Dania. Because of his military mind, he would be helpful in organizing the defense of Sandala. In the end, Baldor convinced the monarchs that keeping some of the enemy busy in Palaton would aid everyone's cause. What he said was true and no one could deny him the right to be present to defend his homeland.

King Sorbonne repeated his offer for safe harbor in the castle, stressing that all were welcome to remain in Danigh as his guest and ally for as long as they wished. King Darvus gratefully accepted. Queen Endoreen was torn, but in the end Drayen convinced her to wait until the Shala arrived before she decided. By the time they arrived, Gleneden might be overrun.

Drayen was equally successful in getting Baldor to wait until the Shala appeared. They could provide an escort that would ensure his safe return to Palaton. Now all they had to do was wait – for the Shala, for more pigeons, and for the invaders.

After the meeting in the Great Hall, the man went back to his room. It was his first chance to be alone since the pigeons had returned. When he went to retrieve the messages earlier in the day, Baldor had sent two scribes with him, forcing him to wait to read the message designated for his eyes alone.

He crossed to the balcony where the light was better and sat down. Reaching inside his cloak, he withdrew the bound piece of leather, unrolled it carefully then sat back and began to read.

As the words passed before his eyes, a chill began to work its way down his torso. He knew that putting what he read into action would bring about his own death. Once the target was assassinated, he would never leave the palace alive.

He rose and looked out at the view. Dania was a beautiful land, he thought, gazing fondly at the lush countryside and the majestic mountains that ringed the city. The Emperor only chooses the best or the easiest to conquer, he thought. He smiled. He would have liked to have seen this glorious city captured, but he was honored to have the opportunity to serve the Empire.

CHAPTER 18

DEVON'S RUN

It was the hounds that worried Devon most of all. He had ridden hard the past few days, his powerful warhorse taking him across Sealand at a furious pace. Thanks to his horse and his own knowledge of the countryside, he had been able to pull ahead of his pursuit by several miles.

He found a low slung, long bed wagon, and guided his horse recover aboard to allow it time to recover. He forged ahead, driving the team of oxen hard as he approached the rugged terrain of Oreon. He picked his way rapidly through the mountains then held on for dear life as his steed fought the currents of the Orlon River. Once they set foot on Palaton's soil, he chanced several hours of rest. But the hounds were always on his mind. They were tireless, infused with a corrupt energy that could eventually run him into the ground.

His horse's hooves pounded the dry flatlands of western Palaton's red earth, causing dust clouds to swirl in the air. The border to Dania lay just ahead. Home, if they could maintain this pace, was only a day or so away.

Finally, he thought, spying familiar hills. Relief flooded through him. His horse needed rest from his weight and he needed a respite from riding. But yet, the hounds...

Again, he glanced nervously over his shoulder. Sweat dripped down his forehead, etching a furrow in the grime caked on his face. Shading his eyes from the boiling sun, he searched the flats for signs of puffs of dust rising from the gritty hardpan. He could see none and knew his gaze stretched five miles or more across the barren flatlands. He could outdistance the other riders and run their mounts into the ground. No horse in all the lands could match his stallion.

Still, he worried. He knew that as he climbed on foot into the welcoming forest, the rapacious beasts would continue their race across the flat land, steadily closing the gap. Once they reached the hills, they would eat up the ground, barely slowing as they raced up the slopes and through the trees. Their progress would be quick and his would not. So, he might die, falling victim to those awful black beasts with their yellow eyes and foul odor of rotten meat, with their fangs dripping decay and death. He might die because of their relentless pursuit. Unless...

If he were far enough ahead, he might reach the falls and their promise of salvation in time. He climbed with greater purpose now, envisioning the point where the mild stream was joined by a larger and much colder river fed by glacial run-off. Together, the two pulsed rapidly as they accelerated downhill then crashed furiously over a steep drop, creating a new, violent beginning some one hundred fifty feet below. Nothing could survive a jump like that. The force of the falls would drive a man down, refusing him the opportunity to surface, drowning him. Devon smiled.

He would have to leave his horse. Once he reached the stream, he would wade with the stallion for part way then turn him loose on the other side. With luck and the gods' blessings, the hounds might lose the scent and the horse would make it home. He certainly knew the way, having delivered an exhausted, injured or unconscious Devon on more than one occasion. Now should be no different. The hounds were after him, not his horse.

For him, there was little choice. He had to get back. He carried a message in his mind that no animal could communicate. There had been no time to write a coherent letter in any detail. He would HAVE to make it back; too much depended on his return.

Coming to the foothills, he began to work his way up the slope. Together, the man and horse carefully picked their way across treacherous shale and up into the trees. After thirty minutes, the forest thickened making riding impossible. He dismounted and he and his horse started running. Small rivulets were crossed quickly, though they stopped at one to slake their thirst and snatch a few minutes rest. He was tired to the bone.

He was so tired, his body depleted by lack of sleep and weak from hunger, he could hardly stand. He hadn't eaten anything resembling a meal in four days.

He forced himself to stand, knowing if he lingered too long he would fall asleep and with sleep came death."Come, Shadow," he called to the stallion, grabbing its reins and guiding it forward.

He came to a massive thicket. Seeing no easy way around he momentarily panicked, thrashing furiously with his heavy sword, hacking wildly at the tough, wiry weeds that blocked his way, careless of the sound of snapping bows. Though long and tall, the underbrush was not as thick as he had assumed, so he burst through suddenly, nearly tumbling into a small ravine.

Anxiety took hold of Devon. He knew that any advantage he had was rapidly diminishing. He reached a small clearing that afforded a quick glimpse of the land below. He saw the reddish puffs of dust now, probably two or three miles from the fringes of the forest. They would reach the trees about the same time he would come to the stream. He was shocked to see two riders following close behind the hounds, and realized they must have brought extra horses. He turned from the ledge abruptly.

Now on more level ground, he remounted and pushed on quickly. He tucked himself low against the horse's back, trying to dodge branches that whipped past his face and arms. His cloak was nearly torn from him as a sharp limb ripped his shirt and drew blood. He ignored it and they raced on. The brave stallion, strong heart to the last, blazed his own trail. His breath wheezing, the steed pounded past tall pines, leapt over fallen logs and charged up and down steep ravines, while branches creaked and popped whenever he crashed against them. Soon, the animal's flanks were lathered with sweat and foam. Devon whispered words of encouragement, all the while fighting the urge to look back and, worse yet, to stop and listen.

At long last the trees opened before them. They raced across a wide expanse toward a line of bushes that straddled the river he sought. Approaching the water, Devon slowed his mount, guiding him carefully down the bank and edging him cautiously into the water. The icy mountain runoff, a stark contrast to their heated run, chilled them. He turned south and dropped the reins, letting the horse choose his footing freely. They had gone about a mile down the stream before he heard the hounds.

It's going to be close, he thought, urging the horse ahead. He wanted to free his steed now before the fanged monsters saw him, but he had to be close enough to the falls to be able to reach it before the dogs ran him down. Staying alive to deliver his message was all that mattered, even if it meant sacrificing his horse, he reflected with heavy heart.

With great relief, he saw the bend that marked the last few hundred yards to his goal. He rode on a little further and then dismounted. He grabbed his waterproof pouch, but left everything else save his weapon. He could not afford to be weighed down when the time came to swim for his life. He checked to make sure his hunting knife was fixed securely against his side then stared up at the exhausted horse before him.

"You're on your own now, Shadow," he said as he stoked the horse's side."Take care" He wanted to say more, but there was no time. The hounds' snarls were growing louder.

"Home!" Devon ordered as he spanked his horse's rump. Shadow did not hesitate. He too, heard the dogs' unearthly cries. He bolted up the far bank and disappeared into the trees.

Devon did not wait to watch. He moved as fast as the slippery river stones would allow. He cleared the bend and thanked the gods that the falls were closer than he remembered. He paused, looking back. He wanted his pursuers to see him, to chase him and finally to witness his death leap over the edge.

Then suddenly, the hounds burst into view. They spied him and their bays crescendoed. They wanted to sink their fangs in him, rip him to shreds and slather his blood. Devon turned and hurried on, comforted that they wouldn't get the chance.

It wasn't far now, the roar of the falls increasing with each step. He glanced back one last time, pleased to see the two riders who had tracked him close behind their hideous dogs. He raised his sword in a final gesture of defiance. I will never die by your hands, he seemed to imply, then hurled his weapon towards them. He waited a moment, then turned and jumped.

CHAPTER 19

ARMIES ACROSS SANDALA

Katar's forces had beached the boats on the southwestern shore of the Sea of Death. A small contingent of warriors remained to guard the vessels while the rest of the *kosh* began the rapid trot to the seashore. It was seventy-five miles away but they stopped to rest only once. Now he stood on the lee side of a low bluff at the edge of the sea.

Katar, garbed in his leather war tunic, walked to the top of the dune and looked out at the blue-green water sparkling in the sun. The wind was low and the ocean calm. Looking to the far horizon, he saw a sea empty of any ships.

Pael, Katar's second in command, trudged up the higher ground and stopped alongside his *kosh* leader. He studied the glimmering expanse as well."At least we arrived first, if they even come ashore here."

"We must assume they will. Tahjeen wouldn't send an entire *kosh* on a fool's errand." Katar looked at the long stretch of smooth beach, broken only by the meandering river they had followed the last ten miles."It's the only realistic invasion site. Swamps run all along the southern coastline and the steep cliffs to the north make any landing impossible."

He turned to the stocky Pael, a build rare among the Shala. "Set large bonfires every two hundred paces along this stretch. Have two warriors tend each site, one to keep the fire burning and one to run messages. Perhaps we can make the invaders believe a large army is waiting for them."

Pael dipped his head in acknowledgement and trotted away, slogging through the soft sand that made up the dune. His spotted leopard loped along by his side. He passed two women who were waiting at the bottom.

Katar signaled for the two warriors to join him. After they scampered up the incline, he spoke to the younger woman first.

"Sonoria, take a half dozen warriors and scout the desert north of the river. Our flanks are vulnerable. Establish a safety zone so there are no surprises," Katar explained. She nodded, her shoulder-length dark hair bobbing slightly. It blended in with her walnut-colored skin.

After she retreated back down the dune, Katar faced the second warrior. Her light blond hair mirrored his own, one of several characteristics he shared with his sister.

"Take a like number and search the land to the east and south."

"Do we engage if we come upon the enemy?" Lanai asked, her head tilted slightly in her usual way.

"Only if they can be completely destroyed. But if it's a large contingent, leave someone to watch their movements while the rest of you continue on."

"I understand. Be safe, brother." She turned to leave but he reached out his hand to stop her.

"There's more," Katar said. Lanai's eyes flashed yellow in surprise.

"Your path is also the direction they're likely to take as they move on toward Danigh," Katar explained.

"We're not going to hold them here?"

Katar shook his head, his eyes turning a somber brown."If this invasion force is similar in size to the one that landed in Seadawn, there will be far too many. Instead, our task is to slow them down and give Toman and Katrine's *koshes* time to get to Danigh and increase the fortifications there."

Comprehension dawning, Lanai's eyes turned orange as eagerness for battle took hold."You want me to look for places where we can ambush them?"

Katar smiled."Your enthusiasm betrays you, sister," he teased as several colors danced across his eyes. Then he turned more serious. "No doubt they'll send scouts ahead so the sites can't be anything obvious. Look for places where we can nip at trailing supply wagons; narrow spots where we can cut a portion off from the rest then retreat quickly after we've inflicted some damage. Locations like that."

"Like sites I would use when I ambushed a certain older brother?"

"Exactly," Katar said. "You've a good imagination when it comes to that. Why else do you think I picked you?"

Lanai laughed."Anything else?"

"Be vigilant, sister."

"Always, brother," she said then turned away.

He watched her and her dark panther head down the small dune, her head still tilted. Though he trusted every man and woman in his *kosh*, it was a comfort to have someone with you who knew your mind so well. He doubted either contingent would encounter the enemy, but he wanted every possibility explored.

Turning back he stared at the vast expanse of blue then let his gaze drop to the waves rolling towards him as they journeyed to shore. They crashed below, their white foam clean and bright. How soon they would be running red with blood?

Later that same day, Gable stopped his *kosh* just inside the mouth of the eastern cavern. Outside the entrance, the rolling plains of Gleneden stretched wide, prairie grass rippling from the caressing breeze. Like Katar, he sent scouts to survey the immediate vicinity, and while waiting for their return, he called for his lieutenants. It was time to discuss strategy and determine how to hide an army in plain sight.

Gable had his own ideas, but input from the rest might produce additional and perhaps more effective strategies. Warriors moved deeper into the passage, creating room for the ten or so who started to gather. Gable waited until everyone was settled, his own golden mountain lion stretched out beside him.

He inhaled deeply, his older face bothered, marked by more worry lines than he had sported only a week earlier.

"Our task is challenging," he began at last."The Queen wants us to infiltrate the four kingdoms of Oreon, Palaton, Sealand and Gleneden. But at the same time, we need to keep the enemy guessing as to our numbers and identity until we know exactly what they are up to." Gable paused, inviting suggestions.

"Small bands would be the best," said a younger, lithe warrior. Others murmured their agreement.

"I concur," Gable said then explained their three tasks.

"We need information - determine the enemy's numbers, their types of arms, modes of travel, and anything else that would be of use. We need to know how the civilians are reacting. Are they being harmed or enslaved, or forming resistance groups?" He paused to let his comments sink in then continued.

"We must also undermine the enemy whenever possible — destroying weapons and supplies, disrupting communications, eliminating patrols if we can do so without being seen. Essentially," Gable said, "We must create confusion."

He waited a moment to gauge their reactions, and was pleased that none of the younger leaders displayed disappointment that open battle was to be avoided.

"Finally, we will assist if we can. Perhaps provide food or healing, maybe help them organize, let them know there is cause for hope."

An unusually muscular Shala called Cordon raised his voice. "Gable, as you outlined our situation, I did some basic mathematics. We could divide into five equal groups. One would protect the cavern, and the others target one of the four kingdoms."

"That still leaves a very large group," interrupted a young warrior named Tyrol.

"I am not finished," chided Cordon, his eyes reflecting the greenish yellow of irritation. The younger man's eyes turned pink as he reddened in embarrassment, realizing his youthful enthusiasm had betrayed him.

"Each large group can divide again, one for each of the three tasks."

"It is the seed of a good plan," Gable replied, nodding his head. "Break into smaller groups and refine it. We will meet again in one hour."

Everyone broke quickly into random groups, eager to further develop the overall plan. Inwardly, Gable was glad for Tyrol's impetuosity. His embarrassment would keep other young warriors in check rather than risk similar ridicule.

Gable decided he would keep Tyrol with the group that stayed at the cavern. It would not please him but he would understand the lesson. More importantly, others would as well.

Devon let the water drive him deeper. The pain in his ears was nearly unbearable as he sank lower. It grew dark, making the opening in the rock wall barely discernible. He let the chilly, swirling waters push him toward it then started swimming hard, aiming for the dark hole just ahead. With a last, desperate stroke, he propelled himself into it. Once inside, the pull of the current eased and he kicked strongly, using his hands to pull himself along the tunnel's sides. Lungs almost bursting, he nearly sobbed when he saw the water lighten, and a moment later, he bobbed to the surface and gulped the life giving air inside the underground cavern. Slowly, he drug himself out of the water and lay completely spent on the cavern floor.

He was shivering. Cold, too cold, he thought. He had to get warm, but had nothing to start a fire with, no food or supplies. I cannot fail now, he thought."Please," he begged, his voice altered by chattering teeth, "not now, not after I have come this far." He was exhausted and so very, very cold.

The two men watched for over an hour. They stared at the tons of churning water below, and knew that no one could survive such a desperate leap. The hounds paced back and forth around the edge of the large, churning pool. They were barking and snarling furiously, slobber dripping from their fangs.

"What should we do about them?" the younger of the two men asked.

Raston grew thoughtful. He looked back the way they had come. "We'll hunt for food in those woods. They need to eat soon. It won't be what they hungered for, but it will do."

"Will we wait for the body to float to the surface? General Taro will want proof." His tone of voice betrayed the younger man's worry.

"There will be no corpse rising out of that. He's being pounded to pieces. Even if he surfaced, he would be unrecognizable. The Commander General will be more than satisfied."

"Are you sure?" Tallic asked his inexperience and self-doubt showing.

"He gave up his sword!" Raston barked as he brandished the discarded weapon."Do you not understand? At the last, the great Devon Longstreet, Dania's legendary sentinel, gave up his sword. He chose suicide, violating every code he ever lived by. His body is not needed. Not with this!" Raston held the weapon high, watched the sunlight reflect off the jeweled hilt, and grinned. He was not a man whose looks were improved by smiling. Instead, his lean, sharp features, stretched taut across his face, reminded one of a death's head.

In a field thirty miles east of Sealand's western border, Commander General Taro paced inside the tent that served as the command post. He was awaiting the arrival of the day's messengers bringing the latest news from each of the three offensives. For the better part of an hour he had been pouring over a map spread across his table. Red arrows indicated the thrust of the different divisions.

According to yesterday's reports, General Blugar's forces were driving toward Gleneden's capital, Milhune. Initially, there was little resistance, but as word spread, more Gleneden soldiers appeared and an organized defense was taking shape and slowing their progress. Not by much, Blugar had assured him via the messenger, but slowed nonetheless.

Whitehock's divisions were having great success as they raced across Oreon. The lowland population centers were poorly defended and easy targets. Eventually they would have to subdue the pockets of people in the mountains, but that could wait until the major part of the war was over.

In contrast, Starcher's divisions in Palaton were having a rough go. Resistance was stiff, as if they had been forewarned. The Palatonian soldiers were competent, but since their numbers were half the twenty thousand Starcher had unleashed on them, victory was only a matter of time, and Taro was filled with anticipation for today's reports.

Satisfaction coursed through him. Once Oreon and Gleneden were secure, Taro would combine most of those divisions with the one that now fought in Palaton, leaving only enough soldiers behind in the occupied territories to guarantee that martial law would be obeyed. Even allowing for casualties, Taro estimated that thirty thousand soldiers would be joining the two divisions held in reserve. Together, that group of roughly fifty thousand would attack Dania from the southeast.

Taro's element of surprise was the invasion force that should be landing on Dania's west coast at anytime. Another one hundred thousand soldiers would disembark and begin smashing their way toward Danigh.

Of course, the message from his spy in Dania was unexpected. The presence of a Shala in Danigh was a complete surprise. Drayen was clever to disguise himself as a blind man, and to have married the Gleneden Queen. It might mean that there would be Shala warriors in the vicinity as well, and that would be an even bigger problem. The legends about them were undoubtedly exaggerated, but they would add to the numbers opposing him.

Still, Taro was satisfied. He had done the only thing he could do. The assassin had better strike quickly. With any luck, his actions would throw the leadership of Sandala along with the Shala into disarray.

A messenger arrived, interrupting his thoughts. Upon entering, a chair and some water was provided before the anxious Commander asked him, "Which front?"

"Oreon, Sir." The man replied, still out of breath. He reached inside his tunic and withdrew a piece of leather. The General took it, his eyes narrowing, adjusting his focus as he began to read. Slowly, a smile spread across his face.

"Already to the far border? That is excellent news!"Taro rubbed his hands in satisfaction, nodding with his entire upper torso. "How are the townspeople reacting?"

His breath more under control, the messenger was able to answer in complete sentences."They are weak and completely unprepared."

Taro nodded. That was a fortuitous development. Palaton seemed forewarned, making him think Devon Longstreet might yet have found a way to relay his findings, but with Oreon such a smashing success it looked like Raston had caught up to him after all.

He looked across at the messenger."Thank you," Taro said. "Have another runner sent to me in an hour."

"Yes, Sir," the young man said and departed quickly.

Commander General Taro did not anticipate messengers arriving from Gleneden or Palaton for several hours. Waiting was one of the more unpleasant aspects of war. Some things could not be hurried. A man could only run so fast.

So far, other than the lone Shala at Danigh, everything was going as planned. Taro smiled to himself, wondering when the second surprise would occur and what form it would take. These major offensives never went without a problem. It was only a matter of time.

CHAPTER 20

THE CAVERN

Devon' eyes fluttered open. A motion startled him as his vision adjusted to the dim light. It was only the campfire's shadows dancing across the ceiling of the cave. Sitting up, he felt his body for broken bones, but discovered only bruises then realized his clothes were dry. He grew uneasy, looking all about, as he wondered who had made the fire.

The pool of water that came from the shaft leading to the falls was off to the right. Devon dimly recalled rough hands pulling him toward the fire but his memory was hazy. Looking to the left, his slow scan of the cave slammed to a stop and his heart began to stampede in his chest. Staring from across the fire were the yellow eyes of a mountain lion.

The beast looked like the offspring of an ancient cave Lion. It had huge fangs and a long, velvety tongue licking its chops, perhaps at the prospect of devouring him. Devon shivered despite the sheen of sweat that glistened from his skin. To his shock, the cat yawned, stood, and launched itself onto a shelf above, where is disappeared into the darkness.

Unnerved, Devon fought to regain a degree of calm. He renewed his survey of the cavern. Fearful of moving lest he rouse another cat lurking in the dark, he turned his head slowly.

On the floor were the marks of many cats, and human footprints dispersed among them. Oddly, some of the human steps were on top of the paw prints, as if they had come in later, while others showed that the cats' great feet had trod upon those of the humans.

With his mind still clouded, Devon was unable to decipher the significance of the scene. A sound from the shelf where the cat had originally disappeared brought his gaze back around to the left. There, looking down, was the strangest man he had ever seen. A moment later, the huge cat reappeared.

Devon stared at the tall, imposing figure. Hair, brown like the dead leaf of an oak, cascaded past his shoulders. Equally dark skin covered well-formed muscles and Devon concluded that he would be a deadly opponent. But the eyes shocked Devon the most. They were translucent – totally lacking in color.

The man jumped down and the cat followed, returning to its former place of rest on the opposite side on the fire where it stretched out and studied Devon behind feral eyes.

The stranger's words chased his thoughts away. "Your name," he commanded.

Devon studied the man before him and realized he wasn't merely tall, he was exceedingly tall."Devon Long-street," he finally answered.

"Where do you come from?"

"Dania."

"Why are you here?"

Devon felt himself growing irritated by the questioning."I swam."

The stranger ignored Devon's sarcasm."How did you come to be here, to use this access into the cavern?"

"I have finished answering questions," Devon replied as he crossed his arms in defiance.

Briefly, the man's eyes flashed red, and then once again turned colorless but with that occurrence, everything suddenly made sense to Devon. Once again, his heart began to pound. Like most sentinels, Devon was aware of the legends about ancient warriors who could fight and defeat any man in combat, of men with strange eyes that changed color, of fearless men with huge cats for companions - Shala.

"You are Shala," Devon blurted out before he could stop himself. Inside, he was afraid that if these creatures were Shala then the invasion did not portend a local war, but an intercontinental struggle with the potential of thousands dying.

The man tilted his head to the side. "Yes. I am Shala. Now I ask you again, how did you come to be here, to use this entrance to the cavern?"

This time Devon didn't hesitate. He uncrossed his arms, relaxing his stance."I am an emissary from the Danian King. There have been incidents, rumors of small bands of marauders. I was sent along with other sentinels to travel through the various kingdoms and report back on what we saw."

Devon paused, but the Shalaen nodded encouragement so he continued.

"I was sent to Sealand. The people were afraid and barring their doors to strangers." Devon went on, telling him of his conversation with Talgar and of the invasion.

"I was forced to flee and have been running ever since, chased by two men and some vicious hounds from hell that followed and never let up. I raced for the falls, my only chance to escape and make it back to Danigh with my message."

Devon paused briefly, remembering the harrowing chase and struggle to survive the falls. "All of us who work closely with the King know of this access and others like it."

A sense of urgency spread over Devon's body with desperation not far behind. He had to convince this man, this Shala. "I MUST get back to the king. He has to be informed. This invasion – there are thousands. The army is massive."

"You may come with us," the Shalaen answered.

"No, not unless you are going to the capital."

"It is fortunate for you that we are. If not, you would go where we go."

Startled, Devon realized that he wasn't being escorted. "I am your prisoner?" he his narrowing.

The man looked back at him. "We are here for the same reason, Devon Longstreet. Come. We will feed you."

"When will we leave for Danigh?"

"When he arrives," the Shala replied.

"Who is he?" Devon asked, with furrowed brow, but the man had already leapt to the shelf, the lion quickly following. The big animal turned back, looking at Devon as if to ask, are you coming?

Devon realized that his worst fears were coming true. All Sandala was under attack and about to go to war. How many places were being invaded simultaneously? Dania could be in the midst of a great fight even now. But if the invasion was only being launched at Seadawn, there was still time – time to raise an army and to fortify the borders. He scrambled up the shelf and followed quickly after the tall Shalaen and his huge cat.

Tired of waiting, Devon moved toward the mouth of the cavern looking for the two Shalaen leaders he had been taken to earlier. They had been unwilling to talk with him then, but he was determined to make them listen. Finally, he saw them crouching just inside the cavern opening.

He approached cautiously, still wary of the huge beasts resting beside them. He began to address the one called Toman, the dark-haired leader who was built like an oak tree, but checked himself, remembering that the woman, Katrine seemed to be in command. She was an inch or two taller than the Sentinel, with sleek muscles that added to her beauty.

"With respect," Devon started, only to be interrupted by the strange look the two Shala shared.

He tried again."I must speak with you."

She glanced quickly at Toman then back at Devon. "My eyes are yours," she said.

Devon paused, his mouth partway open to speak, but her words befuddled him. She saw his confusion.

"It means that I will not mask my feelings by making my eyes clear," she explained."They will reflect the color of my emotion so you may see my heart."

Oddly touched by her gesture, Devon cleared his throat and began again. "I am not trying to thwart your plans, but it is imperative that I be allowed to go. I need to deliver my message to King Sorbonne in person."

"He has already been told," Katrine said simply.

He rocked back, startled by the revelation."By whom? When? I only found out myself less than a week ago."

"Most likely by the Gleneden Queen," Katrine replied, shrugging her attractive, shoulders. Her long, curly blond hair bounced with the motion.

"She's in Dania? But how would she know?" Devon blurted.

"She is in Dania because King Sorbonne called a Clave. She knows because her husband told her," Toman explained.

"The blind man? Drayen?" Devon said, still not comprehending. His stoic face was surprisingly confused.

"He is not blind," Katrine explained. "His eyes are as colorful as ours." As she spoke her eyes whirled, spinning a vast array of colors for his benefit. "He covers them in public for reasons that are obvious."

Devon was shocked. Drayen was Shala!

At the realization he abruptly sat, his mind reeling. King Sorbonne would believe Queen Endoreen, but the other leaders might need more convincing, assuming they were present at the Clave. Darvus was a bit of a buffoon, though a decent enough man. Baldor, on the other hand, was impossible. He might demand additional proof.

The two Shala turned their attention back outside the entrance, as if waiting for something. Devon cleared his throat in an effort to regain their ear. Toman looked back at him but Katrine kept staring straight ahead.

"It may not be enough," Devon said emphatically.

Now Katrine turned around as well. "What do you mean?"

"Besides Queen Endoreen, only Sorbonne heeds the Prophecy. Darvus might be swayed but Baldor will require concrete evidence. Accepting Shala will be difficult if not impossible for him, but he will be receptive to what a sentinel has to say. I need to be there."

Katrine started to reply, but a warrior came running up to them from outside."He comes," the warrior announced.

"Who..." Devon started to ask but Katrine cut him off with a sharp motion of her hand.

"Be silent!"

Toman and Katrine stood up and walked out of the opening into the full light of day. Devon followed, refusing to allow a stern look from her to deter him.

He used the time to study her closely. Judging by her athletic physique, she could use the various weapons she carried. A small scar that ran across her bold nose did not detract from her beauty. She was striking! A full head of long blond hair that ran wild. Here was a woman who could hold her own with any sentinel.

His musings were interrupted when two figures and a huge, black panther emerged from the forest. Both were on horseback and as they grew near, Devon realized that one person was a young woman. The other was obviously a Shala warrior.

Once they drew closer, the ruggedly handsome rider, who was exceptionally tall even for a Shala, went directly to Katrine and Toman. To Devon's amazement, they bowed low from the waist. He was even more startled when Katrine knelt and presented her sword to the new arrival.

The male rider leaned over, grabbed Katrine's arms, and lifted her effortlessly to her feet. "Ever vigilant, Katrine, Toman," the man said acknowledging them both. "I'm sorry you had to wait but, ah," he glanced at the woman with him, "a lot has happened in the past couple of days. Keep your honorsword,

Katrine. The three of us will share command."

Katrine, beaming with pride, quickly resheathed her sword. Toman nodded impassively, seeming to expect no less.

"Who is he?" Tahjeen asked, jutting his chin in Devon's direction.

"Devon Longstreet," Katrine answered."He's a sentinel and in a great hurry to relay a message to King Sorbonne."

"A Sentinel! Your kind is known to me. What's the message?"

"I have come from Seadawn. It is the site of a massive invasion. King Dawad has allied himself with the Surmese. Last week hundreds of ships approached the coast. Judging by those numbers, they will field an army of at least a hundred thousand, perhaps more. You can see why I need to get to the King immediately."

Devon studied the reaction of the Shala who stood before him. His eyes flared from blue to red and back again.

"Everything you describe is already known, Devon Longstreet. My brother was told last night. He will relay the information to your king." Tahjeen noted the confusion of Devon's face but said no more, turning instead to Katrine and Toman.

"Are there other humans with you?" he asked, and when Katrine shook her head, he went on."Then we will leave for Danigh immediately. The sentinel can ride my horse so he can keep up."

Katrine was intrigued by the woman who waited patiently behind Tahjeen. "Who is she?"

Before answering, Tahjeen went to the woman, took her hand and brought her forward. Katrine was shocked when Paca went over and rubbed against her.

"This is Ariann. She is the youngest daughter of King Darvus." He paused, noting Katrine's expression, and his eyes whirled their dazzling colors. "Paca says she is the one."

Finally, the Shala halted. Ariann and Devon commiserated over the soreness caused by the prolonged trot. Their backsides ached from the constant pounding against the saddles.

They dismounted and sat down to rest. Ariann noticed that the Shala were barely panting. These people are amazing, she thought then reminded herself that they were not people. They were a different race entirely.

As Tahjeen approached, Devon spoke."May I ask how many

warriors came with your two commanders?"

Tahjeen slowed his step and Devon watched as the Shala seemed to take his measure."Ten thousand," he eventually replied.

Surprised, Devon glanced around."It doesn't seem like that many,"

"The rest are coming now," Tahjeen said as he walked over to sit by Ariann.

Moments later, Devon's mouth fell open. Approaching in their loping style, one huge cat after another drew closer. There were different kinds in varied colors – panthers, tigers, lions, cougars, leopards. Some were black, while others were tan, gray, spotted and striped. A handful were pure white. They dispersed among their Shala counterpart who gave them water and food.

"I had no idea there were that many inside the cavern, "Devon commented.

Tahjeen shrugged."It is a very large cavern."

Ariann watched the exchange. Since they had joined his Shala friends, she had been watching Tahjeen closely. It was obvious the others had great respect for him. Younger warriors glowed with pleasure when he acknowledged them, while more seasoned veterans were comfortable and relaxed in his presence, yet deferential.

Earlier, she thought she had detected a hint of jealousy toward her from Katrine. Perhaps the woman hoped to marry him, or maybe they had once been lovers. But Tahjeen showed no outward sign of affection for her now. Then again, perhaps Shala never did. Devon's question roused her from her musings.

"Will they be enough?" Devon asked Tahjeen.

"Who can say? Warfare depends on many things," he answered," including luck."

"But even with the Danian army added to your numbers, the odds are at least four to one, probably higher."

"Such odds would result in a Shala victory," Tahjeen stated simply. "But one thing we are all taught about warfare, "he paused, looking at Devon, "never count on the obvious."

Tahjeen noted Ariann's overt observation. "Would you like something to drink?"

"I will get it myself, thank you," she said, her eyes filled with defiance. She saw amusement tug at his features before he turned and walked away.

"My Lady," Devon said, "you seem hostile?"

"He presumes too much," she replied curtly.

"Hmmm. If I recall your account correctly, he has saved your life the life of your family on at least two occasions; he protects you now in a countryside filled with enemies; and he and the rest of his kind are willing to die for all of us if that is what it costs to keep us free. You are right. He certainly is presumptuous."

Devon's ironic tone was not lost on Ariann. She glared back but he merely shrugged then got up and moved away as well, leaving her alone. She closed her eyes and took a deep breath, willing calm to return to her soul. She felt overwhelmed by the circumstances. It wasn't just Tahjeen; it was everything –the invasion foremost on her mind. Things were happening that she had never dreamed possible.

Paca came up to her as if sensing her despair. With his big head he pushed against her hands.

"He wants his ears scratched," Katrine said, offering her a biscuit as she sat down. Ariann took it and found it sweet, even delicious. She finished it then began rubbing the big cat behind his ears. A deep purr began to rumble from his chest, and Paca lay down beside her.

Katrine watched."What?" Ariann asked when she saw the odd look on the other woman's face.

"If anyone else," Katrine said eventually, "anyone at all save Tahjeen touched that animal, he would be bitten, clawed, perhaps even killed!"

Ariann was surprised. She looked down at the ferocious beast lying meekly by her side.

Katrine marveled."There is no doubt," she said, "that you are the one."

CHAPTER 21

ON TO DANIA

After another hard pounding in the saddle, Ariann was relieved when Tahjeen stopped and directed everyone to get something to eat and drink from their packs. It was late in the afternoon, the sun was fading and even the Shala were breathing hard. They had been steadily climbing, making their way up the eastern slope of the Learing Mountains.

Wearily, Ariann guided her horse to a small clearing and began to dismount when strong hands gripped her waist and lifted her gently to the ground. She turned and was drawn into the whirling colors of Tahjeen's eyes. As she held her gaze in some childish attempt at defiance, a humming vibration began inside her head, growing into a roar then suddenly stopping, bursting free into a peaceful calm. Through his radiant eyes, she watched as scenes flashed past — a village filled with children with colorful eyes; a stone structure where she saw herself holding an infant; a sleeping room where she lay nestled inside Tahjeen's arms; and the two of them sitting side by side, wearing crowns, while all around them, Shala kneeled.

She blinked, and the connection severed. She let her head fall forward and rest against his chest. Her trembling slowly subsided but she felt strange and disconnected. She looked up at him again, but his eyes were now translucent. The beautiful, fluorescent pink was gone. She yearned to be close to him again. She ached to see the pink come back to those eyes.

Tahjeen nodded, as if he shared what she felt and was equally sorry that the feeling had passed. He found a place for them to sit. "Are you all right?" he whispered gently.

For a moment the intensity of the exchange was overwhelming and robbed her of speech. She knew that everything about her life had just changed. She had shifted onto a different path and was headed in a new direction. She nodded finally, looking up at his face. This being who sat beside her, who could kill three or four people in seconds, who could run faster than a horse and probably lift one as well, had said they were destined to be mates. Now, finally, she believed him. The realization left her with questions…many, many questions.

"What do you want to know?" he asked as if reading her mind.

She thought for a time, wondering about his past, his family, the customs among the Shala. She also wondered how he had come to be the leader of the Shala military. Finally, she found her voice.

"Who are you really? Are you their general?"

Sighing, he searched for a way to begin. His mind drifted back to his abrupt departure from the crater just three days ago.

"I am someone my mother hoped would mature. She knows I can lead but thinks I lack empathy. I'm easily angered and it can blind me from seeing events or people clearly."

Tahjeen paused, but Ariann waited patiently, pleased with his openness.

"And, yes, I am in command of the Shala military." He paused, studying her."I've spent a lot of time studying humans

- what you are like; how your cultures differ; how your governments work, so that I would be in a better position to draw conclusions about those whose fate is entrusted to us."

"And have you drawn any?"

Tahjeen's somber eyes darkened, as he took time to choose his words. Finally, he looked back at Ariann. "You use your young, ignore your elders, and cheat your friends."

Ariann lifted an eyebrow in surprise."I have heard more glamorous descriptions."

Tahjeen stared back at her. "I do not mean you specifically."

"Do you find anything admirable?" she asked.

Tahjeen shrugged. "A shred of ingenuity, a passion for life, and, if you are any example," he said as his eyes returned to a more friendly blue, "inquisitiveness and bravery." He shook his head. "Humans are filled with many contradictions."

"One might wonder," Ariann said smiling, "why you bother to protect us."

"True," Tahjeen replied, recalling his meeting with the king of the *fels*. "But in the end, I do not question my ancestors. If they say we are to protect humanity then we shall."

A muffled growl interrupted them as his *fel* padded up to them. The huge panther casually approached Tahjeen, pushing his large head against his back.

"Hello, my beauty. What have you been up to?" As Tahjeen talked to him, he turned and bumped his own forehead against the cat's then exposed his throat in a sign of total trust. Paca responded by licking his neck, enjoying the salty sweat accumulated by the brisk travel. Tahjeen laughed then laid his arm across the cat's broad back.

Ariann was eager to continue their conversation."I am curious, though. Did you find much difference between the kingdoms?"

"Only in Gleneden and Dania," Tahjeen answered."Gleneden is understandable because of Queen Endoreen's wisdom, but I look forward to meeting Dania's King. He has moved his people to embrace taking care of the whole, not just the individual."

"Perhaps it is possible, then," Ariann interjected, "for a human leader to make a positive difference. If so, it is a hopeful sign."

"Indeed. This appears to be a kingdom filled with much promise."

"Any other conclusions?" Ariann asked, still curious but also wanting to extend the conversation.

"Many. Humans are greedy, petty, short-sighted, and prone to violence," he answered lightly, more gaiety in his voice.

"But surely we humans must have some endearing characteristics?" Ariann teased back.

Tahjeen continued smiling, but a deep purple cast to his eyes revealed a seriousness that matched his words."Ah, yes - a tremendous will to live and the potential for great loyalty. Some even possess a desire to learn and grow. I'm not completely convinced you merit our protection and the possible loss of Shalaen life that that implies, but I am also not sure you don't."

"You seem to have concluded a great deal," Ariann said, surprised that she agreed with much of what he said.

"The question is what good will it do me? I'm destined to a life of doing my brother's bidding and making my estimable mother happy," Tahjeen said as he absently scratched Paca's ears. His *fel* contentedly responded with a loud purr.

"I can understand the devotion to your mother, but why your brother? Is he older?" Ariann asked curiously.

"Yes. And while I am devoted to my mother for the reason you implied, it's also because she is the Queen of Shala. One day, my brother will be the King."

Ariann was dumbstruck. Her mouth opened but no words followed. The Queen! By the gods! That meant that Tahjeen was a prince, not the heir to the throne, but a prince nonetheless. It drew her back to the visions she had seen minutes before. She spoke, verbalizing her thoughts.

"A few minutes ago, when I looked into your eyes, I saw many images of things that have not yet happened."

She saw his surprise as his eyebrows shot up and his eyes spun hues of gold and sea green. "Ariann, it means you have the Seer's gift!"

She jarred to a stop, pinning him with her eyes. "What does that mean?"

He tilted his head and nodded, as if confirming his own conclusion. "Some humans," Tahjeen spoke reverently, "when they interact strongly with a particular Shala, can have visions of the future." She could hear the excitement in his tone, but she shook her head, clearly troubled.

"What's wrong?" he asked.

"One of the images was of the two of us, wearing crowns, while Shala kneeled, and how can that be if your brother is the heir?"

He sat back and looked away."If you truly have the Seer's gift, your vision indicates that I'll rule the Shala, not Drayen. That could only happen if..." He swallowed hard as he forced the thought away, and turned back to her.

"I only know," he said in a somber tone, that life ebbs and flows like the ocean's tide. Each wave brings something different ashore. Nothing stays the same."

CHAPTER 22

STRATEGY

Two days had passed while the Clave members awaited the Shala's arrival. The monarchs were in an evening planning session, refining their strategy for Dania's defense. King Sorbonne wanted Baldor's military advice before he left for Palaton. They were seated in the great room when a member of the King's Guard burst in.

"My Lord," he said, near breathless from his run, "Master Cullen says you must come see this."

Concerned by the alarm on the man's face, the King rushed to follow him, the other rulers a step behind. The retinue went out onto the large balcony and walked over to the ledge where Cullen stood and pointed out into the night. There in the distance, beyond the city and into the darkened countryside, were hundreds upon hundreds of campfires, as many as stars in the clear night sky.

Drayen moved closer to the King's side, a smile forming at the corners of his mouth."The Shala have arrived, Your Highness." Sorbonne heaved a sigh of relief. He nodded and clapped Drayen's shoulder. There was even a small hint of a smile forming at the corners of his mouth.

After a time, the rulers went back inside with a noticeable lift in their spirits. Everyone started to talk at once then deferred to King Sorbonne who had put both hands up asking for quiet.

"My question is for Drayen." He settled his gaze on Queen Endoreen's husband. "Should we send a delegation with a formal greeting and an invitation to join us?"

"That will not be necessary, my King."

Startled, everyone turned at the sound of a new voice coming from just inside the far door.

"Devon!" Roland cried, jumping to his feet and rushing over

to greet the man they feared lost to them forever. The two embraced warmly and before they parted, Sorbonne was also at Devon's side.

"My friend," said the King, clasping Devon's forearm."I have rarely been so pleased to see someone." For the first time in days a broad smile spread across the monarch's face. "I must admit I feared the worst. But forgive my manners," Sorbonne added, gesturing toward the large table where the rest were seated."Please, come and join us. Everyone will want to hear your story."

Devon interrupted him."Excuse me, Your Highness, but I did not come alone." Turning back toward the entrance, he waved someone forward. For the first time, the King noticed another person hanging back in the shadows. Devon caught his look. "King Sorbonne, allow me to introduce the younger daughter of King Darvus, Lady Ariann."

"Ariann," King Darvus leapt to his feet and rushed over to his daughter. Surprise and relief flooded his face."Thank the gods! Achates told me you would be all right, but I still...oh, blast, daughter it is good to see you." Darvus hugged her fiercely and Sorbonne watched some of the weight of the past few days lift from his shoulders.

Darvus drew back, taking a long look at Ariann. A grimace came to his face as he vocalized his shock."But your appearance," Darvus said. "This tunic, and, and there's dust and grime all over you!"

Ariann smiled and chuckled."The former was fashioned by a practical Shala and the latter is a result of the hard ride to get here quickly."

Still standing, King Sorbonne spoke, bringing their reunion to a tactful end."I am sure both of you have much to tell us. Devon, we are all eager to hear. Let's rearrange the chairs so everyone is near the warmth of the fire." Several chairs scraped the cobblestone floor as they were moved to accommodate the two new arrivals.

"So," he continued once they were all settled. "We saw the lights of the Shala's fires," he said, gesturing toward the drapes that hung in front of the balcony. "I assume you came in with them. How...where did you find them?"

Devon smiled as he spread his hands out on the table in front of him. "In truth, Sire, they found me. The Surmese chased me out of Seadawn and into Dania. Eventually I evaded them by jumping the falls." Sorbonne nodded knowingly.

Nodding toward the balcony, Devon continued."It was the Shala that warmed and fed me. They were already in the cavern."

Sorbonne lifted an eyebrow and looked around at the other monarchs. "Indeed," he enthused."Well, thank the gods!"He turned his attention back to Devon."We want to talk to them. How soon can that be arranged?"

Devon smiled."I wouldn't think it should be much longer, Your Majesty. Their leader left the camp at the same time we did and is making his way here as we speak. He, ah," Devon paused, his smile growing into a full blown grin, "he wanted to test your defenses, so he took a slightly different route."

Sorbonne sat up, his face registering alarm."But he could be mistaken for the enemy and harmed, possibly killed."

Abruptly, Ariann laughed before she quickly put both hands up as if apologizing."I doubt that very much," she said, drawing surprised looks from Darvus, Baldor and Sorbonne. Suddenly, all their attention was drawn to sounds of scuffling coming from the outer balcony. King Sorbonne's concern was eased when Cullen's laughter filled the air. A moment later, the heavy drapes were pushed aside.

Sorbonne's eyes widened at the sight of the individual that strode into the room. He dwarfed every man present by ahead and a half. His long arms and legs were well muscled. His skin, as dark as weathered oak, was contrasted by a shining silver helmet and an ivory-colored leather tunic. Wire mesh draped across his eyes and shoulder-length white-blond hair flowed out from underneath his helmet.

Like a prowling panther, he circled them. No one said a word. All heads turned to follow him as he moved around the room. When he came to Drayen, he stopped. The Queen's husband stood and Sorbonne was surprised that Drayen's height was a match for the Shala standing in front of him. Drayen had never seemed so tall.

Then the warrior removed his helmet and everyone gasped. Except for Drayen's short brown hair, they were a mirror image. "Vigilance, brother," the newcomer said.

Before King Sorbonne found his voice, Drayen acted. "Tahjeen!" he said with deep emotion then quickly pulled him into a backslapping hug. When they finally stepped apart, their eyes were flashing with bright, warm colors.

"Two years is a long time to be without one's other half," Tahjeen said. Drayen nodded, as Queen Endoreen approached. She reached out and touched Tahjeen's face. He bowed low and offered a warm smile.

"I have missed the reckless abandon with which you enjoy life, my friend," the Queen said. "Drayen is so serious." Tahjeen straightened and smiled back, his eyes pink and his expression soft.

Drayen turned to the others, raising his arm as he gestured to the tall warrior beside him."My Lords, may I present my twin brother, Tahjeen."

Once formal introductions ended, everyone moved into the Great Hall that now served as the war room. A large wall map of the continent of Sandala was posted on the near side, and smaller maps of individual kingdoms were spread across the massive table. King Sorbonne invited Devon to tell his story. The sentinel strode to the large map.

He let one hand rest on the kingdom of Sealand. "I had to enter Seadawn surreptitiously. The main gates were heavily guarded and anyone allowed in was thoroughly searched. I made my way to an inn owned by a good friend, another Sentinel. We talked and in time, he and I agreed that Dawad has formed an alliance with a foreign power. Most likely," he paused for effect, "the Surmese."

Looks were exchanged and several stirred, unease fostered by the disturbing information."That is not good news, not good news at all," Baldor said, shaking his head several times."Are you positive?"

Devon nodded."The next morning I was. Just after dawn a huge Armada sailed into Seadawn's harbor and landed along the surrounding coast. There's no mistaking their long bowed boats made for ramming" He turned to King Sorbonne. "My Lord, I estimate they off-loaded ten divisions."

Gasps were heard around the room. They were too stunned to speak. So far, they had assumed roughly fifty thousand of the enemy. If Devon were correct, another fifty thousand were unaccounted for. Sorbonne said what everyone else was thinking. "The rest are most likely on their way to Dania. "The room grew silent as each ruler contemplated what might be happening now.

Devon interrupted Sorbonne's musings."Sire, what is the situation in the other kingdoms?"

Sorbonne rose and joined the sentinel at the big map of Sandala. Quickly, the Danian ruler summarized. Pointing out the different locations, he explained that Oreon had fallen and Gleneden's capitol was surrounded. Palaton was giving ground slowly and King Baldor was going back tomorrow to personally lead the resistance.

"As yet," Sorbonne concluded, "we have not been attacked."

"We believe that Dania is their prime target," Drayen interjected. "And they are trying to isolate it completely by defeating the others first."

Tahjeen stood up."If I may?" he asked, gesturing to the map. Devon and King Sorbonne moved aside to give him access. One strong, dark hand covered what was Gleneden." A Shala *kosh* is already here. It will split up and infiltrate the other three kingdoms as well."

With his other hand, he pointed to Dania's western coastline. "Another *kosh* was sent here to meet a second invasion."

A collective gasp escaped from all the humans in the room. "By all the gods!" Baldor exclaimed."A second armada?"

Tahjeen saw the sick looks on their faces. Despair and hopelessness hung over the room like a dark cloud pregnant with rain.

He studied them, trying to judge their readiness for the next bit of bad news. One way or another it did not really matter. They had to be told.

"The enemy will leave a token force behind in the conquered kingdoms, sending the bulk of his army to join the divisions that attack Dania," Tahjeen announced.

Ever the keen militarist, Baldor wanted rationale for Tahjeen's conclusion. "What makes you think that?" His brows furrowed, his concern obvious.

Tahjeen considered the question for a moment, choosing his words, understanding that these rulers knew very little about the Shala, of their long obsession with documenting their military history. All the enemies and battles fought since their first appearance in Sandala was part of their library archives. Every Shala who chose life as a warrior spent years studying those engagements. As a result, he was an expert about Surmese fighting strategy.

"The Surmese first came to Sandala nearly seven hundred years ago," Tahjeen told them."Both then and now they have shown it is not in their nature to take prisoners. It requires fewer soldiers to control civilians." No one said a word, each sobered by the vision of mass graves filled with Sandalese soldiers.

Breaking the silence, Sorbonne finally ventured a question."By a token, are you talking a thousand? Or more?"

"Your Majesty," Tahjeen said quietly, his face filled with empathy, "even if a few thousand are left to occupy each kingdom, and several thousand more have been killed in battle, the force invading Dania is likely to be over eighty thousand strong."

King Sorbonne blanched. Growing heavy with the sudden weight of imposed reality, the king's shoulders sagged. He turned and looked at Drayen "You said that four to one odds would result in a Shala victory. But we might be facing seven to one?" Bleakness gripped his face as he said the words, as futility began to seep into his soul.

Drayen did not answer, but exchanged a glance with Tahjeen. His brother nodded then turned and noted Sorbonne's expression. He read the body language of a proud and noble ruler who was facing the realization that his country might soon be lost.

"Your Highness," Tahjeen said, quoting the prophecy, "The Shala stand ready to 'dance with death'."

He moved away from the wall map, drawing closer to the rulers seated at the table. Ariann was frowning, though it was not her place to speak, she challenged, "Even if it means you will all die?"

"Ariann, please," her father said, his words delivered in a stern tone. She bowed to him quickly, embarrassed by her own outburst.

"It is why we exist," Drayen interjected. Tahjeen's eyes narrowed as he looked at him curiously, surprised that his brother didn't mention other possibilities. But Tahjeen knew his brother was not trained in military strategy and perhaps had not fully analyzed the options.

"There are alternatives," Tahjeen said.

Across the table, Baldor nodded. "Yes," the Palaton king

agreed. "There are many ways to win a war. He directed his gaze at Tahjeen. "What is it you have in mind?"

Tahjeen went back to the big map on the wall and pointed again at Dania's western coast."If the Queen Mother is correct, and there is another armada on the way with a second invasion force,"

"Then we are doomed," Roland interrupted.

"Not necessarily, my young friend," Baldor said without rancor, then looked back at Tahjeen. "I think I understand. May I?"

Tahjeen nodded. Now Baldor stood up, moved to the map and pointed at Gleneden."If Dania is truly their main target, and if token forces are left behind here in Gleneden, we could conceivably retake the defeated kingdoms." He turned to Tahjeen. "Could one *kosh* do it?" he asked Tahjeen, who quickly nodded.

."At the same time," Baldor continued as his fingerspointed in a new direction,"we could move on Palaton before my army is destroyed. Again, with Shala assistance we could defeat the enemy there, driving a huge wedge between the forces preparing for an attack on Dania's eastern border and those sweeping through Oreon and still present in Sealand." As he spoke, as he moved his hand boldly along the Tanon River, marking the area where the Surmese army might eventually be confronted.

"And," King Darvus chimed in as he sat up, his growing excitement obvious to all, "since the Surmese have chosen to ignore our mountain people, with Shala help we can form some very troublesome resistance fighters wreaking havoc on whatever force he leaves behind in the lowlands."

"Or at the very least," Baldor interjected, "prevent the enemy from controlling the mountains which would further disrupt their plans and increase their vulnerability."

King Sorbonne finally spoke up."I like everything you are suggesting, but that still leaves Dania with over a hundred thousand of the enemy to fight. What do we do about them?"

Tahjeen smiled. "If Gleneden and Palaton are regained, Your Highness, the invaders face a serious problem." He gestured broadly at the map. "If they ignore our actions and conquer Dania, the rulers of Sandala will be able to regain the other four kingdoms. The enemy will have wasted many lives for little gain, and will still face an army and a civilian populace ready to fight back."

"So you think he will turn some of the divisions back toward the other four kingdoms to try to stop us?" King Sorbonne said.

Tahjeen nodded."It would be sensible, especially if another invasion force is attacking from the west."

Finally, Drayen entered the conversation. His tone was subdued and his face worried."The only weakness in your argument is the coastal invasion force. Our Shala *kosh* could defeat a force twenty thousand and neutralize thirty thousand, but what if there are as many as the first group that landed at Seadawn?"

"Then a difficult decision awaits us," Tahjeen answered."We could fight, but we lack the forces to win and Dania would fall."

"But what other choice do we have?" Sorbonne asked.

Tahjeen took a deep breath and shook his head. He was reticent to utter the words."Desert the capital and live to fight another day."

Roland leapt to his feet."Either way, Dania falls! Either way we lose." Anger played across his face. He looked severely at the other rulers."Today, we are the only kingdom still free and unoccupied. Does that not strike anyone else as ironic?"

Sorbonne stood as he sought words to calm his son."Roland, think about what you said a few minutes ago. 'We are doomed,' were your exact words. To stand and fight when losing is certain, that is a foolish waste of life."

But Roland shook his head."At least we would die with honor," he said, his voice trembling, "not running away like whimpering, beaten dogs." Tahjeen could smell the young man's anger. It pulsed across the room and assailed him. Had he been a weaker man, he would have been cowed. But before he could answer, Cullen intervened.

"Think, lad," Cullen urged, placing a strong hand on Roland's shoulder. "Do you want to lose your land forever, or just temporarily?"

Roland looked at his mentor, weighing his words. Cullen continued. "The Shala have a saying, 'just because you can whip five men in a fight, doesn't mean you should stand in front of a two thousand pound bull.'"

"What do you know about Shala sayings?" Roland asked, his shoulders slumped dejectedly.

"A great deal, lad. I lived with them for many years and was married to a Shala woman."

"What?" Roland exclaimed. Both he and his father stared open-mouthed at Cullen.

"Why else do you think I can best you in a sword fight? I have been trained by the best," Cullen growled.

Then Queen Endoreen stood and gained everyone's full attention, as her melodious voice reached out to them. "My Lords, we have a great deal to consider. It would be wise to let these decisions wrestle in our thoughts while we sleep. Tomorrow, everything will be clearer. I suggest we meet in the morning following breakfast."

"That's wise counsel, your Highness." King Sorbonne said. He turned to Tahjeen. "You are welcome to spend the night. We can have a room prepared."

"Thank you, Sire, but I will go back to my campfire and return at first light." He looked at King Darvus and walked over to him as the others started to leave.

"Your Majesty," Tahjeen said, "when you saw me earlier, I was an old man with bad eyes and a long gray beard. I am sorry I could not reveal myself to you then."

"What?" Darvus said with disbelief. "You were Sir Dron? I, I..."

"Yes, Father," Ariann interjected. "It was also Tahjeen who brought me safely back to you."

"Well, I don't know what to say, except thank you, of course." Darvus stood there shaking his head, looking up at the tall young man.

"Someday soon, my Lord, we will need to discuss another matter," Tahjeen said, glancing at Ariann. "But that must wait. I bid you both good night." Amazed, Darvus stared after him while Ariann hurried away to hide her rapidly reddening face.

As everyone began heading to their rooms, Tahjeen joined Drayen and Endoreen. He had more to discuss with them which required some time alone. But he'd also missed his older brother deeply and wanted to bask in the comfort of his closeness. Drayen's quiet strength was calming and increased Tahjeen's confidence and resolve, both of which would be challenged in the days ahead.

As they moved down the hallway they passed several servants whose jaws dropped open at the sight of the imposing, strange-eyed warrior.

"Your entrance made quite an impression," Drayen said once they were behind the closed door of their sleeping chamber. Endoreen moved about, using the candle lit by the maid to ignite several others. Shadows shifted, as gradually the room was suffused with more light.

"As intended," Tahjeen answered, walking over to his brother and gripping his shoulders. "Two years is far too long for twins to be separated." He studied Drayen for a time, absorbing the physical closeness. Their eyes swirled with affectionate hues.

Finally, Drayen spoke. "You just don't like getting so much of mother's attention."

Tahjeen saw the humor reflected in his brother's eyes and smiled back. "Well, I never was her favorite son, probably one too many trips beyond the crater," he said, referring to his childhood excursions to the outer edge of their island home, a practice that was highly discouraged.

Drayen laughed. "Yes, but that independent streak has served you well. I like your plan for taking back Gleneden and Palaton, even if you did let Baldor get the credit. What else do you have in mind?"

The smile faded from Tahjeen's face. "We need to convince King Sorbonne that we are saving his kingdom by avoiding a direct military confrontation. The second invasion is imminent, and in numbers similar to the first. Katar's *kosh* will have no chance against an army that massive. It would be a waste of Shalaen lives to try."

Drayen frowned. "But what other choice do we truly have? The prophecy is clear. What will Katar do?"

"Through a *lais* last night he was told to divide his forces into large raiding parties, and stall the enemy with rapid attacks and retreats, stinging them like persistent bees. Katar will continue that strategy until they reach the western pass. That will slow the enemy's advance and pare their numbers as well."

"Will that be enough?" Drayen asked.

Tahjeen paused, his eyes turning slate gray, revealing regret. "No. We don't have enough warriors to turn back an army that size," he lamented. "We have no choice except to let Dania fall and retake it at a later time. To face the Surmese head on would mean total defeat and the possible extinction of the Shala. I don't intend to let that happen."

Queen Endoreen sighed audibly. "I foresee a tremendous loss

of life in trying to retake Sorbonne's kingdom. Do we know if it's even possible?"

Tahjeen frowned and shook his head. "No," he replied. "But it's the only legitimate alternative and the one thing the enemy is least likely to expect. Their numbers are vast. We must keep them guessing and keep encugh of us alive to be able to defeat them when we finally fight them openly."

Is it possible to co-exist with these Surmese if we are able to regain the other four lands?" Endoreen asked.

Tahjeen shook his head. "There's nothing in their military history that would lead me to believe that."

"Do you really believe in the feasibility of retaking Dania?" Drayen asked.

"We must. It is truly the heart of Sandala with its mineral resources and agricultural riches."

"Why do you think it will be so difficult to convince Sorbonne to evacuate? He seems prepared for the eventuality," Drayen said.

Tahjeen inhaled deeply before he reluctantly uttered the words he had been avoiding. "Because there is more to the plan than simply leaving."

Drayen raised his eyebrows and Tahjeen could see alarm capture his face. "Go on," Drayen said.

"We must eliminate what the Surmese want." Tahjeen began to explain. "Every home and crop must be burned, every productive piece of manufacturing removed or destroyed, and every man, woman and child evacuated. Nothing must be left."

"By the gods!" Endoreen whispered.

Drayen looked at his younger brother then exhaled deeply and sat down.

Tahjeen continued. "If we leave them nothing to live on, they will be forced to bring in supplies in order to survive. Those long lines of food and materials will be vulnerable." He could see Drayen's mind working, analyzing his explanation.

"You plan to attack them and capture what they are bringing in," his brother said.

Tahjeen nodded. "Those replenishments can be used to sustain the refugees and eventually rebuild Dania. Ultimately, the Surmese will have to come out of their stronghold in Danigh, cross the Learing Mountains. and attack us on our terms. If they do not, their numbers will dwindle and they will starve to death inside their conquered city. These walls," Tahjeen said, gesturing around him, "will become their tomb."

Endoreen stood, a solemn look on her face. "Tahjeen, you must explain this to King Sorbonne now. We cannot allow another hour to pass without his understanding what he must do. Drayen and I will come with you to help convince him. His heart must believe in the necessity for him to successfully persuade his people."

Tahjeen bowed, impressed with her ability to understand his overall strategy and battle plan.

Before they went to King Sorbonne's quarters, Tahjeen sought out Cullen. Once he found him, he wasted little time. "Fetch Achates and the rest of my original party. They belong back among the Shala," Tahjeen said.

"Are you spending the night inside the castle?"

"I'm not certain. Queen Endoreen and Drayen are going to help me convince a king to destroy his realm. That may take some time."

Cullen bowed deferentially. Tahjeen had changed since he had seen him last. As a youngster, he had been as carefree as any Shala could, and always deferred to his older brother in matters of leadership. It was correct behavior for one who was not meant to be the king. But now, there was a resident steel in the way he held himself. He radiated authority and strength. Cullen knew that both would be crucial in the coming days.

"So tell me, Aldo, what did they talk about?" the man asked. He had entered Aldo's room by the passageway the youngster had shown him earlier that day.

"I'm sorry, sir," the boy said, yawning. "They were jabbering about invading forces and those funny looking warriors called Shala. It went on for so long that I got sleepy and..." His voice trailed off as he looked up at the man sheepishly.

The man turned away and muttered an oath. With only rulers allowed to attend, it was likely that strategy had been discussed. He had asked the boy to eavesdrop, but this worthless young pup had fallen asleep. Blasted luck!

"That's all right, lad," he said, masking the disgust on his face as he turned back to Aldo. "I will still pay you for your efforts." He placed a tiny ruby in the boy's palm then folded the small fingers over it. "Remember," the man said, "this is our secret."

Aldo nodded, his eyes growing large as he reopened his hand and looked at the beautiful stone. "I'll remember."

"That's a good lad. You go back to sleep now. I'll try to talk to you again tomorrow." The man turned away, hiding his disappointment. He opened the closet and disappeared inside it.

Later, on his way back to camp after a tense and ultimately explosive meeting, Tahjeen reached out with his mind for Paca. He wanted his soothing companionship, to lean against the silky hide and absorb his resiliency. The exchange with King Sorbonne and his son had been draining as well as emotional.

The degree of Roland's anger and frustration surprised him. He left grateful for Sorbonne's wisdom and ability to take the long view. Tahjeen realized that he liked the king of Danigh. It made the sacrifice he would demand of his own people more palatable.

Though the plan for Dania's survival was harsh, it was, they all eventually agreed, the only way. Popular and easily recognizable, Roland would set out for the largest farms and villages with a group of Shala escorts. Through his efforts to spread the word, the people would hopefully be persuaded to organize rapidly.

To Sorbonne fell the task of informing the Danigh citizenry, especially the craftsmen and artisans who would be vital to the rebuilding effort. Wagons had to be loaded with the critical machinery and materials. Families had to select only the most vital necessities, and all of it had to be accomplished quickly. Some of Tahjeen's warriors would assist and speed the process.

Tahjeen and the King decided that the moment a wagon was ready, it would start on its way to the cavern entrance. Tahjeen wasn't naïve He knew it would be a monumental effort, but absolutely necessary to secure Dania's future. Therefore, they would make it work. There was no other choice.

A flash of black bolted out of the bushes nearly knocking him over. "Paca," Tahjeen said, greeting his *fel* with a warm smile and pink, adoring eyes. "I have missed you too."

For a few moments, he clung to the big cat, feeling its strong heart beat against his arms. The rumbling in the animal's chest as he purred washed a welcome wave of calm across Tahjeen's soul. He sighed. Being separated from his twin for so long had been hard. It was like living a life half full, with a heart that frequently skipped a beat. His mind would be working out a problem then run into a mental wall he could not get beyond. Drayen's intelligence was often needed to complete his thoughts, and his brother hadn't been there. Only his *fel* could take up enough of the void and make him feel almost whole. If something happened to the big panther, Tahjeen knew would be lost.

Nothing is going to happen to me, his *fel* said. Tahjeen smiled.

"Come on, my furry friend. Let us see if we can get some sleep tonight."

CHAPTER 23

A CIRCLE OF FRIENDS

King Sorbonne's castle slid from view as Cullen meandered down the twisting cobblestone streets of Danigh. Most shops had closed for the evening and few people were about. Glowing lamps, hanging from posts throughout the city, helped light his way.

It wasn't long before he reached the outskirts of the city and approached the inn where Achates and the rest of Tahjeen's small traveling band were staying. The dimly lit tavern was oddly quiet. Small groups of patrons were scattered around, their heads bent close as they talked in whispers. The rumors of the Surmese invasion must have spread already, Cullen thought. Or perhaps it was the startling appearance of the Shala.

It was easy to spot the young men. They were settled at a table on one side of the tavern. When they first sighted the strange Shala, the locals had given them a wide berth and the tables near them sat empty. It was Achates who saw him first.

"Cullen!" he shouted. "How many years has it been? Look at you, all dressed up like a prim noble!" Achates took Cullen's outstretched hand in a strong grip.

Before Cullen had a chance to respond, Langwyn clapped a big hand on his shoulder as his eyes flashed a mixture of merry colors. "Cullen, you old dog, what have they done to you? There's too many new worry creases on your bald head."

Everyone laughed as the rest of the party moved to welcome him. Hands were shook and backs slapped then he joined them at the table. A bar maid headed their way but Cullen shook his head and waved her off. This was not the time to dally, he mused.

"It's good to see all of you," Cullen said, "though I wish the circumstances were different." The others nodded back soberly.

"Tahjeen sent me," Cullen explained. "We're to return to the

Shala encampment tonight then I'll tell you what I know about recent events."

"I understand you're close to the Danian King," Achates said, finishing off his pint of ale. "What's he like?"

Cullen took his time, thinking about the man he had come to deeply respect. The death of his wife some years earlier had nearly brought him to his knees. The tragedy had driven him to a dark place where he foundered for years. When Cullen first arrived in Dania, the king was just beginning to claw his way out by immersing himself in the work of creating a more progressive realm. "He is fair-minded and intelligent, and receptive to the prophecy. We are fortunate to have him as anally," Cullen finally said, looking into Achates' brown eyes.

"If war comes, can we count on his soldiers to do their share?" Langwyn asked, his eyes turning the opaque rust of expectation.

"We've been training hard," Cullen answered, nodding his head. "They have been my responsibility for a long time now, so yes. They won't disappoint you."

The others at the table smiled, pleased to learn of Cullen's role with the Danian army. Cullen had given everyman at the table bruises when he had resided at the Shala homeland. Training alongside them when they were boys, he had sent them sprawling on more than one occasion. Though he was human, Cullen's prowess with the sword was legendary among the Shala. Any soldier supervised by him would be formidable.

"Settle your bill so we can be on our way," Cullen said. "We need to catch every bit of rest we can." Chairs scraped the tavern's wooden floor as the young men rose and left to gather their belongings. While he waited for their return, Cullen surveyed the clusters of men scattered about the room. Where ever his gaze drifted, heads turned away. No, he thought, the Danians are leery of the alien Shala. Too bad, since the tall warriors bore them no malice, and would no doubt save the lives of some of the men present in the room.

Within a few minutes, and Achates and the rest rejoined Cullen in the tavern's main room. Moments later they headed out the front door and were on their way to the Shala encampment.

A short while later, they walked up to the friendly campfires of the Shala. Though often taciturn, Shala could also be sentimental and it showed now in their delight to see the four warriors who had gone with Tahjeen. They were eager to hear about their encounter with the Surmese. Several examined Morgan's healing wounds. Many of the older warriors were deeply pleased to see Cullen, and it wasn't long before a celebration was underway.

The haunting sound of Shala singing soon filled the night. At first light-hearted and boisterous, the tunes eventually turned somber as the reality of the situation drove away the songs of levity. Family and loved ones were recalled, along with their sober duty. One melody describing the Shala homeland, reminded some that they might never see it again.

Over an hour had passed in this fashion before Tahjeen and Paca walked out of the shadows and joined them. He was equally pleased to be reunited with his four companions, and for a time he shared his news with them. Then one warrior with a rich baritone began the Dance of Death lament. Others joined in with a drum like chant, punctuated at intervals with a footstomp on the ground, followed by a lunge that mimicked the thrust of a spear. When the song finally ended, the night was sober.

Katrine and Toman stood up. "It's time for everyone to get some rest," Katrine said. She watched as Toman indicated who took first watch before she walked over to Tahjeen. "How did it go with the Sandalese?"

"They understand the gravity of their predicament," Tahjeen replied.

Toman joined the small group and Tahjeen invited them to sit down and enjoy the fire. Once they were settled, he told them about his meeting with Sorbonne and his son.

"Can the boy-man be counted on once the fighting starts?" Katrine asked, looking from the dancing flames to Tahjeen's face.

"Cullen has been his mentor so he's more prepared than most," Tahjeen replied.

"Still, he bears watching," Toman interjected with a thoughtful look. His eyes radiated the dull orange of caution. "He's spent his young life waiting for the chance to rule, and now, to willingly give it up, even if he will get it back some day, well..."

His voice drifted off as the rest considered the implication. Tahjeen recalled the *King of the fels'* warning – a trusted ally would betray them. Would Roland be the one? No, he decided.

Roland traveled with Shala escorts now. Betrayal was unlikely to come from such circumstances.

"Still," Katrine said, "a Shala companion for him might be wise."

But Tahjeen shook his head. "He trusts us very little as it is. That would only serve to drive him further away."

The matter settled, the small group became silent, staring into the fire. One by one, they drifted off to bed until only Achates and Tahjeen remained.

Achates watched as Tahjeen stirred the hot, glowing embers. He saw a change in his Shalaen friend though less than a week had passed. He wondered if the responsibility of leading the Shala army was the cause, or if the maturity had been there all along, lying dormant beneath a youth filled with wild abandon. Being the younger brother of the Shala heir did have its perks, one being the luxury of growing up slowly, and occasionally skipping lessons on diplomacy and other affairs of state.

He had known Tahjeen over four years, watching him emerge from his teens as a finely chiseled young adult. His toughness was legendary as was his love of adventure and his quick, analytical mind. While a few thought Tahjeen arrogant and easy to anger, Achates knew better. Tahjeen drove himself mercilessly, and over time the training turned him into a warrior whose fighting skill was second to none. It was not arrogance but complete confidence that no one could defeat him because he had sacrificed and trained harder than anyone else.

Achates understood that Tahjeen's anger was only with those who behaved with stupidity. Stupidity, not ignorance, for he had all the time in the world to help someone learn who lacked knowledge or expertise, if they had the desire. Younger Shala warriors loved following him, hoping for lessons on any kind. A natural teacher, Tahjeen knew when to praise, when to correct, when to push and when to call someone out for lack of effort. And even when anger threatened to derail him, he worked hard to control those emotions.

Achates also wondered what had transpired while he was alone with Ariann. He smiled at the thought of being challenged by that inquisitive and independent young woman.

Tahjeen looked up from the mesmerizing flames, his colorful eyes changing like a prism from white to yellow to green, before settling into the warmth of a brilliant blue reserved for friends.

Achates drew himself closer to the fire's warmth. "I have a question," he said, "a serious one actually."

Tahjeen smiled. "And from such a serious fellow."

Achates smiled back. "I was wondering how you got on with Ariann?"

The blue in Tahjeen's eyes changed quickly into a kaleidoscope of colors. "Ah, I forgot," Tahjeen said. "You have not heard."

Achates' mouth dropped open in astonishment as the flashing display of colors told him what Tahjeen had not yet put into words.

Tahjeen grinned and nodded. "Yes, my friend. She is the one."

Before Achates could find his voice, Langwyn arrived, striding into camp with his sleek Seepah by his side. "Ah, a nice warm fire."

Langwyn settled himself. He watched, bemused when Seepah and Paca greeted one another with rough tongues and then began to groom each other.

"Where are the others?" Tahjeen asked.

"Morgan and Palance are on watch and Duhron is bringing dinner. Chai scented a wild boar and the two gave chase. He asked me to make sure the spit was ready." He smiled as he relayed the message, his eyes glowing lime green with humor.

Achates stood up. "I will check on Morgan and Palance. We will finish this discussion later." The look he gave Tahjeen implied that he wanted to hear all the details.

Langwyn called after him. "Tell them the cats will replace them as soon as they feed." Achates nodded then disappeared in the darkness, though had they wanted, Shalaen eyes could watch the glow of heat that his body gave off until he was nearly a mile away.

Seepah and Paca both got up and walked over to their masters. Tahjeen smiled at the big beasts then shifted his gaze to Langwyn. "I believe it is customary that the one who mentions 'food' is also privileged to do the feeding."

Langwyn grumbled, but rose and went to a heavily wrapped cache. Reaching inside the waterproof cloth, he pulled out two haunches of dried meat and tossed one to each cat. The huge beasts wasted no time devouring their meal.

"I am missing home already," Langwyn said as he crouched

back down by the fire. "And now with the invasions, it may be a long time before I see it again."

"You just miss Apoleen," Tahjeen said referring to the Shala maiden Langwyn courted.

"Yes, I do. But I also miss our crater, the food, and the absence of biting insects," he said as he slapped his forearm. A rumbling stomach shifted his focus. "I hope Duhron gets back before too long. I am hungry."

"You are always hungry," Tahjeen replied.

Langwyn looked across the fire at his friend. Tahjeen seemed subdued, as if his mind was elsewhere. "Something vexes you."

Tahjeen took a deep breath then sighed heavily. "The weight of responsibility is always heavy." The recent conversation with King Sorbonne and Prince Roland plagued him. It was a lot to ask - to flee the capital and destroy their land. And Katar's losses at the western shore would be staggering. Even if his plan worked, it would still be very hard for Dania's leaders to find it in their hearts to thank him.

"I am worried about Katar," Tahjeen finally said. "Very worried." He stared hard at the fire, as if a solution was somehow hidden in the flames.

"Katar is a brilliant leader and highly capable warrior. I doubt anyone could beat him in hand to hand combat, except you," Langwyn reassured him. "He will be all right."

But Tahjeen shook his head. "He faces terrible odds. An armada carrying a hundred thousand soldiers will land on the shores that Katar guards. Even Shala have limits."

Langwyn did not reply. He was reeling at the scene Tahjeen described. One hundred thousand men against five thousand Shala? No wonder Tahjeen was so gloomy. What would Katar do? What could he do? He felt a coldness invade his heart.

CHAPTER 24

ASSASSIN

It was a short night for everyone, dawn coming as it always did, early and unrepentant. This time Tahjeen entered the main gates of the city. Though the guards had been forewarned, they still drew back at the sight of him. No doubt the presence of his *fel* had something to do with their reaction. Not knowing when he would be returning to his camp, Tahjeen had elected to bring Paca along. Achates accompanied him as well.

Entering the wide hallway leading to the Great Room, Tahjeen made his way directly to Roland whose eyes widened upon seeing the huge animal. "Meet the other half of the Shala army," Tahjeen said.

Roland acknowledged the tall warrior with a curt nod. "I would not want to face him on any battlefield."

"Nor will the Surmese," Tahjeen answered. "There are a dozen Shala just outside the main gates to escort you. Cullen is among them. Perhaps his presence will help convince some reluctant citizens."

For a long moment Roland stared hard at Tahjeen. Seconds bloated as tension filled the air before he finally replied. "I'm ready to leave as soon as I get my horse."

Tahjeen nodded. "Good luck. Cullen will explain how you can contact me if it proves necessary." Roland bowed slightly then took his leave.

Tahjeen watched the young man depart. He shook his head. Perhaps Toman was right about Roland but he couldn't proceed with any enthusiasm if he mistrusted every single ally. He took a deep breath then moved headed towards the Great Room.

As he entered, he noted that all the rulers and their assistants were present. Most were startled at the sight of Paca. Several mouths dropped open, and a few others turned, speaking quickly to the person next to them.

The sheer number of people in the room shook Tahjeen. Doubt assailed him once again. There were too many people which meant too many possibilities for treachery. His mood darkened. He wondered if all generals were plagued by this much suspicion.

King Sorbonne interrupted his thoughts. He opened the morning session by asking Tahjeen to review the essentials of what had transpired in their late night meeting held only hours ago. Tahjeen obliged and when he finished, everyone at the table was silent. To willingly lay waste to your own kingdom was nearly impossible to contemplate. After a long pause, Baldor spoke.

"What of our plans regarding Gleneden and Palaton?"

Tahjeen did not hesitate. "I command two *koshes* of five thousand. One will accompany you. Their commander is Katrine. She has been fully briefed."

"She? A woman?" His incredulity was obvious as his eyebrows nearly disappeared into his hairline.

Tahjeen regarded him strangely then took the measure of the rest of the people around him. None of them grasped what a Shala warrior brought to a battle. Reaching a decision, he turned to the big cat. *Come Paca,* and in seconds the animal stood and walked toward him.

Over nine feet from his nose to the tip of his tail, each paw as big as a dinner plate, and jaws that could rip a man's head off, the animal was terrifying seen so close up. While the rest shifted uncomfortably, doubt still lingered on Baldor's face.

Tahjeen turned to King Sorbonne. "Could someone fetch a side of beef?"

Sorbonne was surprised, but quickly issued the order. Tahjeen paced in front of the large map of Sandala while the others, trying to be patient, began talking quickly to one another. Finally, two servants came in with the carcass. Tahjeen directed them to put it down in a far corner nearly thirty feet away. Paca watched with curiosity until Tahjeen turned to him and made a fist. The panther growled and lowered himself. His back legs bunched and the muscles rippled along his dark form as he gathered himself to spring. Abruptly, Tahjeen swept his hand toward the beef and the cat leaped. Covering the distance in the air, Paca landed on top of the carcass, jarring the table where everyone sat. Using his sharp claws and teeth he began tearing the beef apart. Pieces of carcass flew around the room. Everyone was stunned.

Tahjeen watched briefly then turned to Baldor. "Many of our warriors are women. Half are cats like Paca. All of them," he paused for effect, "are Shala."

Baldor swallowed then nodded.

Tahjeen began the briefing. As he talked, heads swiveled at the occasional sound of crunching bones as the cat ate his fill. The *fel* looked back at the humans, raw meat hanging from his jaws. If the big cat could generate an expression, he almost looked amused.

At the long table, one of the assistants watched the frightening beast swallow. He knew that somehow, someway, he needed to get another pigeon off to his Commander General. They had underestimated the prowess of the Shala, but more important, laying waste to the kingdom of Dania could ruin all their plans. He turned to Baldor, whispered something in his earthen stood up.

The room was suddenly filled with the panther's angry roar. *Traitor* the animal said. Tahjeen spun around, saw Paca start to rise then noted the assistant backing away from the table.

"There is an enemy among us," Tahjeen declared, pointing and starting for the man. But before he reached him, the assistant yelled, "now!"

It happened too fast. No one could react in time as a guard posted near the table and standing directly behind Drayen lunged forward with his sword. Still distracted by Tahjeen's action, Drayen did not realize his peril. With all his weight behind the thrust, the guard drove the sword completely through the unsuspecting Drayen. A second later, Paca was on the assassin, his jaws closing on his throat while his hind legs eviscerated the man.

Queen Endoreen screamed. Beside her, Tahjeen staggered then shoved the traitor away roughly. Moments later Achates raced into the room with a half dozen palace guards.

Drayen was still sitting, a startled look on his rapidly paling face. He glanced down at the sword protruding from his lower chest. He raised his head slowly then reached out towards Endoreen and she took his hand. His mouth formed words but no sound passed his lips. She watched, tears streaming down her cheeks, as the colors in his eyes begin to fade until all that remained was a milky white.

Across the room Tahjeen cried out then collapsed in agony. Paca dropped the grisly mess of the guard's remains, and ran to his master. He nudged him once with his bloody forehead, mewing softly. Satisfied that Tahjeen was breathing, the huge animal turned and began to stalk the traitor.

There was no time to run, but still the traitor tried. He had taken only two steps when Paca caught him and with one swipe of his claws, tore his arm off at the shoulder. Before Paca did any further damage, Achates ordered him to stop. He wanted this man alive, at least long enough to interrogate him. Achates went to Tahjeen.

The younger brother, now Shala's sole heir, was very pale. His breathing was labored. Among his kind, if a twin's sibling dies before the former has wed and formed the chemical union with his mate, he would die as well. The bond formed in the womb was intricate and mutually dependent. It was the strongest blood tie there was among the Shala. Achates knew that Tahjeen's death was only a matter of hours unless something was done quickly. He looked up, his eyes seeking and finding King Darvus.

"Find Ariann," Achates said to him. "Bring her here now!"

Tahjeen was laid gently on a bed in one of King Sorbonne's private rooms. Everyone left, leaving Achates alone with Ariann. She was stunned by the turn of events. He walked over to her then guided her to a seat and knelt before her.

"I have sent for some of the Shala to guard this room, and for one of the women to instruct you in what you must do, "he said.

She was bewildered and uncomprehending. "I do not understand."

Achates took a deep breath then explained as best he could. As he spoke, her eyes grew wide, tears forming then spilling down her face. "He will die?" She was incredulous.

"Yes, and quite possibly all of Sandala with him. Ariann," he went on, "you must do this." As if to add emphasis Paca padded over to her, and pushed against her with his large head.

Achates watched the exchange. "Even Paca knows what must be done."

In the outer hallway King Darvus was beyond furious. "I understand what you are saying!" he bellowed. "I am not an idiot. But this cannot be allowed. It is...it is indecent! The Shala may be important to us but they are not human. It would be an abomination, an unholy union defying all the gods in existence!"

His faced was blotched with red as he sputtered and gesticulated. Katrine let him rant. Nothing in Sandala would prevent the union from taking place no matter how vociferously Darvus argued. If necessary, all ten thousand of the nearby Shala would march through the city's front gates to put an end to any interference. Standing next to Devon, King Sorbonne caught her attention, inviting Katrine to join them by the far window.

"Do you want me to have him restrained?" Sorbonne asked.

Katrine shook her head. "Let him occupy himself with his own tongue, Sire. In the meantime, the Shala act. Ariann is willing and being prepared as we speak."

King Sorbonne's features revealed the depth of his worry. "This alliance between us is fragile. Baldor's loyalty is still in question and the Shala are temporarily leaderless. It could all fall apart."

"There are two things we can do to prevent that," Katrine said, "and the one involving Ariann is already underway. Let us deal with the other now and interview the traitor before he dies from his wounds. Then," Katrine explained, "We will know where Baldor stands."

King Sorbonne looked at Devon and after the latter nodded his assent, all three headed back into the Great Hall.

As they approached the heavily guarded room, Katrine signaled to Toman. When informed of Drayen's assassination, she knew instantly what could happen to Tahjeen and was more than relieved that Ariann had already been called. She moved quickly to protect the surviving heir to the Shala throne. A dozen Shala warriors along with their ferocious cats guarded the room where he rested.

"Lock the castle down," Katrine ordered. No one is allowed in or out without your permission. No one!" Toman nodded curtly then hurried away.

The remaining leaders and their assistants remained in the Great Hall. They were still reeling. Queen Endoreen wept quietly as aides tried to comfort her. Baldor paced, nervous and visibly shaken. The assistants look frightened. To one side, the injured traitor lay between two menacing Shala. Though they had stopped the flow of blood from his severe wound, they had done nothing to ease his pain.

Katrine, Sorbonne and Devon approached him. Before either the King or Katrine could move to interrogate him, Devon interceded. "Would you allow me?" he asked.

Clearly, he meant to do it. Katrine's eyes flashed purple, her eyebrows raised. She waved him forward.

Devon stationed himself by the traitor's side. "Who ordered this done?" he asked.

Despite the pain, the man smirked. "King Baldor, obviously."

King Baldor charged the man. "That is a lie! I would never..."

Devon put his hand up, cutting him off. He turned back to the injured man then drew his knife. The others watched in fascination as he moved the tip toward the terrified man's eye.

"I will ask you one more time. Who ordered this done?"

"I already told you!"

Devon did not hesitate. He pushed the blade a half inch into the man's eye. He screamed in agony as Devon withdrew the knife. The man's breath came in short, ragged gasps. He begged, "Please stop. I will tell you what you want to know."

Devon moved the knife to within an inch of the good eye. "I'm waiting."

The man gathered himself then shouted, "I do the bidding of the greatest ruler on earth; bless his name, High Lord Klaron, Emperor of the Surmese!"

Briefly, Devon studied the man then drove his blade through the other eye and all the way into the brain, killing him. He wiped his knife off and stood up. "There was nothing more he was going to tell us," Devon said, his words ending the matter. There were shocked faces all around from the traitor's execution but Katrine smiled and nodded her approval.

Devon walked over to Baldor. The man stared back at him, unafraid. "I tell you truly, I had nothing..."

Devon spoke, forestalling additional words. "I know. "Then he looked towards King Sorbonne. "Your Majesty, do you recognize the guard?" He pointed to the bloody, tangled mess that Paca had made of him.

The King went over to the dead man, whose head, at least, was still in one piece. He removed the helmet that hid his face. "I have never seen him before."

"We will no doubt find the body of the real guard someplace on the palace grounds," Katrine offered.

"Maybe not," Devon said. "These Surmese are very careful."

Baldor approached them, tentative. "That assistant had been in my employ for nearly two years. He came from Sealand, highly recommended by King Dawad."

"So, Dawad's treachery is even more extensive that we first thought," King Sorbonne commented.

"He will pay in time," Devon remarked bluntly.

Baldor looked at Devon quizzically. "How did you know that I was duped?"

Devon offered a wry smile. "Your thoughts are an open book, my Lord. It's not in your nature to be duplicitous."

Baldor looked surprised as he considered Devon's words then he turned to Sorbonne. "What will happen to our plans now?" Baldor asked. But Katrine answered instead.

"As promised, you will leave within the hour with my *kosh*. Some things have changed," she said, looking around the hall, "and some have not." She walked out of the room, heading in the direction of the chamber where Tahjeen rested. Devon excused himself then followed after her.

King Sorbonne followed Katrine with his eyes. "You have lost a general, but not your leaders."

"If all goes well, the 'general' will be back tomorrow," Achates said as he entered the room." He would expect everything to proceed as planned. Shala walk in each other's footsteps all the time. Katrine will replace him, as Tahjeen has replaced Drayen as our future King. You forget that they have but one purpose, my Lord, to save the people of Sandala."

"I had not forgotten," Sorbonne said, "I just…" his voice trailing off because he could think of no adequate words to describe the Shala.

CHAPTER 25

THE RITES OF UNION

Juna was almost finished explaining. It had been difficult at first, for one as inexperienced as Ariann, to listen to the intimate details of the Shala Union Rites, but with so much at stake, she forced herself to ignore the embarrassment and her own ignorance. There was no time for frivolities. Instead, she concentrated, clinging to Juna's words, forming images in her mind in accord with the older woman's description.

Sexually, Shala men and women were not identical to humans. Functionally, the act still worked but there had to be some accommodations, as Juna was now relating. Ariann knew she was blushing deeply.

"We will wake him with this potion, but then you must act quickly and gain his complete attention. His will is very weak because of his brother's death. He could easily lapse back into unconsciousness and you must not let that happen. The rest is as I described. Now disrobe."

Ariann did as she was told. She felt as she looked, completely naked and vulnerable. She blocked out the presence of the Shala women in the room, focusing instead on Tahjeen and saving his life. Then she recalled the earlier visions she had of the two of them together, of their child, of wearing crowns, and she was suddenly calmed by the realization that this was meant to be. She did not resist when two women guided her to Tahjeen's bed where Juna was administering the potion.

"Remember," she heard Juna remind her, "Once joined, you will remain so for several hours."

She was lost in the color of his eyes — ever changing hues swirled in mesmerizing patterns that held her fast. She could feel him drawing strength from her, as he wound himself tighter and closer in their embrace. As the minutes slipped by, she felt herself changing deep within. It was as if they could see inside each other, watching as one part of her personality met and conquered something in his then a portion of his brought about a similar reaction in her. Sometimes segments met and united, neither one dominating, but blending into something more complimentary and powerful.

Then she was inside his mind and emotion drowned her senses as she saw how truly beautiful he was. She journeyed through his memories reliving parts of his life, gaining knowledge in the exchange. She felt his pain, his deep sense of loss brought about by his brother's death. He was drowning in it, nearly devastated. Tahjeen reached for her, desperate, needing a lifeline in order to survive. She reached back.

Now she knew him, really knew him. And he knew her. She could not imagine a greater closeness between two beings. They were now a part of one another and both were morphing into something different, stronger, better. Suddenly, deep within him, she felt a humming begin. It increased in strength, becoming a vibration that played along both their bodies until in a rush he was coursing through her, flooding her veins, swallowing her with his eyes, and sharing an ecstasy she had not thought possible.

Shortly after sun-up, the meeting started. During the long night, Toman had received news from Katar, and everyone was anxious to hear the details. Toman was starting to speak when Ariann and Tahjeen walked into the room.

She glowed. Her long blond hair, once straight and rather plain, was now lustrous, cascading down her back in soft waves. She also seemed taller, more regal. Her face was flushed with energy and life. Her father stared in astonishment. Tahjeen walked by her right side and Paca on her left.

He was more robust, his muscles larger and rippling with every stride. The sharpness in his rugged face was gone, replaced by a serene, gentle countenance. Still, sadness tugged at his features for all to see. His once wild white blond hair was now a mirror of Ariann's. Everything about Tahjeen projected power and authority. Then he spoke, his voice richer and deeper, resonating in the Great Hall. "Please, Toman, continue."

Places were quickly made for them at the table, thoughtfully distant from where Drayen had sat. For a long moment, Toman could only stare, spellbound, but then he found his voice once again.

"It is as you foretold. A large Surmese armada waits off the western coast. Judging by the number of ships, Katar estimates a force similar in size to the one that landed at Seadawn."

King Sorbonne asked why they had not landed, and Toman smiled wryly. "Katar had hundreds of fires set along the coastline. The fleet arrived during the night, no doubt saw the fires, and presumed a large a force awaited them."

"They will land," Tahjeen announced. "They may wait a day…perhaps two…then they will begin their march on Danigh."

Directing his gaze at Toman, Tahjeen told him to contact Katar again that night. "Tell him to delay the enemy as best he can with minimum risk to Shala. I want as many of his *kosh* alive as possible. Have him send some of his forces on ahead, burning crops along the way," Tahjeen shifted his attention to King Sorbonne.

"Your Majesty," Tahjeen said, looking him in the eye. The King appeared stunned. The armada's arrival on the western coast was now a reality and had shaken him to the core. "You must begin the evacuation of your city now! Those who travel light should assemble by the city gates at noon. Shala will escort your people to the cavern."

The King stood, glad to finally take some definitive action though he had never dreamed it would be like this. "My scribes have already gathered the most essential documents. I will personally contact the major artisans and craftsmen and they can help spread the word."

"Some Shala will join your Palace Guard in escorting you." When King Sorbonne hesitated, Tahjeen explained. "The Surmese may have other assassins. Only one would be unusual."

Sorbonne nodded, but sadness covered his face. He walked over to the new Shala heir, reached up and placed a firm hand on the tall man's shoulder. His face became steely as he squeezed firmly then excused himself and left to begin his difficult task.

Tahjeen turned to Ariann and nodded slightly. She shared a brief, intimate smile with him then turned towards Queen Endoreen. "Your Highness," she began, "tonight we will contact Gable and tell him of the change in tactics that involve the retaking of Gleneden. Do you want the Shala to escort you to your capital, or would you rather travel with us to the Shala homeland?"

The Queen found Ariann's low voice soothing. She was aware that it was deliberately projected that way, but found it comforting regardless. It did little though to salve the pain of Drayen's death. Much that she had gained in the initial union on their wedding night was lost. Endoreen was a hollow echo of the past, diminished, a paper-thin remnant of what she was just one day ago. But she was still astute and understood what was behind the question.

Choosing to retreat to the island home of Tahjeen and his people, would be retiring from life, and becoming a recluse, though no one would hold it against her. If Endoreen went to Gleneden, she would be telling Tahjeen and Ariann that she felt capable of leading her people in their fight against the Surmese. The thought of peaceful solitude was compelling and seductive.

Sitting up straighter, Queen Endoreen looked across at Tahjeen and Ariann. Mustering courage, she told him, "I was the Queen of Gleneden before I knew Drayen. I am still that person. I belong with my people." She paused, briefly looking away, then continued. "Perhaps after this war is over, I will still be welcome in my husband's homeland?"

"You will always have ground to claim there. It is your right and our privilege," Tahjeen said, humbled by her strength and self-sacrifice. It would have been easy to give in to grief. That she chose not to was admirable.

Queen Endoreen rose. "I will go now and have my assistants begin preparations for the journey."

Tahjeen and Ariann both stood and bowed as she took her leave, watching the sad and elegant monarch for a few moments before they turned their attention to King Darvus, the only ruler remaining.

"Sire," Tahjeen said," I mentioned two days ago that there was a matter we needed to discuss."

"Yes, I recall. I assume you were going to ask my permission to wed my daughter."

"No," Tahjeen said simply. "I was going to tell you that events revealed that Ariann and I were destined to be mates, but that the choice was hers."

King Darvus reddened as he fought to control his anger. "In our world, the father is the one who decides."

"In your kingdom, that is true. But among the Shala, it's the woman who makes the decision," Tahjeen replied. His voice was calm yet the strength behind it was intimidating.

Darvus looked at his daughter. "I take it you agreed?"

Ariann looked back at him with a serene confidence that he found unsettling. There was no dispute that whatever had transpired between her and Tahjeen had changed her irrevocably. "Yes, father. I did."

Darvus glared back at her, wanting to rant but held back by her demeanor. She was no longer the quiet, meek girl he once knew. Where Leona had been the outgoing daughter, the one who took charge and whose laughter shook the draperies in the royal hall, Ariann had been bookish and introspective. There had always been an elusive quality about her that made him uncomfortable. The young woman who sat in front of him now radiated confidence. He shook his head.

"What's done is done," he said, waving his hand in the attempt to end the discussion.

"There is a favor I have to ask," Tahjeen said.

"There will be no dowry!" Darvus bellowed, his shoulders straightened in outrage.

"None is required," Tahjeen replied, his eyes momentarily blazing cardinal red before he went on. "We need your leadership to help organize events at the cavern entrance. With so many people and possessions, it has become dangerously chaotic. Would you be willing?"

Tahjeen's request was a result of Ariann's advice. Her father was a man who needed to feel valued, and he was a good organizer. This could go a long way in smoothing the rough patch between them.

"Why, yes. Yes! I will do that," Darvus said, surprised, but obviously pleased.

Tahjeen thanked him and bowed deferentially. "Can you leave before noon? Several Shala will guide you."

Darvus stood up. "Of course. I will be ready shortly. "He excused himself and left quickly, filled with purpose.

Tahjeen watched him leave then felt Toman's gaze. He looked at his lieutenant. "What is it?"

Toman sighed and shook his head. "I am glad I do not have your responsibilities. I detest such political gamesmanship."

Tahjeen shrugged. "Tonight Gable must be told of the change in plans and that Katrine is on her way to Palaton."

Toman nodded. "Yes, my Prince. What else must be done?"

For a moment Tahjeen was surprised and a bit shaken by the formal address, but he continued. "Send some of your *kosh* to join Katar's forces to defend the western pass. The remainder will guide people to the cavern."

Toman paused. Tahjeen saw his hesitancy and knew something was weighing on him. "Speak your mind, Toman."

"Must the cavern entrance be destroyed? The possibility bothers me. I know the Surmese might stumble across it with so many people making their way there, but losing a major route to our homeland might cost us heavily in the future."

Tahjeen paused, taking in the unhappy look on Toman's face, imagining the all too obvious trail that several thousand people and hundreds of wagons would leave.

"Be ready to destroy the entrance, but not the entire tunnel. With counter attacks occurring in Palaton and Gleneden, it is doubtful they will be able to spare the men to dig it out." Ariann reached across and laid a hand on Tahjeen's arm, garnering his attention. He looked at her, inquisitively.

As was her usual practice, she was busy contemplating contingencies while the two men talked. She was unused to having her opinion sought, but Tahjeen smiled, his eyes a warm, deep hue of lavender, providing the encouragement she needed.

"Prepare a series of collapsible sites," she said. "Leave only enough warriors behind to trigger them if it proves necessary. Even if the Surmese dig through the first blockage, a second will frustrate them and another will make them realize it is fruitless," Ariann concluded.

Toman smiled. The more he saw of Ariann, the more he liked her. "A wise suggestion, my Lady. I will have some warriors start on it at once."

Tahjeen and Ariann watched him go, their eyes sweeping the empty chamber.

"A good start, my love," Ariann said, turning her gaze to him.

Tahjeen nodded, pleased that it had gone well, but knowing that the harder part lay ahead. And for him, a most difficult task to be sure, for tonight he needed to contact the Queen Mother and tell her of Drayen's death.

His face betrayed him to the observant Ariann. She reached out for him, touching his arm, silently seeking an explanation. Tahjeen sighed then covered her hand with his own. When he looked at her, his eyes were tree-bark brown with grief. "Just remembering that tonight I must tell my mother."

Pausing, Tahjeen looked away, recalling the previous day's events, and his failure to sense Drayen's danger in time. "I cannot believe he is gone."

"I wish I'd had the chance to know him," Ariann said.

Tahjeen nodded. "You would have liked him a great deal. We were very different. He would have made an excellent king." Tahjeen closed his eyes, willing the grief to ease its hold on him.

"As will you," she insisted, caressing his arm. "Have you noticed the deep respect Toman displays in your presence? And the other rulers are truly inspired when you talk with them."

"They did the same for Drayen," he said quietly, looking down at the table.

"No, Tahjeen. They did not. They liked and respected him, but you they hold in awe."

He looked at her once again, the brown gradually fading into a rich pink. "If what you say is true, it's because of you. You not only saved my life, you also gave me parts of yourself that have made me a better Shala. Perhaps that's what they see in me now."

She smiled back at him, shaking her head. "No, Tahjeen. I saw it from the beginning - first with Achates, then Toman and Katrine then Devon and now with all the royals, even my own father. You command attention without trying and obedience without insisting. You are the leader your mother envisioned."

He smiled back at her then grew serious once again. "The Queen Mother will take it very hard."

CHAPTER 26

PALATON

Devon Longstreet stole a glance at King Baldor as both men stopped to switch to a third horse. Keeping a fresh mount was the only way they could keep up with the Shala. Baldor's face showed signs of strain but Devon guessed it was caused more by concern for his kingdom's fate than the grueling ride.

Devon saw Katrine approaching and smiled, recalling her earlier reaction when he had asked to go along when her *kosh* left for Palaton. "Why? Your interests are in Dania," she had answered.

"My loyalty is to King Sorbonne," Devon had replied. "My interest is in you."

She had been taken aback; at least that's what he thought the rainbow of colors dancing across her eyes indicated. Her answer had been a sharp nod before she rushed off. He didn't hesitate but raced after her.

Once back at the Shala encampment, Devon had watched Katrine give the initial orders. Her five thousand warriors had formed ranks quickly. The *fels* and their Shala counterparts divided into separate groups. Once they set off, Katrine had run alongside him, explaining that the *kosh* was further subdivided so a few terse orders could send groups racing off to different tasks.

It was also apparent to him that while all carried the same weapons, each group took additional specific items. Some carried extra water, while others had bundles of replacement arrows. One group had heavy food packs strapped to their back. Devon saw some laden with unlit torches and another with extra spears. A final group held the reins of extra horses as they ran.

The previous morning, they had raced through the eastern pass then flooded down into the foothills. Both small and large streams were crossed efficiently. With indifference, the Shala warriors charged through thick underbrush, pushing small trees and heavy bushes aside. Nothing seemed to slow them.

Rests were infrequent and brief. Each time they stopped, a warrior brought Baldor and himself fresh horses and gave them a few swallows of water. By late afternoon his backside was aching from the constant pounding atop the saddle.

By the end of the first day, they had passed through the mountains and were headed across the lowlands towards Palaton's western border. Near sunset, an advanced scout had returned with a sighting of the Surmese army less than a day's ride ahead. Katrine gave the order to alter course. It would cost them time, but it would avoid the risk of discovery. To be successful in defeating the enemy inside Palaton's borders, the element of surprise was vital.

Even when the sun dropped below the horizon and night was descending swiftly, the Shala's keen vision allowed them to continue on. Devon realized they would camp close to Palaton's border. He was surprised when Katrine ran back and announced that they were stopping, but he didn't argue. She knew their limits far better than he.

A Shala warrior took his horse after he dismounted, leaving him free to exercise his stiffened limbs. Walking around the area, he was again impressed at how quickly they established their camp, deployed their sentries and served food and water. Devon took pride in his prowess as a sentinel, but there was much he could learn from the efficient Shala.

They were now situated in a heavily forested area, not far from a stream. As yet, no fires had been started to ward of the evening's cold. Devon paused to watch as hundreds of Shala disappeared into the trees. Looking around, he realized that if strangers stumbled upon them they would have no idea that there were twenty five hundred warriors and a similar number of huge cats in the vicinity.

He saw a young warrior carrying a small torch approach Baldor and went over to join them. "Sire," the warriorsaid to the king, "*kosh* leader Katrine requests your presence."

Devon and Baldor were led across the clearing towards a group of boulders tucked beneath a rugged cliff. Katrine was sitting with several of her lieutenants around a small fire. Their big cats lolled nearby, feasting on something no longer recognizable. Devon's thoughts flashed back to the grisly display of

Tahjeen's panther less than forty eight hours ago. The memory was unsettling so he pushed the image from his mind.

"Your Highness," Katrine said to Baldor, "we've stopped early to rest for battle and to discuss strategy." She beckoned for Baldor to sit next to her and ignored Devon, but another Shala brought food and two cloaks to further ward off the night's chill. She might be ignoring him but she obviously expected him to be there. He sat down, pleased but trying to not let it show.

"Later tonight," Katrine continued, "we will send advance teams ahead. Can you tell us, Sire, how the border will be defended?"

Baldor shook his head. "Because of the invasion, it's difficult to tell. We had garrisons stationed at the main bridges, but some may have been called away to fight, or worse."

"Can we cross it elsewhere?" Katrine asked, looking pensive.

"Of course. But the Tanon River runs along the entire western border." Baldor's swept his hand in a wide gesture. "It's wide and the current is treacherous. We can only access it with boats."

Katrine nodded, thinking. "How many bridge crossings are there?" she eventually asked.

"Three," Baldor answered then picked up a short stick and began to draw a crude map in the dirt. He marked where they were then placed one pebble by a secondary crossing at a smaller town and another at the major crossing.

"This is Pandor, which we presume will be heavily guarded. Further south is the last crossing," Baldor concluded, as he added another stone, "but it's another day away."

"Then we'll head for the smaller town further north," Katrine said without hesitation. "We'll assume the Surmese presently hold it so we'll have to fight our way across." She then told Hadel, one of her lieutenants, a well-built man in his mid-twenties, to lead the advance group and scout the area.

"One more thing," Baldor said, interrupting. Katrine paused and looked back at him.

"There should be boats on both sides of the river. People often choose to ferry across that way rather than pay the bridge toll," Baldor said.

"Unless the Surmese have taken them to the far side and have them under guard," Katrine commented. She looked back at Hadel. "Find this out as well."

Hadel and his tawny mountain lion left but two other lieutenants remained. One, Isador, went to her pack and retrieved a long roll of leather, which she then spread out close to the fire's dim light. A detailed map of Palaton was revealed.

"Now Your Majesty," Katrine said, looking at Baldor expectantly, "please describe the general layout of your capital and tell us of your city's fortifications."

Baldor didn't hesitate. "Some forty years ago my grandfather rebuilt the castle. He was a skilled and creative engineer, a man ahead of his time. A maze was fashioned within the city to baffle invaders. He also had wide streets narrowing at strategic points so an attacking army could only pass through two at a time." Baldor pointed to a large open area in the middle of the city. "Hidden behind public food marts are sliding walls that give the farmers access for their wide wagons. They were common knowledge among the local citizens, but never open during daylight hours, lessening the chance that spying eyes might discover them."

As Baldor continued his explanation, Katrine nodded to herself, a smile starting to tug at the corners of her mouth. Devon observed all of this, studying the city map as closely as Katrine. Palaton's military readiness was impressive. He hoped it would be enough.

Katrine awakened them an hour before dawn. The Shala were up and ready to begin the run to the northern bridge. Devon saw Hadel standing in the background and went over to him. "What did you find?" he asked the taciturn young man.

"No boats," he said, "and a small scouting party that we easily avoided. The Surmese have about a thousand soldiers on the other side, guarding the bridge."

Devon nodded then looked expectantly at Katrine who had been listening to the exchange. She was idly stroking tieback of her huge *fel*.

"Are you always so inquisitive Devon Longstreet?" she asked.

"I never presume there is nothing left to learn," Devon replied.

For a time she studied him through translucent eyes then she bent to gather her weapons. "We are ready," she announced a moment later. "Please mount your horse."

With the scout team somewhere ahead, the main body moved steadily without fear of discovery. Several hours later after they had stopped for a light meal, Katrine came over to where he and King Baldor were sitting.

"Later tonight, Sire, two groups will swim across the river and eliminate the bridge watch. Once secure, the rest of us will move quietly across the bridge. We'll surround the enemy camp and use stealth and surprise to eliminate them. All the cats save mine will be kept back so none of the Surmese animals raise the alarm."

"But the river current is treacherous, impossible to swim," Baldor said, his face registering a mix of concern and confusion.

Katrine smiled and shook her head. She was surprised by how he continued to underestimate them. "Hadel's group swam across earlier, Sire," she commented wryly.

The stunned expression on Baldor's face spoke volumes.

Several minutes later, they moved out to travel the remaining miles to the forest on the near side of the bridge. The sun was approaching its zenith, its heat waves blurring the land ahead of them. Baldor and Devon removed their heavy cloaks, but the Shala continued running, indifferent to the broiling sun. Devon noticed the sweat staining their leather tunics, as stains began spreading down the fronts and backs. At least they're human, Devon thought then was startled by the sudden realization that no, indeed, they were not.

Two hours later, they arrived at their destination.

CHAPTER 27

A QUEEN'S GUILT

All across their island home, the Shala began mourning as news of Drayen's death spread. He had been beloved and respected – a serious, humble and kind young man.

For Queen Mardra, the only good news in Tahjeen's message was his own salvation thanks to Achates' quick thinking and the presence of a woman named Ariann. She wondered how the union had changed her one remaining son and what this human woman was like.

Now, alone in her private chambers, the Queen was filled with grief and self-recrimination. She should have known the prophecy could not be changed. Guilt haunted her as she recalled that fateful day when the High Priest and Priestess had first revealed the second half of the Prophecy to her:

Ever vigilant, the watchers watch.
The five lands grows richer, prosperity abounds.
Rulers live and die, humans laugh and cry.
Ever vigilant, the watchers watch.

Ever vigilant, the watchers watch.
The sun turns water into dust.
Rich green land becomes dry sand.
Then rains come and torrents fall.
Men rejoice, and raise their voice.
Still vigilant, the watchers watch.

Ever vigilant, the watchers watch.
Twins are born to a Shala Queen.
One will die before he's King,
the other gets the golden ring.
Fair-skinned strangers on the prowl,

Ever vigilant, the watchers run.
They race the word to the Shala Queen.

Still vigilant, the watchers watch.
One King lies, Danish's the prize.
Kingdoms fall to rise again.
Caverns' pride is a human tide.
Where a brother dies by a brother's hand
Ever vigilant, the watchers watch.

If you take the staff you'll feel the wrath
Of the Shala when they rise.

When she first read this part of the Prophecy, she realized that over five hundred years of peace might be coming to an end. In her family's line of succession, she had been the third Queen in the past five centuries. While it was possible that the Prophecy might be referring to a future Queen, her instincts told her otherwise. When she gave birth to twin boys, she knew for certain that war was coming to Sandala and the Shala would be called upon to fulfill their duty.

Still she resisted the sacred words, trying to turn aside what her husband Artur had told her was inevitable. With only her mother and Artur present when her sons were born, she made a decision, swearing them to secrecy. Seeking to save her son from the death the Prophecy foretold, she tried to alter the future. The first born child with the white blond hair, the one who would inherit her crown, was told by all including him, that he was the younger of the twins. By switching him with Drayen, who would become king instead, she hoped that both of her sons would live full and vibrant lives. But her deception had not fooled the gods, and Drayen had paid the ultimate price for her folly.

Was her action so difficult to understand? Wouldn't any mother go to such lengths to ensure the welfare of their children? Artur had pleaded with her, even warned her of risking much by playing with fate, but the Queen was not immune from common desires, so she didn't listen. All she could do now was pray that her actions didn't have further consequences, and that Tahjeen would not be lost as well.

CHAPTER 28

FLAMING ARROWS

Late in the day, Gable's seven foot, muscled frame was stretched out on top of the hill. He and the two lieutenants, who lay beside him, were being careful to keep their profiles low. His long brown hair, sprinkled with gray, fell across his back in a single braid.

The three men watched the Surmese tents that dotted the plain below. Tomorrow, their army would launch assault on the capital city of Milhune. In the distance, Gleneden troops were digging in for what would probably be their last stand. The Surmese had already slaughtered nearly half their forces, leaving roughly three thousand left to fight.

"What is your count?" Gable asked Mylander, the older of the two beside him.

"Around twenty thousand. Nearly two divisions of Surmese. The Glenedians have fought hard but they're heavily out-numbered," Mylander commented, shaking his head.

Gable turned to the younger lieutenant, Xander. He was short by Shala standards, measuring a mere six feet six inches. "Take two hundred and fifty archers around to their right flank. Shortly after darkness falls, a flaming arrow from our side will be your signal to open fire." Gable still held hope. With any luck, they would chop the enemy's numbers significantly. "Stay out of range of their weapons."

"Do we return here?" Xander inquired.

Gable shook his head. "When you're finished, send two hands of runners to find the others coming up from the south."

The young man nodded then quickly crept back down the hillside.

Mylander stared out at the Surmese encampment. "Two hundred and fifty arrows let fly a dozen times. If half find their mark..."

"We will eliminate the remaining Surmese as soon as the others arrive," Gable finished the sentence for him. He knew as well as Mylander that far tco many of the enemy would still be alive after all the arrows fell.

"I am actually looking forward to that," Mylander commented.

"I have another task for you," Gable said. He saw curiosity in the yellow green color of Mylander's eyes.

"We need a Glenedian commander. Later tonight when most of them are sleeping, you must enter their camp undetected and commandeer one of their leaders."

Mylander's eyes turned egg yolk yellow in surprise. "That could prove tricky."

"We will create a diversion to draw their attention elsewhere. But the Glenedians must know what is going on. We need to meet with someone in authority."

Mylander nodded. "I know some younger warriors whose talents would fit the task you describe."

Gable watched as Mylander retreated back down the hill then turned his attention back to the enemy's camp. Caressed by a soft breeze, the grass on the plain swayed. The scent of food cooking on the enemies' campfires drifted up to him.

For a time he studied the Surmese. Their army was efficient, with disciplined soldiers and first rate equipment. According to his brother, who had *laised* with him early this morning, they did not surrender.

Gable wasted no time rousing the rest of his party after waking from his dream talk. Because there was still time, he had Cordon's sister to drink the elixir so she could *lais* with him before the new day dawned. Cordon was told to re-gather the four thousand Shala warriors who were spreading out across the four kingdoms. They were to get to Milhune and reunite with Gable's force as fast as possible.

Together, the five thousand Shala could destroy the Surmese army surrounding the capital city. But if the Surmese attacked before Cordon and the rest of the *kosh* arrived, only Gable's group combined with the Gleneden soldiers would be in place. Even if half the arrows did find their mark, they would still be engaging far too many to have a chance of winning. A lot of Shala would die and thousands of humans along with them.

He refocused his gaze to the south. Somewhere out there,

who knew how far away, another four thousand Shala were working their way back to him. Gable sighed and his eyes radiated the frosty green of hope, hope that they would arrive in time. Beside him, his golden *fel* growled quietly. *Be calm, Coba. Nothing has been lost yet,* Gable told him. But the big cat betrayed his tension by pacing.

Gable gave the signal and the flaming arrow raced high across the night sky. Several guards among the Surmese saw it and shouted the alarm. In seconds, their camp was alive with activity as thousands of soldiers poured out of their tents. Gable snorted his pleasure. He had not anticipated such good fortune. The enemy was silhouetted against the backdrop of their camp-fires, making easy marks. Gable knew that more Shala arrows would find their target because of it.

Suddenly a new cry of alarm broke out among the enemy below as the first flight of arrows from Xander's group reached them. Screams now filled the night, and Gable heard the thumping twang of his own group as they fired the next wave of lethal missiles. As more Surmese fell, the rest frantically sought cover. To one side he could see a Surmese officer organizing archers to return fire. Gable smiled, he knew they wouldn't come within a hundred yards of any Shala.

Some of the Surmese who sought shelter ended up clumped together in a mass that offered a prime target. As the next volley from Xander's side rained down, the screams crescendoed. On the far side another Surmese officer was barking orders, organizing a cluster of men to charge towards Xander's group. They moved forward slowly, shields raised in front of them, leaving their backs unprotected. It was from that direction that Gable's men mowed them down with their third volley.

Soon the enemy gave up all pretenses of fighting back, withdrawing instead under the cover of supply wagons or running to the rear and jumping behind boulders several hundred feet away. If they had only had more men or more arrows, Gable knew they could win total victory this night.

As it was, once the supply of arrows was exhausted, Gable estimated that nearly six thousand Surmese lay dead or dying. It was far more than he had hoped for and might give the enemy pause before they launched their assault on the capital.

Gable's gaze swept toward the Gleneden encampment. He longed to talk to their commander, let him see a friendly face

and know that he wasn't alone. Besides, their military leaders
needed to know of Tahjeen's plans to retake all the kingdoms
except for Sealand. He glanced up at the night sky, willing time
to pass quickly so Mylander's small raiding party could complete
their task.

They crept forward, silent as muted night. Those with light
colored hair covered it with dark leather, and their naturally
darker skin made them nearly impossible to see. The Gleneden
soldiers were oblivious of their nearness, as they dashed past the
trench filled with sleeping soldiers. In another ninety feet they
reached the tent of the commander. With the stealth typical of
all Shala, they slipped inside.

As one hand covered the commander's mouth, two others
pinned his arms. He awakened, staring blearily at the two men
before him. A candle provided the light that allowed him to
gradually see their eyes. His alarm showed as he stared in disbelief.

"Make no sound. We are not here to harm you." The warrior
who spoke watched the man closely, and was pleased to see no
fear in him. "Your Queen, Endoreen, has talked of us. We are
Shala." The commander's eyes widened in disbelief, but fright
was still absent from his gaze.

"I will remove my hand if you give your solemn word you
won't call out," the young Shala warrior said.

The Gleneden commander glanced from one to the other and
quickly nodded. Slowly, the warrior removed his hand. "May I sit
up?" the commander asked quietly. The other Shala released the
man's arms.

For several moments, the commander studied each warrior,
looking at their colorful eyes and their long, dark bodies, shaking
his head all the while. Finally, he spoke again, barely above a
whisper. "Was it you who attacked the enemy shortly after
dark?" he asked.

Each warrior nodded.

"How many of you are there?" the Glenedian asked.

But the Shala who had covered his mouth shook his head.
"We are here to take you to our camp. Our leader must speak
with you."

"Now?" the commander asked, surprised.

Both Shala smiled briefly. "Soon. Come, prepare yourself."

The Gleneden leader rose from his pallet, reached for his

sword then stopped, looking to the Shala for approval. They shrugged. One of them went to the tent flap and peered outside. "Not yet," he said as he watched what was happening outside the tent.

Suddenly cries could be heard in the distance, coming from the enemy's camp. More flaming arrows were striking the tents, setting them on fire. From the Gleneden trenches, soldiers were stirring and looking out across the plain to where the Surmese were located.

"Now," the Shala warrior said. The three left the tent quickly, and dropped behind it into the darkness. They ran, guiding the commander toward a line of trees several hundred yards in the distance. Once they reached them, they turned sharply left and started working their way ahead, parallel to the Surmese encampment. A few minutes later, they turned at aright angle and entered a heavily treed hillside.

It was hard for the Gleneden leader to see, the thick-branched trees effectively blocking out the moonlight, but the two Shala steered him unerringly as they continued to move swiftly along. He was breathing more heavily now, feeling the effects of the gradual climb.

After they covered over a mile, they emerged into a small clearing. A moment later, they stopped and the commander was startled when a dozen or more Shala materialized out of the darkness. A small torch suddenly flamed, held low to the ground to limit its range, casting eerie shadows on the faces of those who surrounded him. An older Shala stepped closer.

"I am Gable. Thank you for coming." Gable studied the human as if waiting for something. The commander realized he was expected to introduce himself.

"I am General Ronkier, commander of Gleneden's army," his shoulders sagged as he added, "at least what remains of it."

"Please," Gable gestured to a nearby log, "sit. There is much we need to discuss."

CHAPTER 29

THE BRIDGE

On the west side of the bridge, a dozen Shala slipped unseen into the Tanon River's turbulent water. With powerful strokes, they made their way across in less than twenty minutes. Though the current was strong, they succeeded in maintaining a direct course to the other side. Armed with only their knives, they moved silently up the bank.

Half a dozen sentries patrolled the bridge, blind to the danger below. A similar number were grouped a short distance from the span and they rotated with the bridge sentries every hour. None of them slept. They would be relieved half way through the night so they could sleep.

A noise caused one of the men to stand up and peer into the darkness. "I think there's something out there," he said. As he turned back to his comrades, he saw dark forms materialize out of the night. Before he could utter a cry of warning, a strong forearm wrapped around his neck and clamped down hard on his throat. He was lifted off his feet. He bucked and kicked while clutching desperately at the vise-like grip that was squeezing the life out of him. He did not see as one by one his colleagues' bodies went limp as death claimed them. All he saw was a burst of light then an ever-growing darkness.

The rest of the swimmers were climbing horizontally along the side of the bridge, hidden from the guards. A low whistle from the other Shala, now finished with their grisly task, gave the signal to attack. They launched themselves onto the bridge in unison, aligned in pairs to make sure that no sentry had the chance to utter a sound. Noiselessly, save for the lone birdcall, the Shala took the bridge.

A warrior raced to the far end and signaled the rest of Katrine's forces. In moments, twenty five hundred warriors raced silently across the bridge, with Katrine and her huge beast leading the way. Baldor and Devon waited in the rear, not wanting the sound of their horse's hooves alerting the Surmese encampment. They were accompanied by several Shala and two thousand five hundred impatient cats. In the midst of the ferocious beasts, their own horses were nervous. The cats paced, eager to join their warrior partners on the far side, but managed to give the horses a wide berth as if sensing they upset them.

On the other side of the river, Katrine and her *fel* slipped into the first tent. Six of the enemy slept soundly, two of the men snoring as they lay on their backs. She put her hand out, signaling her cat to wait. In rapid succession, she slashed the throats of the two men nearest her. Another man stirred and her lethal companion was on him instantly, using his huge jaws to tear his head off at the neck. With blinding speed Katrine threw her knife as a fourth man reached for his spear, and with two devastating paw swipes, her *fel* dispatched the last two. In tents all around her, other Shala were similarly engaged.

Though the Shala were silent killers, it was only a matter of time before a Surmese awakened in time to raise the alarm. At the sound of voices and clashing metal, Baldor and Devon spurred their horses onto the bridge, the *fels* racing ahead them. The time for stealth had passed.

The king and the sentinel arrived as deep-throated Shala war cries shattered the night. The enemy was under attack on all sides. Knives flew and swords thrust, as men and Shala fought hand to hand in close quarters.

Atop his powerful horse, Devon leapt into the fray. He slew two of the enemy with quick swipes of his long sword while with a thud, his mount bowled over another and crushed him underfoot. He spurred his horse forward where a dozen Surmese had a *fel* surrounded. The cat huffed as it dodged one lance then brought its carrier down, his claws making a ripping sound as they raked the legs of one soldier. Focused on the animal, the others did not see Devon's charge. He ran one soldier through with his sword, pulled the bloody weapon free, and then another man screamed as Devon severed his arm with a vicious slice. The *fel* took advantage of the sudden distraction and crashed several men to the ground in one powerful leap. His fierce jaws made quick work of them. The rest began to scatter, trying desperately to evade Devon's furious onslaught and the cat's terrible claws.

Across the encampment, Surmese battled the cats and Shala and the two men astride their horses. They had no chance against the swift, ferocious strangers with the fiery red eyes; no adequate defense against the huge cats that tore through them; and no chance against a King whose land they had invaded.

In less than an hour, it was over. The encampment grew quiet. The only sounds were quiet murmurs among the warriors and panting cats. Shala warriors went from body to body making sure that the fallen enemies were dead. Devon saw Baldor survey the carnage, a look of grim satisfaction on his face. But Devon had seen a lot of death and felt no pleasure in the slaughter.

Katrine found him several minutes later. She was drenched in blood but all of it belonged to the enemy. She looked him over for injuries and nodded when she found none. She turned and checked King Baldor as well.

"Survivors?" Baldor asked her, the excitement of battle still etched on his face.

Katrine shook her head. "It was as Tahjeen foretold. The Surmese do not surrender."

"Did you, er, we lose any?" Baldor asked.

She heard the concern in his voice. "Two warriors and one cat," she answered simply. "Take the opportunity to rest, your Highness. The commander's tent is being searched for any plans or maps. We'll take some of their supplies and destroy the rest, but we move out within the hour."

Devon watched Baldor, recalling the king's initial reaction to a female commander, let alone female soldiers. What a fool the king had been, Devon thought. In the distance, he noticed several leopards eating their human kill. Bones crunched as they gorged. He shuddered, greatly relieved that the Shala were on his side.

Katrine left to check on the rest of her *kosh* and Devon hurriedly joined her. "Are all your victories so one-sided?" he asked.

She flashed him a quick look and snorted. "This was child's play. To attack a sleeping enemy in his own tent..." she shook her head, her golden locks swaying gently, "child's play," she repeated.

They took a dozen steps before she spoke again. "Word will travel quickly, and each time it will be harder."

Devon grinned.

"What?" she challenged, annoyed by his smile.

"Word can't travel anywhere if there's no one alive to spread it."

Katrine looked at him, her eyes gradually turning a light shade of pink. She smiled back and he was struck by the fact that he had never noticed how tall she was. She dwarfed him by at least six inches. As they continued walking among the warriors, he realized that he didn't mind at all.

CHAPTER 30

GABLE'S STAND

"We have close to three thousand men," General Ronkier said, warming his hands at the small fire the Shala had started. "Unfortunately, almost half are wounded, most seriously. We expected the enemy to attack in force today, but your surprise may give them pause."

"I hope so," Gable said, offering the General a hot drink to ward off the night chill. "I'm sorry we don't have a healer with us so we could improve the odds. Between us we do not have enough to stop them, but another four thousand Shala are on their way and those numbers will be enough."

Gable's eyes swept across the group seated around the small fire. "Unfortunately," he said, shaking his head, "they may not arrive for a day or two."

General Ronkier lowered his eyes and looked away. "The Surmese won't wait that long."

"I know," Gable said, "which is why we need to make some adjustments."

General Ronkier breathed deeply and sat up straighter. He lifted his gaze, looking directly at Gable. "What do you have in mind?"

Gable nodded, pleased with the man's courage. "I suggest you relocate to inside Milhune and take stations along the walls. Some of my warriors will replace yours in the trenches and the rest will divide in two and attack their flanks."

"But you'll be heavily outnumbered!" the General said, his eyebrows lifting in alarm.

"It may buy us the time we need," Gable answered. "If nothing else, it will delay their attack on the city."

"No slight intended, sir, but even with your full complement, the odds are long." Gable knew that the General saw no possibility of victory against the size of the army they faced. "As long as the rest of my command arrives in time," Gable said, his eyes turning steel blue in determination, "victory is certain. Be sure of that. Even if they are too late to come to our aid, they will retake the city."

Gable looked at the General and his eyes turned faintly purple with regret. "But we'll not be alive to see it."

The General nodded, still finding the turn of events difficult to comprehend. "Very well, then," Ronkier said and stood up. "If you will return me to my men, we'll start to move out under the cover of darkness."

"Good," Gable answered. "The warriors who are replacing yours will accompany you. The rest of my team will move into position along the enemy flanks. If they do attack tomorrow, we will be ready."

Devon watched as Katrine's warriors rifled through the Surmese supplies. After taking what they could use, they destroyed whatever was left. Unconcerned about holding the bridge, they left it unguarded. Surmese corpses were the only sign that the Shala had been there. When Devon registered his concern, Katrine shrugged and said that the dead bodies would provide a strong deterrent to any thought of pursuit. He couldn't argue with her logic.

With the search of the Surmese tents concluded, Devon, Baldor, and Katrine's *Kosh* raced on toward Palaton's capital. They skirted several small villages seen burning in the distance. Devon was pleased that Baldor's people had chosen resistance rather than surrender.

Longstreet knew Palatonians were a rugged lot; loyal, honest folk who consisted primarily of farmers whose labor in the fields produced strong, well-nourished bodies. Baldor's kingdom was efficiently run and he ruled with a fair hand. Citizens appreciated that, and whenever soldiers trained in the countryside, the civilians welcomed their presence and fed them well. It wasn't surprising to Devon that not only was Baldor's army providing stiff resistance against the invaders, but the populace was as well.

Katrine's scouts reported back that the Surmese army had been forced to fight their way through the countryside. The progress they made toward the capital was proving costly. Evidence of battles was frequent. The sight of vultures circling in the distance occurred several times throughout the day, once directly in their path. When they came upon the scene, the big cats chased away the vultures, but ignored the rotting flesh.

Devon was shaken to see that a significant number of Baldor's soldiers lay strewn about the killing ground, but judging by the amount of dead Surmese among them, his men had fought well. He took advantage of the opportunity and complimented the king.

"Unfortunately," Baldor said, glowering, "that isn't good enough since we can't match their numbers. I can only hope that the four thousand left to guard the capital have remained inside the city walls. If they were enticed to aid their fellow soldiers," he paused rather than state the obvious.

"Sire," Devon said. "Your army is superb. They will stay where they were ordered."

Earlier, when Baldor explained his city's fortifications and defenses to Devon and Katrine, they had been impressed and it had given her an idea. There were really two walls an enemy had to overcome. First was an outer wall that was heavily gated. A walkway ran along the ramparts where defenders could launch spears and arrows. Every one hundred paces there was a tower with stairs that crossed under the street directly behind the bulwark. They emptied out on the far side of a second wall, where defenders could climb up another walkway and renew their attack. Inside each set of stairs was a device that once triggered, collapsed the steps so the enemy could not follow.

Katrine explained to Baldor that she planned to send a third of her forces into the city to help with the inner defense. The rest of the Shala would attack the enemy from the rear, forcing them inside between the two walls and into a killing zone. In the narrow confines with no cover or avenue of escape, it could be a full-scale slaughter.

King Baldor expressed his approval of the plan. "It greatly reduces the potential loss of Palatonian and Shalaen lives, and might even leave the inner city intact. Only the stair access to the outer towers would be in need of rebuilding."

"And with luck," Devon added, "few civilians would be harmed, a fact they would not only appreciate but remember. "He knew it would earn Baldor mountains of goodwill in his declining years.

"But first," Katrine said, sobering them both, "we have to get to the capital before the Surmese."

The one day reprieve Gable hoped for did not come. The next morning the Surmese army attacked with a vengeance. They formed line after line of infantrymen armed with spears, shields and swords. When they drew within a hundred yards of the trench, they began a headlong charge, their pounding feet raising a billowing cloud of dust, and their voices sounding a hair-raising battle cry. At one point, the Surmese commander ordered his archers to fire their volleys but the arrows did little harm. At that moment Mylander's Shala attacked the flanks.

With incredible speed the Shala warriors sprinted toward the startled enemy. Their onslaught disrupted the neatly charging formation, as the three hundred warriors crashed into the rows of attackers. Amid the confused shouts of the enemy and the screams of the dying, the Surmese started to regroup, trying to divide the Shala into smaller groups that they could surround and overwhelm. But the Shala broke off and raced away. From out of the dust their retreating feet kicked up, the cats, growling furiously, came charging through.

The effect was terrifying. Some of the nearest Surmese turned and ran, but enough stood their ground and fought. Blood flew as warriors' flesh was torn by lethal claws. Men grunted and gasped, fighting in vain against razor sharp fangs. Along the outer edge of the various lines, nearly every soldier died.

But as the cats moved deeper into the enemy ranks, some were slain, their ear-shattering death roars bringing a numbing grief to their Shala bondmate. The death toll on both sides began to mount, until finally, the *fels* were called back to rejoin the rest of the Shala. To Mylander's sorrow, only two-thirds returned. Still, another two thousand Surmese lay dead.

Breathing hard, the Surmese left standing regained their momentum and the stalled charge surged forward once again. Gable watched as the distance between them narrowed. It dawned on him that he was going to die today. He glanced at his three hundred warriors and then at the thundering horde bearing down on him. In the trenches, they had little chance against a force so large. Knowing the odds were better in the open ground, he cried out, "attack." Shala and cats alike leapt onto the higher ground, earth flying from the force of their feet. The grim-faced warriors raced forward, side by side, shields in front and weapons drawn.

Then, like an unexpected breath of fresh air to a suffocating man, Gable saw Cordon's forces hurtling over a small rise. He watched as they stopped and drew their powerful bows. Their unleashed arrows tore into the enemies' flanks with heavy thuds and hundreds of Surmese dropped in their tracks. Immediately, the Surmese commander yelled at his men to form a defensive circle, but it only made them easier targets. Another volley slammed into them and more soldiers fell.

Gable halted his group, his eyes radiating the deep blue of appreciation and relief. He watched as a thousand of Cordon's warriors broke off from the rest and began running towards his small line of defenders. Another thousand raced around the enemies' rear and in minutes the invaders were surrounded. The air seemed alive with the buzz of flying arrows. Men gurgled in death from shots that pierced their necks. Others grunted when the heavy Shala projectiles drove deep in their chests.

At long last, Cordon called a halt to the rain of arrows, pausing to see if the enemy would surrender. But when the Surmese realized the attack was no longer coming to them, their commander barked out the order to charge. Cordon responded in kind.

The ground shook as both sides pounded toward one another, and when they met, the crunching sound of the massive collision reverberated across the plain. There were no more commands, only guttural cries and grunts as they warred. The Surmese were experienced fighters, hardened veterans of numerous empire-building campaigns. But they had never faced a Shala and were no match against the flying feet of the guardians of Sandala. It was as if the enemy had been caught by a terrible tornado.

Shala spears zipped through the air, pinning some of their targets to the ground. Shala swords swooshed against Surmese shields, splintering them. Swords put up in defense were cracked in half. Hand to hand engagements ended quickly, the humans unable to turn aside the alien strength. Everywhere, moans of the injured and screams of the dying floated over the blood-caked earth.

From his viewpoint atop the city's walls, General Ronkier watched the slaughter. Most of the enemy was killed at a distance by the strong Shala arrows. The thousand or so who managed to avoid the shafts ran forward toward the dark warriors and their terrifying beasts. They were cut to pieces by swords and claws.

When it was over, less than two hundred Shala from Cordon's party died. From Gable's nine hundred, over eight hundred were alive to carry the recapture of Gleneden forward.

General Ronkier was filled with gratitude. The legendary Shala his Queen had once described had saved the capital. He doubted her account of their existence, but the deadly skills attributed to them had been difficult to believe. After today, any lingering misgivings were gone.

With the capital secure, the next few weeks could be dedicated to eradicating the enemy from every corner of Gleneden. With the Shala's help, it would be done.

Smiling, Ronkier turned to his aid. "Open the larders and prepare a feast. Those warriors will be hungry and I intend to see that Gleneden feeds them well."

CHAPTER 31

THE SECOND ARMADA

General Swota, the one-armed leader of the Surmese western invasion force, waited a day and a half before he launched his attack. Safe aboard his ship but plagued by uncertainty over the size of the force that lay in wait, he was hesitant to charge blindly into a potential slaughter. Once bold and tactically brilliant, he had morphed into a battle-weary, cautious commander, which he took pains to hide from the Emperor.

He had wanted more information and spent most of the previous day crammed into a cabin with his lieutenants, grilling them for ideas. By the afternoon of the following day, the Admiral of the fleet ended Swota's dalliance. With words sizzling with derisiveness, he ordered the General to launch the attack immediately. If he failed to establish a solid beachhead, he was to turn over his command to the next in line and follow the only honorable course left open to him - commit suicide.

From a large sand dune, Katar watched as hundreds of smaller boats laden with soldiers headed toward shore. He thought it odd that the invasion was taking place late in the afternoon, but it suited his circumstances. The cover of darkness worked in the Shala's favor.

With supplies limited, Katar had ordered his warriors to save their arrows. They would use them in hit-and-run attacks and, if fortune shined upon them, they would circle back around and remove them from the dead for reuse at a later time.

Katar was popular with his *kosh*. Those who followed him appreciated his plain speaking, direct manner. Younger than the other *kosh* leaders, he seemed more like a big brother than an uncle to the warriors he commanded. It didn't hurt that he was handsome and cheerful, with long, lustrous black hair that had turned more than one maiden's head.

He had never been a dreamer, and the reality facing him now

shoved any lingering good cheer deep inside him. It did indeed appear that nearly a hundred thousand soldiers were dis-embarking. He was under no illusions. His *kosh* could do a lot of damage over the next week, but even if they cut down half the enemy, the fifty thousand left was still too many to defeat in open combat.

He stood and slogged his way back down the dune where his friends waited. Before reaching them, he signaled the twenty five hundred Shala men and women to begin their rapid withdrawal. Half would venture north, the rest south. Together, they would hound the advancing Surmese army from both sides as it marched towards Danigh. They would implement that strategy this very night. The big cats, however, retreated several hundred yards inside the dense forest, where they would wait for the enemy. Under the cloak of darkness and hidden within the trees and brush, they would take a bloody toll before the night was over.

Katar reached his companions. "It begins," he said. As one, they turned their back on the sea and began to run.

After the fifth wave of boats had come ashore, Field Commander Nybol, a younger veteran whose chiseled face was still unmarred by scars, was eager to move over the dunes and begin his assault. He was furious with Swota's cowardice. How the Emperor could assign this old cripple was past his understanding. A campaign of this magnitude deserved the leadership of those whose hearts were still wedded to war.

Nybol now understood that the fires the enemy had set were a simple but effective ruse. Still, he had no idea of the numbers they faced, so he moved cautiously up the dune then lay on his belly and crawled the last ten feet. What he saw surprised him. Below the dune, sand stretched for another fifty yards then disappeared into waist high flora. In another hundred yards trees appeared, bent sharply toward the east by the stiff, coastal winds. They grew denser, gradually multiplying into a forest. Across the span no one was visible. Where was the enemy? Somehow, he had to find out. The Admiral had been quite clear on the matter. Field Commander Nybol loped back down the way he had come and headed for General Swota.

After listening to his report, the General made his decision. "Order the advance team across the dunes and into the far trees. If they come under fire in the open, they are to hunker down where they stand. They will not, under any circumstances retreat." Nybol saluted before he hurried off to begin the advance.

Within five minutes, a thousand Surmese soldiers started the short climb up the dune. This time the General joined the Field Commander and went up to watch what might unfold.

The soldiers spread out along the wide stretch of flat, sandy surface. They did not slow when they entered into the shrubbery but continued working their way toward the trees.

Both men waited. Nybol had anticipated spears or arrows or a sudden wall of rushing warriors. But there was nothing. When the advance team reached the trees, two thirds of them held back, lowering themselves into defensive positions while the remainder continued through the trees and into the forest.

For several minutes nothing happened. Nybol sensed that the General, like him, was filled with tension. Then they heard the first screams, followed by more, impregnating the air with sounds he could only compare to the rape of a thousand maidens. A yellow flag was waved by one of the men still waiting at the edge of the trees. It was a signal requesting what to do next. On the word from General Swota, Nybol stood up and waved a red flag back at them. Immediately, the remaining two thirds charged ahead, disappearing among the trees.

Once again, several minutes passed then more shrieks began to fill the air. Shouting was heard but the meaning was indecipherable. The screams continued on, interrupted on two occasions by guttural, inhuman cries that raised the hair on Swota's arms. The shouting gradually lessened then stopped entirely.

Suddenly, a small group of soldiers broke out from the trees and came running across the sand. Most were bleeding and as they drew nearer, the General could see deep, ugly claw marks running down their arms, across their faces, chests and backs. One man's arm dangled loosely from his shoulder, attached by only a few tendons. Another man dropped to the ground, bleeding from a terrible gut wound, his intestines visible.

The men on the dune ran forward to the injured soldiers. The General grabbed one who appeared relatively whole. "What was it?" he asked the stricken man.

"Huge mountain lions or leopards," the man said, panting heavily. "We killed two, I think. But there were hundreds of them."

"Were you outnumbered?" the General asked, frowning.

"Maybe," the man bent over, and spit blood, "I'm not sure, sir. But one man against a beast like that has no chance."

Swota let the man go, and then turned to the Field Commander. "Ready half a division." He looked over his shoulder, noting the setting sun.

"Five thousand men?" Nybol asked, surprised. "Now? The sun is almost down. It would be prudent to wait until morning."

Anger suffused the General's face. "You saw the look on the Admiral's face. If we wait, both of us will have our throats slit before the sun has set." Nybol was furious. It was suicide to send more men into the forest at dusk with visibility growing worse by the minute. But he also knew what would happen to him if he failed to do it.

"Bring the grelags as well," the General ordered.

Ten minutes later five thousand Surmese marched over the dune. Soldiers carried several dozen cages filled with the ugly, slithery creatures were carried by a like number of men. They moved across the sand and approached the forest's edge. Quickly, handlers opened the cages and one by one the half snake, half lizard abominations were released into the trees. The soldiers hurried after them.

Even though they had heard them twice before, when the screams started the General flinched and Nybol looked away in disgust. But this time, however, there were also hideous howls from dying beasts. The sounds continued until darkness fell.

Gradually, soldiers started to trickle out of the trees, their shapes clearly visible under a full moon and a bright, starlit sky. The General turned to Nybol. "Give me a report as soon as enough men return to get a coherent account."

The Field Commander nodded and watched Swota return to the beach. He heaved a sigh then headed toward the flat expanse of land that lay before him. He started counting the soldiers as they appeared, noting the one good sign – none of them were running.

A half-hour later, Nybol came back over the dune, and made his way to the large fire and blue pennant that marked the General's location. Swota saw him coming and motioned him to a spot away from the rest of the officers.

"Sir," Nybol started to say, "Over three thousand men have

established a front several hundred yards into the forest. The grelags were very effective, killing many of the beasts. The fighting was intense, many dying on both sides before the animals suddenly left. One officer said it was as if..." he paused, scratching his cheek.

"As if what?" the General growled impatiently.

"It seemed like they were being ordered away, as if someone was controlling them," the Field Commander concluded.

"Humph. It wasn't darkness that drove them off?" the General asked.

"No sir. Besides, animals like that have excellent night vision. According to the officer, they all left at the same time, as if called." The Field Commander waited.

"Very well," Swota said. "We have only half the men ashore so far. Start moving all of them," he pointed at the mass of soldiers stretched out along the shore, "to the other side of the dune and into the forest. I want that front reinforced. We will push further into the interior in the morning once all the men and supplies are ashore."

"Yes, sir," Nybol said then moved off to deliver his message and get the men moving.

Over breakfast, Tahjeen and Ariann met with King Sorbonne and Queen Endoreen. Since Baldor was gone and Darvus coordinating efforts at the cavern entrance, they were the only rulers left.

Tahjeen could tell that the two were eager to hear what had transpired the previous day, so he wasted no time in relaying last night's information. As servants placed the last plate of bread and cheese on the table, he began.

"Queen Endoreen," Tahjeen said, "the Surmese surrounding your capital have been destroyed." He paused momentarily, nodding at a maid who filled his cup full of steaming coffee. He sipped carefully and continued. "Over the next few weeks Gable and his team, along with your own forces, will work to eradicate the enemy from every corner of Gleneden."

Endoreen exhaled, visibly relieved and followed with her first smile in three days. "Thank you, Tahjeen. Bless all the Shala." She took a small chunk of cheese from the plate being passed around. "When do you think I'll be able to return?" she asked.

"There is no reason to delay," Tahjeen answered. "We can have some Shala escort you there at once."

"I would like that very much," she replied, but made no move to leave just yet.

Tahjeen swallowed more coffee as his gaze shifted to Sorbonne. "Your Majesty, Katar reports that the Surmese landed yesterday afternoon. Near nightfall, five divisions were on the beach. Soon after, a small party went inland to scout and the cats destroyed them, but a larger force followed. They released a lethal creature, much like a lizard, that was very effective against the cats. Katar was forced to call them back when too many were being slain."

Sorbonne nodded thoughtfully as he reached for a warm, thick slice of bread. Before he could reply, Tahjeen added, "Early this morning several Shala infiltrated the Surmese camp and killed their General. He was foolish enough to have a flag marking his presence flying above his tent."

The King's eyebrows lifted in surprise. "Do you think that will hamper their progress?" Sorbonne asked.

Tahjeen shook his head. "It's doubtful, Sire, but the two-day delay is helpful." He paused to slather a piece of bread with butter before he shifted subjects. "Sire, how are your people responding to the evacuation?"

King Sorbonne frowned. "As expected, some were resistant, but the presence of your warriors helped convince them. For most, the difficulty is deciding what items are essential and what can be rebuilt easily." He stared at the warm bread in his hand before he continued. "They are worried about simple necessities, like food," he said wryly and took another bite. He chewed and swallowed then added, "I'll go back into the city today to inform the last sector, even though I'm sure word has reached everyone by now."

"Your presence will no doubt help with morale," Ariann said.

The King nodded.

"A messenger from your son's party *laised* with us last night," Tahjeen said, and the King's face lit up at the mention of Roland. "Most farmers are reluctant to leave their land, but he has persuaded them to at least go into hiding. If they refuse to burn their crops and homes, he is having it done for them."

Sorbonne grimaced. "His popularity will no doubt suffer."

"Yes," Tahjeen agreed. "But truthfully, Your Highness, it helps if some of the populace stays behind. With fewer numbers on the roads, those who do leave can travel faster and the caverns will be less crowded."

"He was told to return in two days," Ariann said. "His life is even more important now in case..."

King Sorbonne finished the sentence for her, "In case I do not live long enough to see Dania reclaimed." Neither Tahjeen nor Ariann said anything at the simple statement of fact but they shared a furtive look. "What of King Baldor?" Sorbonne eventually asked.

"He fares well, Sire," Tahjeen answered. "They will reach the capital sometime today. The opposition has been minimal, though they've seen evidence of costly battles as they've passed through the land. Tomorrow will provide many answers," he concluded.

Encamped on shore, the Surmese army was rudely awakened when trumpets began blaring. That only occurred when there was an emergency. Something had happened! A crowd was gathering outside the General's tent.

When word reached Field Commander Nybol, he was shocked. Someone had gotten into the General's tent and murdered him! It was impossible. In a few minutes he joined the Lieutenant Generals at a hastily called meeting. They were standing just outside General Swota's tent.

"There were tracks before some fools walked all over them, there were tracks," one of the commanders said. "It wasn't those awful beasts. It was a man – a rather big one judging by the size of his footprint. One guard was found dead on the perimeter, along with the guard outside the General's tent."

Another commander spoke up. "How could that happen? An extensive perimeter was established. They could not all have been asleep."

"Are you suggesting traitors? Spies among us would be impossible!" A third commander interjected.

"There are no traitors," the first man said. "Only lackadaisical sentries and some of them will hang today."

For a moment the other men were silent then Vikor, a shorter, squarely built man with bristling gray hair stepped forward. "That would further undermine morale," he said.

"Damn morale! We cannot allow such laziness to go unpunished."

"I think," replied the shorter man, "we would benefit by giving the enemy more credit."

"What are you saying?"

"I am saying that we are plagued by unknowns. First, there were the wild felines that slaughtered several thousand of our men, followed by their sudden disappearance, and now, the assassination of our General. We face a foe of surprising ability, so let us not be too quick to blame our own men. After the debacle with those beasts, morale is suffering and that needs to be acknowledged."

The other man started a rebuttal but before he could voice it, an older, slightly built man named Rolav, spoke. "Gentleman, first things first. We need to decide on the General's replacement then inform the Admiral. I agree with Vikor that morale is suffering. We must act quickly to project confidence."

No one offered any disagreement, so he continued. "Vikor is the senior Lieutenant General. Therefore, he should assume command. Is that acceptable?" Again, no one disagreed. "Very well, then." He turned to Vikor. "What are your orders General?"

Vikor gave them a small, wry smile. "First, bury General Swota. Next, send a message to the Admiral informing him of what has happened. When both of those things have been done, we will move on to Danigh." The others started to leave, but his voice stopped them.

"Another thing. No one will hang this day." He stared hard at the other men, imposing his force of will on them. One by one, they looked away.

As the group of leaders broke off, one volunteered to handle the burial and another took responsibility for getting word to the admiral. The rest went to muster their units. None of them challenged Vikor. He made the deceased General seem soft by comparison.

Only Rolav remained. "Congratulations, General," he said to his lifelong friend and ally.

Vikor nodded. "Thank you. You are now the second in command. Keep an eye on Tobol; he could be behind this assassination. Transfer some of your men into his command, enough to do what needs to be done should that prove necessary."

"Do you want him removed now?" Rolav asked.

Vikor shook his head. "No. Morale is a concern. Another assassination or well-planned accident would harm more than help. But watch him carefully."

CHAPTER 32

HIT AND RUN

It was late morning when the first attack came. The Shala struck with the same suddenness experienced when moving from the absolute calm of a hurricane's eye into the wind-whipped madness of the outer maelstrom. Deadly arrows crashed into the enemy's right flank. When the huge army wheeled around to defend that side and return fire, the ferocious *fels* assaulted them from behind. When the Surmese split their forces to face both challenges, several hundred Shala rushed them from the original front and rear. Less than five minutes later, the Shala broke off, rapidly disappearing into the surrounding forest, leaving over two thousand dead in their wake.

General Vikor met immediately with the other commanders. Rigid and tense, Tobol was the first to express his anger and frustration. "I told you we needed advance scouts! This could have been prevented."

Vikor looked back at him coldly. "Do you forget so quickly what happened to the five thousand men we sent ahead when we first landed?"

Tobol stared back with a similar degree of iciness, but remained silent.

Field Commander Nybol, who had been charged with the previous day's scouting parties, stepped forward. The other lieutenant generals glared openly at his boldness.

"General, if I may?" he asked.

Vikor nodded, his eyes still cold enough to freeze rain.

"This is the first time we have actually seen some of their warriors. They are of a different kind."

"Explain yourself," Vikor commanded, a lifted eyebrow revealing his intrigue.

"They are unbelievably fast. The front line of my unit was eliminated before we could react. They have considerable height and strength. I parried a blow from one but the force knocked me off my feet. I would have died except he turned away suddenly and left with the rest."

"Did you manage to kill any?" Vikor asked.

"A few, but only because they were cut off from the rest. We surrounded them with over twenty men." He paused, shaking his head. Worry lines creased his forehead.

"What?" the General asked.

"When the last one was killed, only five of my men remained. Three of them killed eighteen men, General, eighteen!"

"Impossible!" Tobol said sarcastically, ready to add another acerbic comment when Vikor interrupted him.

"Take me to them," the General said. "I want to examine one for myself."

The Field Commander bowed then led him to the outer edge of the Surmese soldiers. A group of men were gathered around a fallen enemy, but dispersed when they saw the officers heading their way.

Vikor walked up to the nearest body and knelt beside it. The man appeared young, probably in his late teens or early twenties. He was tall and physically well-developed, and Vikor noted his dark skin. He looked up for a moment then waved the rest of the officers away until he was the only one near the still warm body. He reached out to the man's eyes and used his thumb to roll back one of the lids. The dead eye was glassy white.

Vikor was one of only a handful of Surmese who knew what that meant – Shala. Centuries before, his distant ancestors had come to this continent, determined to continue the expansion of their empire. The Emperor had sent an army of one hundred thousand to conquer Sandala. That effort had ended in failure. Less than one thousand lived to tell the tale and provide descriptions of the terrible warriors who had defeated them – Shala.

This time, doubting the accuracy of the history books but never-the-less respecting them, the latest Emperor sent two hundred thousand to do what one hundred could not. Vikor looked back at the corpse, hoping that the huge army they had brought would be enough.

He rose quickly and walked over to a group of officers waiting off to the side. "Our march to Danigh may be a war of attrition. It is distinctly possible that our enemy lacks the numbers to launch a direct assault or they would have done so. We must expect more of the same tactics."

"We have already lost half a division," Tobol reminded him. "How many days are we from Dania's capitol?"

Vikor barely hid his dislike for the man as he answered. "Three, unless our progress is slowed appreciably."

"But at that rate," Tobol blustered, "when we reach the city half our men could be dead. That is unacceptable." His face reddened as he clenched his fists. "You must do something!"

"Oh, I will, Tobol," Vikor answered, nodding, irritated at the man's lack of control. "Tomorrow you will be at the front of our lines with your men. You can personally assume responsibility for our protection. I will be in the middle, in a better position to give orders to all units in case we are attacked in the same way."

Tobol paled but there was nothing he could say. He had demanded something be done, and Vikor had responded. "As you command," he said, venom dripping from every word.

Vikor turned to Rolav. "From now on I want all sides shielded so we are not decimated by arrows again."

"General," Rolav responded quickly. "Their bows are powerful. The arrows passed right through the shields."

"Then use the width of two shields!" Vikor shouted back. "Have a thought everyone!" His eyes bounced from one officer to the next, his voice laced with anger. "We are Surmese. The greatest fighting force in the world! Every man on the edge of the lines will use two raised shields. The men in the next line will point their lances outward ready to deflect the wild beasts. If the warriors attack, open your ranks and swallow them in mass so they can be killed!"

He stared hard at each of them. The officers bristled at his reprimand but their backs straightened and they stood taller. He had challenged their heritage and pride. Every single man was determined that the next attack would yield far different results.

Late that afternoon, Katar attacked again. The alterations Vikor had ordered made a difference. The arrows were not as effective and the Surmese lances brought more than fifty of the big cats down, but the rest started to leap over them, landing in the middle of the ranks of the Surmese defenders. There they took a deadly toll. When the first group of Shala warriors was drawn into the middle and surrounded, Katar immediately sent in reinforcements in to neutralize the effect.

Once again, after just a few minutes, the Shala withdrew. Their losses had increased dramatically. Over three hundred Shala saw their life's blood emptied into the earth. A similar number of *fels* died as well. When Field Commander Nybol finished his count, the Surmese death toll was again almost two thousand. He didn't know whether the General would treat it as good news or bad and was not anxious to find out.

CHAPTER 33

BALDOR'S RETURN

"Thank the gods!" Baldor said when Shala scouts returned with the news that the Surmese had not yet reached his capital. His relief was palpable.

"Bring a fresh horse!" Katrine ordered to a nearby warrior. "Sire, the enemy is not that far away. You must ride on now. Even so, you will arrive only an hour or two ahead of them."

Baldor nodded, dismounted then took the reins of a fresh horse in hand. "Once I get to the capital, give me a little time. Remember, I am sorry to say, I never accepted the Prophecy and dealt harshly with those who did. I'll need to prepare them, explain who you are."

Katrine realized that Baldor was embarrassed. "I under-stand," she said. "Hopefully, once inside your city's walls, you'll have the time you need. In the meantime we'll fall back out of sight until we know what the enemy is going to do."

"It's late in the day," Devon offered. "It's likely that they'll wait until first light before they begin to attack."

Katrine's eyes radiated a dull orange as she stared across the rolling hills. "One can hope."

Baldor rode closer to her. "I will see you inside the capital." He urged his horse into a gallop and a dozen Shala warriors fell in behind him.

Over one and a half divisions of Surmese soldiers neared Palaton's capital just as the sun was dropping below the western skyline. They stopped several miles away and as Devon predicted, began to set up camp. They gave no indication of launching an immediate attack. From all appearances, they were establishing a defensive perimeter, starting bonfires, and preparing to settle in for the night.

Katrine and Devon worked their way toward the edge of a forest that stood less than a mile from the enemy's camp. While he stood guard below, she climbed a large pine tree. When she reached the top she had a clear view of the Surmese army. It was soon obvious that they were settling down for the night. However, several men were headed for the line of trees where she and Devon were hiding. She descended from her observation point.

"Some of them are headed this way. We should withdraw." She did not want Surmese scouts getting anywhere near them. She could kill them easily, but their failure to return to camp would alert the enemy just as effectively as if they had seen a Shala and sounded an alarm.

"Will you attack them tonight?" Devon asked.

Had she been less sensitive to the lives of her own warriors, she would have ordered a night attack, taking the enemy by surprise and eventually destroying them.

"The cost would be too great." She eyed him boldly. "Though if it is our duty to defend you, I won't throw lives away unnecessarily."

Devon nodded. He liked the plan she had formed earlier to trap the Surmese between the double city walls. It would result in far fewer deaths. He knew she also had to obey Tahjeen's instructions to keep as many of her warriors alive as possible. They would face a far bigger and more important battle in the future. They could not afford to waste lives.

He was unaware that earlier she had said as much to some younger warriors who were filled with anticipation and eager to fight. She chastised them for showing their inexperience, explaining that they would have plenty of opportunity in the future once the effort to regain Dania began. They grew subdued when she mentioned the size of opposition they would be facing, and they realized they would be lucky to survive at all.

As they re-entered their main camp, Katrine went to the nearest lieutenant and told him to have the night sentries set up an extra wide perimeter. "I doubt the Surmese would launch an assault on the city tonight, but I we can't afford to take that chance. Be very careful. They have entered the forest as well."

Another warrior brought Katrine food and water. She sat down, thankful for the opportunity to rest before the fighting. Devon sat nearby, watching her.

Across the plain and inside the city's inner wall, King Baldor met with his chief commanders along with those who would stand watch that night. Aware of the Shala's keen night vision, he spaced one between each Palatonian sentry. The Shala would sound the alarm far sooner, but he wanted his own men to share the responsibility for alerting the rest of the city.

Baldor had spent a harried hour explaining the battle plan to his commanders. He had told them that he trusted these strange warriors with his life, which they had already saved several times. It was slow going at first, not surprising considering the depth of his earlier denial regarding the Prophecy's validity. His attitude was well known and etched in the minds of those closest to him. Reversing their prejudice at this late stage was a challenge, but he prevailed.

His commanders were drawn to his strategy. They had seen many of their friends fall in battle, and while grimly determined to defend the capital at all costs, they were relieved when he explained that victory was possible without a steep loss of life. Still, some found it hard to believe that the Shala outside the gates would be able to keep most of the Surmese pinned inside the first great wall.

He took this opportunity to remind his officers once again, of the importance of letting as many of the enemy as possible inside the first line of defense. "Use your arrows to kill as many as you can, but protect yourself at all cost. I want you alive to fight once the outer gates have been penetrated."

He paused, studying the faces around him. All eyes were focused on him, as they should be, but it pleased him nonetheless. "There is room enough," he continued, "to take in thousands of soldiers between the first and second wall. Once that happens, and on my signal, the Shala beside you will join the fray. I assure you, their main force will take care of any enemy still outside the wall."

He stepped away, looking at his men and the Shala around him, at the mayor standing off to the side, at the many women in attendance being given last minute instructions by the city's leaders, at the shopkeepers and craftsmen who were boarding up their windows. He swelled with pride. What a hardy people the Palatonians were. It was a privilege to be their king.

He walked back to finish addressing them. "Several days ago, we feared Palaton would be conquered, defeated and absorbed by a foreign power. Tonight, I give you my solemn promise that will not happen. Palaton shall prevail!"

The responding cheers were deafening.

Shortly after dawn the Surmese attacked. A huge battering ram, centered at the front of their assault lines, came rolling forward. The huge wooden wheels groaned and creaked under their heavy burden. The men propelling it walked to its side and rear, protected by a wooden roof attached to the top of the mechanism. Though Shala archers could have reached the rest of the marching soldiers, they did not fire, but instead let the enemy draw nearer.

Once they closed the distance, the Surmese bows twanged as they fired a heavy barrage of arrows at the outer ramparts. The Palatonians responded in kind, shooting only enough to give semblance of a credible defense and saving the rest until the enemy cleared the first wall.

In minutes the battering ram reached the massive gates and its rhythmic pounding began. Scaling ladders were thrust forward and slammed against the wooden walls. Grunts erupted from the throats of the Shala warriors as their powerful arms flung the ladders aside, forcing the enemy to rely on the ram.

For a time, the gates withstood the assault, but wood began to splinter and crack after each thudding blow. That was the signal that prompted the outer defenders to race to the towers' stairs and retreat to positions behind the second wall. A pin was pulled and the last stairway collapsed in a roar, leaving a heap of rubble and thick dust floating through the air. In the next moment a thunderous crack assaulted their ears as the front gate shattered. Seconds later, the enemy started pouring in.

Katrine and Devon, along with half her *kosh*, were bent low and running next to the trees and bushes that lined the main road to the city. The rest of her warriors were doing the same on the opposite side of the road. When she saw the first gate fall, she immediately ordered her warriors to attack. Sprinting onto the broad boulevard, they raced forward, launching themselves at the rear of the invaders. Inside the main gate, those on the front line of Surmese were momentarily confused when confronted with a second wall just thirty yards away. But the lead commander grasped the situation and divided them, sending half racing in each direction in search of another entryway.

Pressure from Katrine's warriors driving hard from behind, began to jam the Surmese close together. Sweating men bumped against one another, cursing and grunting as they fought for space. Lacking room to maneuver, they found it hard to turn and fight. Panic began to fill their ranks.

At the front of the assault, the push from behind forced the Surmese forward into the killing ground. They flooded in rapidly, inundating the area. The Palatonians responded, firing in mass. Hundreds of arrows whizzed towards easy targets, slapping into meaty arms and legs or bouncing harmlessly off enemy shields.

The battering ram appeared but the commander signaled his men to drop it inside the wall. Until another entrance was located, it would only slow them down.

For the next twenty minutes, both Shala and Palatonians fired arrows into the enemy horde. As the onslaught rained down on the Surmese, they grew desperate to escape the deadly arrows. Finally, they found the second gate and a hundred Surmese raced back to retrieve the battering ram to begin the next assault.

As they pounded away on the second gate, the ability to maneuver between the walls grew difficult as bodies piled up beside the ram. Each time a man went down, he was replaced by another from the seemingly endless supply.

On and on the rugged Surmese pounded the ram against the inner gate. If they broke through, they would be inside the city. Baldor watched, gripping his sword so tightly that his knuckles were white. Racing from his vantage point, he crossed an open area and headed towards a large body of his soldiers. "Slide the false wall aside and hide yourselves behind it!"

With the sound of the false wall grinding to a close fading behind him, he hurried on to the next intersection. "Push this wall over there and close off the exit!" he yelled. He watched, knowing the placement would force the enemy down a narrow, dead-end lane. More of his men lay in hiding behind that wall as well.

He set another half dozen traps before he dashed back to his observation point near the second gate. He arrived just as the Surmese knocked several heavy planks aside and were poised to shatter the rest of the barrier.

Now the Shala, their supply of arrows exhausted, began leaping from the wall, throwing themselves into the enemy's midst. Blood and bodies flew as they smacked into the enemy's ranks. Screams and groans of the injured and dying intermixed with guttural Shala war cries. Ragged breaths burst from the mouths of warriors as they fought for their lives. Still, because of their sheer numbers, many Surmese forged ahead. Enough worked their way past the Shala to break through the new opening and into the heart of the city.

For a time, Baldor watched. His heart pounded against his ribs when he saw hundreds of Surmese race unimpeded down the main street before he signaled his forces to attack the next group. Swords clashed and metallic clangs reverberated across the square. Baldor' forces challenged the enemy's right flank, driving them in the opposite direction, as they hacked and pushed, slowly herding them toward the dead end street.

Between the two walls, all was madness. The dark warriors were everywhere. Terrified Surmese screamed as leopards, cougars, lions and jaguars tore into them. The original Surmese commander, still alive and surrounded by an elite group of battle-scarred veterans, yelled out orders for some of the men to turn and fight the new onslaught from their rear. Amidst the noise and chaos, not enough heard. Inch by bloody inch, Katrine's forces steadily forced the rest between the walls.

Suddenly, a number of Surmese broke free on the left side, and Katrine and her *fel* raced to intercept them. Her knives were gone, buried in the chests of two soldiers, so she was armed only with her sword and shield. One man still carried his spear and was using it to fend off the big cat. Katrine faced him first, her sword clanging as she sliced the spear in two. Hearing gravel crunch behind her, she turned as the second soldier lunged with his bloody weapon. His blow thumped against her shield and she felt a sharp sting in her upper arm. A moment later, she was thudded to the ground, fighting off another attacker who had grabbed her by the hair. She twisted quickly, driving her sword through the man's chest, but her shield was ripped away. Three more Surmese charged her, their blades rising high, yelling like they had lost their minds.

Devon launched himself forward, his shield out in front, and crashed into the trio that threatened Katrine. He rolled back to his feet quickly, ready to parry, but Katrine had already sliced off one attacker's head and her terrifying *fel*, snarling in fury, had ripped the other two apart. She paused only to offer Devon a grin before she leapt back toward the mass of soldiers who were trying to squeeze out of the main gate. She never got there.

The Surmese commander had singled her out and jumped in front of her. The rage inside him was revealed by the fury that contorted his face. He launched himself at her, his sword ringing with a flurry of strokes, all the while looking for an opening for the knife in his other hand. She parried one after another, her breath rasping louder with every move. The two grappled, grunting with the effort, their strength evenly matched, before she finally flung him back. His feet slid, crunching the gravel as he stumbled. Katrine gulped air, the gash on her arm aching and she felt fatigue setting in. She wondered how much blood she had lost.

You are not that tired, a beloved voice spoke inside her head. *Your wound scarcely bleeds.*

Katrine smiled and then laughed. She felt renewed and with a surge energy attacked. Now the commander danced back and forth across the ground as the strange, exotic looking, wild-eyed female in front of him slashed at him a dozen different ways, until a long, attractive leg whipped out and swept his feet out from under him. He turned to break his fall and a second later when he looked back, Katrine's sword was pointed at his heart.

Everything stopped. For brief seconds he recalled his wife and family back home, his hope for a higher rank, and the delicious wild game he had eaten for dinner the previous night. He marveled at the odd combination of thoughts, hardly unusual for someone whose life was spiraling past. A roaring hurt his ears then he looked down in disbelief. She had run her sword through his chest.

In the heart of the city the first group of Surmese to breach the second gate arrived at an open plaza. Their feet slid to a stop, grinding the dirt and gravel into the cobblestone lane. They were silent save for their whistling breaths as they stopped and looked around. The stores were boarded shut and no one was visible. The entire place was deserted. They could hear yelling and the clash of weapons in the distance, but that was all. A creaking noise snapped their heads around and they watched as a long wall on the right slid open. A second wall to the left did the same and when hundreds of Palatonian soldiers came roaring through they had no more time to watch or think. Shields and swords banged together as they met the Palatonian onslaught. Dust began to rise as the combatants blurred together amidst the chaos. Pain-filled cries and triumphant yells blocked out thought. There was time only to defend or die.

In the back of the city another contingent of Surmese grew frustrated as the street they were racing down grew narrower with each bend. The sound of their pounding feet lessened as they were forced to thin their ranks, the passageway allowing room for no more than two or three abreast. Progress slowed. At the head of the line, the leader turned the corner and stopped. The men behind him muttered their complaints as they were shoved against him. But he held his ground. Ten feet in front of him two huge cats, a tiger and a spotted leopard stood growling. They snarled, baring their teeth, saliva dripping.

He gulped and his throat went dry. Something whizzed by his ear and a man behind him cried out then another smacked against the hard ground as a second arrow buried itself somewhere in the dense pack of bodies. Slowly, the big cats began to walk toward him.

Despite the fury of the battle at the dead end street, King Baldor managed a smile. With nowhere to run, the Surmese had grown desperate. Baldor felt a sharp pain in his right leg but couldn't take the time to look. Without taking his eyes off the man in front of him, he plunged his sword to the rear and heard a grunt. While he worked to withdraw his blade, he used his shield to block an enemy's frontal attack. Once his sword was free, he parried with the man several moments before he found an opening for a killing plunge. He barely had time to take a deep breath before another enemy took his place. Sweat poured off his face. He was starting to feel a little desperate himself.

Then he heard the welcome sound of an animal's roar. He didn't know whose *fel* it was, or which Shala had come to help but they were certainly welcomed. More roars erupted from the throats of fighting cats, and Baldor saw the blur of a dozen tall figures racing by him and into the enemy's ranks. Blood began to spurt in all directions and the coppery smell filled his nostrils. All around him the street's pavement grew slick.

A long, powerful dark hand gripped his forearm and pulled him back from the melee. Baldor looked up into blazing red eyes that suddenly softened into a friendly blue. "Please, your Majesty," the Shala whose name he thought was Lysander said, "let us finish this mess for you."

CHAPTER 34

KATAR'S CIRCLE OF FIRE

General Vikor scanned the ground that stretched before him as far as the eye could see. Burned! All of it burned. The thick layer of smoke rising from the ashes turned breathing into a hacking, labored chore. Each step his soldiers took kicked more soot into the air. The charred smell almost gagged him. It was a nightmare.

In the middle of the night they had awakened to the smell of smoke. In the distance fires lit up the night sky. The wind carried it away from the main camp so they were in no immediate danger, but they had marched only about ten miles today when they came to the torched land.

After another hour of walking, Vikor pulled his chariot to a stop and jumped off. Trudging back to his second in command, he told Rolav to call a halt. "We will camp here and give the smoke a day to dissipate. We will choke to death if we march all day in this mess!"

Vikor was disgusted. Yet he had to admit that the enemy's new strategy was ingenious. They had slowed his army while managing to destroy any food the land might supply. The only plus was that the land around his troops was clear for a mile in all directions making a surprise attack impossible.

He beckoned to a nearby Field Commander. "Send for ascribe and ready a dozen birds. We need some messages dispatched." The commander hurried away to do his bidding.

Hidden from the Surmese eyes, Katar watched them come to a halt. He nodded to himself, pleased at the outcome. Only a fool would try to march through the charred land and hot embers. He had achieved another day's delay.

The night before when the *lais* message informed him of the alarming losses incurred the previous day, Tahjeen decided to change tactics. He needed something to counter the Surmese commander's strategy. Katar was relieved. He had no desire to repeat the lesson. In a war of attrition, his team would be the loser.

But Tahjeen was an astute militarist and had planned his next two moves. Tonight, while the Surmese slept, the Shala would attack from long range with half their supply of arrows. With a bit of luck, his archers could cut deep into another half a division of the Surmese fighting force.

Tahjeen's second move was already underway. A sizeable number of Kater's *kosh* were sent ahead into territory that was not yet burned. They would lay an arcing string of dry wood gathered from dead trees and ground debris in the surrounding forests. When the Surmese decamped in the morning, and started marching once again towards Danigh, the Shala would wait until the enemy was far enough inside this circle before they ignited the fires that would surround them. With any luck, many Surmese would die before they could escape the flames.

All Katar could do now was wait, and be glad it was not the rainy season.

Commander General Taro of the Emperor's army was not happy. It no longer mattered to him that Oreon was completely conquered, save for a smattering of people in the mountains, or that his headquarters now rested inside Dania's borders. He was disturbed by the reports from the second invasion force that they faced daylong delays because of the enemy's tactics. But even that did not bother him as much as the total absence of information from Gleneden. He had no idea what was happening there. For nearly thirty-six hours he had heard nothing from them. The last message proclaimed that a division was sitting at the doorstep of Milhune, the capital of Gleneden. But for the past day and a half, not one word!

At least we are poised to capture Palaton's capital, he thought to himself. He looked about, searching for a runner. "You there," he said, spying a young man who was walking past, "come over here." The soldier moved quickly towards him.

"Use my standard to garner quick passage through the ranks, and find the Field General. Tell him to come see me at once!"

"Yes, sir!" The young man saluted then hurried away. Within five minutes, the Field General arrived with several of his officers.

"Good, good," the Supreme Commander said wasting no time on any courtesies such as liquid refreshments or a seat, he went on. "It's time we move out and head for Danigh. I am not going to wait for additional forces to arrive from Palaton or Gleneden. We have nearly thirty five thousand as it is. Give the orders."

The Field General saluted and turned to leave, but the Supreme Commander stopped him. "General," he asked, "what is all that smoke on the horizon?"

"It appears the Danians are setting their fields afire, sir."

The Supreme Commander shook his head. Burning their crops? What would these people do next? Irritated, he went back toward his tent and ordered his aides to start packing. He strode past the tent, finally stopping at a nearby ledge where he could look back over the plain they had recently crossed. He stared to the northeast. What is going on in Gleneden, he wondered?

The great feast was over in Gleneden, and Gable had already dispatched some of his warriors in multiple directions to rid the land of any remaining Surmese. Hundreds of miles away in Palaton's capital, the feast was just beginning.

Baldor was stunned by the carnage. The Surmese had been decimated. Shala arrows had slaughtered thousands inside the first wall, and inside the city, the fierce cats had hunted down and slain a similar number. The flashing swords of the Shala, and his own soldiers to be sure, destroyed the rest. The maze of his grandfather had been responsible for the great victory in the city proper. Remarkably few Palatonians had been killed.

Katrine's group, blocking the outer gate effectively, had prevented any escape. But it had been costly. Over a thousand Shala had fallen to the determined enemy who refused to surrender. All things considered, it was a great victory. And without the Shala, Baldor knew, it would never have happened.

He watched as Katrine and Devon climbed the steps to where he stood surveying his city. She was smudged and battered. A nasty cut on her right arm needed tending and she was limping slightly. She no longer carried a shield. He wondered if she was too tired to carry it or had lost it during battle. Long-street was cut in a dozen places, none which looked life threatening.

Baldor reached out, gripping her forearm. "Ever vigilant, Katrine." he said, using the Shala greeting as a sign of his appreciation.

She smiled back wearily. "Ever Vigilant, Your Highness.

Now that you have your capital secured, we must see to the rest of your kingdom."

"Time enough for that tomorrow. I have four thousand men ready to do their share. Let your forces recoup, and allow us have the honor of weeding out the Surmese," Baldor said.

To his surprise, Katrine nodded. "I will have five hundred of our healthiest accompany you. The remainder can rest, or assist if necessary. We will heal those we can."

Then Baldor surprised her by smiling. For once his stern countenance disappeared. "I think you will find the city most welcoming. I have already sent word to every inn. Tonight we will feast in your honor." He was beaming.

Katrine's face broke into a smile. Baldor realized that despite being covered with grime and blood, she was quite attractive. One glance at Devon told Baldor that the sentinel did as well.

Vikor's soldiers marched forward steadily. Their eyes swept the land around them, looking for any sign of the enemy.

The attack with deadly arrows during the middle of the night had unnerved them. How were they to defend against such tactics? It left them suspicious of everything, especially now as they moved through a beautiful landscape untainted by fire. It seemed too good to be true.

General Vikor was unwilling to send scouts ahead, knowing it would be a futile attempt ending in their death. So they were forced to march forward blindly. His anger grew at having his actions manipulated by the Shala. He who controls the war, he thought, controls the outcome. Somehow, he must find a way to take the initiative.

After hours of traveling, they entered a pastoral area several hundred yards wide. High grass swayed back and forth, tugged gently by a light breeze. Trees and thick undergrowth encircled the open area.

After more than half his army had moved into the expanse, Vikor smelled the smoke. Seconds later, the horses began neighing. He jerked his chariot to a stop and glanced around. He saw the first flashes of fire off to the left.

He glanced behind and saw smoke billowing from the trees. He was about to order his troops to veer to the right, but flames suddenly leapt from that side as well. He did not delay another second but put the lash to his horses, forcing them forward to the only opening left. Still a hundred yards away, the hooves of his horses pounding furiously as his chariot bounced along precariously, he saw fires igniting dead ahead. It would be impossible for all of the divisions trapped inside the circle of flames to escape.

Moments later he was through the opening, joined almost immediately by field commanders and captains on horseback. Those marching on foot were not so fortunate.

He pulled to a stop well beyond the wall of fire now closing behind him, the heat building as dozens upon dozens of his soldiers started racing through. Some were suffering from mild burns, while others, their clothes burning, stumbled to the ground, rolling over and over, desperately trying to staunch the flames. He watched, horrified and helpless, as thousands of men trapped inside the burning ring began to fill the air with their screams. The unmistakable smell of burning flesh fouled the air. Behind him, he heard someone spew the contents of his stomach onto the ground. A few of the officers on horseback bravely jumped back over the ring of fire. Some returned carrying coughing men with them, but too many did not come back.

Time seemed to slow. Burning men flung themselves across the fire line. Others hurried to them and tried to beat out the flames with whatever they could find – blankets, packs, clothes off their back. Some tossed dirt on top of the men on fire, and all the while Vikor's ears were bombarded with the incessant screaming.

Afterward, they did what they could. The handful of physicians who had escaped the flames went from man to man, placing salve on burns that were less serious. But more often they were forced to look with doleful eyes at the officer who accompanied them. When they shook their head, the commander knelt beside the charred warrior and put an end to his suffering.

Vikor was not a vengeful man. He believed that too much emotion robbed a man of reason and led to poor decisions. But for the first time in his life, he wanted to ride madly after the foreign savages and tear them apart with his bare hands.

"The final count is in," Tobol said several hours later. He wasted no time with greetings but got immediately to the point. We have six divisions left and in condition to fight." Tobol looked disgruntled, but then he always had a sour look about him.

"The fire was very costly, General," Rolav remarked. "We lost nearly a third of our men. I recommend that we camp for several days and tend to the wounded."

For a time, Vikor said nothing. His initial fury was now under control and he was thinking rationally. There had to be a reason why the enemy was avoiding a direct confrontation. His earlier suspicion that the enemy had limited numbers was a certainty. To compensate, their ingenious use of fire and knowledge of the terrain, were proving to be effective weapons against Vikor's huge army.

Their purpose was to delay, so slowing was the last thing he could afford.

"We will move out at once," he said, turning back to the two men. "We will not let these devils rest nor give them time to hatch further insidious plots. I want us on their heels and marching up their backs!" With his last words he pounded his fist into his palm.

Tobol and Rolav nodded sharply then turned to convey the orders. After they walked a dozen paces Rolav spoke. "This is madness," he said. "He will kill us all."

CHAPTER 35

A KING COMMANDS

When he first arrived, King Darvus found the gathering at the cavern in near chaos. Many of the civilians were frightened by the Shala and ready to bolt and run. Despite their best efforts, the Shala leaders were unused to being diplomats. They seemed abrupt and unfriendly to the nerve-wracked citizens.

The problem was compounded by the heavy rush of farmers from the countryside and the craftsmen and artisans from the city demanding the privilege of being first in line. Darvus asked the Shala to assemble leaders from both groups. A dozen men stood before him now, eyes haunted and suspicious.

"King Sorbonne asked me to organize the procession through the caverns," Darvus said in his most commanding voice. "I need your cooperation."

"And who might you be?" a rough looking farmer challenged. A nearby Shala moved toward the man, ready to enforce some respect, but Darvus stayed him with a quick gesture.

"I am King Darvus III of Oreon." He met the gaze of each man in turn. "You are no doubt aware that your Prince Roland is betrothed to my oldest daughter, Princess Leona. That is why my family and I were in Danigh when the invasion began. My own kingdom is in grave peril at this very moment."

He paused, summoning all the inner resources he could find. "Citizens of Dania, hear me. Now is the time to draw strength from one another, to put our individual desires aside and work together for the security of all. We face a daunting task and I need your help."

The men studied him as his words sunk in. His regal clothes were dusty and torn, and his short, dark hair was speckled with gray and no longer neatly combed. But his stance was wide and commanding and his gaze fierce. Finally, an older master craftstman spoke. "What is it you require?" he asked. Others around him nodded.

"Your cooperation and expertise," Darvus answered, not allowing relief to show on his face. "We need to proceed through the cavern in an organized manner. We must give thought and care and not have panic rule the day."

An elderly farmer, standing with the help of a roughhewn staff, stepped forward. "I believe it would help if we were at the entrance, instead of these strange-eyed warriors." He looked at the nearest Shala. "I mean no offense." His remarks seemed to bounce off the stoic young man.

"That is an excellent idea," King Darvus replied. "But before we do that, I suggest we consider this as well. First, we must keep the people moving and Shala warriors every thirty paces or so can help that occur – not through threat but with encouragement and assistance." The men in the group considered that for a moment then began to nod.

"Second," Darvus continued, "we should keep families together so their children or elderly are not lost." The men continued nodding. "Lastly," Darvus added, "we should organize admission. Farmers bringing wagons of food should be interspersed between groups of city folk so supplies are available up and down the caravan."

The men looked at each other. The old farmer and the master craftsman moved closer together and began to confer. Another man from the city joined them. After a few minutes of talking, they came to an agreement.

"It will be as you ask," the farmer said. "We will station ourselves near the entrance and with your help, oversee the procession. We will disperse the supplies and citizens as you suggest."

Darvus nodded, greatly pleased. "Warriors will be placed nearby to help with any who object to your authority. "The King then asked to talk alone to the three who had emerged as leaders. The rest of the men moved toward the cavern entrance.

The farmer, staff in hand, looked hard at King Darvus. "What haven't you told us?" he asked.

Darvus smiled grimly, impressed at the wisdom behind the aging eyes. "The time may come," King Darvus said, "when necessity forces our hand. Decide now if women and children go first, what crafts are indispensable, what citizens absolutely must be saved."

"Could it come down to that?" the master craftsman asked, his eyes widening in disbelief.

"Truthfully," King Darvus said, "I do not know. But panic must be avoided at all costs. We must be prepared for anything."

The three men looked at him, comprehending perhaps for the first time, the extreme peril they were in.

"Gentlemen," Darvus said, "you may be required to survive outside of Dania for a long time. You may also have a great deal of rebuilding to do when you return. Please keep that in mind as you decide upon priorities."

The farmer watched the back of King Darvus as he retreated toward a group of Shala gathered under some trees. His mouth tasted foul, turned so by words he had hoped never to hear.

"Palaton has been regained," Tahjeen told King Sorbonne the next morning. "Baldor himself is leading the roundup of any Surmese that remain."

"Thank the gods!" Sorbonne said, his sigh of relief audible. Slowly, a smile crept across his face. "So far the plan is working. Have you heard anything from your forces in the west?"

Tahjeen smiled. "Katar has managed to eliminate at least a third of the Surmese army. But that still leaves a sizable force. They camped in the foothills of the mountain last night. They attempted to breach the pass at dusk, but Katar's warriors turned them back. I have sent Toman there to add further support."

Sorbonne looked at Tahjeen, an almost apologetic expression on his face. "A moment ago I said 'thank the gods'. I should have said, thank the Shala. We can never repay you for what you are doing, for what you are sacrificing."

"We are doing our duty, Sire, willingly. You're sacrificing a great deal as well."

"Homes and businesses can be rebuilt, crops replanted, but the dead cannot be raised, my friend. So, thanks are greatly deserved."

Tahjeen bowed slightly. "You may not feel so appreciative when we set fire to your capital tonight."

The smile faded from King Sorbonne's face. "I understand the need but that will not make it easier to witness." He stopped, imagining the city he loved and his beautiful palace inflames. All that he had worked for and preserved, and everything that reminded him of his beloved wife was inside the castle walls.

Losing it would be the most difficult thing he had done since burying her.

"So the last of us will leave tonight at sunset?" the king asked.

Tahjeen nodded. "Oman's scouts located the other part of the Surmese army on your eastern border. They've encamped for the night, but they're close enough to the caverns to cause concern. It would be too dangerous to delay any longer."

"My son returned last night," Sorbonne said, changing the subject. "The people became more cooperative as word spread about the Surmese invasion and their initial successes in the other kingdoms."

"He will be a fine King one day," Tahjeen said, hoping to put some life back into Sorbonne's eyes, "but he's not ready yet." Then he turned his head. Someone had been listening and was now running away down the hall. Tahjeen excused himself and hurried to investigate.

Aldo held his breath while the tall man passed by at the far end of the hall. It was a long way but Aldo knew that the Shala had incredible hearing. Finally, he relaxed and exhaled. He had to find his friend's assistant. He hadn't seen his friend for days, not since that night he had given him the ruby. He finally had something to tell him.

Ten minutes later Aldo was in the part of the castle where his friend had stayed. Maybe he could find... there! It was his assistant. He raced after the man and caught up with him just as the door began to close.

"Wh--?" the assistant started to say, but Aldo pushed him into the room then closed the door.

"Sir," Aldo said," I need to find your master. The man you work for. I have something important to tell him."

"Oh, you do now. Well, he is... ah... he has left the palace and you are to tell me instead."

Aldo looked at him, doubt spreading across his young face. "He never told me that."

"Because he didn't have the chance. He had to leave in the middle of the night. But I'm empowered to reward you for your efforts, depending on the message," the skinny assistant explained.

Aldo's eyes grew wide at the prospect of another gem. He was sure it would add to Roland's jealousy. "All right," he said.

"So, young man, what is this important news?" the man asked.

"I know where we are going tonight," Aldo answered quickly.

The skinny man laughed. "Everyone knows where we are going — to escape through some caverns."

Aldo did not laugh. "Yes, but, I know where the caverns are. Do you?"

The man narrowed his eyes, realizing the value of this knowledge, if in fact the boy actually knew. "Where are they?" he asked Aldo.

Something about this man bothered Aldo. He had liked the other man, but this assistant was not very pleasant. Suddenly he decided that this wasn't such a good idea after all.

"I will be back in an hour with a map," Aldo said, then started for the door.

"How would you like to be the next King of Dania?" the man asked.

The words stopped Aldo in his tracks. He looked around, his eyes beginning to shine in wonderment.

CHAPTER 36

STANDOFF

General Vikor stared at the Learing Mountains, made brilliant by the sun. Reaching eleven thousand feet, draped in a blanket of snow at the uppermost peaks, they were impressive.

"General," a young officer said as he approached from the camp below. Vikor turned and acknowledged him with a nod.

"Sir," the man continued, "the cooks request fires tonight."

Vikor gave it a moments thought. A hot meal would be nice for a change. "Yes, go ahead," he said and watched as the young officer hurried back down the hillside. Passing him on the way up were several of his Lieutenant Generals.

As they came near, one of the men, who showed great promise based on his performance the last few days, stepped forward. "General," he said with great deference, "I have a theory as to why we have not seen the enemy for the past day and half."

Vikor raised an eyebrow, suddenly interested. He gestured with his hand indicating for the man to continue.

"I think they are all up there, sir, waiting for us to enter the pass. The site may be perfect for an ambush."

General Vikor took a deep breath and let it out slowly, enjoying the freshness in the air that the earlier scorching of the earth had temporarily taken away. "I agree, commander. That's what I would do. I suspect a lot of us will die up there tomorrow." He turned and looked squarely at Tobol.

"What would you advise?" Vikor asked him.

Tobol eyed him suspiciously, wondering what trap the General was laying for him. "I would send a large force up there, perhaps a division, enough to draw the enemy out. If they are up there, they would not allow that many to get behind them. Whether they attack or not, we will have our answer."

"That could cost us another ten thousand men!" Rolav fumed.

Tobol ignored him.

Vikor laughed without humor. "You are right, Rolav, yet what else are we to do? If we only send a handful and the enemy is there, they would stay hidden and let them pass. Where are we then?"

Vikor turned back to Tobol. "I want to talk with you. The rest of you are dismissed." Rolav looked at him, clearly puzzled, but he left with the others.

As soon as the rest were out of earshot, Vikor wasted no time. "I do not like you, Tobol. I never have."

Now it was Tobol's turn to chuckle mirthlessly. "The feeling is one I share."

Vikor gave him a quick, sharp look then moved to within inches of his face. "Understand something. You are alive because I choose for you to be and there are only two reasons that compel me to keep things as they are. The first is that you are a good military strategist, as you just demonstrated. The second is because you are the only one capable of leading this army to victory if something should happen to me." Vikor watched him chew on what he was being told.

"What do you want from me?" Tobol finally asked.

"I want you to learn that you do not lead by whining or by emphasizing the negative," Vikor spoke with vehemence and Tobol backed up a pace.

"The most important consideration," Vikor continued, "is that we accomplish what the Emperor charged us with. Do you understand what I am saying?"

Tobol stared back for several moments, his jaw clenching and unclenching. Finally, he replied. "Yes."

"Good," Vikor said curtly. "When the officers dine together tonight, I will inform them that I have selected you to replace me if I should fall in battle. Rolav will be your second in command."

"Rolav will not like that," Tobol said quickly.

"Rolav knows his weaknesses. He will understand." Vikor paused, carefully assessing the man before him, measuring his commitment. Finding it acceptable, he continued. "My last piece of advice, should all this come to pass, is that you listen to him."

Tobol's brow furrowed. He found himself fighting his usual urge to point out Rolav's shortcomings, rather than his strengths. He hated admitting to himself that Vikor was right, but he knew that he was.

"All right," he said, nodding. "I will faithfully do as you ask...should it prove necessary," he added hastily.

"I am glad we understand each other," Vikor said. He turned back to face the mountain pass then squinted his eyes. He focused on the small opening in the distant promontory. He tried to imagine the forces that had been secreted there, awaiting them.

From this distance he had no idea how wide the access was. A narrow one could be defended for days by a relatively small group of men. He sighed in disgust, knowing there was but one way to find out. He looked back at Tobol.

"Get a division ready to advance on the pass. Have them move up the mountain until they are within a few hundred yards of the gap. I want to know how large the opening is."

Now it was Tobol's turn to study the pass. He, too, tried to discern its geography, and reached the same conclusion as his commander. There was no point waiting for the morning to garner this last bit of information. He nodded curtly to Vikor then went back down the slope towards the Surmese army. Cooking fires had already sprung to life, the telltale columns of smoke belching upward from a half-dozen locations. He began salivating, and wondered briefly if it was caused by anticipation of a warm meal or of the beginning of the assault on the capital of Dania.

Katar stood, heartened by the sight of Toman and his warriors as they approached. The Surmese army appeared to be preparing for a massive assault in an effort to break through the Shala defense. The arrival of additional warriors was welcome indeed.

Katar left his vantage point overlooking the pass and worked his way down the steep incline and headed toward the new arrivals.

"Vigilance, Toman. I must admit I'm pleased to see your ugly face." Katar smiled as he spoke and Toman rewarded him with a hearty laugh.

"Vigilance to you, Katar. Tahjeen told me that you might find use for some familiar faces."

"He has the right of it," Katar replied. "Our spears have been well-bloodied." The two Shala walked a short distance away from the main body of warriors then settled on a rough boulder just off the main trail. Katar sent for food and water.

"He also told me you have cut their numbers significantly," Toman said. He accepted a water skin and drank deeply. Katar waited until he finished before he replied.

"We have, but the cost has been high. We did ourselves no favor by killing their original commander." Toman raised his eyebrows in mild surprise.

"His replacement," Katar continued, "is more than capable. His tactics have inflicted a lot of damage, but more than that, he is relentless. With your team here now, we can hold the pass for several days, but he is determined to break through. Despite our presence, as well as yours, he will eventually be able to accomplish that."

Toman shook his head and remained quiet. Katar saw that he also had deeper worry lines marking his features.

"How fares Tahjeen?" Katar asked, unsuccessfully feigning disinterest.

Toman smiled. "The change in him is remarkable. It is strange," Toman said, looking thoughtful. "I always thought he was more of a natural leader than Drayen."

Katar couldn't hide his interest. "What do you mean?" he asked.

Toman considered his words then went on. "As expected, the union with Ariann transformed him. Still, everything about him is more imposing, and more regal. I would have thought the effect of the union to be less, having Drayen's change for comparison."

Katar nodded. After Drayen's marriage to Endoreen was consummated, many noticed that he hadn't changed that much.

"Perhaps this Ariann had more to give him to begin with," Katar said.

"Perhaps," Toman replied. "But it's truly striking. It's true, her gift has calmed him, given him patience, but" Toman shook his head, "I almost feel like kneeling in his presence."

"Really!" Katar said as his eyes turned egg yolk yellow in surprise. "Well, I doubt he would want that and he will not get that from me." A wide smiled creased his face.

Both men laughed. Then Toman sobered and looked apologetic. "Do not misunderstand, Katar. I loved Drayen and mourn his loss."

"We all loved him," Katar said wistfully. "There was an aura of kindness surrounding him that affected us all."

"Maybe that's the difference," Toman said. "Tahjeen radiates strength and assurance that makes you feel invincible. His exudes power." He looked back down the mountain trail at the city far below. "Yet he also shows a gentleness I had not seen before. That must be from Ariann," Toman concluded.

Katar smiled as memories came flooding back. "He has always been gentle, Toman. He just hides it well." Toman shrugged.

A younger lieutenant approached Katar, and whispered in his ear. Katar nodded and turned to Toman.

"Eat quickly," Katar advised, "they are readying for another attack."

Toman ate fast, after accepting a meat roll and biscuit from a nearby warrior. He consumed it in a matter of moments. "We are to delay them only for this evening," he told Katar, "then retreat under the cover of darkness. Tahjeen wants no slaughter of Shala to mark this spot. We are to race to the other pass and once through it, destroy it. That should provide King Sorbonne and his people with the time they need to reach the caverns and make their escape."

Katar nodded, pleased by the news that he would not have to sacrifice the rest of his warriors protecting the evacuation. The task assigned him had been difficult and deadly, but he understood its importance. Privately, he had been afraid that he would not see Tahjeen or his homeland again and he was relieved by Toman's explanation that such was not the case after all.

A warrior called out to him. "They are coming. They have more cages of those nasty creatures."

Katar turned back to Toman. "We've exhausted our supply of arrows so set your archers on both sides of the opening. My team will deal with any of the enemy who make it through your barrage. Watch out for their small lizards – their bite is fatal. Be sure to advise the *fels*."

Toman nodded his understanding before he left to disperse his team. Katar called his warriors forward to the nearside of the pass. Multiple lines of warriors formed an arch from one side of the passageway to the other. The lines would rotate in and out as they fought so they could constantly meet the Surmese with fresh defenders. Guttural yells announced the onslaught of the determined enemy as they rushed the pass yet again. Katar's eyes swirled with a mixture of reds, blacks and oranges as he braced himself for battle.

The Commander General slammed his fist against the wooden table. The messenger backed quickly out of the tent. First no word from Gleneden, then the army in the west loses over a third of its men, and now this – no word from the two divisions in Palaton over the past two days!

"By the gods!" the General yelled aloud, but deep inside a kernel of fear was growing. Like Vikor, he was among the few who knew about the Shala. He had heard of the legends and read the historical archives. But surely, he thought, two hundred thousand soldiers were enough to defeat them.

Well, it will be done, he mused. We will start over if we have to but we will conquer Sandala. He paced, praying his words weren't hollow, knowing the consequences to his career and his life, if he was wrong.

Tobol bunched his men, twenty abreast. The pass was too narrow to allow a wholesale rush of ten thousand men at once. The first twenty raced forward and threw themselves into the slot face first, landing on their shields. Their backsides were shielded as well, offering some protection. Directly behind them, archers fired a deadly volley into the ranks of the defenders. The arrows hummed through the narrow gap, some banging harmlessly off Shala shields. But duller thuds accompanied by grunts and moans meant that many found their mark. Steadily, the Shala began to fall.

The first line then stood up and repeated their mad, leaping rush. This time when they hit the ground, spear throwers had replaced the archers. They whistled through the air, some crashing against the thick shields while more Shala fell as the long blades found their mark.

The third time the Surmese surged forward, prostrated themselves on their shields, and released the grelags. The scaly creatures snaked forward, their lethal fangs dripping venom as they sought their prey.

Toman's archers were ready and let fly with arrows. Most of the nasty creatures were pinned to the ground, writhing in their final death throes. But a few made it through and still more Shala cried out.

The onslaught was relentless. When the first group of twenty shield bearers was finally decimated, they were replaced, and that action repeated as the supply of men, arrows, spears and grelags seemed endless. Grudgingly, inch by bloody inch, Katar's forces were pushed back and the death toll on both sides mounted.

At long last, the Surmese began to fall back. Most of their division was strewn about the pass; bodies piled three and four deep in many places. The earth was slick with blood, dead soldiers lay contorted at odd angles, and broken weapons littered the ground.

Katar was breathing heavily, his face drenched in sweat despite the chill of the higher altitude. He was unhurt but covered in blood. The fighting had been fierce as the Surmese General had thrown soldier after soldier at them.

Toman found him leaning against a big rock. "Are you all right?" he asked, noting the consternation on Katar's face.

Katar shook his head. "You can train a lifetime and still be unprepared for so much death." He paused, his face registering additional grief. "I lost Britta," he said dejectedly, referring to his beloved *fel*.

Toman said nothing. There were no words of comfort that could begin to ease that pain. Instead, he gripped the forearm of his friend. They were quiet for several moments then Toman spoke again. "We must start our withdrawal."

Katar nodded and pushed himself away from the rock. They started to turn away from the carnage and head towards the capital when a grelag lurched out of its hiding place and launched itself from a nearby ledge.

CHAPTER 37

EVACUATION

King Sorbonne was the last Danian to pass out of the gates of his beautiful city. Sprawled ahead of him was a wide, meandering line of crafters, artisans, merchants and government officials. Shala warriors straddled the sides of the serpentine group of heavily laden refugees, ready to give assistance to any in need, and to infuse the emigrants with a sense of safety by their presence.

After a few hours they approached the summit of the mountain pass. A Shala warrior caught up with King Sorbonne and pulled him from the line of travelers. The warrior talked quietly, his words only for the King. Both Roland and Aldo noticed their father's activity, and moved off to the side of the steep trail to wait for him. At one point in the conversation King Sorbonne looked towards them and when he spotted Aldo, fixed him with a stern look.

"What have you done Aldo?" Tahjeen overheard the king shout at his youngest son. A moment later Sorbonne had the boy's shoulders in his grasp and was shaking him. Tahjeen looked at the Shala who had kept a rear guard and noticed that he was holding something in his hand.

"You always ignore me," Aldo cried. "It is always Roland, Roland, Roland."

"What are you talking about?" Roland demanded, joining the dispute.

"Your Majesty," Tahjeen said, trying to project some calmness. "May I help in some way?"

Sorbonne looked at him, his face a mixture of anger and sadness. "One of your warriors discovered that someone had been leaving a trail for others to follow, dropping bits of gold cloth every so often. It was Aldo's doing though I cannot imagine why."

Tahjeen looked at the scraps of cloth in the warrior's hand. The pile was significant. "You got them all?" Tahjeen asked. The warrior nodded back.

Suddenly Aldo tore himself away from his father. "It won't matter anyway. I gave him a map."

Furious, Roland stepped toward his brother. "Who did you give a map to?" Roland shouted.

"Leave me alone," Aldo cried, but Roland grabbed his arm roughly.

"Why should you get to be king?" Aldo yelled back. "Maybe I want to be king! He told me if I helped him I could be the king after father died."

Roland was incredulous. "Who was this man?" he demanded, as Aldo started to struggle again.

"Let me go!" Aldo blurted, wrenching his arm violently and breaking free. Without thinking where he was, he bolted, his feet precariously close to the edge. His second step pawed at the air as the ground disappeared beneath him. Roland leapt after him, his hand reaching out to grab a fistful of shirt, but it slipped from his grasp. The terrifying scream raised the hair on Sorbonne's neck as he stared at Roland's empty hand.

Tahjeen moved quickly to the side of the cliff and the king joined him a moment later. Together, they looked down the mountain where Aldo's body lay battered and broken on the rocks hundreds of feet below. The King sobbed and Tahjeen grabbed him, holding him firm so in his grief he could not follow his youngest son. Slowly, he led the king away, walking him towards safety.

"We will recover his body, Your Majesty, and bury him properly." Tahjeen said before he ordered another Shala warrior to accompany the king and ensure his safekeeping. Two others left to retrieve the boy's body.

Katar was not a particularly sentimental man, but he found he could not leave Toman's body behind. He wanted to honor the fallen *kosh* leader by taking him back to his homeland for burial. When he asked for volunteers to carry the body, he was not surprised when hundreds of warriors came forward.

Despite the unexpected tragedy, speed and stealth were still necessary and he could delay no longer. Once Toman's body was bundled in extra tunics, Katar gave the order to withdraw. The Shala hurried silently down the mountain road.

In the distance, the night sky was glowing, lit by the fires that burned in Danigh. It wasn't long before the air was filled with particles of ash and soot as the wind turned in their direction. Katar altered course, taking his forces away from the wind and skirting the southwestern edge of the city's boundary.

They raced along, glancing back and forth to the walls of flame burning behind them. They were concerned that the Surmese might discover the pass abandoned and immediately move through. Katar was not worried the Surmese might catch them, but he did want sufficient time to block the pass that lay ahead on the eastern slope of the mountain range. He hoped, however, that the Surmese would not discover their retreat until the morning.

In less than an hour, Katar's combined forces had passed the far side of the burning city, and were entering the foothills of the Learing Mountains. The Surmese had yet to appear, so he called for a brief rest. Everyone was thirsty, parched by the hot, dusty air. The cats especially needed water.

The warriors sat facing the distant fires. There was an endless sadness in watching a beautiful city burn. It left them downcast and stifled conversation. The flames did not reflect off the deep purple dominating their eyes. They were filled with regret and sorrow. Katar hoped that he would get to be part of Danigh's rebuilding. Most of his life had been spent training tonight, to repel those who threatened Sandala's survival. It would be far more satisfying to get to do something constructive to counter the carnage of battle. Yes, he would like that very much.

Just before sunrise, they reached the pass and joined the Shala warriors and Danian citizens who were already there. Katar saw Tahjeen in the distance and headed for him. As he approached, he was struck by the change in Tahjeen. He looked older, taller, stronger. His hair rippled down his shoulders and the power of his gaze was undeniable.

"Vigilance, Katar," Tahjeen called as his friend neared. His eyes whirled a warm blue at the sight of his childhood companion.

"Vigilance, Tahjeen. We came as quickly as we could." Katar knelt before the man who would one day be his King.

Tahjeen grimaced, his face a mixture of embarrassment and irritation. "Please, Katar. Get up," he said, bending forward and pulling the man to his feet and into a warm embrace.

"The civilians are resting, " Tahjeen explained after he released him. He pointed at a large ledge several hundred feet above the pass. *"Mo'els* are gathering to concentrate on that protuberance. Once they bring it down, I'm hoping it will bring more of the mountain with it and block the pass."

Katar nodded. Tahjeen looked at the warriors around him and realized that there were far fewer than there should have been. "Where's Toman?" he asked, his concern deepening.

Katar couldn't look at him, and instead fell to his knees once again. How much pain can one heart stand he wondered? He looked back toward a small group of Shala that now sat beside the wrapped body of their fallen leader. Slowly, he raised his arm and pointed to the bundle.

Tahjeen's gaze traveled to where Katar indicated, widening in comprehension. Murky purple washed through his eyes revealing his grief. Then oranges and reds replaced them, as anger overtook him.

"Curse the gods!" Tahjeen said hoarsely, as he threw his pack down violently. First his brother, then the king's son, and now a good friend – all with the war barely begun.

Initial anger was replaced by a stabbing pain. Toman had held a place in his heart that was now filled by aching sorrow. "Why Toman?" he said aloud to no one in particular. "What reckless chance did you take this time?"

"None, Tahjeen," Katar answered. "He fought with wisdom and efficiency. It was a grelag. No man could bring Toman down." He watched as tears fell unchecked from Tahjeen's eyes. Katar felt a sorrow he had never experienced before, empathy so deep he was dazed.

Tahjeen finally found his voice. "The price of duty is very steep. First Drayen, and now Toman. How many of his team survived?"

"Nearly half," Katar said, finally getting to his feet. "He was a good leader. He wanted me to tell you that he did his duty."

"And did it well," Tahjeen replied emphatically. He paused, looking back at the bundled tunics that held Toman's body inside them. "Thank you, Katar, for bringing him home. "His words were whisper quiet but Katar heard them.

Tahjeen looked more closely at Katar and for the first time saw the sadness in his eyes. He chastised himself for being selfish and insensitive. "How did your *kosh* fair?" Tahjeen asked.

The colors of grief radiated from Katar's luminescent eyes. He took a deep breath before he sighed deeply. "At last count we have nearly a thousand left to fight."

Tahjeen was humbled and his eyes spun colors rich with humility. "A steep price in any circumstance, but a miraculous victory as well. Over thirty thousand Surmese no longer draw breath."

Katar nodded. "I know. But I lost Britta. My soul is empty without my *fel*." He looked back at Tahjeen and despite his own grief, wanted, somehow, to comfort his suffering friend. "War has no friends," Katar said, "only ambitious devils who lost their souls a long time ago."

Bitterness drenched Tahjeen's face, turning his eyes a brilliant orange. "Well, it has an enemy now," he said. "Mark me, Katar, from this day forward I will do everything in my power to end the stupidity of war. The Shala will no longer live merely to sacrifice their lives. We have a new purpose, a new calling – we must rid man of his lust for power and the violence it breeds!"

Katar looked at him, and after a long moment, bowed low.

Shortly after dawn the Surmese discovered that the Shala had abandoned the western pass. Vikor wasted no time and gave the orders to rush his divisions through. He was not prepared, however, for the sight that greeted him on the other side.

The capital was a charred ruin. Fires still burned in parts of the city, and hot embers were smoking everywhere. He was furious, plagued by an unfamiliar feeling of impotence. Now there was no city worth capturing, and worse, another food source had been destroyed.

He was struck again, by the wisdom behind the strategy and wondered if the Danian King made the decision or if the Shala were behind it. Either way, the damage was done another unplanned difficulty added to the many they had already faced.

As they drew nearer to the city's outskirts, Vikor saw a red flag waving in the distance. It was the unmistakable sign of one of several Surmese spies insinuated throughout Dania prior to the invasion. He ordered several men to go forward and bring the spy directly to him. Within a few minutes, the man stood in front of him.

"I am General Vikor. Have you anything useful to tell me?"

The man bowed. "General, my name is Felad. I was Argenor's

assistant before he was discovered and slain. I have two pieces of information that are pertinent." The man paused, and Vikor impatiently waived him on.

"Yes, General," he said, bowing again. "First, Argenor was successful in having the Shala prince and husband to the Gleneden Queen, assassinated as ordered by the Commander General."

"Excellent!" Vikor enthused.

"Secondly," the spy continued, "although the city was completely evacuated last evening, I have a map of their escape route in my possession." He went on to explain that the party was heavily burdened, and Vikor's army might still be able to catch them.

The General quickened at the spy's announcement and snatched the map from his hand. He wheeled around and called out to his two commanders. "Olav! Tobol!" The two men hurried to his side.

"Have the men drop all extraneous supplies and make ready for a forced march. The enemy is within our grasp. They are less than a half-day ahead and are moving slowly. More importantly," he said grinning wickedly, "I know exactly where they are headed!"

Tahjeen, with Paca at his side, walked over to where Roland was sitting. He studied the King's oldest, and now only, son carefully. "Your father needs you," he said quietly.

"Right now," Roland said, shaking his head bitterly, "I am the last person my father wants to see." Then he stood and moved past Tahjeen, seeking another place where he could be alone with his thoughts.

Tahjeen sighed. The tragedies of war were difficult to predict and even harder to swallow. He sensed someone watching him and turned. Ariann stared a moment longer then walked toward him.

She looked at the edge of the cliff where Aldo had fallen. She shook her head. "That boy was plagued by jealousy, but neither the King nor Roland could see it."

She paused, and Tahjeen knew something else was bothering her. "What is it?" he asked.

Ariann squared to face the imposing gaze of the deep blue eyes she loved. "Bitterness and anger fill Roland's heart. He has changed into a man we don't know."

Tahjeen nodded, moving closer, dwarfing her as he placed a large hand around her waist. "We'll have to watch him closely. The betrayal could come from any royal."

Ariann sighed. "I know, but I'm even more worried about King Sorbonne. I don't think he believes he'll see Dania again, and now, with Aldo's death," she paused, shaking her head once again. "A man can will himself to die if he perceives he no longer has a viable reason for living."

Though Tahjeen smiled, his eyes flashed the colors of sadness. "You're observant and wise, and your counsel is always welcome." He drew her close, drawing strength from her nearness.

"We need Devon Longstreet to return," Ariann said suddenly, surprising him. She turned in his arms and studied his face. Tahjeen had changed since she had first met him nearly two weeks ago. Had it only been two weeks Ariann thought? It felt like years.

The earlier version of Tahjeen was one of an intense, wild thing, ready to uncoil and attack. Drayen's death and his subsequent union with her had changed all that. The wildness was replaced by a sense of calm and poise. The intensity lay hidden beneath a newfound gentleness, though it could still be seen in his eyes when they turned a fiery red. She could still feel the raw power radiating from him, constantly aware of his capacity for violence, but it was controlled now by the confident leadership that pulsed with every breath. The merge with her had created a being that even other Shala were hesitant to approach.

"Roland blames himself when there is no cause," she finally said. "Devon's presence might steady him, displace his anger."

"I was afraid that might happen," Tahjeen replied. "Even though Aldo's death was prophesized. There was nothing Roland or anyone else could have done to prevent it."

Ariann nodded.

"I'll have someone *lais* with Katrine tonight. She can bring Longstreet back to the crater."

He approached his father quietly. King Sorbonne was seated unceremoniously on the end of a wagon. To Roland's eyes, he looked defeated, tired and old. He sat down beside him, and stared out at the distant sight of the burning capitol.

"I am sorry I was not able to save him, Father."

Sorbonne was silent for a few moments then finally spoke. "We lost him a long time ago to neglect that is entirely my fault," Sorbonne said, chastising himself. "You have nothing to apologize for."

"You cannot alter the past, Sire, nor disavow the grief of my mother's death. You were, and always have been, a good father."

Tears welled in the King's eyes but he forced himself to meet his son's steady gaze. "You are a good son. All that any man could ever hope to have. You will be a fine King, though I have left you with a terrible legacy. Regaining what we have abandoned will be the challenge of your lifetime." Sorbonne paused to look back at the once lovely capital one more time.

"Why torture yourself, Father?" Roland said, noting where his father looked. "We'll rebuild it – make it even grander."

Sorbonne turned back to his oldest son. "That task will fall to you alone, my son." King Sorbonne got down from the wagon then resumed walking away from the only home he had ever known. In the city below, towering flames leapt from the rooftops of homes, stables, shops and the castle itself. Had he seen it, he would have wept at the site of the tall spire above the palace as it leaned sharply to one side then tumbled to the ground.

"Concentrate!" Katar growled as he strained mentally. He was at the forefront of a wedge of ten Shala warriors, the focal conduit aimed at the massive ledge poised above the pass. They were tightly grouped, arms around one another's shoulders, all eyes closed except his. They had spent long minutes staring at the target, committing the image to memory. That accomplished, they closed their eyes and began to focus internally.

They were *mo'els*, or movers. Most all Shala were blessed with unique gifts beyond heightened sensory abilities. Tahjeen could heal and communicate telepathically with animals. Others, like the ten who now labored mentally, could move objects. The more minds involved, the larger the object that could be 'pushed'.

The rock ledge was wedged tightly into the side of the mountain, but it lay in a prime position above a large pile of precariously balanced boulders some fifty feet below. If they were able to topple it, and with a little extra luck, it would bring a substantial part of the mountainside down with it, completely blocking the eastern pass. The enemy's attempt to follow would grind to a halt.

As their concentration intensified, a low humming vibration started, and gradually grew in strength. The tip of the ledge dropped a few inches, stalled then dropped another foot. Sweat poured off Katar and the others as the ledge dipped another foot then slowly started to slide. Gravity took hold and its momentum propelled the huge slab toward the boulders. Through the distance, they could hear it crash heavily into the rocks, starting a small avalanche that gradually gained speed. Then, a large part of the entire slope broke free and began to slide. At first, it sounded like the water of a babbling brook, but as tons of hillside came rushing behind it, headed directly for the pass, the babbling crescendoed into the roar of a thunderous waterfall. The ground rumbled and shook, forcing Katar and the others to fight for balance.

When the noise stopped and the dust began to settle, Katar leaned heavily on another warrior and smiled for the first time in days. "Well done!" Tahjeen complimented, grabbing Katar's shoulder. "And not a moment too soon." He pointed back down the mountain where two miles in the distance the Surmese army could be seen approaching at a trot.

Roland walked up to the Shala. "Let them feast on the ashes of Danigh," he said grimly. Unlike Katar, he was not smiling.

Tahjeen understood his dismay. "When all of this is finished, the Shala will be there to help you rebuild."

Roland turned away from him. In his heart of hearts he felt the city would never, could never, be the same, no matter how hard they worked to make it so. Too much had transpired. Too many wounds could never be fully healed.

"Come," Tahjeen said to Katar and the nine other *mo'els*. "Climb aboard this wagon. You've earned the rest. "None of them argued. The task had been arduous and drained their strength. A few hours to relax would rejuvenate them.

Tahjeen then spoke louder so others nearby could hear. "It is time…"

He was interrupted by shouts. A Shala was running toward them rapidly, and from the looks of the sweat on her body, she had been running hard.

"Vigilance," she panted once she drew close. "You must hurry. The Surmese on this side of the mountain have been spotted on a forced march toward the caverns. Some of our warriors are preparing to harass their flanks to slow them down, but there is no time to waste."

Tahjeen directed everyone to start running, and those who could not were picked up and carried by the Shala. Anything unnecessary was abandoned where it stood. Clothing and other sundries were tossed out of wagons so those too young or too old could climb aboard. Some of the crafters objected when their supplies were tossed aside.

"You'll have no need for them if you're dead!" Tahjeen told them gruffly. Katar started to get down from of the wagon. "Don't be foolish," Tahjeen said, "You haven't the strength, "and pushed him back on board.

They were still over ten miles from their goal. To come this far, Tahjeen thought, only to have everything unravel now. No! By all the gods of Sandala I will not let that happen. He raced ahead searching for Ariann. When he found her, he took her hand just as he had done days before when they were being chased by marauders. She flashed him a quick smile and gripped his hand hard.

CHAPTER 38

INTO HELL ITSELF

Vikor was driving his men hard. Though they were nearly spent from their assault on the western pass, he would not let them rest, not when he knew the enemy was so close.

After his forces had covered the first several miles into the foothills, a lead scout on horseback had come galloping back. He brought the welcome news that the enemy was insight, resting at the top of the pass on the eastern slope. They were no more than four miles away.

The General wasted no time. He left his chariot and took a horse from one of his captains. In moments he was riding among his divisions, spurring them on with words of encouragement. He reminded them of their comrades who had been burned alive and promised vengeance against the enemy that he had grown to hate. He drove his forces mercilessly but they responded.

After a half-hour, he looked toward the top of the pass once again, grinning in satisfaction and anticipation. They were closing ground fast. Their goal was in sight, barely a mile away. Then before his eyes, the mountain began to move.

He watched in growing concern that morphed into naked rage as a ridge above the pass began to crumble. He cursed the gods and his own impotence as a wall of soil and rocks broke free and began sliding down the mountain. More boulders and earth joined the avalanche as it gained speed, knocking aside any trees that were in its way. It thundered into the pass, rocks and dirt flying everywhere. The strength of his fury was futile as the opening high above him disappeared behind a dense layer of dust.

Many minutes later, Vikor stood alone, some distance away from his commanders. He stared hard at the cloud of dust still drifting above the massive pile of debris that buried the pass. To be thwarted once again when he nearly had the enemy in his grasp was infuriating! He trembled, so great was his anger.

He turned back and looked down at what once had been a lush, green valley but was now a scorched memory. It was unfathomable that a people would go that far to resist being conquered. Joining the Empire was something most kingdoms found satisfying, once they became accustomed to sacrificing some small freedoms. He could not begin to understand civilizations like this.

He was discouraged though he would never allow his men to see it. These Shala devils had frustrated him at every turn, matching every strategic move with an even better one. Would nothing go right on this campaign? Would the Commander General insist on his resignation? Would the Emperor demand his execution?

No matter how many times he reviewed his decisions, he could find no flaw in his thinking. He hoped that the invasion was proceeding successfully in the other kingdoms. At least that wasn't his responsibility. Failures there fell directly on Commander General Taro's shoulders.

In the meantime, he would replace his misgivings with action. He would get the eastern pass re-opened, fortify his camp and establish a well-protected supply line to the seacoast armada. But his important task would be to track the Shala. He knew that the war was just beginning. He was determined to do everything he could to find them. Wherever they went, whatever hole they crawled into, he would root them out. If he had to follow them into hell, he would find them and kill every last one of them.

As they raced down the mountain to the cavern entrance, several wagons overturned. Two were completely destroyed, forcing the strongest Shala to carry extra burdens. Some citizens fell down as they ran, and one man broke his leg as he tumbled head over heels. Tahjeen had his hands full preventing wholesale panic.

For all that, along with the several times they had to stop and let the humans rest, the contingent made surprisingly goodtime. Tahjeen thanked the gods that so many had already been evacuated, making the size of the last group manageable. They would make it to the caverns unscathed. The entrance was in sight and his sensitive ears detected no sounds of battle. Still, his warriors had taken positions all along both sides of the line of evacuees just in case.

He and Ariann stepped away from the running throng, and watched as the last of the harried travelers staggered forward. King Darvus was stationed by the large opening, along with a group of Danian citizens, and they could be heard offering encouragement. He had completed his task with great sensitivity and efficiency, and Tahjeen was impressed and grateful.

"My Father has found a purpose," Ariann said. She turned back to Tahjeen. "Thank you."

The tall Shala smiled back at her. "It was your idea, *Sha*," he said using the intimate Shalaen endearment. "And fortuitous," he added as King Sorbonne and his wagon passed by. Despite Roland's efforts to help his father regain his resiliency, the King looked haggard and frail. "We'll need his leadership in the event King Sorbonne is unable to rally himself. Prince Roland will have to walk a delicate line in the coming months."

Ariann nodded, understanding the difficulty the young man faced – how much to push his father, deciding how much he should take control of himself, or if he should assume leadership entirely. It was too soon for Roland to know what the right action would be.

Suddenly, Tahjeen cocked his head and listened. Several seconds passed then he looked up anxiously. "Hurry, Ariann. Get the last of them inside. Many are running this direction. It may be our warriors, but the Surmese might not be far behind."

She caught up with the end of the procession and began urging people forward. Tahjeen ordered the few Shala still outside to help the last of the civilians before he turned and raced toward the sounds he had heard moments before.

Together, he and Paca sprinted down a well-trod path traveled by the many evacuees over the last few days. He had gone less than a half mile when he saw hundreds of Shala trotting towards him. It was the part of Toman's *kosh* that he had left to guard the caverns. He slowed to a stop and waited for them.

"Vigilance, Regon," Tahjeen called out to Toman's second in command as he approached. "How far behind is the enemy?"

The young man, still in his teens, dipped his head. "Vigilance, My Lord." Tahjeen grimaced at the show of respect, yet another, unhappy reminder of Drayen's death.

"The enemy has altered course," Regon continued. "They

turned on to another road that leads to the pass. They seem very familiar with the lay of the land."

Tahjeen nodded. "The marauders spent several months in this kingdom so I'm sure you're right. But they won't be pleased when they find that route blocked."

All the warriors had arrived and were now grouped loosely around Tahjeen and their young leader. "You've done well," Tahjeen said to them. "And though this war has just begun, it's now time to take the Danians through the cavern and to safety. But heed my words. Our task is far from over. We'll soon return to finish what the Surmese have started."

Pleased murmurs came from dozens of determined Shala along with the haunting growls of a like number of big cats. Tahjeen turned abruptly and began running back up the trail to the cavern, the rest of the Shala close on his heels.

Ariann was waiting for him and he smiled at the sight of her. He sent the rest inside while he told her that the Surmese had veered off toward the pass. "They won't like what they see when they get there," she said. "What do you think they'll do? "She looked worried.

"They may start to dig away the blockage, or turnaround and look for us. Maybe both. To be safe, we'll collapse the first site, and leave warriors in place to collapse additional ones if necessary."

"How long will it take us to reach your homeland?" she asked. "I'm concerned about food and water."

"There are water cisterns and caches of food along the way to supplement what the Danians brought with them. Some may lose a pound or two, but no one will starve. The first part of the journey will take a week or more. The second part will be completed in a few days."

"There are two parts? I thought it was a direct route?"

"To my home, yes," Tahjeen answered. "But there is not enough room there to accommodate all these civilians. We'll be transporting them to a nearby island. That will take several days."

"Is anything there ready for them?" Ariann asked.

"No," Tahjeen said. "They will have to make some adjustments."

Ariann's eyebrows arched. "Oh, I would think so."

They took a last look at the dense forest around them then

turned as one and disappeared inside the cavern. Neither saw the figure emerge from the dense undergrowth and then reach inside a bag and retrieve a homing pigeon. Quickly, a message was fastened to its leg and the bird was tossed upward into the air currents and sent on its way.

About the Author

Cathy Benedetto is a writer, artist and avid reader. Her love of science fiction and fantasy helped inspire her trilogy about the mystical race of warriors known as Shala. Her favorite authors, Anne McCaffrey, Robert Jordon and Orson Scott Card, have spun stories that shifted Cathy's imagination into high gear.

A retired high school Vice-Principal, Cathy was also a successful athlete who was a five time softball All-American, and AAU basketball All-American. She was a member of the U.S. Women's basketball team that played in the World University Games in Czechoslovakia and the Pan American Games in Canada. While coaching, her girls' basketball teams won two Washington State Championships. Cathy has been published in "Women In Sports" and in the Bellevue Journal American.

Originally from the Northwest, Cathy moved to Kentucky in 2003. The former coach enjoys supporting the Kentucky Wildcats women's basketball team, often writes at her cabin near Lake Cumberland, and loves fishing on her pontoon boat. A special joy is playing with Liz, Lily, Kendall and David.

by Jason Walters

At the edge of the known world, two desperate armies struggle for the right to siege a city that has never been taken. Terrible magics are unleashed and the fate of empires hangs in the balance. Highdome and his crew of cutthroats, monsters, and mutants don't care. They just want to stay alive. But when sorcery backfires and the fury of the Vast White desert is unleashed, the men and women of the Red Regiment must look inside of themselves to find the strength to survive.
[Dark Military Fantasy, ages 14+]

by Dirk Vandereyken

In a small village, a necromancer stands trial. At the center of the universe, the Spider that wove All watches intently. Webs are spun in the courtroom, of magic, of lies, and of scandal. The mage Baour argues that he supercedes not only man's laws, but god's! What he truly wants may only be uncovered through testimony. As strange magics meet strange deaths, can the reality behind it be unmasked? And should it?
[Fantasy Legal Thriller, ages 18+]

www.BlackWyrm.com

Albrim's Curse

by Trevis Powell

All young Albrim wanted to be was a master bowman like his father. Then a savage attack on his home cost him his family, his arm, and his humanity – all at once! Crippled and contaminated by the Curse, his beloved Gran leaves him in the care of Mute, a giant warrior dedicated to protect-ing humanity from the depre-dations of the Quarg. Albrim does what he can to assist his master and redeem himself. But can a werewolf ever really recapture his humanity?
[Epic Werewolf Fantasy, ages 14+]

Gran's Secret

by Trevis Powell

Her son is dead; her grandson Cursed. Gran has to send him into hiding to protect him, and to protect others from him. But there are those who hunt Weres to use for their own evil purposes, and they are backed by the resources of kingdoms.
When these hunters begin snooping around Gran's village, there's nothing a sweet old lady can do to protect her grandson from such people, is there?
Apparently, you don't know Gran.
[Epic Werewolf Fantasy, ages 14+]

IMMORTAL BETRAYAL

by Paul Lewis

Darien, viking and explorer, braves the treacherous seas to discover new lands. That changes when he falls in love. But his world is shattered when he learns she has already been promised her to another. Darien's loyalty is put to the test as he battles vampires and werewolves. Darien finds himself having to choose between the woman he loves and his very soul. With tragic romance, heart stopping thrills, and plot twists, *Immortal Betrayal* aims to please. [Tragic Fantasy Horror, ages 14+]

IMMORTAL BURDEN

by Paul Lewis

Immortal Burden picks up where the first book in the immortal series, *Immortal Betrayal*, left off. It is now the 14th Century. To keep Darien from taking drastic measures he is summoned by Joshua, the first vampire, with a proposition. In exchange for his help Joshua will give him what he wants most. Darien is hesitant, but he would risk everything for a now distant dream. [Tragic Fantasy Horror, ages 14+]

www.ingramcontent.com/pod-product-compliance
Lightning Source LLC
Chambersburg PA
CBHW060537260626
47161CB00003B/944